True Heart
Peggy Nicholson

HARLEQUIN®

TORONTO • NEW
AMSTERDAM • PARIS •
STOCKHOLM • ATHENS • T
PRAGUE • WARSAW • B

ISBN 0-373-71025-9

TRUE HEART

Copyright © 2001 by Peggy Nicholson.

This edition published by arrangement with Harlequin Books S.A.

® and TM are trademarks of the publisher. Trademarks indicated with ® are registered in the United States Patent and Trademark Office, the Canadian Trade Marks Office and in other countries.

Visit us at www.eHarlequin.com

Printed in U.S.A.

To Christina Canham, fearless on the foredeck,
fearless in the kitchen, frequently admirable,
perpetually amusing. Closest to a little sister
I'll ever have. Chrisso, how I'll miss our
Girls' Nights Out. Sail on, kid, but don't be a stranger.

PROLOGUE

KALEY BOSWORTH DANCED straight out of the doctor's office that afternoon and bought a double armload of sunflowers. And beeswax candles—every last tall, creamy-white fragrant candle that the florist had in stock. Fifty-seven, in all.

Now they stood in unlit readiness on the counters to either side of the door that led from her kitchen to the attached garage. From there they spread out over the other counters, the marble-topped central work island, the table in the breakfast nook. She'd even set candlesticks at the doorway to the butler's pantry.

More candles beckoned the eye into the pass-through pantry, then on to the dining room, to its long, lace-covered mahogany table, where the remaining tapers stood in two silver candelabra. Between the candelabra on the table, she'd placed a cut-crystal punch bowl, filled to overflowing with the sunflowers, entwined with pink honeysuckle and roses from her own garden. Color and a blaze of light to match her mood.

The table was laid with their best sterling and china. Champagne stood iced in a wine bucket for Richard, along with a bottle of sparkling cider for herself.

All she needed was her husband to help her celebrate. Richard was only ninety minutes later than he'd said he'd be that morning—still well within his self-imposed margin of two hours, after which he'd usually phone to say that some case had delayed him and she shouldn't wait supper.

But tonight he hadn't called.

"So, any minute now," Kaley half sang as she stood by a window in her darkened living room, hugging herself, bouncing on her toes with impatience as she peered down to the distant street corner.

Headlights knifed through the summer dusk with swift assurance. Streetlights rippled over a sleek, sliding shape—a dark blue convertible swung around the bend and arrowed straight for the house. *"Yes!"* Kaley snatched up a box of matches and ran for the back door.

She lit the first half-dozen candles, then, as their flames grew, she threw the light switch. She bit her lip as she heard the rumble of the garage door rising. *Hurry!* Another dozen candles leaped into flame, washing the walls in flickering gold. *Hurry, hurry!* She tossed a spent match in the sink, struck another, laughing breathlessly at her own foolishness—too many candles!

Yet, a thousand wouldn't have been too many.

Fire touched wick after wick as the garage door rumbled down. She set the candles in the breakfast nook ablaze. A scent of warm wax and honey wafted upward—incense of thanks and joy.

Two dozen or more to go; she'd never finish in time! Kaley knelt to light the candles on the floor as the back door opened.

"Huh?" Richard Bosworth stopped short in the doorway. "Good God, Kaley." He frowned. "What's all this?"

"Oh, this...?" She twinkled up at him. "Guess you'd call it a celebration." Touching a match to another candle, she shared a smiling secret with its kindling flame. Kindling, yes—exactly so. Such beauty! Such a miracle!

"Looks more like a three-alarm disaster waiting to happen. Candles on the floor? Is that really necessary?"

She felt her smile tighten ever so slightly and drew a

slow breath. "Ran out of counter space." She backed away into the pantry, lit the candles on the sideboards.

He dropped his briefcase on a chair and followed. "What am I missing? It's not our anniversary. Nobody's birthday." He paused in the door to the dining room, taking in the flowers, the lavish table set for two, the blue velvet dress she wore. She lit the tapers in the first candelabrum. The flames struck his fair hair to ruddy gold, picked out the chiseled planes of his handsome face.

Showed her his lips thinning and his eyebrows drawing together.

"So?"

"So…" She looked up at him over the flames that mirrored her inward glow. "Something *wonderful* happened today."

"Yes, I gathered that. What?"

If only, just this once, he'd go along with her mood. Especially this once. "I'll tell you, but first, if you'd open that bottle?"

"Dom Perignon," he noted, lifting the bottle from the ice. "Whatever your news, isn't this a bit over budget?"

He'd treated himself to two cases the year before, when he'd made partner at his law firm. And now it was her turn to rejoice. "For this occasion? I don't think so."

"Your department head—what's the old bat's name? Henley? She decided to retire," Richard guessed. "You're next in line for the job."

"I am, but this has nothing to do with teaching. Nothing like that."

"Then tell me. You know how I hate surprises." He covered the bottle's cork with a napkin, drew it with a deft flick of his thumbs. The soft *pop* promised bubbles, but something somewhere, had gone flat.

She held the crystal flutes for him to fill, biting her lip as she studied his impatient frown. He did hate surprises, much as she loved them. Her fault, this. She should have told him the instant he walked in the door. Now she stood torn between blurting out her news and waiting for a happier moment, perhaps after his first glass?

"Come on, spit it out." He lifted his flute. "What should I toast?"

Why was she worrying? Once he'd heard… At least, once he'd gotten used to the idea… She rallied her smile. "Kiss me first?"

"That bad?" Still, he kissed her—a wary, closemouthed kiss, precisely measured. "*Tell* me."

"Well…" She took a breath. "You know I had an appointment this afternoon, with my gynecologist."

His eyes swept from the candles, to the flowers, back to her radiant face. No one could ever say that Richard was slow. He shook his head. "No."

"*Yes!* I told him I was a week late. That's unusual for me, so he tested and—and—" Her words jumbled into breathless, pleading laughter. *Come on, share this with me.* All the worries and setbacks she'd suffered through at his side, all the ambitions she'd applauded, the triumphs she'd celebrated. She'd been there for Richard every step of the way, and now couldn't he just—

"*Shit.*" He tipped his glass back and gulped, blew out a breath, then smacked the flute down on the table.

She stared at the champagne splash marks darkening the lace, she ought to get a cloth and dab them dry before they soaked through and marred the perfect, polished mahogany beneath.

"I'm pregnant, Richard. *We* are. And you know how long I've been wanting this. You said once you made partner—"

"You're on the Pill! How could this have happened? Did you stop without telling me?"

"Of course not! I'd never—"

"So you forgot—skipped a couple. Of all the careless, idiotic things to—"

"I didn't! I didn't forget a one." She set down her own glass untasted. "I had that awful earache—five weeks ago, remember? I couldn't get an appointment soon enough with my GP, so I stopped by a walk-in clinic and the doctor prescribed tetracycline."

"So?" Richard turned his back on her to pace down the length of the table, then swung on his heel to glare. "What's that got to do with—"

"Some antibiotics interfere with contraception. I never knew that, and the doctor didn't tell me."

"I'll *sue* him. And the pharmacist, too—negligence pure and simple. By God, they're going to regret—"

"*Oh,* no." Shaking her head, she met him halfway down the table—clamped her hands over the forearms he'd crossed on his chest. "No. Maybe they were careless, but we're not suing anyone. Not when the results were just what we wanted anyway."

"Who says—"

"*You* said! I wanted to start our family the year I finished college, but you said we should wait. That our condo wasn't big enough, remember? You said it was no place to raise rugrats." She shook him gently, smiling pleadingly up into his face, trying to spark some warmth in return. "Then when we moved to our house on Cottonwood I asked you again. And you didn't tell me no, Richard. You just said we should wait. That you were so close to making partner, that you needed all your concentration and energy to focus on that. That if I'd only wait till you made it, we'd be rolling in bucks and you'd have more time to help me with midnight feedings."

"I never—"

"You *did!* That's exactly what you said... So I did. I waited again."

He twisted away from her to resume pacing, yanking at the knot in his tie as if it was strangling him.

"Then once you made partner last year," she said to his back, "you know I said it was time. And remember what you said? You said that now that you'd made partner, they'd want to see you perform."

"That's precisely right." Richard ripped off his tie and dropped it onto a chair back, from which it slithered to the floor. "I'd made it to the big time, but that meant I had to bring in business if I wanted a place at the trough. It meant cultivating the right people, throwing the right kind of parties. I needed you beside me and I needed you to sparkle. It's hard to wow anybody, babe, if you look like a little blimp."

"So you asked me to give it another year," Kaley agreed levelly. "Which I did. But now I'm pregnant and I've been waiting eight *years*. Now it's my turn. *Our* turn for family—or what's it all been for? What good is all *this*, without family to fill it?" She swept a hand to include the whole house, so much bigger and grander than anything she would have chosen.

Richard stood not listening to her but staring off at the far wall. "You said you took tetracycline.... A drug—a powerful drug, Kaley. Did you happen to ask your gynecologist about side effects?"

She closed her eyes for a moment. *Oh, no. Please, please, don't go there.* "I...w-what do you mean?"

"You were on it at conception. What's tetracycline do to a developing fetus? Did you ask him that?"

Yes, they'd gone over that. She swallowed around the jagged lump in her throat, clasped her hands before her and said huskily, "He said that the odds were g-good—*much* better than good—that our baby is developing normally. That no...no permanent damage had been done."

"Ah!" Richard's finger came up to jab the air between

them. "That's what he said, no damage? But will he *guarantee* it? No? No, of course he won't! He's not entirely a fool. He knows that if anything went wrong, I'd sue him for everything but the fillings in his back teeth—and he knows I'd win."

"Richard, *please.*" Her knees were trembling; she was trembling all over. Kaley pulled out a chair from the table and sat. "Nobody could ever guarantee that—"

"Well, if he won't guarantee a healthy baby, ask Dr. No Problem if he'll agree to support it for the rest of its life if it's hopelessly retarded." He leaned down to look into her brimming eyes. "No? He won't do that, either? Then why should I—should we—risk it, babe, *if he won't?*"

"Because it's ours!" Kaley cried.

CHAPTER ONE

One month later

FEARFUL OF FALLING ASLEEP at the wheel, Kaley opened the car window to the cold rushing air. Now she stretched her gritty eyes wide and said softly, "Kaley Cotter."

No. That sounded apologetic, and she owed apologies to no man. "Kaley Cotter," she proclaimed, lifting her chin. The night wind sucked her name through the open window, sent it spinning and tumbling across the desert behind her humming wheels.

"Cotter, Cotter, Cotter," she chanted, squinting into the headlights of an oncoming truck, the first vehicle she'd encountered for twenty miles or more. "My name is Kaley Cotter." Again. After eight years as Kaley Bosworth. It would take practice before it sounded right. Her car shuddered in the truck's slipstream, then surged on through the dark.

Roughly two hours to go. She'd reach Four Corners, where the southwest border of Colorado touched the borders of three other states, by dawn. "Then home before eight," she comforted herself. She could make it. "Kaley Cotter's coming home."

Where she should have stayed all along.

"Kaley Cotter and *daughter* are coming home," she amended, one hand slipping off the wheel to cup her flat— still utterly flat—belly.

Or possibly Cotter and son.

But something told her this baby would be a girl. "Love you either way," she murmured, lashes drifting lower. Boy or girl, healthy or damaged, her baby would be welcome.

As she would be welcome at the Cotter family ranch. "Home," she half whispered, stroking her stomach, "is where, when you've got no place else to go, they have to take you in."

Suddenly, her head dropped forward with a sickening jolt. She gasped and jerked upright just as the off wheel bit into the roadside gravel. The car swerved wildly, then straightened to the road.

"*Whew!*" Kaley shuddered, rubbed a hand along a thigh roughened with goose bumps, and shook her head to clear it. That had been closer than close! If there had been an oncoming car... "Not good." Las Vegas, where she'd obtained her quickie divorce this afternoon, was five hundred miles behind her. She should have stopped in Page for the night, but like a wounded rabbit intent on reaching its own burrow, she'd found that no intermediate bolt-hole had looked safe enough. She'd sped past every possible motel until there was nothing left but rock and sand and stars and the pale road beckoning her eastward, home to Trueheart, then the ranch in the foothills above it.

KALEY MADE IT into Four Corners without further mishap, and pulled in at a truck stop for a cup of coffee to go.

Coffee. She frowned down at her stomach as she turned away from the cash register. She'd sworn that no matter how she craved it, she wouldn't drink another cup for eight months. Her baby had taken enough abuse already in the first four weeks of life, without having to put up with her mother's caffeine habit.

On the other hand, any sensible baby would agree that sharing one last cup of stale brew beat running off the road at seventy miles an hour any day. *Last one, I promise you.*

Let's just limp on home, then I swear I'll never touch another—

"Um, excuse me?" A woman loomed at Kaley's elbow as she stiff-armed the exit door. She was tall and blond, with a rueful smile. "I saw you pull in and I noticed you seem to be heading east and I was wondering if…"

THE BLONDE'S NAME was Michelle Something; Kaley hadn't caught the last half. Her car radiator had sprung a leak, she'd explained, forty miles back down the reservation road, and rather than stop in the middle of nowhere, she'd crept on to the truck stop, pausing to let it cool off each time the needle on her temperature gauge kissed red. She didn't dare push on to Trueheart, but she had a restaurant there, customers who'd be expecting their breakfast, so if Kaley would be so kind? She could send somebody back to collect her car once the morning rush was over.

Kaley was glad for the company. "I've been driving on snooze control for the past hour. Just talk to me and it's you who'll be doing the favor."

"Where are you headed," Michelle asked as they swung out onto the highway. "Durango?"

"No, Trueheart. At least, that's where I turn north. The Cotter ranch." It warmed Kaley just to say the words. Four generations of Cotters had held that patch of upland valley and now her baby would make the fifth. Heading home. Once she was home, she could face anything. Let go of the protective numbness that had carried her this far, and collapse.

"You're a friend of Jim Cotter's?" Michelle turned to prop one elbow on the dash.

"His sister," Kaley admitted. "So you know him?"

"Two eggs over easy with a double order of hash browns, half a bottle of ketchup, and if I were a cradle robber…"

Kaley stole a glance at her smiling passenger. Elegant rather than cowgirl-pretty like Jim's usual sweethearts, the blonde was perhaps five years older than his twenty-seven. But there was a certain level of...sophistication? Experience? Whatever, the cool, wry confidence beneath Michelle's surface warmth made her seem half a generation older than Kaley's younger brother.

"You're a teacher over in Phoenix, I think he told me. Married to—um—a lawyer?" Michelle continued.

Kaley winced. "Was..." Might as well say it. There was no keeping your life private in a small town like Trueheart. Still, she hadn't expected to have to fess up so soon, or to a stranger; had yet to shape her explanation or polish her delivery. Gray as the fading night, a wave of desolation washed over her. Richard was history now, a story to be told, not a man to wait up for, supper cooling on the table night after night. Not always a considerate man, maybe, but still, her man. *Was.*

"Oops!" Michelle said lightly, though a ready sympathy lurked under her humor. "Was a teacher? Or was married to a lawyer? I'm sorry, don't answer that. Either way, it's none of my biz. Me and my runaway mouth!"

"No, it's okay. I was married, but that's all over now. I passed through Las Vegas yesterday."

"Wham, bam, we'll be happy to stamp that paper for you, ma'am," Michelle said, "God bless them. And good for you. Once you decide to yank the bandage off, it's best to do it fast."

"Yes..." Kaley supposed it was. In her case, it certainly was, once Richard had given his ultimatum.

Abort it, Kaley, and let's forget about this. We don't want a defective child.

Or any child at all, Richard. Why had it taken her so long to see that?

Because I didn't want to see. I was happier blind, living

in hope. But once Richard had made it clear that no matter how she pleaded or argued, there'd be no marriage counseling, no compromise and no reprieve, that it was his way or the highway, she'd had only one choice. She'd chosen the road home to Colorado.

"So is this a short visit, to regroup and decide what next, or…?"

Kaley shook her head decisively, her straight dark auburn hair swinging from shoulder to shoulder. "No, I'm home for good." *Never should have left.* "I own half the ranch, though Jim's the active partner and I'm the silent one." Despite Richard's complaints, she'd contributed half her salary as a high-school English teacher these past eight years to keep the ranch operating. Jim had supplied the manpower and all the daily decisions; she, the vital cash. That was the very least she could do if she wanted the ranch to stay in the family. Jim had had the hard part after their father passed away, running a five-thousand-acre spread with little help. Not like the old days, when a ranch was a family enterprise and families were extended and capable.

She'd always assumed that if they could hang on through just a few hard years, Jim would choose one of his local sweethearts, a mate with ranching in her veins, and they'd start raising their own brood of cowhands. And when at last she and Richard started a family, she'd have sons and daughters to contribute to the tribe. Sons and daughters who'd happily summer at the family spread, learning to ride and rope and round 'em up as had so many Cotters before them.

So much for blithe assumptions. So much for dreams. Kaley grimaced.

Finally she'd had to face the reality that her husband didn't want children. Never had. Never would. As Richard pictured the universe, he was the sun, and she the adoring planet that spun around him. Any lesser satellites would be, at best, distractions; at worst, costly and tragic nuisances.

"I see," murmured Michelle into the bleak silence. "Well, to be perfectly selfish, I'm glad. I think Jim could use the help. Whenever I've seen him this past summer, he's been looking frazzled. That hand of his is an absolute sweetheart, but he reminds me of a pet tortoise a roommate of mine had years ago—sort of dried up and deliberate. I have a hard time picturing him getting his boot up into a stirrup, much less catching a calf."

Kaley glanced at her in surprise. "You've met Whitey, too? How long have you lived in Trueheart?" She'd tried to make it back for two or three weeks every summer. Alone, since Richard always begged off. But these past two years, she'd been working on the master's degree she needed to maintain her teaching accreditation and her schedule of classes had prevented her visiting. *Haven't been home since Dad's funeral,* she realized with a pang of guilt. A lot could change in eighteen months.

"Just over a year," Michelle said. "I bought Simpson's café down on Main Street. It's Michelle's Place now—best breakfast in southwest Colorado, if I do say so. Gourmet suppers on Friday and Saturday nights, with plans to expand to six nights if I can ever find a decent sous chef."

"Just what the town needs," Kaley said approvingly. "A serious restaurant. When I lived here, a hot date was steakburgers for two at Mo's Truckstop out on the highway."

"Still is, for the older crowd," Michelle admitted. "And most of the truckers and cowboys. But some of the younger set are giving me a chance. Then there are the yuppie commuters moving up from Durango, plus the dudes and the tourists."

Whenever Kaley and Jim spoke on the phone, Jim complained about the way southwestern Colorado was changing. Five-acre ranchettes replacing working cattle ranches. Outsiders moving in with money that the locals couldn't hope to match. Values they didn't want to match. Ideas of ways to "improve" a country that the natives liked just the way it was and always had been.

So far the cattlemen north of Trueheart were holding their own, with most of the changes confined to the town, Jim had reported. Suntop Ranch, the largest outfit in this part of the state, seemed to exert some sort of gravitational pull, holding the smaller ranches like Kaley and Jim's Circle C safe in its orbit. So far.

Still, as the land folded itself into deeper and greener valleys, steeper ridges that lifted toward massive peaks, looming dark against a rosy sky, Kaley looked fearfully for signs of change. She ticked off each familiar landmark as she came to it with a sigh of relief. On her left the sign to the Ribbon River Dude Ranch—guests still Welcome. Then to her right, the turnoff to the private airport with its bluff overlooking the distant town, where courting couples parked on summer nights to "watch the planes take off." Then they were coasting down the foothills into Trueheart, past Mo's Truckstop, past the tiny Congregationalist church with its modest white steeple, where, once upon a time, so long ago it almost seemed like a fairy tale, Kaley had planned to be married.

And if Tripp McGraw had really wanted to marry me? She touched her stomach and tipped up her chin. Well, he hadn't. And if he had, she wouldn't be carrying this precious passenger. Much as they'd hurt at the time, things worked out for the best. Would do so again, she told herself firmly.

Michelle glanced at her watch as they turned onto Main Street. "Speaking of breakfast, I hope you'll let me feed

you a magnificent one. Eggs Benedict maybe? Or buck-
wheat pancakes with native berries?''

"Some other time I would love that," Kaley assured her.
"But I want to catch Jim before he rides out for the day,
so..."

Michelle made a ticking sound with her tongue. "He
doesn't know you're coming?"

"No." Kaley had hoped till the last day—till the very
last hour—that she and Richard could work things out.
She'd have felt disloyal airing their differences—temporary
differences, she'd been so sure—before her younger
brother. Especially since Jim had never, in all these years,
quite warmed to his brother-in-law. Why give him further
reasons to disapprove, when what she wanted was a larger,
happier family, not a family divided?

"No, I didn't tell him, but it doesn't matter." There'd
always be a place for her and hers at the ranch. A wave of
weary gratitude washed over her as she braked the car before Michelle's Place. She was luckier than so many single
mothers. Because no matter how desperately lonely she'd
been this past month, she wasn't alone. She could count
on her brother, count on her welcome, count on her bedroom being there, bed made and pillows fluffed, her favorite childhood books lined up on her shelves, her great-
grandmother's old pine wardrobe standing ready for her
clothes. Whether she deserved it or not, she had a place in
the world, reserved in her name. While such a sanctuary
waited, she'd count herself among the lucky.

"Well, if it turns out you miss him," said Michelle,
opening her door before the car had stopped, "don't hes-
itate to come back into town and let me feed you."

"Thanks." Though if she missed Jim, it was bread, butter and milk, then she'd crawl upstairs for a hot shower
and a round-the-clock collapse.

Michelle gathered up her purse and overnight bag,

swung her long legs out of the car, slammed the door and leaned back in the open window. "Thanks again, Kaley." She glanced aside as a red pickup tooted its horn and turned into her parking lot. "And here comes Sam Kerner, riding point. I'm going to get no end of grief that there's no coffee waiting."

The local vet, a big-animal specialist. Likely as not, Sam was stopping in to Michelle's on his way home from tending a sick cow. Kaley smiled wearily. Her landmarks were all holding true.

"And Sheriff Naley," Michelle added as a gray pickup followed the red into her lot. "Kaley, if you ever want to just…talk. About anything at all? Breakups are tough—I should know. Anyway…" She shrugged and smiled her wide, rueful smile. "I live upstairs here and the coffeepot's always on. Stop by any ol' time." She glanced back the way they'd come. "Oh, now, here comes a customer to die for. Do you know Tripp McGraw?"

"Vaguely. Well, guess I should let you get cooking." Kaley revved the engine, lifted a hand in farewell as Michelle hastily straightened. "See you!" She had barely time to swing out from the curb before Tripp's oncoming truck. It loomed up in her rearview mirror, its driver a dim, wide-shouldered shape beyond the glass. He was towing a horse trailer behind, she noted, as she accelerated and he slowed for his turn. But no—oh, no—he'd only slowed to wave to Michelle and now he was driving on.

He followed her for a block or two, and Kaley drove with hunched shoulders, hands clenching her wheel, though she was being silly. There was no way Tripp could know this car was hers. She'd been dodging him successfully for years.

Still, she averted her face as she made her turn north toward the mountains, and she let out a pent breath when he drove toward the east. "Whew!" she whispered, and drew in a shaky breath. Downhearted and tired as she was this morning, he would have been one local landmark too many.

CHAPTER TWO

KALEY DROVE the last ten miles to the ranch in a haze of
exhaustion. The early sun shining in her eyes made her
squint, and once her lashes drooped, conscious thought dis-
solved into drifting images, the present blurring with vivid
memories of the past. A fine herd of Black Angus crosses
on Suntop land—the Tankerslys always had the best. Five
pronghorn antelope on a hill overlooking the highway.
Buzzards riding an early morning thermal to the south—
something dead over there, maybe? No snow on the peaks
yet in August, but soon, soon. She hadn't skied in years,
used to love to, but maybe this year… *With a baby coming
on, Kaley?* For a moment she'd actually forgotten!

On her left now was the road to the McGraw ranch. The
McGraw brand was burned into the arching plank sign-
board: M Bar G. Brands… *His should have been a comet,
a shooting star…*that way he used to touch his scarred
cheek when he encountered someone unexpectedly, or
when he was sad or uncertain… She'd caught his hand
more than once, drawn it down to her lips and kissed it…

Her left front wheel dropped into a pothole in the road—
Kaley yelped her surprise and took a firmer grip on the
wheel.

Sunlight gave way to shadow as the road passed onto
National Forest land. Aspens shivered in no breeze at all
along the flashing creek, their leaves here and there already
gleaming golden—getting late. Too late. *Jim will have ridden out by now.* But maybe Whitey would still be puttering

around the kitchen. He'd have some harsh things to say about Richard; he'd never approved of her marrying a lawyer. Harsh things to say to her, too. Kaley smiled. Coming home.

"And here we are," she informed her tiny passenger as a line of barbed wire slanted down the hill to define the border of Cotter land. She frowned—a post leaning badly there, hadn't Jim noticed? *At least now he'll have some help.* She ought to be able to ride and work till Christmas, anyway, as long as she was careful. She certainly meant to pull her weight—her lips curved in a rueful grin. *Guess that'll just get harder and harder, for a while.* Still, though she was claiming sanctuary, she had no intention of being a burden.

At last she came to the private road to the ranch. The house wasn't visible yet, but after her car topped the second low rise, she looked down into the valley and let out an audible sigh. Home at last!

IT WAS EIGHT BY THE CLOCK in her car when Kaley stepped out, stretched her aching limbs and trudged to the kitchen door. Suddenly she was just as glad Jim would likely not be home. She was too tired to explain anything. Tonight, after she'd slept, would be soon enough.

She entered via the back door and walked through the mudroom, then stopped in the kitchen doorway. "Jim!" Dressed, not in his usual Wranglers and boots, but in a pair of town-going trousers and, wonder of wonders, an ironed shirt. His hair not as shaggy as usual, but clipped close to his head.

"Kaley! You got my—" Her brother paused, frowning, to set the mug of coffee he'd been drinking on the counter. "You can't have gotten it yet."

"Gotten what?" She stood blinking stupidly, still waiting for the whoop and a hug that should be coming.

Jim made no move to close the gap between them. "My letter. But there's no way, when I only mailed it yest—" The scowl on his tanned face deepened. "Whitey called you! Why, that old mule-headed, *son* of a—"

"Nobody called me. What's going on?" She nodded at his clothes. "Somebody died?" A funeral. That could be the only explanation for such attire on a workday.

"No." At last he moved toward her, to brush the skin under her lashes with one work-hardened fingertip. "You look done in, sis. Come sit down. Want a cup of coffee?" He guided her toward the kitchen table, swung a chair out for her.

She stared at the battered canvas duffel bag that rested on the floor beside it. Their father's air force bag. It had survived Vietnam along with him, then come home to be bequeathed, years later, to his son.

The bag looked stuffed full. Her eyes skated along the scarred linoleum from the bag to Jim's unbooted feet. "Jim, what's— You sent me a letter about…what?"

"Here. Sit." He pressed her into the chair, moved his bag out to the mudroom—as if she'd forget about it!—then busied himself, avoiding her searching gaze, fixing her a mug of coffee from the pot on the stove. "Guess you missed it. My letter's probably hitting your mailbox today. But what are you doing here?"

Apparently she'd have to talk first. She let out a long-suffering sigh and propped her face in her hands. "That's not my mailbox anymore, Jim. Not my address. I've left Richard. Divorced him yesterday in Vegas."

The mug Jim had been offering her dropped from his fingers—smashed on the floor, hot coffee spattering their feet and ankles. He stood gaping, then closed his eyes, shook his head and said softly, fervently, "Crap… Crap, crap, *tell* me you're joking!"

"No joke." She could understand surprise—she was still

in shock herself—but horror? "You never liked him any-way, so— Jim, what's *wrong?*"

He crunched through the bits of pottery to yank out the chair opposite hers and collapse into it. "Crap." He broke into bitter laughter, then stopped abruptly. "Who says Cot-ters never have any luck? It's just that it's all the wrong *kind* of—"

She smacked the table flat-handed. "Tell…me…what… was in that *letter?*" He lost that black smile; his dark eye-brows flew together, and she added hastily, "Please? What did you want to tell me?"

His eyes stopped flashing and dropped to the table. He reached for the sugar bowl, lifted the lid and clinked it aimlessly back into place. "Monday after next, Kaley, what date is that?"

"Hey, I've driven all night. I'm too tired for guessing games."

"It's my birthday. My twenty-eighth."

She studied his face, the same dark-lashed, navy-blue eyes as her own, meeting hers half in pain, half in angry challenge. What was she missing here? "Yes. I'd forgot-ten."

"I'll be twenty-*eight,* Kaley." He scowled when she still didn't get it. "You can't join the air force any older than that."

"Oh…Jim!" He hadn't mentioned that ambition in years, not since she went away to college. She'd assumed it was simply a teenager's dream, long left behind. He'd grown up on their father's tales of his flying adventures in the war. Hadn't Jim noticed, as she had, how carefully those tales had been edited? Their father had told them of the good times—the wonderful friendships forged in war-time, the sun on snowy clouds like castles in the air, the feel of a jet answering as sweetly to the yoke as the best cutting horse to the rein, the thrill of night landings on an aircraft carrier in the open sea.

But Kaley had seen her father's face when Jim had asked him what it was like to loose a clip of bombs on a peasant village—the instant change of subject and mood. Hadn't Jim once stopped to think that their father had left that all behind as quick as he could? He hadn't stayed in the service; he'd done his duty, then come straight home to Colorado, back to what mattered. "I didn't realize," she said carefully as Jim continued to glare his defiance. "I thought—"

"That I'd grown out of all that? Changed my mind, decided I'd rather punch cows the rest of my life than pilot a jet? You've always believed what you want to believe. Dad needed somebody and it wasn't going to be you— you'd already run off to college and married your city slicker. So who did that leave holding the bag?"

"But Dad couldn't do it alone." The illness that had finally claimed him had sapped his strength for years before the end. "There was no way he could have kept the ranch going without your help."

"I know that." Jim rubbed a big hand tiredly up his face. "And I didn't begrudge it while he was here. But he's gone now, so what about *my* dreams?"

What could she say to that? "If I'd known you had any—" She stopped at his harsh laughter. "I mean any apart from ranching. But you didn't *tell* me, Jim. I thought you loved it here."

"You thought I felt the way you do," he said flatly. "Just because I didn't whine didn't mean I was happy."

She let out a slow breath. Another thing she hadn't seen, just as she'd missed Richard's true feelings about children. Was she that selfish and blind?

"I tried to make a go of it," Jim continued, lifting the lid to the sugar bowl once more and dropping it, raising it and clinking it down again. "Tried hard since Dad was gone. I don't want to lose this place any more than you do. But I don't want to be chained to it, Kaley. Looking up when the jets fly over from Colorado Springs, wishing I was up there, not stuck down here with a jar full of pink-eye ointment and an irrigation ditch to muck out."

She put her knuckles to her mouth and bit down, thinking hard. "Will it help any now that I'm back? That should free up some of your time. Maybe we could go halves on the chores…" At least, once her baby was delivered they could, if Jim would be patient that long. "If you took private flying lessons, maybe rented a plane?" But that could hardly be cheap and money had been tight around the ranch for years; they were just barely holding their own with her teaching salary added to the ranch's profit… And now that she'd no longer be teaching… *I'll have to think.* There had to be some way.

Jim shook his head. "I wish you'd gotten that letter. This was easier to say long distance." He sucked in a deep breath and let it out on four simple words.

"I've already joined up."

WHAT NOW, WHAT NOW, what now? Kaley wondered, scrubbing a hot washrag over her face. She'd had to excuse herself and go upstairs, as much to gain time to think as to freshen herself. *What am I going to do now?* If she'd had a day to think things out—even half a day—but in reality she had less than an hour. Jim was due at the induction center by noon.

He'd signed the papers and for the next four years, he belonged to the air force; she might as well ask them for one of their jets as for her brother back. He was as good as gone.

And he'd said they had more things to talk about. *I'll say!* Kaley glanced down at her stomach, then grimaced.

No, that wasn't fair, to mention her baby now, when there was nothing he could do to help her. It would only make him feel guiltier when he felt bad enough already. Braced on the cool porcelain, she leaned over the sink, staring down into the darkness of the open drain, like the hole Alice fell down to Wonderland. She'd dropped into a whole new country. Not the safe and comforting one she'd been fleeing to, had counted on for the past miserable month.

It isn't fair!

No. She sucked in a breath and held it. She was the one who hadn't been fair, telling herself that Jim was satisfied with his life. *Time to grow up, Kaley.* Mothers really ought to be grown-ups. She touched her stomach for luck, squared her shoulders and went back downstairs.

Jim was sitting out on the back stoop, staring off toward the high country. She sat down beside him, their shoulders brushing, glanced at him and had to smile, he looked so miserable. "It's not *that* bad, flyboy. I'll manage." Somehow. "Me and Whitey. You've done it for years. Now it's my turn."

His Adam's apple bobbed painfully and he shook his head. "I haven't told you the half of it yet. Wish I'd kept a copy of that damn letter to show you now."

What could be worse than his leaving? "What else?" she said lightly.

"You remember after Dad died, when I told you we'd have to have more cash to keep going? That the books were in much worse shape than he'd let on. When I asked you for more money and you couldn't let me have it?"

She nodded. "I'd just paid for my first semester on my master's degree." And she and Richard had just moved into a bigger, fancier house out in Scottsdale. Richard had set his heart on it, had said it projected the right kind of image for his new position in the firm, and they'd already put the money down when her father died.

She winced, remembering. "I felt awful about that. But you got a loan anyway, in the end, a third mortgage from the bank."

Jim put his head down on his forearms, which were resting on his knees. "Not from the bank, Kaley. That's not where I ended up getting the money."

"But you said—"

"I lied, all right? The bank wouldn't risk a third mortgage, what with the loans they hold on us already."

She felt her heart stutter. "Where did you get it, then?" Jim had wanted a chunk—forty thousand.

"Borrowed it from Tripp McGraw."

"Tripp." Her hands felt cold—icy—and the day darkened. Someone was feeling very sick to her stomach. Kaley dropped her head between her knees and gulped air.

"Kaley?" Jim thumped her back. "Hey!"

"How could you?" Anyone in the whole wide world but Tripp McGraw! "How *could* you?"

"I could, 'cause he would, and we *had* to have that money to keep going. And that—this—is why I didn't tell you. You didn't want to know."

"No, I didn't. Don't." She'd closed the door on Tripp McGraw nine years ago, when he'd broken their engagement, and she'd never looked back. Hadn't dared. The only way to happiness had been to pretend Tripp didn't exist. Never had. "We have to pay him back immediately!"

"That's what I suggested in my letter. We'll have to sell. To him, if we don't find a higher bidder. He'll deduct his loan from the purchase price and—"

"Are you out of your mind?" Kaley pushed herself upright to stare at him. "Sell the *ranch?*" Four generations had struggled to hold this land, and now Jim was going to trade it for an airborne toy? A shiny toy that was only his on loan from the government?

"Yes, sell it, why the hell not?" Jim stalked off the steps and wheeled back again, eyes blazing. "*You* don't want it—you're an English teacher, not a cowgirl now! I'm supposed to hang on to your dreams for you if you won't do it yourself? You call that fair?"

Slowly, Kaley shook her head. "No..." She put one hand to her stomach, the other to her cheek and found it wet—knuckled the tears away and tried to smile.

"So what exactly do we owe Tripp, and when is it due?"

CHAPTER THREE

WATCHING LONER WALK INTO the buyer's trailer had been harder than Tripp would have thought possible.

"Loads well," Huckins noted with satisfaction as the stallion followed his man up the ramp, ears pricked, dark intelligent eyes taking in the new conveyance with his usual bold curiosity.

"Yep." *All my horses load well.* That the Californian should be surprised wasn't the best of signs. A horse that feared the ramp—well, that said more about the animal's handler than it did about the horse. *Should have insisted he ride him before I agreed to sell.* Watching Huckins in the saddle, Tripp would have known for sure if he deserved the stallion. If he had the patience, and the know-how, and the appreciation that he ought.

For Pete's sake, McGraw, that's just a damn horse! Not your virgin daughter.

Smartest, fastest, finest cutting horse he'd ever owned. With more cow sense than a twenty-year-old bull. Tripp had bred him himself, begun gentling him within an hour of his foaling. Loner and he had had the best kind of understanding.

The back gate of the trailer was swung shut with a careless bang. Tripp winced inwardly and set his back teeth. *I owed him that much, to watch Huckins ride.*

Too late now. He brushed his thumb across his shirt pocket, and the folded check rustled softly. Cold comfort at this moment. He'd never dreamed this would hurt so much. Never dreamed he'd need to do it.

Huckins had first phoned him months ago after Loner had ranked a close second for the National Cutting Horse Association World Champion of the year. The Californian had offered a truly astonishing sum should Tripp ever care to sell.

Back then, selling Loner had been unimaginable. Downright laughable. The chunky buckskin was going to be Tripp's foundation sire for a line of cutting horses the likes of which had never been seen before. McGraw horses that would spin on a dime and give you eleven cents change. A line of cutters that would bring the ranch a second source of income, to offset the sickening swoops in the cattle market.

Instead, here he was, cashing Loner in like a forgotten check he'd found in the back of his wallet. Because there was one thing in the world Tripp needed more than the country's finest cutting horse, and that was land.

Tripp swallowed and found his throat aching. "Well..." He held out his hand. "You've got a long drive ahead of you."

"Don't worry about him, McGraw. I'll treat him well. Like the prince he is."

You do or you'll find me on your doorstep! "Sure." Tripp turned on his boot heel and walked. *Land,* he reminded himself, trying to drown out the sound of Huckins's pickup starting up behind him. *Land*—that magical, crucial word. No, make it two words. *Enough land.*

Maybe he'd stop by Cotter's, before he went home, cheer himself up. Plant his feet on the land Loner had bought him.

JIM WEDGED his duffel bag onto the floorboard of his truck and closed the door. Walked around to the driver's side, and stood, fingering the handle. "I hate to leave you like this. It isn't right."

"Can't see you've got much choice." And by now Kaley was swaying with fatigue and shock. She just wanted him gone so she could crawl up to bed. *Sleep first, figure it out later,* she told herself. "Stop worrying. I'll be all right." Somehow. She shuffled forward and hugged him fiercely. "Now, go knock 'em dead, flyboy. Make me and Dad and Whitey proud."

She waved till his pickup had topped the first rise, then her shoulders slumped and her smile flattened to a trembling line.

Closing her eyes, she stood, hearing the quiet creep in around her. Each time she returned, she marveled how quiet it was out here. It had never mattered when, come suppertime, there'd be family at the table. One hand crept to her stomach, then she turned and went inside.

AFTER SHE'D USED UP all the hot water showering, Kaley wrapped herself in a white terry-cloth bathrobe, the one she'd taken from her mother's closet after her death. It had been Kaley's for years now, since she was fourteen. Had accompanied her to college, then out to Arizona. But Richard had never liked it, so on one of her visits she'd left it here, where it belonged. One more raggedy, comforting landmark waiting for her return.

Lying on her bed, she bit the sleeve, her nose brushing its fuzzy nap. *Oh, Mama, what now?* To come home—and find it yanked out from beneath her feet just when she needed it the most! Tears trickled down her cheeks. She flung her forearm across her eyes, mopping up the flow, shutting out the awful day. *Sleep now, figure it out later.*

SHE LAY ON HER BED, listening to the approaching engine— a shiny black hearse idling into the backyard. Whitey sat behind the wheel, with her father riding shotgun—same way they'd always driven the ranch truck. They'd come to tell her about her mother's fall. "Too sassy," Whitey said. "That was always her problem. If she could have saddled a locomotive, she'd have tried to ride it."

Her father nodded bleakly.

"We thought we'd take your baby, too," said a man dressed in a doctor's green surgical scrubs and mask, coming in the kitchen door behind them. "That'll save a second trip."

"Aaah!" Kaley sat up, heart lurching, breath coming in terrified pants. *"Oh…"* She stared around her old bedroom. *Horrible* dream, somehow worse for its silliness. She pulled in a shuddering breath and tried to hold it. Let it out in a gasp. Couldn't have been asleep for long—the angle of sunlight slanting across the windowsill had barely changed. "Only a dream," she muttered, rubbing her stomach.

A bad-luck dream.

No! No, not at all. Simply foolishness—nothing but exhaustion and stress.

Knock-knock.

"Whitey?" She swung her legs off the bed and stood—wobbled and caught hold of the footpost.

Knock-knock-knock!

Whitey, of course. Jim had told her he'd been staying in town all this week at his widowed sister's. They'd had an awful fight when Jim had decided to sell out. After she'd slept, Kaley had intended to drive down and find the old man, tell him to come back, stop worrying, everything would be fine. So he'd saved her the trouble. And this was the reason for her nightmare; she'd woven the sound of his approaching truck into her dreams.

The knock came a third time as she reached the bottom of the stairs. *What's he knocking for?* Whitey owned the kitchen—owned them all and the ranch, too, by right of seniority and survivorship. He'd been her grandfather's hired hand and best friend. *Knocking 'cause he's on his high horse—he's still mad,* she realized, crossing the mud-room. But not with her. She opened the door with a big smile. "*Hey,* you—"

Not Whitey. Her gaze collided with a chest that was younger, broader, harder, that blocked most of the door-way. With a big fist poised in the act of knocking. Her widening eyes lifted to a face she hadn't seen close up for nine years.

Tripp.

His hand unfisted and rose on to his face. He touched his scarred cheekbone with his knuckles, then his hand whipped aside, aborting the motion.

That scar like a comet, a shooting star, which he hated and she'd loved. A radiating tracery of fine white lines, starkly vivid now against his reddening face.

Reddening because he knew that she knew the why of that gesture. It was a holdover from childhood, a reflexive attempt to shield his face from the eyes of a stranger, from the eyes of someone he didn't trust. A sign of surprise and dismay.

I thought I cured you of that.

His hand came to rest on the doorjamb alongside her head. She'd forgotten how much taller he was than she. She'd always loved that about him, his size and strength. "I thought you were Whitey." Belatedly she realized she was standing there in nothing but her old bathrobe, its coarse fabric stinging skin that had suddenly gone achingly, wincingly, alive.

"Kaley." Her name came out in a croak, and Tripp shook his head—more wonder than denial. His hazel eyes drifted down over her, were veiled by dark lashes as his gaze dropped to her naked feet.

Under the pressure of that gaze, she stepped back, her hands moving to her belt, instinctively tugging it tighter. She felt her own cheeks go hot. Damn, she'd wanted time to nerve herself for a meeting with him! And she'd gone to bed with wet hair—it must be a mess.

"What are you doing here?" he asked as his eyes traveled back to her face.

He had no right to look at her this way. He'd willingly, ruthlessly, wastefully forfeited that right nine years ago. "Not selling to you, that's what." *Jim shouldn't have borrowed from you, and you should have had the decency not to loan!* But that was all in the unmentionable past and would stay there. "I'm not selling to anybody," she amended.

"You're—? But—" Another wave of ruddy color swept his face. "Now *wait* a minute!" He advanced into the room and she retreated the way she'd have dodged back from a hot stove—then frowned. She was in no mood to be pushed around in her own kitchen.

"Your brother and I have an understanding," Tripp growled, reaching for her arm.

She retreated another step. "He didn't check with me, Tripp."

"He said you didn't care. That you'd be delighted to sell. That he had full power of attorney."

"He does, but he was wrong—dead wrong. I'm not selling."

Tripp had gone so pale the scar had vanished on his cheek. He caught her shoulders as if to shake her—she narrowed her eyes at him and tipped up her chin. *Don't you dare!*

Instantly he let her go. "I sold my—" He tried again for a level tone. "I sold a stallion this morning, Kaley, to raise money for the down payment on this ranch."

"This ranch isn't for sale."

"I can't get him back."

"I'm sorry, Tripp, but what am I supposed to do? Give up my home, instead?"

"Yes! It's not your home anymore. You don't need it, can't keep it the way it should be kept, and I can. You damn sure *should* sell it!"

"Well, I won't."

Eyes locked, they glared at each other as if the first to blink would lose all. He'd been twenty-four the last time she'd faced him. Nine years of Colorado weather, the hard, outdoor life of a rancher, had burned the last hint of boyhood out of him, leaving him fined down to taut muscle and hard bone. Unsmiling. Once he would have seen the humor of them facing off like a couple of cursing cats. No more.

Just as her eyelashes shivered, he spun away, looked wildly around the kitchen as if in search of something to smash or punch, then swung back again. "Did Jim explain this to you? This didn't happen overnight. I bailed him out May before last—loaned him forty thousand for six months."

"Yes, he told me." Not two hours ago. Jim had borrowed Tripp's money and used it to buy early calves in the spring, meaning to fatten them and sell them in the fall. His hope had been to make a big enough profit that he could afford to hire a manager for the ranch, leaving him free to enlist in the air force. *"I risked big, yeah, Kaley, but the payoff could have been terrific!"*

Could have been. If the price of beef hadn't dropped through the basement. Had Jim sold at that point, he'd have ended up worse off than he started, by the time he reckoned in feed, labor and overhead. Better to hold the calves till the following fall and pray their price would rise.

"But he couldn't pay me off come roundup," Tripp continued. "So I let the loan ride for another year."

"That was very…considerate of you," she admitted.

"Considerate! What were my choices? Calling my loan and ruining your brother, since he hadn't a hope in heaven of paying? Or doing without money I could have used myself for another year?"

He'd been extremely generous—or extremely crafty. Ruthlessly foresighted. Because Tripp hadn't simply let the loan ride—he'd forced Jim to sign a further contract. "You may have done without your money for a year, but it bought you a first option on our land." An option to buy, if ever Jim decided to sell. Tripp had an unbreakable right of first offer, first refusal.

"You're blaming *me* for that?" He advanced on her till he stood towering over her. "What was I supposed to do, Kaley—give your brother a free ride for your sake? For auld, sweet lang syne?" His hand rose until the tip of his callused thumb touched the corner of her mouth, then his thumb stroked up across her cheekbone and feathered away. "You think it meant that much to me? Forty thousand dollars' worth?"

The taunt stung like a lash. His touch burned—it wasn't a caress but an insult. He was using his bulk to intimidate her. She hit out blindly, fighting for space. "Or to me?" *Do you think you meant that much to me?*

"Hey, if I ever thought that, you set me straight a long, *long* time ago," he jeered softly. "How long did it take you to find a new man?"

As if *she'd* been the one who hadn't cared? Who'd broken the faith. She threw the answer back in his face. "Two months!" Richard had found her in Europe two months after Tripp's letter had broken their engagement, leaving her stranded and heartbroken in a strange land. Two months, though it had been another ten before she'd agreed to marry.

"Fast work, hotshot."

She'd had enough. "You want fast? Let's see how fast you can get out of my kitchen—off my land!"

His head rocked back an inch as if she'd slapped him; a muscle ticked beneath his scar. He didn't budge.

If he didn't back off, give her room to breathe, she'd go wild. She prodded his chest with a forefinger. "I said...*out!*"

He looked for a moment as though he'd explode—then his anger sucked inward. "Big words." He brushed her hand aside. "You order your husband around like that? Wear the pants in your family, do you, cowgirl?"

"I don't!" She shook her head, but she couldn't deny *something* had gone wrong with her marriage. Or had never been right.

"Wear spurs when you ride him? Mexican rowels?"

From out of nowhere the image arose of her on top—sobbing, laughing, rising and falling like a rider on a bronc, while Tripp's big hands cupped her, caressed her, guided her, clamped her to him as he arched—no eight-second ride that one. Walled off in the back of her mind for nine years, the image hadn't been softened or fuzzed by review. It was as vivid as if they'd made the memory only last night. Her body throbbed and tightened; her nipples rose against her robe's coarse fabric. *"Out!"* she whispered, eyes watering with the heat of her blush. Tired as she was, she was no match for him. Not for him and her memories, too.

He shook his head. "We have to talk this through, Kaley."

Her voice cracked with startled laughter. "You call this *talk?* And whatever it is, no, we don't. Not this minute. I haven't slept in two days, Tripp." Damn. Pleading for mercy. Where was her pride?

Somehow her weakness reached him, where resistance had not. His eyes narrowed, focused on her face in a different way—seeing her in the present, perhaps, instead of the past? He opened his mouth on a question, then shut it again and nodded. "All...right. That's fair enough."

When had he ever been fair? But ask that, and she'd launch them straight into round two. She didn't want to fight; she wanted to creep upstairs and collapse.

"Then I'll see you tomorrow," he added, when she didn't speak.

Not if I see you first! She turned her back on him and stood hugging herself, tears of sheer exhaustion springing to her eyes.

Behind her, she heard him let out a deep breath, almost a sigh. Then his boots moved lightly to the door, and it closed behind him.

Still she stood, too tired to move. His engine muttered off toward the ridge...died away to...nothing.

The silence crept back and embraced her.

CHAPTER FOUR

"EEEASY, SUNNY. 'Atta boy," Kaley murmured, backing the little chestnut down the trailer ramp. When his hooves reached solid ground, she rubbed his warm red shoulder while he snorted and shook his shaggy head. "*Good* fella." The chunky quarter horse was the most docile ride of Jim's string. On this, her third day home, Kaley was still taking it slow, working up to her brother's hard cases. She tightened the gelding's saddle cinch, then tied him to a tree at the side of the unpaved turnaround that marked the end of the logging road and trailhead to Sumner's Peak.

Five miles up-mountain, on the far side of the forested ridge, lay Sumner line camp, headquarters for the Cotter cattle's summer range. She'd chosen to drive an extra seventy miles round this spur of the mountains, bringing the trailer as close to the camp as she could, rather than ride the direct route from the southeast, which would have meant a trek of some thirty miles as the crow flies. Her thighs weren't up to that yet. Neither did she care to stop overnight in the line cabin, as that longer ride would have required.

Just find Whitey and bring him home; that would be sufficient unto this day. She collected her hat and Levi's jacket from the ranch truck's cab, then turned to her mount. What the old man must be feeling, to have retreated as far as the line camp! He was seventy-two this year. Too old to wake up and find himself without a home.

"Not a good feeling," she informed the chestnut as she

swung her leg over the saddle and urged him toward a gap in the trees. Her heart ached for the old man. She knew precisely how he felt.

Yesterday she'd gone looking for Whitey in Trueheart. A day late, but after her disastrous encounter with Tripp, she'd slept the clock 'round, and woken at noon.

By the time she'd eaten lunch, then yawned her way into town, it had been nearly three. Then she'd lost another hour at Emma Connelly's, eating homemade cherry pie and listening to the old woman's complaints.

Whitey's elder sister had been widowed for twenty-three years. Time enough to decide that she knew precisely what shelf of the refrigerator the butter belonged on, and exactly in what order she cared to read the sections of the *Durango Herald*. At seventy-six, Emma figured she was old enough to know that a grown man ought to make his own bed, ought to close a box of crackers once he was done with it. And as for her brother's nasty spit jar for his tobacco chaws? Or that mangy old dog of his?

Whitey had been eating Sunday dinner with his sister as long as Kaley could remember. But apparently sibling affection and forbearance stretched only so far. Emma had never imagined herself saddled with her brother full-time, any more than Whitey had pictured ending his days without a job, cooped up in town.

By the fourth day of his self-imposed exile he'd retreated from Emma's guest bedroom to an army cot in her drafty garage. Three days later there'd been the final blowup— something about Whitey's attempt to do a load of his own laundry, Emma's unimpeachable, but roundly ignored, advice about never mixing blue jeans with white shirts and red bandannas—and Whitey had packed his duffel, growled something about the line camp and stalked out.

Emma doubted she'd see him before the snow flew, if then, stubborn old coot.

Considering that she'd had tears in her eyes when she'd said this, Kaley couldn't find it in her heart to blame the woman. Because even in good times, Whitey was best taken with a large dose of wide-open spaces. Given the claustrophobic confines of a spinster-fussy cottage festooned with crocheted lace doilies and silk flower arrangements, and considering what must be his present mood of black despair, Kaley was sure he'd have tried a saint, much less his loving sister.

Kaley only hoped that he wasn't driving the cowboy up at Sumner camp half-crazy, too. Adam Dubois. Kaley had never met the man. He was a stranger Jim had hired in the spring, and who knew how patient he'd be with an unexpected guest, especially when that guest was an elderly, endlessly opinionated cowboy. Line camp men took jobs in the high country for a reason. As a breed, they tended to be loners, happiest without company.

And even if—faint hope—all was bachelor bliss above, Whitey was too old for these remote and rugged mountains. He needed his own soft bed in the little house Kaley's grandfather had built for him forty years ago out back of the barn. Needed a propane heater at night, a hot bath when he wanted one, decent meals and proximity to somebody who cared for him.

So here she was. Kaley ducked under a low-hanging branch and tightened her knees; the chestnut surged uphill, ear tips almost touching with alert interest, hooves clopping softly on the dirt trail. It was nearly noon now, though she'd left the ranch at dawn. Assuming that she'd find Whitey in camp, rather than have to hunt him down out on the mountainside, still they'd be driving bad roads home in the dark.

Of course there was one advantage to this. She'd miss Tripp again.

She'd managed to duck him all yesterday. He'd come by once while she was in Trueheart and left her a note on the back door. Just four brusque words: *We've got to talk.*

Then he'd returned after supper. She'd seen him from the slope of Cougar Rock Pasture, where she'd walked out to admire the sunset. Standing motionless under the trees, she'd watched Tripp hammer on her back door, then open it. She'd clenched her hands to fists at that. *Thinks he owns the place already?* They would have to talk.

He'd emerged in a minute, apparently satisfied that she wasn't hiding within, to stand glaring around the property.

He'd stalked to the barn, no doubt figuring she was feeding the horses or chickens, then moments later he'd reappeared, a tall, unmistakably masculine shape in the gathering dusk, broad of shoulder, narrow of hip, turning slowly on his long horseman's legs, staring out across the darkened pastures and slopes that he meant to own.

She should have gone down to him. No use making things any rougher between them than they already were. Not when, thanks to her brother, Tripp had her dead to rights.

She couldn't bring herself to smile and do it. Not yet.

She needed time to get the bitter pill down and keep it down. Bitterness piled on top of old bitterness, but still, there it was. Thanks to Jim she owed him. Owed him bigtime. All the wishing in the world wouldn't change that, any more than it had changed his mind nine years ago.

Tomorrow she'd have to face him and work something out.

But that was tomorrow, and today was today, Kaley reminded herself, squaring her shoulders. Today the sky was a color of high-altitude cobalt that Phoenix, with its streams of glittering, smog-belching traffic, would never match. Breathing deep, the cool air fragrant with pine, she tipped her head back to watch a black dot against the blue—a golden eagle, wheeling high above the granite pass toward which Sunny was climbing. She smoothed her palm round and round the top of her saddle horn, and laughed aloud. *Oh, I'm home all right!* However uncertain and terrifying her future, the present was sweet as wine. *Kaley Cotter and daughter are home again.*

THE LINE CAMP STOOD in an alpine meadow, starred with late-blooming asters and goldenrod, encircled by the shivering gold of turning aspens. A one-room log cabin built by Kaley's great-grandfather and added onto by every generation of Cotter since—a lean-to here for feed and tack, a shed for wood there, a rough pole corral that fenced in a small vegetable garden, keeping the crops safe from marauding cattle, if not the rabbits and deer.

Three horses lazed at the far end of the pasture, in the shade of the trees. They lifted their heads and whinnied as Sunny trotted down the slope toward the cabin, then went back to their grazing. The line man would have five horses in his string, at least, Kaley figured. If two were missing, then he was out prowling the meadows. And Whitey must be, too, on a borrowed mount, since he'd driven his rattletrap pickup to the trailhead and left it there.

She tied off Sunny and knocked on the screen door. "'Lo the house!"

Something stirred beyond the sun-spangled, rusty mesh.

"Anybody home?" When nobody answered, Kaley opened the door.

Lying in a bunk against the far wall, Whitey heaved himself to his elbows and blinked. "Kaley?" He swiped a gnarled hand across his unshaven face. "Kaley-*girl?*"

She crossed the bare, dusty boards in four strides. In all the years she'd known him, Whitey had never slept past seven. "Whitey, what's *wrong?*" She knelt beside him and touched his bristly cheek, then cupped a palm to his forehead. "You're sick?"

"Had a wreck yesterday. Nothin' t'speak of."

A wreck was cowboy for a fall. One to speak of. Minor spills didn't count. "You're okay?" She checked the urge to whip off the dingy blanket that covered him and see for herself.

"Banged up m'damn knee."

"Good one or bad one?" A cow had crushed his right knee between a gate and a fence post years ago. He limped badly at the best of times.

His snort was a rueful laugh. "M'good one's not so good now." He touched her shoulder, the shy touch of a child. "What're you doin' here, girl?"

"Come to bring you home. We're not selling the ranch, Whitey. Not if I can help it." She patted his hand, then stood hastily as his eyes glistened. He'd never survive her seeing him cry. With her own eyes brimming, she turned briskly on her heel. "Where's Chang?"

She spotted the circular heap of frizzy white-and-copper hair, coiled in a battered easy chair that was pulled up to the wood-burning stove. Trust Chang to claim the best seat in the house. "Hey, Chang." She stooped beside the ancient Pekingese and warily offered her knuckles for his identification.

A wavering growl issued from somewhere within the furry mound, and one brown goggle eye cracked open to regard her with weary malevolence. "Let's go home, old guy." The mountains were no place for a short-legged lapdog. "Mellowed a bit, hasn't he?" she observed when he didn't lunge for her. Oh, she'd stayed away too long! Even Chang had changed.

"Just losing his teeth and too dang proud to gum you," Whitey grunted. From the shuffling and groaning behind her, he was struggling into his jeans.

"The hand here—Dubois?" she asked without turning. "Any chance he'll be stopping back by for lunch?"

"That Cajun? He never shows before dark."

Meaning that Whitey's presence was probably proving a strain. Kaley's eyes wandered to the bunk on the opposite wall from Whitey's. A book on dinosaurs, of all things, rested on a Mexican blanket tucked to drum-tight perfection. "Too bad. I wanted to meet him."

She'd be needing at least two dependable hands to help with fall roundup. Jim had said Dubois could be trusted, but Kaley preferred to see for herself. Some cowboys had problems taking orders from women. If that was going to be an issue, she needed to know sooner rather than later.

She scratched Chang's tasseled ear and stood. "Guess I'll go catch you a ride." She supposed they could leave Dubois a note, telling him to collect Whitey's mount, which they'd tie off at the trailhead. "Any preferences?"

Whitey grunted. "Shot my preference yesterday. That grullo your dad used t'ride. Ol' fool stepped smack in a badger hole."

Kaley winced. Hence Whitey's wreck and his taking to his bed. More sadness than jarred bones, she'd bet—one more connection with her father gone forever. Apart from which, nothing hurt worse than to shoot a good horse. "I'm sorry."

"Huh! No sorrier than he was."

RIDING ACROSS the flowery pasture, Kaley held a coffee can of grain balanced on her thigh. She reined in Sunny and rattled the oats against the tin. "Who wants to work today?"

A couple of glossy equine heads lifted from the grass, but she had no takers. The sun-burned black grabbed a green mouthful, turned a casual quarter turn as he grabbed another bite, till, apparently without intention, he ended facing toward the trees. He glanced back at her over his rump, chewing insolently, ready to bolt. And the others looked as if they'd take their cue from him. "Come on, you bum." She rattled the oats seductively.

"Which one do you want?" called a masculine voice behind her.

Her thighs clamped together in startlement and Sunny jumped, then steadied as she reined him in again and looked over her shoulder. To find Tripp, his big white-faced bay carrying him down the meadow at a half trot. He was building a loop in his catch rope already. "The paint," she said, her voice steadier than her heartbeat. Think of the devil and here he came riding!

Ears pricked in fascination, the brown and white-patched mare watched Tripp's advance till it dawned on her she'd been singled out. She snorted and spun away—straight into the path of his lazily descending loop. She flinched as it tightened around her neck, then stopped dead and blew out a disgusted breath.

"Thanks," Kaley said as Tripp reeled her in. "What are you doing here?"

He nodded back toward the cabin, where two packhorses now stood in hipshot patience by the corral. "Dubois is about out of salt blocks. And I wanted to see for myself how the grass is holding."

"Neighborly of you," she couldn't resist saying—though it wasn't. He was acting as owner already. So he hadn't believed her when she'd told him she wasn't selling. Or if he had, he meant to ride right over her.

His mouth tightened at her tone. She found her gaze snared by its well-carved shape, the bottom lip full and almost sensuous, the upper lip stern to the point of harshness. The nerves at her nape quivered and stung as the memory came, unwilled as it was vivid—the rasp of his afternoon beard across her shuddering skin, the furnace warmth of his breath at her ear. She looked away.

"Not exactly," he replied evenly. "Jim and I split Dubois's time and wages. He works for both of us."

"Oh." Another thing Jim had forgotten or omitted to tell her in their short while together. Kaley felt her temper kick up a notch. So Jim hadn't even been able to pay a full-time line man? No more putting it off. Tonight she'd have to sit down with the ranch accounts.

"And you," Tripp said as they turned their mounts toward the cabin. "What brings you here?"

She told him about Whitey. "He ended up here," she said with a dark, accusing glance. "Forty years with my family and this is what it's come to. Who knows what he meant to do when the snows came?"

Tripp opened his mouth to tell her that he'd intended all along to take Whitey on, make him welcome. Because she was right. You didn't turn away a man who'd worked his whole life for your family, any more than you sent your old saddle horse to the cannery. Loyalty bound both, hired hand and rancher. And the whole point of this way of life was that, hard as it was, there was always room and grass enough for one more.

He'd made it plain to Jim Cotter that Whitelaw had a job and a home, but he'd been remiss not seeking out the old man himself first thing. He'd been too preoccupied this past week with arranging Loner's sale, with double-checking his forecast of the fall profits as he prepared for the purchase of the Circle C. Tripp felt a muscle tick in his jaw. If there was one thing he hated, it was to realize he'd left something undone that he should have done.

And here it was Kaley, of all people, pointing out his blunder. "I…" He clamped his jaw on his explanation and shrugged. Coming now, it would only sound like an excuse. Talk was cheap and action all. He'd failed to act in time.

He glanced at her bitterly, then when he found that she rode with face averted, he gazed with greedy abandon. Kaley. She didn't look a day older than the last time he'd kissed her, in the spring of that terrible year when she'd come home from college for Easter. Or if she'd changed, it was—impossible as it seemed—for the better. The long, reddish-brown hair that had once hung like a silk shawl to her waist, now swung enticingly at her shoulders. And last time he'd held her in his arms, she'd been angular as a yearling colt. Now she looked curvier—still slender, yet somehow softer. Soft—he remembered drawing his nose across her cheek, soft as a foal's velvety muzzle. He could still feel the creamy smoothness of her breast cupped in his palm. *Don't go there,* he warned himself harshly. *She's another man's woman.*

A woman he'd put behind him years ago. Only fools looked back.

"We have to talk," he reminded her as they reached the cabin. "I came looking for you yesterday." Then again this morning. When he'd stopped by the Circle C and found her car gone, he'd wondered if perhaps he'd dreamed their whole encounter.

Or at least misunderstood. It had crossed his mind, on not finding her for the third time, that maybe she'd dropped by the ranch to say farewell to Jim and to a way of life. If bad luck hadn't sent Tripp stumbling into her path, maybe she'd have cried a few tears and gone her way.

Instead, he'd shown his ugly mug at the worst possible moment. Her refusal to sell had been a spur-of-the-moment token protest against bitter reality. A gut-level, reflexive denial that Tripp could well understand. He'd sooner part with an arm than an acre of his own land.

But given two nights to think it over, maybe her defiance had faded to pained acceptance. So she'd fled back to her husband in Phoenix, leaving Tripp shaken but whole, winner by default.

So much for hopes and dreams!

"We do have to talk," Kaley agreed. "But first I've got to get Whitey home. Maybe to a doctor."

She'd been too long in the city if she thought she'd drag Whitelaw to a sawbones. Short of major blood loss or compound fracture, his generation of cowpokes tended themselves and kept on working. *City girl, go back where you belong.* "I'll help you get him a-horseback," Tripp said bleakly.

She looked for a moment as if she meant to refuse him, then she nodded and slipped off the chestnut. "Let me see if he's ready."

SHE'D NEVER HAVE MANAGED without him, that was sure, Kaley realized a short while later as she watched Tripp lift the old man into the paint's saddle. "All right now?" Tripp asked, stepping back from the mare.

"Right as rain," Whitey growled, looking more than a little flustered.

Kaley bit down on a worried smile. If she knew Whitey, it was his helplessness that was irking the old man, not the pain. Though that had to be considerable. His left knee was puffed to the size of a cantaloupe.

"Where's that damn Chang?" he added.

"Coming." Kaley slipped back into the cabin and brought the pannier she'd padded with a blanket over to the easy chair. "Be nice now, you, if that's possible." She clamped her hands around the dog's fat middle and lifted him, wriggling and snarling, into the basket and shut its lid. "You're lucky a coyote didn't gobble you up, up here." Or maybe the dog was too mean to be eaten.

Tripp's face was carefully blank as he took the basket from her arms and fastened it behind Whitey's saddle, to counterbalance the one that held his clothes. The paint's ears swiveled backward in alarm, but they didn't flatten to her head. Embarrassment rendered Whitey speechless. With a grudging nod of thanks to Tripp, he set off toward the pass, his right hand absently patting the pannier's lid.

"Well..." Kaley untied and mounted. She'd left a note for Dubois along with the brownies she'd baked for him the night before. Meeting him would have to wait for another day. "Thank you, Tripp."

But he was swinging astride his big bay. "He's heavier than he looks," he warned her, nodding at the distant rider, who'd almost reached the top of the meadow. "You'll need help getting him off again."

Nodding grimly, she touched spurs to Sunny's ribs and shot away. Thunder of hooves on the grass, and Tripp was loping alongside her in seconds. She should know better than to hope to lose him so easily. He rode like a centaur, plus his gelding had two hands on Sunny and a stride to match.

Where the trail entered the trees, they reined back to a walk. Resigning herself to his presence, Kaley tugged her Stetson lower on her forehead to shield her eyes. Still, like sunlight on her cheek, she could feel him looking.

"How did an old hardcase like him end up with a useless lapdog?" Tripp wondered. "He ever married?"

She had to smile at the thought. "Not in fifty years, and I think that ended badly. No, he found Chang about eight years ago out on the highway. Had a busted shoulder. All we could figure is he'd leaned too far from a car window and tumbled out, and his owner didn't notice and drove on. Whitey always says he should have shot him."

"Uh-huh," Tripp said dryly.

"Well, he chases cats on command." Trying to explain the inexplicable, Kaley laughed under her breath.

"That's useful."

She'd forgotten how he'd say one thing and mean quite the opposite. All the humor he could pack into a word or two. "Besides, everybody needs somebody to love." Laughter fading, she trailed two fingertips across her stomach.

"Do they?" His voice had lost its warmth.

Don't they? She certainly had. Did. Her fingers twitched toward her stomach again; she flattened them, instead, on her leg. But take her companion now—apparently he hadn't felt the need. Nine years and Tripp still hadn't bothered to find a lasting love of his own.

Or had he? She felt as if she'd have known somehow, but really, how would she? Jim had been only eighteen when she and Tripp parted. Still, in all the years since, he'd known better than to mention Tripp's doings to her.

From the corner of her eye she could see Tripp's elkhide boot resting lightly in his stirrup, the long, muscular length of his calf and thigh. Hard to imagine he hadn't had his pick of the ladies in the years since he'd dumped her. Tripp wasn't film star–handsome as Richard was, and the regularity of his features was forever marred. But the scar that he hated added so much character. Edge. And he had something better than glossy perfection—an aura of strength and presence that a woman couldn't ignore. He wasn't an image, handsome or otherwise, he was a...a force. A man in motion, striding through life.

"When does school start in Phoenix?" he asked, reining his bay closer to Sunny as the trail narrowed.

Their knees brushed and she drew in a feathering breath. So even if she hadn't heard about him over the years, he'd made it his business to learn about her—that she taught school. "It started this week."

"They gave you time off to say goodbye?"

She shook her head. "I've quit, Tripp." And now the trail was narrow enough to give her an excuse. She drew back on the reins and Sunny slowed to fall in behind the bay.

Tripp glanced back, frowning, then wheeled his mount across the path.

She halted with Sunny's nose almost touching Tripp's knee. Funny, but she felt as if she'd been trotting alongside the horses, her breath was coming that fast. *Here it comes.*

"Decided to be a housewife, instead," he hazarded, voice stonily neutral, eyes narrowed. "Reckon a lawyer earns enough for two and then some."

"He does," she agreed defiantly. Not that Richard hadn't spent it just as fast as it came in. On sleek cars, a twenty-thousand-dollar Ducati motorcycle that he had no time to ride, a gym full of shiny weight machines for his exercise room, custom-fitted golf clubs, a collection of antique handguns. Boy toys. But try to explain that to Tripp, who hadn't been a boy since his early teens. By then his father had pretty well slid into the bottle, and it was Tripp who'd called the shots at the M Bar G.

"Reckon he can support a wife at home, and a manager for a hobby-horse ranch, as well."

"He could," she allowed. Tripp was probing closer and closer to the heart of the matter.

"So who're you hiring? Whitelaw's too old for the job."

Closer. She remembered playing blindman's buff with him one night in the barn, up in the hayloft. Standing with a half-terrified giggle frozen in her throat while his arms swept the hay-sweet dark, coming closer and closer. The trembling in his fingertips when they found her at last, tracing the shape of her face...her mouth...her body...as if he'd never touched her before, never touched a woman in all his life. Then her lashes shivering against his lips...her knees turning to butter...

"*Who,* Kaley?"

She blinked and sat taller in the saddle. "I'll manage my own place."

His incredulous smile died stillborn. His dark eyebrows drew together. "And commute to Phoenix on weekends? Reckon you *do* wear the pants in your house."

Reckon I do, at that. She met his gaze squarely. "My house—my home—is here now, Tripp. I'm divorced."

His head rocked back half an inch; his eyes narrowed to slits. Reacting to something sensed in his rider but not visible, the bay threw up his head and snorted, dancing in place.

"So that's it." Tripp's face was wiped clean of all expression, but the starburst scar on his cheekbone faded as he paled. "Why?"

"Why what?" He was mad, she realized as the bay pinned back its ears, half rearing to Tripp's shortened rein. Blazingly mad. But then, so was she. Who was he to demand an explanation?

"Why did you leave him—or did you?"

No, he left me just as you did! Because in spirit, if not in the flesh, it was Richard who'd walked out on their vows—rejected her child and therefore her. But she'd sooner rip out her heart and hand it over than admit that now she was a two-time loser! Touching her spurs to Sunny's flanks, Kaley drove him past the bay. Branches flailed her hunched shoulders. Her hat flipped back and cartwheeled away.

Let him fetch it or let it lie! She urged the chestnut to a tight lope and held him there, huffing and puffing, till she reached the pass, where Whitey and the paint stood waiting.

By the time Tripp joined them at the trailhead and handed over her hat, his temper had vanished behind a wall of ice-cold, courteous calm. And the more she pondered it, on the drive home, the less Kaley could make sense of his response. Perhaps she'd imagined it.

Because how could Tripp be mad, when she was the one who'd been injured?

CHAPTER FIVE

As TRIPP DROVE back from Durango the following evening, his mood was black—dark as the wall of thunder-
heads that towered off to the west.

Feeling like this, maybe it was just as well he hadn't
connected with Kaley today. When he'd stopped by the
Circle C this afternoon, he'd found only Whitelaw in res-
idence. The old man had been gimping about the barn,
using a rake for an improvised crutch, his scruffy Pekingese
pattering underfoot, likely to trip him at any minute.

Kaley had gone to Durango, Whitey had told him when
he'd asked.

Four days home and she was flitting off to the city already. It figured. What didn't figure was why he'd been
so...damn...angry ever since he'd learned of her divorce.
Waste. What a crying waste! were the words echoing somewhere at the back of his mind. He'd always despised a
waste of anything—time, effort, emotion.

But what, precisely, was wasted here? he wondered as
his truck climbed out of the plains toward Trueheart.

Well, his time, for one thing; that was sure. After he'd
spoken with Whitelaw, he'd driven to Durango. Told himself that he needed those tractor parts and shouldn't put it
off another day. But the John Deere dealer hadn't stocked
the crucial bearing, would have to order it special, so that
errand had been entirely a loss. And he hadn't caught even
a glimpse of Kaley, though on his way out of town he'd
swung through the parking lots of two of the larger grocery

stores, where most Truehearters did their serious provisioning. The whole damn day just a waste of time.

The way his dreams lay in waste. Maybe it was just starting to hit him that the purchase had fallen through. That he'd sold Loner for nothing. Wasn't that reason enough for a mood like a black wolf padding at his heels?

To the west, the setting sun reappeared, dropping into the slot between storm clouds and horizon. A red-orange light swept across the hills, bathing the land in ruddy gold, branding the undersides of the purple clouds with rose and ruby. Tripp sucked in a breath of sage-scented air. This— it was moments like this that made the struggle to hold the land, his way of life, worth whatever it cost. Till the sun puddled and sank below the horizon, Tripp simply drove and drank in the changing colors.

Finally, he gave a sigh that seemed to let something go, and reached for the headlight knob. *Don't give up,* he told himself for the hundredth time over the past few days. This was a setback, but it wasn't defeat—not by a long shot, it wasn't.

Because there was no way Kaley could make a go of her ranch. All he had to do was make her see that.

The headlights of an approaching car gleamed like animal eyes in the dusk. Its windshield wipers were still switched on, he noticed as it shot past. It was raining somewhere up toward Trueheart, then. Good, they could always use rain. The longer the grass grew in the fall, the more graze there'd be for his herd in the first half of the winter. If he could put off feeding hay till after Christmas, he could keep his costs down, future profits up. Which was one more reason he needed the Cotter land. Kaley had acres and acres of irrigable meadows along her creek. If he could grow all he needed…was no longer at the mercy of the market price for good hay…

His truck mounted the first of the foothills. The road

ahead gleamed black and shiny, though the shower that had drenched it had passed on already. He crested another rise and now Tripp saw taillights. Possibly Kaley returning from town? His foot came down hard on the gas.

But no, he realized when he'd closed the distance. This was one of those big sport utility vehicles. He recognized it as the one Rafe Montana had bought for his new wife, Dana, and her babies, when he made out its license plate: RbnRvr—the Ribbon River Dude Ranch, Dana's ranch to the west of town. Tripp smiled and eased off the gas—just as the brake lights ahead flared and stayed on.

What the—? He stomped on his own brakes and swore— then groaned as the sport ute wobbled into a skid on the rain-slick asphalt. *"Easy!"* For a moment he thought the driver had the trouble in hand, but then she overcorrected. The sport ute's right wheels dropped off the jagged edge of the pavement, slowed as they hit the gravel and low brush beyond—and the car swerved hard to the right and plunged off the road, bouncing and bounding into a pasture.

"Stay upright, stay *upright!*" Tripp prayed as he braked. And miraculously the vehicle did, coming at last to a jouncing halt sixty feet off the highway.

After parking on the shoulder, Tripp leaped out and ran. Off to the south he saw another car coming and he begged it silently to stop. He could send its driver into Trueheart for help, if need be.

"Dana!" He swung open her door and flinched at the noise—two babies wailing their lungs out. "You okay?" She was twisted around to her right, peering into the back seat as she yanked frantically at her seat belt buckle. "Dana." He patted her shoulder, even as his eyes were drawn irresistibly to the windshield.

It wasn't cracked. Seemed that it ought to be cracked. His heart was thundering, the sound of the babies drilling straight through his brain. *Tears and glass and a wreck in the rain. And nothing had ever been the same after.* He wrenched his mind back to the present, where, thank God, no glass had been shattered. "Dana, honey, hey…"

Blinded by tears, she whirled around and clutched his shirt. "G-g-get me out of this! *Please!* Oh, sweetheart, hang *on.* Mommy's coming!"

He doubted she even knew who he was. "Easy there, e*aaa*sy…" He reached over her lap to unclip the seat belt. Not jammed at all. She was just in a tizzy. And maybe stunned, he realized, noting the disinflated air bag drooping from the steering wheel. That must have blown up in her face. *Rafe is going to thank his lucky stars he replaced her old pickup.* "Easy there," Tripp soothed, helping her down out of the high seat, then holding her up as her knees buckled.

"How can I help?" asked a quiet voice at his elbow. He glanced aside to find Kaley standing there, her fine eyes wide with sympathy. So that had been her in the car behind them.

"Petra and Peter, *please,* somebody look at them!" Dana begged, trying to twist out of his grasp.

"Of course." Kaley hurried around to the far side of the vehicle and leaned in from there, while Tripp opened the near door for Dana and lifted her in.

Strapped into car seats, both her babies were squalling wholeheartedly. Beneath the racket, the women's crooning ran like a wordless melody, a song no man could sing. Peering past Dana's shoulder, Tripp saw Petra—with blood dripping down her chin. His stomach lurched.

A woman weeping…the smell of blood…it wasn't the pain of the glass in his face so much as the terrifying blindness, blood welling into his eyes… He staggered back from the open door and turned to lean against the car's side, his stomach heaving. Scrubbing the back of his hand across his cheekbone, he closed his eyes—saw his mother's tear-drenched face—and opened them wide again. Shook his head to clear the vision. *That was then...this is now.* He sucked in a breath and held it, blew it out, sucked in another and squared his shoulders. Forced himself back to the door. "How are they?"

"Just fine, I think," Kaley almost sang with happy relief. "Shaken up a bit, but everybody looks just fine."

"Petra's bleeding," he protested.

"Bit her lip," Kaley agreed, but her smile reassured him.

"Mommy's crying!" Petra announced to the world with a tearful grimace.

Dana let out a sobbing laugh and continued wiping the tail of her shirt across her daughter's chin. "She is, sweetie. Yes, she is." One hand cradling her toddler's face, she leaned to study the baby Kaley was comforting. "You're sure Peter's all right?"

"His neck seems fine. He's very alert. Truly just startled, I think." Kaley smoothed the baby's red-gold hair, reached for one of his waving hands and held it, her thumb stroking his tiny knuckles. "Aren't you, Peter?"

At the sound of his own name spoken by a stranger, the baby stopped midsquall to gape at her—then scowled ferociously and started again.

"Lungs in great shape," Tripp added wryly. "What happened, anyway, back there?"

"A coyote," Dana said, brushing her short, dark hair off her brow with a forearm. "He just stood there in my headlights till the last second. I thought I could—" Tears brimming again, she shook her head. "I'm so *stupid!*"

"You braked for a coyote!" Lucky her husband was crazy in love with her. The manager of Suntop Ranch didn't suffer fools lightly.

"Of *course,* she did." Kaley flashed him a glance that said *Back off!*

He did, half grinning at her fierceness. Then he set himself to getting this show back on the road, while the women comforted the small fry. He walked around the vehicle, checking for damage, then went for his flashlight and crawled beneath to inspect the suspension.

By the time he'd concluded that the car was roadworthy, the whimpering within had faded to the odd hiccup and an occasional piping comment from Petra. "The car bucked. Like Tobasco bucks with Daddy. I don't want it to *do* that, Mommy!"

Tripp laughed under his breath and leaned back in the door. "Ready to roll, Dana? I'm driving you wherever you want to go." Though it didn't look to him as if anybody needed a doctor.

She swung around and smiled shakily. "Home, of course, but, Tripp, you don't have to—"

"Yes, I do. Do you want to sit up front or back here?" He knew the answer already.

A FEW MINUTES LATER the sport ute bumped out of the pasture and lunged up onto the pavement, bouncing on its heavy springs.

"Stop that!" Petra commanded from the back seat.

"Yes, ma'am!" Tripp had to smile. Not quite three and she was bossing men already. "That was the worst of it. Smooth riding from here."

In his mirror, he could see Kaley's headlights switch on, then she pulled out behind them. He'd tried to tell her that Rafe could drive him back to his truck, but Kaley wouldn't hear of it. "Dana will want him at home," she'd told him in an undertone—then reached up to wipe a fingertip below his lashes.

"What's that for?" he'd demanded, stung by her touch. Nine years since she'd touched him.

"Just…something on your face." She'd headed off to her car.

Something on his face, you could say that—the mark of that day, never to be erased. When he returned to school that fall, the other boys had called him Scarface—till he'd inflicted a few scars of his own. As full of bewildered rage as he'd been all that first year after his mother left, the fights had been welcome.

"My mouth hurts," Petra announced.

"I'm so sorry, sweetheart," Dana murmured in the darkness behind him. "It's all Mommy's fault. I never should have tried to…"

That wreck twenty-five years ago had been his fault. Also on this road, farther along toward Durango. Maybe that was why this was hitting him so hard. On the way into town, in the midst of a rainstorm, he'd spotted an antelope bounding alongside the car. Reaching blindly behind, he'd grabbed his mother's elbow to show her. At eight, he damn sure should have known better.

At least he'd been the one who'd paid, smashing the windshield with his face when the car swerved into a ditch. His mother had only been shaken, though he could close his eyes and still hear her weeping.

Weeping for him, he supposed, and what in the space of a heartbeat he'd become. Because before that day she'd always called him "my handsome," in her honeyed Southern drawl. Her teasing endearment had embarrassed him, even while it made him feel special. He couldn't remember her saying it even once after that in the two months before she'd vanished from his life.

From his father's life. From his brother Mac's life, who'd only been five at the time—too young to lose his mother. Tripp had changed all that, grabbing her elbow.

THAT WAS A TEAR ON TRIPP'S CHEEK, Kaley thought while she followed the sport ute through Trueheart, then out again, heading west. She'd seen the tracks of more tears, and his thick lashes had dried in spikes. *Crying? Tripp? Why?*

Not for Dana, who'd been more frightened than hurt, Kaley guessed.

Because this wreck reminded him of his own? She tried to recall what he'd told her that summer night while they'd lain on a blanket out under the stars, her head pillowed on his arm. It had been a halting story, and not one he'd volunteered. She'd had to coax it out of him, word by reluctant word. And she wasn't sure she'd gotten it all, before he'd rolled up to one elbow and applied his own form of persuasion, to his own ends.

His mother hadn't wanted to take him along, she remembered that much. But when Tripp had pleaded, she'd finally given in, saying she'd drop him at a movie matinee while she did her shopping. Kaley remembered finding it odd that his mother would leave an eight-year-old alone in the city.

They'd never made it that far. Tripp had jogged her elbow and the car had skidded, much the way Dana's did tonight. Except with far worse consequences. "That's how I got my ugly mug," he'd said matter-of-factly, then smiled at her storm of protest.

Surely he was just being modest, she remembered thinking. A scar like that might have troubled him as a child, but now that he'd grown to glorious manhood? When she was seventeen to his twenty-three he'd seemed such a man. Her first man, reducing all boyfriends that had come before to posing children. Surely her man realized how beautiful he was, inside and out. She'd lost the rest of that night, trying to show him.

Sometime later, she'd learned the rest—that his mother had left his father two months after Tripp's accident. Had run off with her sons' pediatrician in Durango. They'd moved to New Orleans and she'd never looked back.

And Tripp's father had never recovered, never looked for another woman. Only for comfort in the bottle.

Kaley bit her lip as she frowned in thought. And somehow, someway, she'd gotten half a notion that Tripp blamed himself for his family's dissolution. Though that was crazy. How could an eight-year-old be to blame?

But I bet I know one thing—where his mom meant to go while she stashed her son at the matinee. If anyone should be blaming herself for what had happened...

Yet, maybe she had shouldered the blame. Maybe in the end, Mrs. McGraw hadn't so much run to her lover as fled from her guilt, emblazoned on her small son's cheek for all the world to see. Every time she'd looked at his poor little face, it must have stabbed her to the heart.

WHEN THEY REACHED the Ribbon River Dude Ranch, Kaley stayed in her car while Tripp and Dana unbuckled the children from their seats. A tall, dark man walked out the back door of the Victorian farmhouse onto the wide deck, called a question, then came down the steps at a bound.

Standing with his big hands on Dana's shoulders, he listened to her for a moment, then swept her and their baby into a fierce embrace. Tripp stood by, examining the stars for the first minute of that hug. Then he shrugged and carried Petra, still babbling and waving her chubby hands, to the screen door, where he passed her to the gangly, teenage boy who'd made an appearance. Returning, Tripp patted Dana's shoulder in passing, said something with a grin to the man who still held her and came on to Kaley's car.

"Reckon Rafe'll forgive her the coyote," he said, straight-faced, as he dropped into his seat next to Kaley.

So Dana was one of the lucky ones, Kaley mused as she drove the long gravel road out to the highway. She felt more than a passing twinge of envy. Not once in the past eight years had she been hugged like that.

And before Richard? Her eyes flicked to her companion. That had been different. That had been all about sex. They'd been young and greedy and couldn't get enough of each other. But their romance had been nothing to build a life on, nothing to last.

Or it would have lasted.

TRIPP DIDN'T SPEAK till they could see the lights of True-heart twinkling in the distance. "Can I buy you a burger at Mo's? I'm 'bout ready to gnaw my boots."

The last time she'd eaten at Mo's Truckstop had been with Tripp, nine years ago, on her spring break from college. Lingering over coffee, hands clasped across the table, they'd planned their modest wedding, which was scheduled for June. By then Tripp would be done with spring roundup, and she'd have completed her freshman year at Oberlin.

Marriage had seemed so easy and right as they'd sat there. So...so attainable. All they had to do was hang on for three more lonely months, then happiness was theirs. Kaley cleared her throat and managed to find a level voice. "Mo's sounds good."

INSIDE THE TRUCK STOP, Tripp chose the same booth they'd always taken—their booth, Kaley had thought of it, way back when. Afraid to meet his eyes and find the memories lurking there, she ducked her head over the dog-eared menu.

"Steakburger with fries?" Tripp asked quietly. What she—both of them—had always ordered.

But she was a different person now, a believer in easy and right no longer. Life wasn't that simple. "Something lighter, I think. Maybe a grilled breast of chicken if Mo—" But no, Mo was still holding the high-cholesterol line. Nothing on *his* menu but cow or deep-fried.

"Go back to the city," Tripp jeered, halfway between teasing and something sharper. "You'll find a yuppie sandwich on every corner."

Wish on. "I'm here to stay, Tripp." She looked him straight in the eye, and ordered a steakburger when the waitress came.

They called a tacit truce over Mo's meltingly tender strip steaks, sticking to small, safe topics while they ate. Kaley explained that Whitey had refused to consult a doctor, so she'd gone to Durango for crutches.

She wanted to know how Tripp had made it down from the high country so soon. She hadn't expected to see him back for a day or so yet, but she learned that he'd ridden only halfway. He'd trailered his packhorses up and back through Suntop land, a shortcut Rafe Montana permitted his closest neighbors.

She asked after Tripp's brother, and learned that Mac was working for a rodeo stock contractor out of Laramie, serving as a pickup man in the bronc events, also doing his own share of bull riding.

Riding those horned freight trains—now *that* sounded like Mac McGraw, macho from his boot heels to his eyebrows. He was devil-may-care, where his big brother was the steady one. The caring one, she'd once thought.

Tripp asked how she'd liked teaching high-school English, so she tossed off a few war stories—the laughable times and the ones where you wanted to tear out your hair in frustration. The kids were the very best of the bargain. All the hurdles the bureaucrats placed between you and actual teaching—that was the worst of it.

"Are you thinking about teaching in Trueheart?" he asked after he'd ordered coffee and she'd wistfully passed.

She stifled a stinging retort, remembering how he'd protested when she went away to college in Ohio, where Oberlin College had offered her a full scholarship. How hard she'd had to work to persuade him that this was a good thing, the smart thing, her getting her B.A. and certification to teach. Because once she was certified, he could run his ranch and she could help him, but if beef prices kept dropping, she'd be able to teach in Trueheart or Cortez or Durango and carry them over the rough spots.

All the same, Tripp had hated her running off to the city. Had said she'd never be satisfied with ranching life after that. Yet now here he was asking, as if he'd thought up the idea himself!

"I've considered it," she said slowly, swallowing her resentment. Teaching *had* been part of her plan when she'd thought that Jim was still in the picture. Her baby would be born in April. Then, assuming that her daughter was healthy, that the antibiotic hadn't…harmed her, by the following September the baby would be old enough to do without her mother for eight hours a day, if an outside job proved to be necessary. Kaley didn't like it, knew she'd hate leaving her baby, but it was no more than most single mothers had to do.

Tripp leaned forward, hands flat on the table. "That's what you should do, Kaley, if you want to stay in Colorado. Take a teaching job here—or even better in Durango. Or Boulder. It'd be more like what you're used to, a real city."

Kaley shook her head. She was done with cities. When she'd settled for a shallow life in the city with a shallow man was when her life had taken its wrong turn. Besides, her plan didn't work anymore now that Jim had flown away. She couldn't both manage her ranch *and* teach.

"You should do that," Tripp insisted, his callused fingertips whitening on the tabletop. "I'm offering the appraised value on your land. It's fair—Jim hired the appraiser himself. You should take your half of the money and buy a nice little house in Durango or Denver or—"

"Or maybe Miami," she cut in. "Or how about Spain?

Would that be far enough for you?'' As his eyebrows drew together, she shook her head. "Get *used* to it, Tripp. I'm not selling." So much for truces!

"You're not selling. Yeah, that's big talk," he snapped. "But the question is, can you *keep?* You understand I can call your loan anytime after shipping day? That it's all due—the forty thou plus interest, all in one balloon payment?''

If Tripp insisted on full payback, there was no way she could keep the ranch—she was as good as sunk. Bad enough to be at anyone's mercy, but to be at this man's? How much mercy had he shown her the last time? "Jim walked right into that one, didn't he?" she said bitterly. "He's always too impatient to read the fine print."

Tripp's face darkened; his scar went pale. "You're saying I *tricked* your brother? Pulled a fast one?''

Whoa, girl! Her temper had grabbed the bit and run right away with her. But this wasn't the cynical city, where slick moves were a given. This was Trueheart, where the Code of the West still held. Where a man would fight for his honor and his good name, sometimes to the death. She drew a breath, sighed it out, and shook her head slowly. No, her brother had been a fool, but he'd needed no help in that, or received any. "No, Tripp, I'm…not saying that. Don't believe it.''

When still he waited with narrowed eyes, she added reluctantly, "Sorry. I'm sorry…I know you're just looking out for yourself. But then, so am I. I want to keep the ranch in my family.'' Below the edge of the table, she touched her stomach for luck. "Is that so hard to understand?''

"Wanting's one thing, Kaley,'' Tripp said bleakly. "Everyone wants. But doing?'' He stood up from the table. "That's another.''

CHAPTER SIX

THEY DROVE halfway back to his truck before either of them ventured to speak again. At last Tripp cleared his throat and said huskily, "Look, I know this isn't easy, but you need to face it. There's no way you can make a go of this. I reckon you've forgotten, how hard ranching is."

"I ranched for almost eighteen years till I went off to college," she reminded him.

"You worked with a father, a brother and a younger Whitey to help you. Now it's you and a lame old man. You won't last out the winter."

"I will!" she insisted, staring down the tunnel of her headlights. "I know it won't be easy, but I will." She had no place else on earth to go. No place she wanted to be.

"Kaley, you'll quit."

Her hands clenched till they ached on the wheel. "You're calling me a *quitter?*"

"Aren't you?" he taunted. "Who walked out on who back there in Phoenix?"

She had half a mind to pull over and order him out. Let him hoof it the rest of the way to his truck.

"Why *did* you leave him?" Tripp probed her silence. "Or did you?"

She shot him a seething glance. He'd maneuvered her as neatly as a cutting horse splits a calf out of the herd. Left her nothing but two bad choices. She could let him brand her a quitter, a woman who'd walked out on her marriage—or she could admit that, yes, once again, she'd failed to hold her man's love. "It's none of your business, you know."

"Yeah?" His harsh laughter goaded her. "Sounds like he left you!"

And so Richard had, in his heart. By rejecting her baby, he'd rejected her. All she'd saved from the disaster was her pride. "He didn't," she said flatly. "I reached the decision. *I* walked out the door. I drove to Vegas and got the divorce. Here I am." The truth, as far as it went.

"But why?" Tripp demanded.

No way was she telling him about the baby! He thought—now—that she wouldn't last till Christmas? What would he think if he knew she'd be five months pregnant by then? In six weeks, come calf-shipping day, Tripp could call in his loan, by the terms of the contract. Somehow she had to persuade him to let it ride for another year. And fat chance he'd do that if he considered her a wounded duck.

"Why did you leave, Kaley?" Tripp insisted. "Did he cheat on you?"

"No." Even to save her pride, she couldn't say that.

Tripp drew a sharp breath. "Did he...beat you?"

"No!" And Tripp apparently didn't mean to stop till he had his answer. So she'd have to brazen it out. Brush him off. "He was selfish," she said lightly. "Okay? Raised as an only child by a doting single mom, and I guess it warped him. Richard always had to choose the channel when we watched TV."

"TV," Tripp repeated, incredulous. "You call that a reason?"

"Not good enough?" she asked flippantly. "Well, he was prettier than me and he knew it. I got tired of that." *I was the one who was supposed to admire, always, always. I wonder if he even saw me, except as his mirror.*

"Yeah, that's grounds for divorce, all right."

"And he was picky," she plunged on recklessly.

"Wanted his eggs fried ten seconds over easy, but if you let them cook for twenty or if you broke the yolk…" And his custom-made shirts had to be ironed just so, or there'd be sulks and tantrums. He'd paid more for his haircuts than she had for hers. And as for the possibility of having a daughter who might be less than perfect? Unthinkable! He'd sooner abort her than take that chance. "Definitely picky," she muttered.

"Yeah, I can see you two had big problems," Tripp said with quiet savagery.

He'd asked; she'd answered. If he didn't like it… Her smile was diamond bright and just as hard. "Hey, what do you care? Sometimes things just…don't…work out." And there, up ahead—oh, joy—was his truck. The end to this inquisition was in sight.

Tripp put a hand to his door handle—looked as if he was as ready to part company as she was. "I care, Kaley, because you came back to Trueheart and wrecked my plans. And you're wrecking them all for nothing! Six months from now you'll be tired of playing rancher and you'll be gone again."

"No…*I won't.*" She jammed on the brakes, stopping with her headlights glaring into the blind eyes of Tripp's pickup.

"Right." He swung his legs out onto the road, then called back through the door's closing gap, "Hey, and thanks for the ride, cowgirl!"

Kaley blinked at the crudeness, felt the heat rise in her cheeks—then his intended meaning hit home. She was the one with her thoughts in bed. "Yeah, and thanks for supper!" she flung back through the windshield, but he'd already slammed his own door.

She backed around in a tight, vicious circle and headed for home.

HARD AS HE WORKED, sleep usually came easy to Tripp, but not this night. He rolled over in bed for the twentieth time. Thumped his innocent pillow, then buried his face in it. Should never have asked her... Would have been happier not knowing...

So what? Go to sleep!

After a moment, he turned onto his side. *Careful what you ask for, 'cause you just might get it,* was what his dad used to say with a bitter half grin. But no, Tripp had needed to ask, and now he knew why Kaley had left her lawyer husband.

Still, Kaley's complaints were hardly sufficient grounds for divorce.

Divorce wrecked lives, burned dreams to the ground, left walking wounded. It wasn't something to be done with a careless smile and a so-what shrug.

Whatever happened to "till death do us part"?

His own mother had hated feeding chickens, hated the mud her husband and small sons tracked through the kitchen every spring when the snow melted. She'd complained that there wasn't a movie theater or a place to go dancing within fifty miles of the ranch.

She'd left on a whim, for no good reason, like a sparrow that lights here, then explodes into flight again, for no reason a man can know or see. Flighty... Flying away with a man's heart... *Pretty women never stay,* his dad used to say after his third or fourth drink, and the old man should have known. *Not with an ugly mug they don't,* he'd add, rubbing his unshaven chin.

Fair enough, or maybe not fair, but it was how the world worked. No use complaining. You played the hand you were dealt.

Tripp turned onto his back to stare at the dusky ceiling. But why was he feeling so bad now that he'd asked and she'd told? He should be feeling good to know for sure—

at long last—that he'd done right all those years ago to break up with Kaley. To finally have it confirmed.

Not that he hadn't had his worries from the very start. From the first time he'd danced with her at that shindig after the rodeo down in Cortez and breathed in the scent of her hair, and his heart had shivered in his chest and his arms had tightened around her till she gasped—then hummed an odd little sound of pleasure that sent the blood rocketing through his veins....

Oh, he'd worried, all right. But try as he might, she'd had a way from the very start of ducking under his defenses—to somehow end up in his arms, laughing up into his face. And once her lips touched his that first time, he'd been hypnotized. Lost. Captive till she cared to release him. Back then he couldn't think, when he was within ten miles of Kaley Cotter. Not with his brains he couldn't.

Only when they were miles or weeks apart could he begin to see the truth. The shape of sad things to come. And worry.

But he'd ignored that worrisome voice at the back of his brain—had tried to ride right over his own doubts by asking her to marry him their first summer, within a month of that first dance. She'd been fresh out of high school, not yet eighteen. She'd cried *Yes!*, thrown her arms around him—then bit her lip like a child and wondered if maybe she should ask her father.

How many times had Tripp wondered what would have happened if, right then and there, he'd dragged her into his old pickup truck and driven off to a justice of the peace?

Instead, he'd wanted her to be sure. Needed her to be sure. So he'd said, *Right, you do that.*

And back she'd come the next day with the word that her father wouldn't give his permission. He insisted she complete at least one year of college before she married.

And Tripp had wondered; was it really her old man

who'd said no—or on second thought, had Kaley changed her mind? Maybe she'd realized, and rightly so, that she ought to shop around before settling for an uneducated cowboy with a sliced-up face.

But when she swore they'd be married the following June, what could he do, wanting her so, but agree? Thanking him for his patience, she'd stood on tiptoe to kiss him—and his doubts had melted away as his temperature spiked.

She'd gone off to college in September and he started to steel himself for how it must end.

Then, that following May, when she asked him to postpone their wedding for a second time while she flew off to Europe for the summer, he'd seen the writing on the wall. Read every word and grimly accepted the bitter truth. Kaley would never be satisfied with a hardscrabble ranch in Trueheart, not after she'd had a taste of the wide, glamorous world. Not any more than his mother had been satisfied.

Sure, maybe she'd return to the States as promised. Maybe they'd even marry, and maybe he could hold her for a sweet, sweet year or two. But she'd never stick, never stay. He'd been a fool to hope she would. A fool to let her into his heart.

Something this good could not possibly last.

And if it didn't last, he didn't want to go into it. He knew what that had done to his father. Better to live whole and alone, than...than shattered like a rain-drenched windshield... Like the tracery of scars on a ruined face....

HOURS LATER, Tripp came awake to lie blinking in the darkness. He held his breath and heard the sound again— a clink of crockery down below, the shuffle of a boot heel in the kitchen?

What the hell? Now that Mac had hit the rodeo trail,

Tripp ran the home ranch alone. He had a hand and a half up at the line camps, but nobody should be— Stealthily he swung his legs out of bed and rose. He found the pair of jeans he'd tossed across a chair, then reached into his closet for the .22 that leaned in a back corner with a shell in its chamber.

Easing barefoot down the stairs, he stepped over the squeaky step, but the one below it groaned softly.

"Tripp?" called his brother's voice from the kitchen. "It's me."

"Figured it was a black bear raiding the fridge," he grumbled as they half hugged, thumping each other's backs, Tripp pointing his rifle away toward a corner, Mac swinging a gallon jug of milk in his free hand.

They stepped apart, grinning, sizing each other up. Mac hadn't passed this way in months. He looked good, maybe honed down a bit on his steady diet of road food. The Band-Aid on his temple and the wrist strapped with a pressure bandage didn't seem to amount to much, not for a bull rider.

"Sorry t'wake you," Mac apologized, turning back to the bowl he'd set out on the table.

"Wasn't really asleep, and if you're thinking about cereal, don't." He should have bought groceries when he was in Durango yesterday, but Tripp hated to shop. "We've got eggs or—"

"It's not for me. It's for Martha." Mac filled the bowl to its brim. "She's sick. That's why I swung out of my way and stopped by."

Tripp frowned. Martha was a black-and-white Border collie that went everywhere with his brother. Friends in Trueheart teased Mac about when he was going to give her a diamond and make it official. And most folks figured she was the brains of the couple. "Where is she?"

"Out by the truck, puking her guts out. She got into

something back of a barn when we picked up a load of bucking stock this morning. I'm scared t'death it was poison of some sort. Rat or coyote bait or maybe insecticide. We stopped by Doc Kerner's, but he's out on a call.''

"Maybe just bad meat?'' Tripp comforted him, following his brother out the back door. Mac without Martha was not to be imagined. "Suppose we could get a hose, try to pump her stomach.''

Mac grunted. "She's been pumping—believe me. Both ends.''

They spent the rest of the night dosing the dog with milk, baking soda, crushed-up charcoal, Pepto-Bismol, when they weren't trying to phone the vet. By morning, she was looking better than they were, after a night of too little sleep and too much worry.

"Reckon she might do,'' Tripp said finally. He sat slouched in a kitchen chair while Mac lay on the linoleum beside the nest of blankets they'd made for the collie, stroking her bedraggled head.

Martha thumped her tail weakly at the sound of his voice.

"Yeah…maybe.'' Mac scowled. "I'd still like Kerner to look at her. Did I tell you she was knocked up last week when I called?''

"You didn't.'' And Tripp could see where this was headed. Mac was en route to his next rodeo, in Oregon, with his usual road partners in tow. He'd dumped Denny and Cam at Mo's Truckstop on his way up to the ranch, and by now they had to be fuming.

"Yeah.'' Mac rubbed the collie's shoulders. "Hussy jumped out my truck window at a stock auction and chased down this big Airedale. By the time I caught up with them, it was a done deal. All silly grins and cigarettes.''

"Airedale-collie mix. Now, that'll be a sight to see. Frizz and patches.''

Mac grinned. "Hybrid vigor, they always say. Like it or not, I reckon I'm going to be a grandpa. But since I've gotta be heading on down the road..."

Tripp sighed. "How long till you pass this way again?" And though he pretended to grumble, he didn't mind. Normally he loved his solitude. That a man could be alone with his thoughts, have the time and quiet to hear himself think, was one of the best parts of ranching. But this past week or so, the place had felt...empty. Hollow. So achingly silent that, once or twice, riding home to an empty house with the twilight thickening around him, he'd almost have sworn he could hear it—the sound of his own heart beating.

KALEY SPENT the following morning riding fence. Every last mile of each home pasture would have to be checked and repaired before the herd came down from the mountains for the winter. Tiring work, with its constant mounting and dismounting, and the barbed wire was hard on her hands in spite of the heavy leather gloves she wore.

Still, she found the work soothed her, and it satisfied. She could stop her horse every so often and look back over her shoulder and see precisely what she'd accomplished— unlike teaching, where you could slog on for weeks, then wonder if you'd made any difference at all. If anything you'd said would lodge in the kids' brains one minute past the three-o'clock bell. But out here... Oh, she'd missed this, the sun on her back and a good horse between her knees. Perfume of pine and the shrill cry of a hawk wheeling far off in a bowl of blue, blue sky. She'd have been happy to stay out all day.

But by afternoon, she could put off the dreaded task no longer. If she hoped to stay happy, it was time to look at the books. She ought to—must—have a proposal in place before Tripp came calling again.

A WORKABLE PROPOSAL didn't come easy. Half past three she still sat before an unyielding computer in the corner of the living room that Jim had turned into an office.

"So...try it this way. What if we sell Jim's steers?" The original source of her woes. These were the grown-up Beefmaster calves that Jim had used Tripp's loan money to buy, which he'd intended to make a killing on last fall. Kaley tapped a few keys on the keyboard to fill in that part of the financial spreadsheet that filled Jim's computer screen. "And we cull our breeding herd from four hundred twenty-eight cows to...say, two hundred?" She winced as she typed in the numbers. Could she ever build the herd up again if she cut it back that far? This solution looked like no solution at all.

Still, play it through to the bitter end. She was testing every alternative she could think of, no matter how far-fetched. "And we still have roughly three hundred eighty-five calves to sell, no change there, and they still average a weight of four hundred fifty pounds. And say the price of beef rises to..."

She bit her lip, typed in another number. Muttered, "No, it can't possibly, Kaley. Don't lie to yourself!" Erased that number and typed in a lower price per pound, then hit the command to process the results and pushed her chair back from the desk. *Please, please, please, just give me a tiny profit! Any eensy profit at all...*

The screen blinked and presented the new figures and Kaley groaned. Even when she cut her breeding stock in half she had a year's-end loss for the third time in a row!

The costs were eating them alive. Between the first and second mortgages on the ranch; the interest on Tripp's loan; property taxes, which had risen again; IRS taxes; wages for Dubois and Whitey; vet bills and building maintenance; the cost of feed...

Yeah, take feed. Last winter had been brutal. Deep snow

by early December had put an end to all grazing, and the
hay her brother had grown hadn't lasted the winter. Jim
had to buy more, but he'd waited till March to do so, by
which time scarcity had driven the price through the roof…

Kaley swiped a hand up through her tousled hair. *He
didn't think very far in advance, did he?* Maybe Jim was
better off making split-second decisions in a diving jet than
predicting beef prices a year in advance. Her brother had
no patience for the slow and steady accumulation of facts
and figures, their methodical application…

"Now, where in blue blazes did you put the hot sauce?"
Propped up on his crutches, Whitey glared at her from the
kitchen doorway. He was making his famous enchilada pie
for supper tonight, and Kaley was wondering if inflicting
a four-alarm plateful on her tiny passenger might be child
abuse. Or were fetuses tougher than that?

*If I had a doctor, I could ask him stupid questions like
that.* Another thing she needed to do, and soon. "I put it
in the fridge, Whitey. Top shelf of the door."

"In the icebox! Of all the consarned places to…you're
tryin' to defrost it maybe?"

She'd rearranged the pantries last night when she
brought in her month's load of groceries. Today Whitey
was doing his best to put things back where he liked them.
She sighed and said mildly, "Want me to find it for—"

"Danged if I do! If you don't stop mollycoddling me,
girl, I swear I'm gonna…" His voice trailed away as he
hobbled out of sight.

She looked back at the screen. He was grumping partly
on general principle. Because he despised anything high-
tech. Cowboys didn't rely on spreadsheets in Whitey's day
but on seat-of-the-pants judgment and hard riding. You
worked from sunup to sundown, from "can to can't," and
somehow you'd scrape by. He saw no reason they should
change their methods now.

But Whitey was also grumbling to hide his fear. Many a time this past year he must have seen Jim struggling with these same dismal figures, and he dreaded the results as much as she did.

What am I going to do? Any way she cut this pie they were in trouble. The best scenario she'd found so far—the only remotely workable one—had her repaying one-half of Tripp's forty-thousand-dollar loan in October, while she used the other half of the fall roundup income to pay off the ranch's past-year expenses. That would leave her with just enough cash in hand for the future, so that if—if!—the coming winter was a mild one...

Oh, yeah, that proposal works, Kaley. Now ask the computer how I persuade Tripp not to demand his money back, when he's got every right... When if we fail, then he wins... Why hadn't some genius invented a spreadsheet for that tiny problem?

She jumped half a foot as the phone rang in the kitchen, then glanced that way guiltily. Speak of the devil! That would be Tripp, insisting they had to talk. It was only fair. They'd solved nothing last night. Talking had only upped the tension between them. She winced as the phone rang again, and called, ''Want me to—''

''Who's this?'' Whitey snarled in the kitchen. ''Uh-huh?'' The vinegar in his voice turned abruptly to honey. ''No...no, just stubbed m'dang toe. Well, I'm fine. How are you? That's good. Yeah. Yeah, she's here. Hold on.'' Setting the receiver on the counter, he reversed himself laboriously on his crutches—then started when he found Kaley standing behind him, her eyebrows lifted in question.

''It's Michelle from Michelle's Place.'' For the first time all afternoon, he smiled.

''Michelle!'' Kaley hadn't forgotten her blond hitch-hiker. Had been meaning to drop round her restaurant when she came up for air from the ranch.

"The very same," Michelle agreed on a note of warm laughter. "Look, this is short notice, I know, but Dana Montana and I were wondering if we could cook you supper tonight."

CHAPTER SEVEN

TWO HOURS LATER, Kaley found herself seated on a stool beside a butcher-block counter in Michelle's kitchen—her personal kitchen, as opposed to the larger one downstairs in the café. A room of blond varnished woods and many windows, with herbs growing on the sill above the sink, and restaurant-grade pots and pans hanging from a rack above an antique six-burner stove. "So what can I do?" she asked happily.

Dana and Michelle had already explained that Wednesday was Girls' Night Out. Each week on this day Michelle closed the restaurant at three, leaving after-hours cleanup to her busboy and bottle washer while she retreated upstairs.

Dana took the evening off from her usual duties as cook and hostess of her own dude ranch, leaving a buffet of cold dishes behind to feed her guests and family. Since this was also her one night a week to forget for a few hours that she was a mother, she left her two babies in charge of her stepson, Sean, with the dude ranch's aging wrangler, an eighty-something cowboy named Willy, to help him ride herd.

"Want to chop the garlic?" suggested Michelle, nose-deep in a cookbook—one of perhaps three hundred that were shelved under the kitchen's central island counter. "We need...um...thirty-six large cloves, coarsely chopped."

"Coming up!" Kaley selected a blade from the well-

stocked knife block at her elbow, while Michelle piled
plump heads of garlic before her. "What are we cooking?"

Girls' Night Out was actually a busman's holiday, which
might more accurately be entitled Foodies Cook In, the two
friends had admitted with sheepishly guilty grins. Michelle
used the occasions to experiment with new recipes that she
hoped to adapt for her menus downstairs. Dana often borrowed their results for her nightly offerings at Ribbon
River. Whatever they cooked, they cooked it in quantity so
that Dana would have a dinner to feed her paying guests
on Thursday night and Michelle would have several serv-
ings to try out on favored customers. Also food for upstairs,
since there was no sweeter phrase to a restaurateur at the
end of a long day than "There're leftovers in the fridge."

"You're in luck tonight," Dana assured her. She was
unloading bags of groceries on the pine table, which stood
under two large windows at the end of the room. "We're
feeding you a square meal. Last week was sauce night—
eight different kinds—but by the time we'd finished ex-
perimenting, we were too whipped to cook something to
go beneath. So we spooned them over toast."

"Oh, please! Over crostini," Michelle protested.

"Any way you slice it, sounds like heaven to a carbo-
hydrate junkie like me," Kaley said, laughing as she
smashed cloves of garlic with the flat of her blade, then
used its tip to flick their loosened skins aside. Tonight felt
like a holiday to her, as well. It seemed as if, lately, she'd
been talking strictly to men. And there was no man alive
who understood the exquisite pleasures of feminine small
talk. Or who knew what it was to be a slave to bread and
butter.

"Then there was the time last spring when we cooked
nothing but desserts," remembered Michelle.

"Strawberries dipped in chocolate," crooned Dana.

"Amaretto chocolate mousse," added her friend with a sensual sigh.

"*Three* kinds of cheesecake, since we couldn't decide which recipe to try." Dana rolled her eyes heavenward. "A-a-and—"

"Stop!" Kaley laughed. "I'm gaining weight just listening!"

"That was the problem." Michelle patted her own board-flat stomach.

There was no problem that Kaley could see. Michelle stood half a head higher than tiny Dana, a good willowy five foot ten in her stocking feet. Dressed in jeans and a checked cotton shirt rolled to the elbows, the blonde looked like a runway model sporting Ralph Lauren's latest cowboy collection. "Well, you know what they say a world without men would be like," Kaley ventured, straight-faced.

Her two companions looked up and shook their heads.

"Full of fat, happy women?"

They burst out laughing and nodded ruefully, though Kaley noticed that Dana's amusement held the slightest reserve. She was having trouble imagining herself happier in a world without a certain man, Kaley suspected. Lucky Dana. Now, Michelle, as far as Kaley could judge from her remarks, seemed to be entirely footloose and fancy-free.

"So what are we cooking?" she repeated as Michelle drained white beans that had been soaking in a pot on the stove, then ladled them into a restaurant-size pressure cooker.

"Tonight it's a cassoulet," said the blonde, clamping the lid on. "I'm always looking for dishes that can swing both ways. I have to keep my local customers happy. But at the same time, I'm trying to increase my tourist and daytripper trade, and those types tend to be more sophisticated in their tastes. Or sometimes the problem is that Trueheart men want tried-and-true, while their wives want something they'd never cook for themselves.''

''So how would you sell both sides on cassoulet?'' Kaley wondered. It was a dish she'd eaten in Paris, that long-ago terrible, wonderful summer after Tripp cut her loose. ''I can't imagine the cowboys round-about would—''

''Ah, but it's all in how you describe it,'' Michelle said with a twinkle. ''When Joe Rancher brings the Little Woman in for a Saturday-night treat, I'll suggest the cassoulet to her in an undertone, telling her it's Gallic cuisine at its finest, an entrée that contains duck, sausage, wine, white beans and thyme and bay leaves. When Joe scowls and asks me to repeat that, please, ma'am, I'll just smile and say, 'Oh, *that?* That's just French chili'—while overhead, I wink at his wife. Works every time,'' she insisted as they hooted their skepticism.

''Till he asks for the hot sauce,'' Dana teased, ''and a bowl of jalapeños on the side.''

''Which he will every time, absolutely,'' Michelle agreed. ''But what the heck, so long as everybody's happy and they keep coming back for more.''

While Dana peeled onions, Michelle drifted to another undercounter cabinet, stooped to examine its contents, then stood with a bottle of red wine. ''A Bardolino, I think.'' She reached for a corkscrew.

Head lowered, Kaley raked her chopped garlic into a pile. ''If you don't mind, I think I'll just have water.''

''Not a drinker?'' Michelle's voice held no hint of disapproval.

Trueheart was a small world. Word didn't creep around town; it flew like the sparks of a wildfire. Still, like it or not, in a few months the truth would be plain for all to see. Meantime, Kaley needed friends, women friends, and confiding was part of female bonding. And these two, though she'd barely begun to know them, somehow she felt—and really, really hoped—that they'd become friends. Because tonight they might be cooking haute cuisine, but she was sure already it would go down like comfort food. She felt at home here in this airy kitchen. Safe among her own kind. So she said quietly into the attentive silence, "Not for nine months or so, I'm not."

Michelle stopped twisting her corkscrew. "You mean…?"

"You do!" Dana cried as Kaley nodded shyly. "Oh, Kaley, that's *wonderful!* Babies are so—" she hurried around the counter to give her an exuberant hug "—so magnificent! Also fun."

"*Magnificent* isn't the word I'd have chosen the last time I helped you change Peter's diaper," Michelle said dryly, but she, too, was smiling. "Congratulations."

"Thank you." It felt so *good* to share her secret with people who were truly pleased for her. Her obstetrician back in Phoenix had hardly counted, since what to her seemed a miracle was to him a daily event. And when she'd brought Richard her precious news, he'd rained down a relentless drizzle of dire predictions and discouragement; her poor parade had been half drowned before it had a chance to hit its marching stride. Now, for the first time since the afternoon the doctor told her, Kaley found herself beaming at her own news. Thrilled all over again.

Michelle had poured out two glasses of wine, then a flute of sparkling water, and now she handed round the drinks. Dana raised hers in a toast. "To a healthy, happy, *beautiful* baby…who sleeps every night through and laughs all day—and to you, Mom!"

"Hear, hear," Michelle agreed. They all sipped, then she cocked a considering eyebrow and said, "I suppose it's your skunk of an ex's? Or…" Her thoughts caught up with her mouth as she blushed beet-red. "*Oops!* Shut up, Michelle. I'm sorry, do *not* answer that!"

"Michelle used to be a Texan," Dana explained with wry humor, deftly deflecting the moment. "Texans shoot straight—and think about what they aimed at, later."

"*Used* to be!" If Michelle wasn't truly outraged, she faked it beautifully. "That's like saying someone used to be German! Or used to be a man! Or used to be right-handed. Believe me, girl, Texas is bone-deep. It's not a state you can move away from. It's a nationality. A state of mind. Just because I ran off to the Culinary Institute of America in New York at eighteen—"

"And lost your drawl," Dana teased.

They were working so hard, raising a smoke screen over the gaffe, that for a moment Kaley simply smiled, sat back and watched their show. She learned that Dana was originally a Yankee from Vermont—Yankees had *no* understanding of the finer points of being a Texan. That Michelle had cooked in a restaurant in Marseilles for a year, then aboard a millionaire's yacht in the Mediterranean for a while. Probably had lost her drawl somewhere at sea...

Finally, as the two women began to wind down and glance nervously at her, she took a sip of water and said, "Of course it's my ex-husband's." Which should tell them two things about her in one, if they were listening.

They swung around to face her and nodded, relaxing at last. Silently saying by their attention, *So tell us.*

"But he didn't want her—wanted me to abort—and I said no way." Kaley shrugged and smiled to show them she was okay. "So we split." Much as she longed to tell them why Richard hadn't wanted her baby, she didn't. Though she felt she could trust them, still, this was her deepest, darkest secret. The fear that rode with her by day and crouched on her pillow in the dead of night.

Besides, perhaps she was superstitious, but to speak of the chance that her baby might be damaged seemed to call the risk home to her. She tried not even to think of it, much less voice the awful possibility.

"He didn't want your baby?" Dana repeated, uncomprehending. "His baby."

"Aha! So he *is* a skunk!" Michelle turned to adjust the flame beneath the pressure cooker as the steam valve rose to its highest level with a tiny shriek. She swung back to lean against the counter. "I hope your lawyer wrote you an ironclad child-support agreement. Though it'll be hard to enforce between states, I suppose."

Kaley looked down, reshaped her pile of garlic with her knife. "Actually, there won't be any child support to quarrel about. We worked out a trade. I've got full legal custody of my baby, forever and ever. Richard renounced all claim to her. In return, I agreed that since she's all mine, I'll support her myself."

"Not only a skunk, but a veritable Prince of Skunks!" Michelle fumed. "Do you know what it costs to raise a child through college years?"

More than she'd make running a half-bankrupt ranch. Kaley nodded gravely. "Lots and lots." But somehow she'd get by, working from can to can't. She had to. They were a family of three now, counting Whitey, and somehow she had to provide.

"Kaley can do it," Dana said with more faith than facts. "And you're right. If he wants no part of his own child, you don't need him or want him in your life. You're better off making a clean break." She picked up Michelle's cookbook and said determinedly, "So...what's next to do?"

THREE DAYS AFTER Girls' Night Out, Kaley still smiled whenever she thought of it. Not only had the cassoulet been a resounding triumph, but she'd made two friends. And she had a feeling that Michelle and Dana would be keepers. People who would matter in her life.

Dana had already solved one of her problems by rec-
ommending an ob/gyn in Durango, a Dr. Cass Hancock,
who'd delivered Dana's two children. A doctor who would
assist Kaley in having a strictly natural childbirth if she
chose, or would allow her any gradation of delivery between that and "Wake me when it's over."

Kaley had made an appointment already. And she had
an invitation for next Wednesday night at Michelle's, as
well, when the menu would be soup, soup and more soup.
The ocean of loneliness and worry that had been lapping
at her doorstep all week had receded a foot or two.

Now all she had to do was face Tripp and sell him on
her payback proposal.

With that thought, the worries came flooding back again.
What if he refused to extend his loan another year? What
then? Kaley grimaced, and looked over her shoulder, at the
fence line she'd checked already. *Let's just take it one
fence post at a time, shall we?*

Tripp hadn't shown his face in days, not since the night
they ate and argued at Mo's. And she hadn't sought him
out, though she really ought to have; they needed to settle
this.

Instead, coward that she was, she'd found it easier to
ride fence. She was checking the Waterfall Pasture today—
had been for the past three days. This was the ranch's second largest pasture, and clearly Jim had left it for last on
his rotation of yearly maintenance. She'd found seven rot-
ten fence posts already today, five the previous day, and
her arms ached from the posthole digger. As did her shoulders, ribs and the foot she'd tried to slice off with one
misdelivered thrust of the digger yesterday. *Nothing like
hard work and awesome bruises to drive your worries out
of mind,* she told herself, and kneed Sunny into motion,
towing the pack mare behind her. "C'mon, Biggie."

Waterfall Pasture was too high and rocky to bring in

supplies by truck, so she'd packed in her posts and tools on a shamble-footed, slow-witted but patient half-Clydesdale mare named Bigfoot, who did the heavy toting around the ranch. Seeing her load the mare with fence posts this morning, Whitey had threatened to saddle up and come along.

But they both knew it was only a threat. Until he could put all his weight on his left leg, he couldn't mount or dismount. So she'd asked him, instead, to use the next few weeks to put all the ranch machinery in tip-top condition for the winter.

That had cheered him. Whitey knew the job wasn't make-work; it was vital. Once the snows came and they started feeding the herd, they'd use the four-wheel-drive truck constantly. The engine-driven feeder box that her father had built twenty years ago, on the bed of the truck, also had to function perfectly throughout the winter if they and the cattle were to survive. The Rube Goldberg device saved the work of one man—meant one person alone could feed the herd from the comfort of the heated truck cab. Even a very pregnant person.

Up the line, she could see three strands of barbed wire leaning out of true. "Dadblast it!" she muttered, quoting Whitey. Another fence post rotted free of its base. Glancing at the angle of the sun she promised herself, *lunch after this one.*

By the time she'd earned her break, Kaley was hot and sweaty and thoroughly whipped. She'd started two holes within feet of the original post, then had to abandon each after the first laborious foot of digging, when she hit an underlying ledge of granite. Her third attempt had proven the charm, but she felt as if she'd been run down by a buffalo.

Sooner or later she was bound to toughen up, but how

much hard work could a baby endure? she wondered as she reined Sunny downhill, away from the fence line.

Kaley hadn't a clue. She could remember her own mother laughing as she told a story one night, when company had come to call and they all sat late at table. About her riding a spring roundup when she was five months pregnant with Jim. Some story about a half-Brahma bull she'd flushed from the bushes who'd refused to be driven. Instead, he'd shouldered her and her horse aside, knocking them head over heels. Kaley's father had been so angry he couldn't decide who he wanted to shoot—the bull or his daredevil wife.

I reckon Mom would say babies can handle plenty. Kaley smiled at the memory of her mother laughing at the table, her eyes sparkling in the firelight, one slender hand resting on her husband's brawny forearm as she spoke, her fingers moving in a slow, unconscious caress, soothing his anxiety years after the event. *Oh, I wish, I wish she were here to tell me herself!* She'd loved life, loved babies, would have loved to hold her own grandchild.

While Kaley rode and remembered, Sunny had brought them to the creek that threaded the floor of the valley. She hung most of her weight on the saddle horn as she dismounted, wincing when her right foot touched ground. Once she'd loosened the gelding's cinches, she watered him and the packhorse, then staked them out on a bank of lush grass. After taking her lunch from the saddlebag, she limped up the course of the stream, toward the sound of falling water.

Some Cotter ancestor, probably her grandfather, had dammed the creek years ago, at several points along its course. The wonderful result was a series of pools strung down the valley like pearls on a string, each of them cascading at its downstream end into the creek or pond below it. Waterfall Pasture was one of the most beautiful spots on all the Circle C, maybe her favorite, at least in the summertime, when she and her family used to swim here.

Then there was that time... Goose bumps stampeded across her skin with the memory. Tripp had met her here once. She'd snuck out of the house after midnight to meet him by the light of a full moon. Their skin had gleamed like molten silver as they cavorted and swam. *Don't think about it,* she told herself crisply, averting her eyes from the wide, smooth rock out in the middle of the pond, where they'd—

She stumbled, came down hard on her bad foot and yelped. Dadblast, indeed! It couldn't possibly be broken, could it?

Not possible, she quickly assured herself. She hadn't the time to be injured, not this year. Still, she took extra care as she settled herself on a rock, a few feet below the waterfall that spilled from the pool above. And she sighed her relief when her weight left her feet.

Heaven. Water clear as diamonds showering down, rainbows dancing in the mist at the foot of the little fall. The drop was only fifteen feet or so, just enough to make a lovely sound. *Warm enough day for a swim,* she thought wistfully, surveying the half-acre pond, though she hadn't the time. She unwrapped her sandwich...savored the first half, bite by sticky bite. Peanut butter and strawberry jam... Dragonflies skimming the pool... Mountains rearing in the distance against a cloudless sky. *Blue heaven!*

Paradise with a nagging undercurrent of pain. Once she'd taken the first edge off her hunger, Kaley found the ache in her foot looming larger, harder to dismiss. Perhaps if she soaked it.

Or was this only a shameless excuse to dawdle? Whichever, she gave into temptation, slipped off her boots and socks—grimaced at the sight of her foot—rolled up her jeans, then eased herself down the sloping rock and swung her feet into the pool. *"Yes!"*

Bracing her arms behind her, Kaley leaned back, soaking up the sun, swishing her toes through silken, foaming water, letting the falls drum its song of endless magic into her brain. *This is why you came back, Kaley Cotter. For this. This. To save this.*

Why, oh, why had she wasted all those years in the city, when she had this to come back to? Why had she lived with a coldhearted man, when she had people back home who really loved her? What in the world could she have been thinking?

I threw the baby out with the bathwater, she realized, swishing her feet. *When I couldn't have Tripp…* Somehow this—this blue heaven—life on a ranch in Colorado, had become hopelessly entwined in her mind with loving Tripp. Once he was gone, she hadn't wanted the other. Couldn't conceive of the other without him. Or so she'd told herself at the time.

More fool she! Eight years a fool, but finally she'd wised up. Come back just in time. If she'd lost this forever, lost it for her daughter…

"But it isn't," she said aloud. "It's not too late. I won't let it be."

With that resolution, her stomach rumbled. It hadn't forgotten the second half of her sandwich, if she had. Kaley opened her eyes, swung around and— *"Aaagh!"*

Instinctively she recoiled from the image—a black wolfish creature crouched by her side, gulping down her sandwich, bound to gulp her next. She recoiled, wobbled, let out a hapless shriek—and tumbled sideways off the rock.

Came up spluttering, aware of what she'd seen at last. No ravening wolf, this, but a Border collie, sitting up on her rock with an expression of horrified guilt—and a wisp of napkin waving from her furry jaw. Kaley burst out laughing. "You little *thief!*"

She swiped both hands over her face, brushing her hair back, and laughed again. "Where the blue blazes did you come from?"

The collie ventured the tiniest wave of the tail she was sitting on, then pattered her black-and-white forefeet, uncertain if she was forgiven or not. She glanced worriedly downstream and Kaley's eyes followed.

Her laughter went out in a *whoosh*. Tripp came striding their way, his face as wonderful a mix of consternation and delight as the collie's.

"So this clown is yours," Kaley said haughtily. As haughtily as a woman could manage sitting in two feet of foaming water, abruptly aware that she'd worn a white T-shirt that day!

"Mac's," Tripp disagreed with the barest hint of a smile.

"She...um...startled me." Kaley tucked a strand of wayward hair behind her ear.

"So I see." His lips quivered; the smile threatened to become a grin. He looked down quickly. "*Bad* dog."

The collie ducked her head and whined, swishing her tail across the rock.

"Not *my* fault. The devil made me do it," Kaley translated for her. "I mean, what's a dog to do? A poor, helpless, peanut-butter-and-jelly sandwich just lying there screaming 'Eat me, somebody! Eat me!'"

Recognizing sympathy when she heard it, the collie brightened. She stood up and stretched her nose toward Kaley, waving her tail in abject apology. Kaley laughed and leaned forward to pluck the scrap of napkin from her teeth. "Mac's, huh?" Dogs and brothers were a safe topic. Tripp was trying to be polite, trying to keep his eyes off her T-shirt by staring over her head—which meant his eyes were fixed on their rock out there in the middle of the pond.

Was he remembering the gritty feel of it against his naked back? Careful of her skin, he'd insisted on taking the bottom, cradling her on his warm, wet, wonderfully muscular length. She'd never made love in that position before. She'd been shy and bewildered till he showed her how, then stunned and triumphant with her power to move him. Her heart beat faster, just remembering. He'd laughed, run his hands up her slippery sides and called her his—

Tripp leaned over and held out a hand. "Come out of there, mermaid."

Her lips parted in shock—that two thoughts could intersect so perfectly, past and present colliding! The water was no longer streaming coolly around her, but steaming. Her blush might bring it to a boil.

His pupils had widened to dark tunnels of memory. She could see her own tiny image reflected there, drenched and dismayed. *It's over, Tripp. You killed it.* This feeling they were feeling was nothing but an echo trapped up here in the hills, bouncing from peak to peak, sad ghost of a word that had died away to nothing years ago.

His hand hadn't dropped to his side. His Adam's apple moved in the strong brown column of his throat as he repeated huskily, "Come out, Kaley. You'll never dry off sitting there."

"True enough." She gripped his hand and let him pull her to her feet, but as her weight came on her bad one—
"*Ooh!*" She staggered, and his arm flexed, holding her up. She clamped onto his forearm with her other hand—and caught her breath. How *could* her hands still know the feel of him, this warmth and delicious hardness, as if she'd touched him only yesterday? *Echoes.*

"What is it? You've hurt yourself!"

"N-not here. Before." She took a faltering step and winced again. "It's just that the bottom's uneven..." Full of rounded, rocking stones. She couldn't stand flat, had put her weight wrong...

Bearing down on his arm, her teeth caught in her full bottom lip, she hobbled into reach. *At last!* Tripp hooked his other arm around her waist and lifted her straight up onto the rock. She let out a yelp of surprise—then laughing terror as they wobbled. He hauled her tight against him, leaned backward from the knees—and after a teetering second in the balance, they stayed upright.

Somewhere far, far away, Martha was barking her excited approval of these antics. He could barely hear her over the roar of the blood in his ears. *Kaley in his arms again, wet and warm, supple as a young aspen.* He dipped his face to her hair, longing for her scent, and the smell of it fresh from a shower came back to him. He closed his eyes, remembering...

"Thanks," she mumbled below his chin. And wriggled, asking mutely for release.

He was crazy. Must have eaten a plateful of locoweed for breakfast. Carefully, still holding her, Tripp rotated on the wet rock, then eased his grasp so she could hobble backward toward shore and safety. His gaze drifted helplessly down over her clinging T-shirt. Her nipples stood sweetly erect from either his nearness or the cold. He clenched his hands to fists and looked aside. No, not locoweed. It was Kaley herself driving him insane, just as she'd always done. *Why the hell did you come back here? To do this to me? Wasn't once enough?*

It sure was for him.

She retreated another hobbling step and his eyes fell to her feet. "Damn it, Kaley!" He crouched and caught her ankle, not gently. "What did you do to yourself?"

"Posthole digger," she muttered, looking off over his head. "It's nothing to speak of. My boot took the worst of it."

Something in him wanted to lift her foot to his lips. Wanted to kiss the ragged crescent of black and purple bruises, kiss after kiss, then move on to her high, delicate instep. Oh, he was mad all right! "Sit down and I'll get your boots."

While Kaley booted up, Martha insinuated herself between them, intent on apology. She licked Kaley's cheek twice, the lucky dog, till Tripp pushed her aside. "Sit, Martha."

Contrite again, the collie sat, nose to nose with her target.

"So that's your name," Kaley said gravely. "Martha."

The collie offered her black forepaw.

"Delighted—well, semidelighted—to meet you," Kaley said, shaking, "even if you did steal my lunch." She laughed as Martha promptly offered the white paw and she shook that one, too.

"Sorry about that," Tripp apologized. "She usually has better manners, but she's eating for half a dozen or so these days."

"*Is* she?" Kaley sat holding the dog's paw, staring into her soulful brown eyes. "Expecting, are we, Martha-girl?"

Martha ducked her head modestly, then tried for another kiss, her pink tongue just flicking the tip of Kaley's nose.

Damn the dog. "Not expecting much," Tripp growled. "Mac says she hooked up with an Airedale."

"Then they'll have brains and guts, if they won't win any beauty pageants." Kaley rubbed the collie's ears. "M-A-R-T-H-A," she mused. "Funny name for a dog."

"Mac named her after a blond barrel racer he courted all one summer, who dumped him for a steer-wrestling champ. I never did figure out if he christened a dog after her out of devotion or pure spite, but either way, this one won in the end. The only lady in Mac's heart now'days walks on four legs.''

A smart man, his brother. Tripp stood abruptly. ''I left my horse with yours. Reckon I'll go get them.''

CHAPTER EIGHT

BY THE TIME he returned riding Dodger, his white-faced bay, and leading Kaley's two, Tripp had himself back under control. He'd sought her out in the first place to talk, and he was darned if she was going to rattle him into retreating without saying his piece.

But honey catching more flies, he might as well ease into it. Tripp unbuckled his saddlebag, drew out his lunch packet and handed it over. "Seeing as how Martha ate yours..." He led the horses off a ways and staked them, taking his time, then returned to find she'd chosen a rock big enough for two and laid out his sandwiches on the opened tinfoil. The collie sat at her feet, black pointy nose aimed at the food like a compass needle tracking true north. "It's all yours," he protested. Last thing he wanted was to picnic with her the way they used to do. "I'm not hungry. Ate breakfast late this morning."

Her lifted eyebrows gave him the lie, but she only smiled and held out a sandwich.

He frowned and finally took it before his stomach growled and betrayed him, but he was darned if he'd sit. So he stood beside her, staring out over her head at the pond, at that damn rock in the middle, wondering if a stick of dynamite would take it out of there, chewing grimly and not tasting.

Or not tasting ham and cheese and bread, but memories. Her wet skin had tasted like gingersnap cookies, along with something darker, wilder, a taste that had stirred him to his depths.

He looked down at the top of her head. The sun danced along threads of copper and chestnut, glinted off strands red as a blood bay's coat. If he plunged his fingers through that glossy mane, it would be hot with the sunlight, heavy in the way all good, valuable things had a heft and a substance to them. He remembered taking two silky handfuls, holding her still while he— Damn it all! He glanced around for her hat—found it tossed carelessly on the grass, brought it back and plunked it on her head. "Sun'll fry your brains, city girl."

"Yeah," she agreed absently, adjusting its tilt, staring off over the valley. "I've been meaning to ask you…" She reached for the abandoned square of tinfoil and folded it in half. "Why'd you loan money to Jim?"

Not for your sake, if that's what you're thinking! Suddenly he was blazing mad. She hadn't wrecked just his plans, coming back, but his peace of mind, too. The curve of her lashes fanned out on her cheeks—he didn't need to remember that!

She tipped her head back to see him. Shadowed by her brim, her eyes glowed dark as the sky at full moon. "Were you hoping he'd fail?" She threw up a hand to stop him when he started to speak. "I don't mean you set Jim *up* to fail in any way, but what were you hoping to get out of this? You could have got a better rate of return if you'd put your money in a stock fund."

"And you don't mean four-legged stock," he mocked her. "You mean the stock exchange." The girl he'd known nine years ago hadn't talked like that. Had known or cared nothing about those things. *I knew you'd fly high, wide and handsome.*

And far, far away. Face it, the girl he'd known back then

was gone, even though the lashes still curved as sweetly on this woman's cheeks, delicate as the wings of a moth.

"I do," she said, refusing to be drawn in. "What were you thinking, lending Jim all that money? You knew..." She drew a breath, looked down, pleated the tinfoil a second time. "You knew he wasn't a...wasn't maybe the best... Didn't have maybe the best mind-set for ranching."

"He was feckless and foolish, yeah." Tripp smiled when she looked up at him, eyes flashing dangerously. "Didn't have his mind on his business, not all the time, anyway, not like your father did. You've got to be steady, Kaley. You can't ranch in fits and starts. You've got to be willing to gut it out, day after day, year in, year out. To do that, you've got to love it—or you might as well leave it. Jim didn't love ranching."

"You're not...being fair to him, not really," she muttered, then lifted her chin. "But even saying half of that's true, what were you thinking, loaning money to a man on the brink?"

"I was thinking either way, I won," Tripp told her bluntly. "If Jim surprised me and turned the ranch around, well...have you seen what's happening to this part of the world?

"I don't know where all these people are coming from or why they can't stay home, but they're coming, all right, and each and every one of 'em wants a five-acre ranchette." His mouth twisted on the word. "They haven't reached Trueheart yet, but those folks are coming, Kaley, slicing and dicing up the rangeland and selling it off. Paving it and putting in streetlights and stop signs and strip malls and golf courses. Bringing in offroad vehicles and boom boxes. Raising taxes to pay for roads we don't want and firefighters and police we were doin' just fine without. Running from the city and bringing the noise and the crime and the crowding and that who-gives-a-damn-about-your-neighbor attitude with 'em. Bringing everything they hate with them, so we can hate it, too.''

She bit her lip and looked up at him, wide-eyed, nodding, and he felt his temper cool. She was with him. "I'd rather have another rancher—any rancher—on my border,'' he said, "than a damn developer. If a fence goes down and my cattle stray, another rancher will cuss and saddle up and help me herd 'em back. If I've got a damn suburbia next door, first time somebody steps on a cowpat, he'll call his lawyer. But this is *my* world, Kaley, and I mean to fight for it. I don't want to live in a world where if I ride down the road wearin' my chaps and spurs people stare at me and point cameras!''

She nodded again, thoughtful, giving him time, letting his anger roll off toward the mountains. "So…if Jim made it, paid you back, you wouldn't have minded?''

"Well, that was second best," he admitted. "Best case was he finally realized he was tired of trying. That he gave up and sold out—to me.'' Tripp didn't want to sit beside her, but he was starting to feel like a fool or a damn politician, standing here on his soapbox, making a speech. He dropped to his boot heels, rested a forearm on his knees and turned to look out over the pond.

Martha nudged his hand with her nose and he scratched her ears automatically. "The only ranches that are going to survive are the big ones," he continued, lowering his voice. "Suntop'll make it—at least while old man Tankersly owns it and Rafe Montana runs it, it will. And a few of the others here about.

"And I could make it, if I joined your land with mine,'' he told her. "You've got the hay meadows and water. I've got the best grazing leases, the best breeding stock by far, the best timber if I have to sell it.'' He had the gumption and know-how and desire to make a go of it, where she

did not. But no use telling her that; she'd always had her
share of pride.

"Put our two spreads together and I'd have more than
twelve thousand acres, which means the state would pay
me a share of the license money if I maintain habitat for
elk and let the hunters in." He grimaced. That would be a
last resort, but he'd do what he had to do to hold his land.
Whatever it took. "Join my ranch to yours, and it means
it's open range clear up to the National Forest, and it stays
that way." *Forever and ever more, amen.* "That's what I
was thinking when I loaned to your brother."

"Just a thought or two," she said wryly.

"Sorry, I ran off at the mouth." He hadn't talked this
much in nine years. Not since the last time she'd listened
with her blue eyes wide and a hint of a smile on her parted
lips. Men didn't dare tell each other their feelings this way,
and even if he'd tried, no other man would have had the
patience to sit still and hear him out.

"I'm glad you did. I know how you feel." Her face was
wistful as she gazed off toward the distant peaks. "You
know in Phoenix, Tripp, you can walk outside at night, and
there're so many lights you can hardly see the stars. The
brightest ones, yes, but not the rest of them. It's like somebody took a great big eraser and rubbed out the Pleiades."

His anger flamed up, as if she'd stirred a dying campfire.
But what do you care? he wanted to ask her. *That would
have killed me in a month, but you stayed on, so I reckon
you liked it. If you felt what I feel, you never could have
left these hills. These stars. Me.*

She sat for a time, head slightly cocked as if she expected him to say more, then she crumpled the tinfoil and
stood. She tossed it up in the air, then caught it two-handed.
"So…with Jim, you were giving him enough rope to hang
himself."

He frowned. Had she understood a single thing he'd said? "I cut him some slack," he corrected her.

She threw the foil again and caught it at chin level, then looked straight over the silver ball and into his eyes. "So if you cut Jim some slack, why not me?"

Because I don't want you anywhere near me, scrambling my brains, turning my plans upside down! Think I'm crazy?

When he didn't shout that, but clenched his jaw on it and said nothing at all, she added hurriedly, "I can pay you some of your money, come shipping day—a good chunk of it. But to pay all, Tripp, all at once, that would skin me."

And once upon a time, you flew off with my heart.

But he was over all that. This was strictly business, or sure ought to be. "The situation's changed," he rasped. "I loaned Jim money for six months. When he couldn't repay, I extended the loan another year. Till this October. Now, here *you* come, saying you can't pay me back. It wasn't a gift, Kaley."

"I never thought it was!"

"And meantime I sold a stud I...valued." That was such an understatement he wanted to laugh for a moment. At least, something like laughter fluttered in his throat. He swallowed it down and went on in a huskier voice. "Sold him so I'd have the cash on hand to put this deal together— make the down payment buying your land."

"I'm *sorry* about that." Kaley stepped closer, searching his eyes, touched his arm gently with two fingertips. "I really am. There's no getting him back, since you won't need that down payment?"

"No." No way in the world. "And who says I won't need it?" he added savagely. "Come shipping day, I can call my loan. Every last penny. If you can't settle up, well, then I reckon there's a ranch for sale."

She took a step backward, hurt as a child who'd been

slapped while asking, "Pretty please?" Tearing her gaze away, she looked out over the pond, her throat working, then she swung back. Her eyes glinted with unshed tears. She squared her shoulders, tipped up her chin. "Reckon there might be, but I read the terms of the loan contract."

"Meaning?"

"Meaning if I have to sell, I've got a month to accept outside bids for the ranch."

"And I've got a month to match any bid you get," he retorted, but his heart sank. She'd always known how to touch him. She knew how to touch him still—she'd gone straight for the weak spot in the deal.

"Wonder what kind of bids I'd get if I contacted the right real estate agents out in L.A.?" she said, but it wasn't a question. "There're super-jocks and rock stars and movie stars snapping up the prime land all over the West. And seems like they've all got more money than God."

Money he could never hope to match and she knew it. But two could burn the barn down and smile as they did it. "You do that, Kaley, if that's what you want." He closed the distance between them in two strides and was glad to see her eyes open wide as he loomed above her. He caught her arm and swung her around. "If those are the kind of stars you want in Trueheart, you go right ahead. Where d'you figure your movie star will build his four-story mansion? Over there?"

He nodded to the slope across the pool. "Great view of the falls and the mountains from there. And how 'bout a couple of guest houses for all his cokehead buddies, right here where we're standing? And what you bet they'll cement the pond and add chlorine so it's safe for city folks to swim?

"Then there're all those bright yellow lights they'll need," he continued relentlessly, "since they'll be afraid of the dark—city folks hate the dark—and the security guards patrolling. And reckon there'll be a road running down there along the creek to go to town. And more roads up into the hills for all their golf carts.''

''Go to hell!'' She pulled away from him, stumbled. Tripp lunged to catch her, but she found her balance and kept on moving, headed for the horses. ''You go *right* to hell,'' she called back over her shoulder.

He stood looking after her but she never turned. *Reckon I'm there already,* he told himself, watching her ride away.

In a spot where once he'd found heaven.

IF TRIPP REFUSED to extend her loan past October, she'd just have to find a way to pay him off, Kaley told herself bleakly, for the hundredth time over the past few days.

That inescapable truth had led her here, to the administrative offices at Trueheart High School. She'd steeled herself and called yesterday to ask if there might be any job openings for an experienced English teacher. Astoundingly, she'd been offered an interview with the principal, Mr. Haggerty. Strange as it seemed for mid-September, apparently he did have an opening of some sort.

She didn't want it.

Perched on one of a row of plastic chairs lined up along the wall, watching harried secretaries bustle hither and yon and sullen students come and go, Kaley realized how much she'd changed. She wasn't the same woman who'd taught tenth-grade English in Phoenix last spring, and done it with competence and reasonable contentment.

She was a new woman. Or maybe, these past few weeks, she'd rediscovered an old Kaley Cotter. The precollege-years one, who'd lived for summers. The one who couldn't wait to spring up from the breakfast table in the morning and run out the door, saddle her horse and ride away. *Have I spoiled my attitude forever, recalling how much I love working outdoors? Being my own boss?*

If so, how cruel to remember what she really valued—
only to be forced to turn her back on it.

But what else can I do if Tripp won't extend his loan?
She hadn't exaggerated when she told him a complete payback would skin her. She could *just* cover his forty thousand plus interest if she handed him every penny she
earned on shipping day—plus most of her divorce settle-
ment from Richard. But that would leave her no cash to
pay off the ranch's other bills, accrued over the past year.
Would leave her nothing to pay operating costs for the
coming year. Leave her nothing for the birth of her baby
and whatever expenses, ordinary or extraordinary, that
might arise.

Tripp's demand spelled disaster unless she found another
source of income. Immediately—yesterday! Which brought
her here to this windowless, fluorescent room with its faint
odor of sweaty gym socks.

"Miss Cotter?" Another secretary hurried out of a narrow back corridor, which must lead to the principal's lair.
Advancing past the counter that divided the room, she
smiled and held out a clipboard. "Mr. Haggerty would like
you to fill this out. He's a little behind schedule, but by
the time you finish this…"

"Of course." Kaley balanced the clipboard on her knee
and stared down at a standard application form.

Which she didn't want to fill out.

But what other choice had she?

Face it. I shot myself in the foot by the waterfall. One
minute she'd been trying to reason with Tripp, negotiate
some sort of reasonable scheme to pay him back. The next
moment…

*I never intended to threaten him like that, threaten to
take outside bids.* Somehow he'd driven her wild. The
words had simply popped out of her mouth.

But once uttered, the threat hadn't backed Tripp down

an inch. Hadn't made him see, as she'd hoped it would, that she was the least of all evils he might find on his doorstep. That for his own sake, he really ought to help her survive the coming year.

Instead, he'd called her bluff as swiftly and ruthlessly as he might have thrown and tied a calf. He was right. She could no sooner sell the Circle C to some L.A. celebrity, who'd turn it into his fantasy-western playpen, a travesty of a working ranch, than she could have stuffed Whitey and sold him for a scarecrow.

The same went for developers, who'd chop the land up into five-acre house lots. Not *her* ranch. Some things were meant to stay intact. King Solomon had known you don't cut the baby in half.

Solomon had also known that if a woman loved her baby enough, she'd be willing to give it up, to see that it stayed healthy, happy, all in one piece.

I'm not selling to Tripp! Not selling to anybody!

Which brought her full circle. She'd have to find the money to pay him back. Kaley gritted her teeth, picked up her pen and tackled the form.

Halfway down the page, she came to the question concerning her status—married or otherwise? She checked ''divorced,'' then sat tapping her lips with the butt of the pen. *And what do I tell Mr. Haggerty about my baby?*

To lie, at least by omission, and say nothing was tempting. Time would tell him.

She couldn't do that.

But if she didn't… Why would the man want to hire a teacher who'd need to take a pregnancy leave in April?

Maybe he's desperate.

If so, that made two of them. She sighed and finished the form.

The door to the outer corridor burst open and a tiny white-haired woman in high heels came rap-tap-tapping into the room. Behind her ambled a lanky, sandy-haired adolescent with an expression halfway between amused and defiant.

"You sit there, young man—*there*—and don't you budge!" The teacher stormed off down the hall toward the principal's office.

So much for Haggerty's schedule. Kaley glanced at her companion, who sat with his oversize hands resting flat on the cover of a fat, zippered folder.

One of the secretaries beyond the counter shook her head at him as she tried not to smile. "Sean, won't you ever learn?"

"I'm learning plenty, Miss Buxton," he countered amiably. "Like where to draw the line," he added under his breath, or possibly to Kaley.

She saw from this angle that he sported a black eye. It gave an odd raffish charm to an already attractive face, much the way Tripp's scar added depth to his looks. Sean. Wasn't that the name of Dana's stepson? But then, it must be a common name.

Sean unzipped his folder, drew out a paper and a roll of tape and turned to Kaley. "Mind holding this a minute?"

Reflexively, she accepted the folder, then watched the boy rise and saunter to the counter. When no one deigned to notice, he coolly taped his poster to the counter side, facing all comers.

Kaley found herself confronted by a photograph of two large boys beating a smaller boy. Or rather, one attacker held, while the other punched. Below the photo was printed a bold headline, which read, Heroes or Thugs? Then followed a paragraph of smaller print that Kaley couldn't read from her seat.

"That's our football team in action," explained the boy in an undertone, seeing her interest. "They won't let me print stuff like that in our school newspaper, even though

I'm editor this year. So that's my personal broadsheet, which I put out as needed. Tell the world.''

"Your last name wouldn't be Montana by any chance, would it?'' Kaley ventured, also in an undertone.

"No, I'm Sean Kershaw. Montana's my stepparents' name.'' The boy leaned sideways to scan her clipboard. "Kaley Cotter—hey, you're Dana's new friend!'' He held out his hand.

"Hi, Sean.'' And what a lovely feeling to know that Dana had described her as such. "You took that photo? It's very…'' She made a face. Not good at all. It made her want to…act. To stop what she was seeing. "Powerful.''

His face glowed with the praise. "Thanks. I want to be an investigative reporter someday. Or maybe make documentaries.''

"Looks like you've got a lot to say,'' she said, and meant it. "But tell me, if you would. How'd you get the shiner?''

Face pinkening, he examined his big hands, their bruised knuckles. "Um… Some photographers kind of hide behind the camera. Tell themselves they're doing their part if they record the moment. But those guys were beating the crap out of that mouthy little geek…so I got my shot, then…'' He shrugged and smiled. "Rafe's taught me to keep my temper. But he's also taught me you don't have to put up with everything you see.''

Good for you. She didn't dare applaud, couldn't help beaming her agreement, was saved by a woman's voice calling her name.

"Miss Cotter? Mr. Haggerty will see you now.''

"WHAT a pompous…*jerk!*'' Kaley declared some time later, collapsing into a chair at a window table in Michelle's Place.

"World's full of 'em,'' Michelle agreed with a wry, welcoming smile. Standing formally at tableside, she was dressed in khaki slacks and a bright red blouse, topped with a spotless white chef's apron. "So what can I do to revive you? Cup of coffee? Slice of pecan pie?"

"A glass of OJ, please. And would you have time to join me?" This late in the afternoon, the café was almost empty. Two women sat in one corner talking hurriedly over their empty plates while a blond toddler squirmed in a high chair between them and a pouting four-year-old sat on the floor at their feet. At the far end of the room, two weather-beaten ranchers slouched in companionable silence, their gnarled hands clasped around cups of steaming coffee.

"Absolutely." Michelle returned in a moment with coffee for herself, Kaley's juice and a plate bearing two brown-edged cookies, which she set between them. "Tell me about your jerk."

"Trueheart High School's principal," Kaley said, careful that her voice didn't carry. "Mr. Haggerty. He wouldn't be an ex–football coach by any chance, would he?"

"Bingo! Ex-Neanderthal, also, in my book," agreed Michelle. "I never turn my bottom toward the man when I'm waiting tables. Unless he's brought his wife along—that tends to slow him down. How'd you run into him?"

Kaley poured out her story between sips of juice and bites of a lemon sugar cookie as thin and sweet as a sheet of frozen honey. "He didn't have a teaching position to fill," she said, ending her complaint. "Or the least prospect of one. I asked him why he suggested I come in to see him. I wasted the whole blasted *day* putting together my résumé, ironing job interview clothes, dithering, when I might have been out doing something useful. He just shrugged and said he liked to know what was available around town."

"Indeed, he does."

"That he likes to keep lots of résumés on hand in case a position ever opens up."

Michelle snorted. "He likes to know that *he's* got—and you want! And he was probably curious to see you, a new lady face in town."

"That's the last time he sees *this* face," vowed Kaley. "He offered to let me substitute-teach—clasped his hands behind his head, puffed out his chest, gave me a great big smug smile and said he guessed he could throw me a day here and there. But that's not going to do it."

"Do what?" Michelle asked gently.

"Pay my bills." Kaley drew a calming breath. "I have some debts to pay off, ranch debts, and I'm starting to think I'll need to take an outside job to ever get on top of them." She felt no need to go into specifics. This was a matter between her and Tripp.

"That would be a lot on your plate once the baby comes," Michelle observed. "You'd ranch and teach—and be a new mom?"

Put like that…she sounded crazy. *Or desperate.* Kaley could feel tears stinging at the backs of her eyes. Much as she'd dreaded taking a teaching job, apparently she'd been counting on it to solve her problems. Now Haggerty had dashed her hopes, thrown her back to square one.

"I'd figured if the school hired me, I'd have to sell my entire breeding herd. All the mama cows and bulls as well as the usual calves we sell off at year-end. No cattle—not much work around a ranch." A Draconian solution that would have broken Whitey's heart, but she'd seen no other. "Then next year, or the year after that, whenever I'd settled my debts, I'd try to build up a new herd again." Although that would call for a new outlay of cash that she might or might not have by then. Once you started living hand to mouth, it was hard to recover. Hard to build for the future with the past snapping at your heels.

"Ouch!" Michelle said quietly. Breaking her cookie in two, she offered Kaley half.

Friendship and kindness and sympathy all in one bite. Kaley wasn't about to refuse. She took a nibble, murmured, "Delicious!" Then shrugged and mustered a smile. "Anyway, it's early days yet to worry. Now that my résumé's whipped into shape, I'll just have to trot it around to the school departments in Durango and Cortez." Either of which would be a dreadful commute, once the snows set in. But so be it. "Now, enough about me. What's new with you?"

They spent a happy half hour in small talk. Kaley told Michelle about sighting Sean.

"He's a handful," Michelle agreed, smiling. "But Dana says he's settling down nicely this year. Finally finding himself, and boy, have the girls found him!"

"Hunk in the making," Kaley agreed.

As for Michelle, one of her customers was trying to give her a reindeer, of all things—or rather barter one in exchange for meals. "He suggested I start a petting zoo out in the parking lot." Michelle snorted. "Said it would attract more customers. No-o-o, thank you! Somehow I don't see myself scooping reindeer poop every morning."

"Madam, *please* curb your reindeer." Kaley giggled.

The party of women and children across the room was breaking up. Michelle pushed back her chair. "Excuse me a minute?"

"I guess I should be going, too. Let you get back to work."

"But we'll see you tomorrow?"

"Wouldn't miss it for the world!" Girls' Night Out looked to be a sanity saver already. Kaley rose, waited till Michelle had turned her back, then tucked several bills under her plate. Friendship was one thing, business another. Then, calling, ''Bye!'' over her shoulder, she sailed out the door.

Straight into the arms of Tripp McGraw.

CHAPTER NINE

"Oops!" she said on half a breath. Hands flattened to his chest, Kaley stood as still as a startled deer in that instant before she bolts. Tripp's hands had gone automatically to her waist to steady her. *So slender, such softness in his grasp!* If fingers had a voice, his would be crying, *Mine!* He needed all his will to hold them still, when they longed to lock tight around her. But if he could control his grip, his pulse was skyrocketing. Could she feel the blood surging beneath her palms?

He eased her back a foot, but still he couldn't let go. "Kaley."

"Last time I looked." She fisted her hands against his shirt, then paused, seeming to realize she had few choices of where to put them till he released her. "Fancy meeting you here," she added wryly.

What was he thinking—that she'd slide her arms on up around his neck the way she used to do? Stand on tiptoe and lift her face for his kiss? His body had its own memories; he wasn't thinking at all! He let her go. "I was down at Hansen's." Trueheart's feed and hardware store. "Figured I'd stop in for a cup of coffee on my way home." At least that was what he'd figured after he noticed Kaley's car parked outside Michelle's Place.

Because they still had to talk. And seeing her car, he realized that Michelle's was the perfect neutral ground. Mac had told him once that a fine restaurant was the safest place to give bad news to a woman.

Not that he had planned what he meant to say. But nothing was settled between them, and when he saw her car his heart had...lightened. Hovered high in his chest like a hummingbird beating its wings. So here he stood, flatfooted in the doorway, knocked off center before he'd even started. The effect she always had on him.

"Well, if you want anything, you'd better hurry." Kaley glanced over her shoulder. "I think Michelle's about to close." She took a step to one side, her eyes drifting past him, seeking escape. "So-o-o...good seeing—"

"Hey." He caught her arm. "We need to talk."

She blew out a breath, wouldn't meet his eyes. "I'm *working* on it! As hard as I can, Tripp, but..." She rotated gracefully out of his grasp, retreated backward a step. "Look, this isn't the best day for me, so maybe we could—" She paused as the door to the café opened and a small boy burst forth, followed by two women, one of them holding a younger child.

"Whoa!" The boy threw out his arms and rocked back on his heels, staring up at Tripp. His mouth formed a perfect *oh*.

"Howdy, son." Tripp smiled down at him. Cute kid, four or five, he figured.

"Mama, look—look at his *face!*" the boy yelled, more fascinated than frightened. He tugged on his mother's arm. "He's gotta scar just like— *Ow!*"

His mother scooped him up, gave him a shake, her own face blushing scarlet. "You don't talk about *people,* Evan! That's rude! I'm *so* sorry. I don't know what's got into him." Giving Tripp an apologetic grimace, she whisked the kid off toward the parking lot, their voices a fading counterpoint of scolding and tearful protest.

The other woman ducked her head and hurried after them.

Out of the mouths of babes... Tripp stood with his face

aimed blindly after the kid, his gaze turned inward, mind filled with a hundred jeering versions of that cry. *Look! Look at him!*

Yeah, go ahead and look. Looking never hurt anybody. Not a grown man, anyway.

A hand cupped his shoulder. He blinked, refocused, on Kaley's face rising to meet his. Lips soft as velvet moved against his scarred cheek—their warmth shafted from there straight to his heart. "Hey, what do kids know?" she murmured, stepping back.

"They know an ugly mug when they see one," he said, but his voice wasn't his own. When she frowned, shook her head emphatically and started to speak, he added huskily, "Doesn't matter. I got used to that a long time ago. Water off a duck's back."

"But—"

"Look…" This he didn't want to talk about, and he sure didn't need Kaley's pity. "Hang on a minute, will you? I'll grab a coffee to go." Not that he really wanted one, but he needed space and time to catch his breath. To get over that kiss.

Minutes later when he stepped out of the restaurant, holding two cups of coffee, he saw that Kaley had discovered Martha. She stood by his pickup's tailgate, smiling and crooning nonsense to the Border collie. Leaning far out as she could from the truck bed, Martha shot out her pink tongue and licked Kaley's cheek. Kaley laughed, kissed her fingers, touched the dog's nose in return.

So much for his feeling a kiss from Kaley meant something special! She was as free with them as she was with her smiles.

Her smile faded to dark-eyed wariness as he joined her and silently held out a coffee. "Thanks."

He flipped the plastic lid to his own cup into the truck bed. "Look…" Though he'd been thinking about little else all week, he'd come to no conclusions. Only that he'd been a damn soft-headed idiot, extending Jim's loan last year. He could have—should have—been tough. Held him to the letter of their first agreement. If he had, no doubt about it, Jim would have gone under last fall. By now Tripp would be owner of the Circle C.

He wished to God it had happened that way. Because Jim wouldn't have been happy losing his ranch, but he wouldn't have taken it personally.

As would Kaley.

In Tripp's experience, women took things too personally. Men could draw blood with their insults or their punches, then laugh about it over a beer. Women got their feelings hurt and held grudges. And since Kaley and he had once been…close, she'd take it doubly bad. No matter what he said, she wouldn't see his refusal to extend her loan as strictly business.

What a fool he'd been not closing the deal last year when he'd had his chance. Tripp liked to think of himself as a hard man—tougher than most—but he was starting to wonder.

When Jim came to him last October, shamefaced and crestfallen at the way he'd blundered, buying those Beefmaster calves to fatten in a falling market, Tripp should have closed him down. Demanded his money then and there. But when push came to shove, all he could think was: he didn't want to live in a world like that.

The Code of the West said that you helped your neighbor. Offered your hand when it was needed, because someday, sure as shooting, you'd need a helping hand, too.

Tripp didn't want to live in any other kind of world. Wasn't even sure he could and still be who he was. So he'd extended Jim's loan.

And to be honest, he'd still hoped he'd win in the end.

That given the time and space—if Jim wasn't shoved till he dug in his heels—he'd realize that he *wanted* to sell.

Tripp had given Jim the time he needed to make up his own mind. Could he do less for Kaley?

And if he did give her time, wouldn't it come down to the same thing in the end? All Tripp had to do was grit his teeth, hang on hard to his hat and his heart—and wait her out. The ordeal would take longer than an eight-second bronc ride. It would probably be rougher—on parts of him far more tender than his butt—but in the end, when the buzzer sounded, Tripp didn't doubt he'd be the winner.

Because she'd never stick, never stay. In the end, she'd fly away. Worse case, she'd be gone by Christmas.

Kaley had given up waiting for him to speak and had turned back to the collie. Now she laughed. "Oooh, *clever* dog!"

Martha held the top to Tripp's coffee cup delicately between her teeth. She offered it to Kaley, her tail wagging a challenge.

"You need to buy this poor dog a Frisbee." Grasping the opposite end of the lid, Kaley waited for Martha to relinquish it. "*Good* girl!" She skimmed it across the truck.

Irritated, he rested his arm along the rim of the bed between Kaley and the blasted dog. "Listen," he growled. "We're nearly to roundup. Weather's holding fine so far, but in a few more weeks…"

Eyes on the dog, Kaley nodded. "I know. I've asked Whitey to hunt around for an extra hand, somebody willing to cowboy for a week or two. You wouldn't know anybody who's looking for work?"

He felt his temper rise a notch. *You don't need another man to ride for you. You need to hand over to me!* "I've been meaning to speak to you about that. Maybe Jim didn't tell you, but I was going to handle roundup for him after he left for the air force. That was part of our deal.''

''But since that's been canceled, you don't need to worry,'' she said quickly. ''I'll do it myself.''

''You?'' He laughed harshly. Roundup was gut-busting work for men who cowboyed year-round! No place for amateurs.

She tipped up her chin. ''I can handle it.''

''How? You haven't thrown a hoolihan in nine years, 'less you've been roping your students!''

''So I'll practice.'' Reaching over his arm, she accepted Martha's lid and tossed it again.

Her forearm brushing across his... The sensation rolled up his arm, tensed every muscle in his chest and stomach. And she did it without a thought, as easy touching him as she was rubbing the collie's ears—and it meant as much to her. ''Kaley.'' He fought the urge to grab her arms and make her look at him. ''I'll handle roundup for you, same as I would have done for Jim. It's a hard job and I don't want to see you blow it, runnin' the weight off the cattle, leaving stragglers up in the mountains to die this winter. Money out of your pocket on shipping day is money out of mine.''

''You will *get* your money, Tripp, one way or another. Stop worrying.''

''I'm not thinking about the damn— Damn it, Kaley!'' He caught her wrist as she reached again for Martha's toy. ''Leave roundup to me, okay?''

At last she met his eyes. ''No. *Not* okay. They're *my* cows... It's *my* ranch. My roundup. But thank you for your concern.'' She jerked her arm an inch or two, testing his grip, eyes flashing blue fire when he didn't let go.

How could he want to shake her and kiss her all at once? ''You can't handle it.''

"Can too." Her lips quivered suddenly, even though she scowled.

Making him want to kiss her all the more. He'd loved her ready sense of humor in the old days, much as the rest of her. "Cannot possibly," he countered, refusing to laugh. He let her go. "But if you're too mule-stubborn to admit it, then you better ride with us. We trade off work nowadays, the outfits around Suntop. Ride up together through Suntop land and bring the herds down the same way. We'll be splitting Dubois's time, anyway." The hand they'd shared up at Sumner line camp. "If you ride with us…" Then he could take care of her, whether she liked it or not.

"I…" He could see her fighting the temptation to tell him to go straight to hell, that she could handle it all by herself. She knew better. "Thank you. I'd like that." She let out a slow breath. "That would be a big help."

Damn right it would! But with her surrender, he felt his own temper ease. "Good. Well, then…" Not that this changed anything between them, but at least roundup wouldn't be a loss or a danger with him there to back her. Good enough for the present.

He should quit while he was ahead.

He drew another breath, his eyes flicking down over her clothes. He'd been aware of them all along. Kaley in a dress and heels was a sight to see, with legs that went on forever. And something about the sheen of those tawny stockings fired a man's imagination. He could almost hear that silky-sizzle of nylon under his hand. Almost feel his nerves leap to electrified attention as she dragged her leg up along his, high as his hip, at which point he'd…

"*You're* all dressed up for town," he observed, searching for something to fill the awkward pause—and felt himself redden, the way his voice betrayed his fantasy.

"I suppose…" She glanced down as if she hadn't noticed, herself. "I went for an interview at the high school. Thought they might need a teacher." She shrugged.

And he felt as if she'd kicked him in the stomach. What the hell was she thinking? *You plan to do that—and ranch on the side?* Whatever she might say, she was no more willing to grind it out—to stick with it—than her brother had been willing. *Or my own mother!* No way could Kaley be serious about ranching if she was already looking for a teaching job.

Just what he'd sensed all along, from the very first day he met her. Tripp drew a shaking breath. No way to vent his anger; it was none of his business. Why should he even care? Hell, he should be happy! When she left, it would be all the better for him.

Martha nudged Kaley's shoulder and she seemed relieved to switch her attention to the collie. She tugged a silky ear, then accepted the lid. "You said she was pregnant?"

"Yeah." He forced the word out.

"Are all her puppies spoken for? I've been thinking I could use a good dog. Haven't had one in years."

"She won't be dropping for another eight weeks."

"So?" She looked up at him, searching his face. Her smile wavered at what she saw there. "I...can wait."

"Eight weeks from now? I reckon you'll be long gone," he said savagely. *You'll never stick, never stay.* "S'pose you could leave me an address. I could mail you one." Not that dogs were ever happy in the city.

But then, happiness—that was asking a lot for anybody these days.

"Eight weeks...eight months...eight *years* from now, I'll still be here." Kaley's face hardened to match her voice. "Better get used to it!"

"Eight weeks from now you'll sell me your ranch and

be on your way." And glad to go. He didn't doubt it for a minute.

"Think so? Well, hope on, hope ever." After grabbing her cup that all this while had been balanced on the rim of his truck, Kaley lifted its lid and splashed the contents out on the ground. "Meanwhile, thanks for the drink." Head high, she stalked off to her car, and Tripp would almost have sworn—almost—that he heard the angry sizzle of thigh rasping against slender nylon-clad thigh.

MIDNIGHT AT the Circle C. Wrapped in her raggedy old terry-cloth bathrobe, Kaley sat at the kitchen table trying not to cry—she didn't know *where* these foolish tears had come from, or why they thought they had a right to fall. Changing hormones, that was all, she supposed, but, oh, tonight they felt like the real thing.

To hold them at bay she was stacking saltines like a house of cards. She'd tried eating them when first she came downstairs, but that was absolutely no use. Her stomach had revolted tonight—wouldn't take supper. Was darned if it would allow her a midnight snack. But at least saltines stood on end better than cards did. She wiped away a tear and commenced determinedly on the third-story floor of her saltine tower.

Never should have kissed him this afternoon at Michelle's! Never would have *dreamed* of kissing him, but when that horrible child had pointed at Tripp's face, she hadn't been able to help herself. Whatever it would have taken at that moment to soothe away his hurt, she'd have done it. Her kiss was the only balm she had to offer.

Don't know whether it made him feel any better, but me—look at me! Here she sat, dripping like the upstairs hot-water faucet, which was sorely in need of a new washer. To remember the taste and scent of Tripp's skin had done her no good at all. The taste of him on her lips had sent her reeling backward through time; that was where she'd traveled in her dreams this night, before she'd dragged herself out of bed. Back to their first summer, when all she had to do to find peace and happiness was bury her nose in Tripp's thick, dark hair, close her eyes and inhale his scent. He'd always smelled like home to her. *Precisely like home.*

Balancing two adjoining walls of saltines with one fingertip, Kaley licked a tear off her upper lip and reached for a cracker to make the third wall. Frowning with concentration, she set that wall in place—let out a slow breath when she lifted her hand and the tower stood.

Then she'd dreamed of Tripp's letter... Of searching frantically for it in Trafalgar Square in London, just as she'd really done, pigeons soaring around her like a whirlwind of lost letters.

Oh, that letter... She remembered smiling with anticipation as she tore it open. He wasn't much of a letter writer at the best of times, and this one had traveled so far to find her, from Trueheart to London, where she'd just arrived to study theater for the summer. This was a special exchange program, awarded to a few students each year on the basis of merit. Not only would winning this grant look good on her résumé, she'd explained to Tripp, but her attendance would earn her extra credits toward a double teaching major, English and drama. She'd explained all this before leaving and she'd thought he agreed it was worth doing. That postponing their marriage till September so she could do so was only sensible.

But reading his letter, her smile had faded to confusion, then incredulity, his phrases leaping off the page, one after another, to stab her to the heart: After long thinking it had become clear to him that they weren't suited for each other... They'd each be wise to find someone else. *You'll be better off without me,* he'd written flatly in closing.

And she'd cried *"No!"* so loudly that the people in the
park around her had stared—then politely looked away.
She'd wadded up the letter, jammed it into her pocket and
fled, running aimlessly. Running from her panic and pain.
Running from the bitter, inescapable truth that if—*fool that
she was!*—she hadn't postponed their wedding in June,
she'd have him now. Tripp couldn't have changed his mind
so easily if they'd been married.

She'd come at last to a street so crowded with rush-hour
pedestrians that she could not run, and by then she'd run
out of breath if not tears. Panting, lanced by a stitch in her
side, she'd leaned against a damp stone building and fumbled in her pocket for his letter—

And found it gone. The last token she'd ever have of
him, if he really meant what he'd said—and she'd lost it!

Back she'd stumbled the way she came, weeping. She'd
wandered Trafalgar Square for hours, stumbling through
clouds of pigeons, blundering through streams of roaring
traffic. But that precious, terrible wad of paper was gone
forever.

The words remained, engraved on her heart. *You'll be
better off without me.*

"Yeah, right!" Kaley murmured, wiping her sleeve
across her nose. *Don't think about it anymore. Does no
good to remember.* She fumbled for the fourth cracker, held
it poised, peering past the tears on her lashes. Completed
the wall.

Losing Tripp's letter had seemed like a hideous omen.
And so, in the end, it had proven.

She'd tried to phone him as soon as she returned to her
room at the dormitory. Had tried again and again and again
all that miserable week. But whether she called morning or
night or noon, the only one who ever picked up the phone
at the M Bar G was Tripp's father.

Sometimes he was too cheerfully smashed to say when

Tripp might be in. Sometimes he was hungover, too surly to find a pencil or remember a word of her frantic messages.

She hadn't had unlimited funds for overseas phone calls. She was there on a grant that barely covered her room and board. She'd made her fourteenth and final call—and reached Mac, Tripp's younger brother.

And it was instantly clear where *his* loyalty lay. Voice stiff with disapproval, he'd told her only that Tripp had hit the rodeo trail. No telling when he'd stop by the ranch again, probably not for months and months. Maybe not till after Christmas.

And no, Mac couldn't say what had happened—hadn't a clue. Tripp's love life, well, that was none of his brother's business. *Just took a notion and went* was Mac's unhelpful version of events. And sure, he'd be happy to forward her letters to Tripp, if Tripp ever called and gave him a place to send them.

Wonder if he ever did. Kaley set the floor of her fourth story in place. The tower swayed an eighth of an inch, then stood tall.

If Tripp ever received and read her pleading letters, they had not swayed his mind.

Kaley lost fifteen pounds she could hardly spare through June and July, missing meals to sit by her phone. Writing him letters till late in the night. Working herself to a frazzle at the theater to forget him, when she wasn't waiting for his call.

By August she finally realized she could sit there and wait forever, but Tripp wasn't calling.

He was gone.

He hadn't loved her enough to wait three months for her.

You'll be better off without me.

Maybe he was right.

In August, Kaley's roommate, another American in the same theater program, a woman of the world at twenty-one, had told her firmly she'd mourned her worthless boyfriend long enough. *Don't you know,* she'd said pityingly, *that when they say you'd be better off without them—it means they've found something better to chase?*

She'd packed Kaley's bag and dragged her off to Paris for a week with friends. And there Kaley had met Richard, who was touring Europe for the summer. Her air of utter indifference had piqued his pride.

And the rest is history, Kaley thought wearily.

History twice over. Now Richard was history, too.

And here I am where I started.

Needing two saltines to make the first two walls of the fourth floor. She placed one and held it vertical with a fingertip. Brought the second up and balanced it at right angles to the first... The tower swayed, teetered—and folded, crackers tumbling every which way to the table.

Kaley burst into foolish tears.

OUT IN THE STARRY DARK, Tripp rotated slowly. Martha had barked and he'd roused himself from where he lay dozing on the couch. Had come outdoors to see why the collie called.

Far off toward the mountains a coyote yipped in sleepy derision. Maybe she'd been talking back.

Whatever had bothered her, it was nothing to worry about, he decided. The chickens weren't stirring in their coop. Beyond the barn in the home pasture, his dark-accustomed eyes could make out two of his string of horses lying down, black mounds on an expanse of charcoal. If something had been prowling, they'd be on their feet, ready to run.

"You wanted maybe to show me the stars?" he asked

in an undertone as Martha came up behind him to thrust a
cold nose into the palm of his hand.

They were worth seeing. Diamonds flung across the
black. Glimmering worlds without end, amen. Looking up
at them, a man could realize his own worries, his own
yearnings, were mighty small. Everything he'd ever hoped
or dreamed, no more than a handful of stardust.

Head tipped to the sky, Tripp turned till he found the
Pleiades. Job's Coffin, his father had called that tiny cluster
of stars. The Seven Sisters was another country name for
the constellation.

By whatever name, Kaley had said she couldn't see them
from Phoenix. For eight years she'd lived without the Pleiades. *Bright city lights were your stars.*

Would be again once she grew bored with the dark and
missed them.

Leaving him behind to miss her, if he was fool enough
to come to care again.

He wasn't. Damned if he'd go through that again. It had
been years after Kaley before he could smile.

That door is locked and bolted, he assured himself,
brushing his knuckles across his cheek.

Where she'd kissed him.

CHAPTER TEN

TWENTY-THREE RIDERS were strung out over more than a
mile of mountainside, Kaley estimated, glancing off to her
left and right. At the moment she could see none of her
companions, only the pale trunks of trees as she rode
slowly through a stand of quaking aspens. But they were
there all the same, spaced roughly fifty yards apart, forming
a long ragged U, a net to scoop up all cattle before it and
send them drifting to the west. All of them riding through
this glorious blue morning, less than an hour after dawn.
Kaley's breath and her mount's made billowing clouds in
the frosty mid-October air. When the sun cleared the peaks
behind them, it would be welcome on their shoulders.

"G-*wan!* Get on, there!" somebody yelled far off to the
south.

Not Tripp, she noted, but a tenor voice—probably one
of the JBJ bunch, whose names, on this third day of
roundup she was just starting to learn.

Tripp rode directly to her left, closer to the center of the
curving line, where most of the cows were encountered. It
hadn't taken her long to realize that she and Sean Kershaw
and a few other riders had been assigned the right-hand
edge of the scoop, the uphill edge, because they were be-
ginners. When cattle fled from the horsemen, they tended
to run either across the alpine benches or down into the
canyons and valleys to the south. Ready to intercept them,

the abler riders rode the center and downhill sides of the line.

Fair enough. Even if her contribution to the total effort was small, here she was, taking part in what must be one of the largest cattle drives left in this part of the world—five outfits working as one to comb the mountain massif. "Thank you," she murmured formally, gazing upward through thinning golden leaves, trembling in no apparent breeze. There could be no finer life than this.

And thank you, too, she mentally saluted Tripp. It was he who had made this possible, inviting her along. Whatever he might have taken away from her in the past, whatever he might take from her in the future, still she should remember: he'd given her this. Three days of bliss so far, with more to come. They'd need more than a week to sift the summer range of every last calf and cow.

"Mine!" called another voice to the south. The distant thunder of hooves faded off the way they'd come—cowboy in pursuit of a bunch-quitter. They were completing the western half of the Kristopherson range today. She'd heard one of the old-timers from the JBJ crew grumbling around the campfire last night, complaining that the Kristopherson cows had no manners. Old man Kristopherson had brought in a strain of half-Brahmas twenty years back that were all high-tailed hell raisers, had no respect for man or horse. "Once your stock takes that attitude, there's nothin' for it. Every heifer sucks it in at her mama's teat, then when she's grown, she passes it on to her calves. No, you gotta ship every last outlaw off to the packer and start again, or suffer the consequences."

The light brightened ahead; they were coming to another meadow. Kaley's mount of the day, Pancake, pricked up his ears and snorted.

"Me, too," she agreed, rubbing the gray gelding's neck.

Meadows were more fun, since you were more likely to find action there. At the thought, she touched the nylon rope that hung below her saddle horn. In three days she'd yet to use it, and that was fine by her. Even in her ranching years, back in her teens, she'd been a four-looper at best. Though she'd practiced diligently for the past three weeks, ever since that day outside Michelle's when Tripp had invited her along on roundup, still she was rusty. And roping a fence post mounted with an old cow skull was a far easier proposition than lassoing a galloping calf. If she had to rope anything, she just prayed no other rider was in view to laugh—and most certainly not Tripp McGraw.

Pancake surged out into the meadow and scanned it as she did. Without signal from his rider, he headed for a cluster of four cows and calves that stood bunched together, midmeadow, warily waiting.

Off to Kaley's right, Sean Kershaw, mounted on a rangy paint, drifted out of the trees. The idea was to drive the cows, but preferably at a walk. Running the weight off the stock was the last thing a good cowboy should do.

"Get along!" Sean called. He pointed a finger at the dusky cow who clearly dominated the group. "Uh-uh! Don't even think about it, you old hussy!"

Kaley let out a high-pitched whoop for the sheer pleasure of it. The gray cow spun around and started off to the west at a trot, bawling her disgust. The others hurried at her heels. Kaley and Sean exchanged grins of mutual congratulation, then she followed her modest herd at a long walk, while Sean loped off to the right.

"And I could be in school!" he called back over his shoulder, shaking his head with the wonder of it.

As an ex-teacher, Kaley had been startled at first that Dana's husband, Rafe Montana, allowed his stepson to miss more than a week of class. She'd mentioned her sur-

prise to Tripp that first day, as they all rode up into the
high country.

He'd smiled and shaken his head in disagreement. "But
what do we want to pass on to our young'uns, Kaley? If I
had a son, I'd want him to learn how to handle himself
among men. How to complete a hard task in the real world,
then lie down tired and satisfied at night, out under a roof
of stars. Better my son push cows in the real world—any
day—than have him cooped up in school, learnin' how to
be a high-tech pencil pusher, moving numbers around a
computer screen. I mean, take a look at this!" He'd swept
his arm to encompass the band of horsemen strung out for
a quarter mile along the ridge, some of them riding with
stern-faced serenity, absorbed in their own thoughts. Others
talked or joked together as they rode, the land rising before
them in big rumpled steps toward the distance-hazed peaks.
"I'd want him to take a *big* bite of this world before it's
gone," Tripp said huskily, "'cause there's none sweeter
than this or likely to be."

He'd tugged his hat brim down over a face flushed with
conviction, then shrugged. "But reckon you don't see it
that way." Touching spurs to his bay, he'd loped on ahead
to ride stirrup to stirrup with Anse Kirby, Rafe's right-hand
man—giving Kaley no chance to say that yes, she did see.
She knew precisely how he felt.

That was the last chance she'd had to speak with Tripp
privately since the start of roundup. In the day, they rode
fifty yards apart. Each night, when twenty-odd riders gathered around the campfire, she shared him with the others.
When Tripp did deign to speak to her, he was brusque and
businesslike, sticking strictly to the matter at hand, which
was cows.

But though he barely seemed to acknowledge her, she
constantly felt his presence. Felt as if he was watching

her—and watching out for her. Why, only this morning when she'd gone off to fill her canteen, she'd returned to her horse and caught Tripp checking her cinches, making sure they were tight. And last night, when for some reason her come-and-go queasiness had kicked in and she couldn't stomach the venison stew, he'd noticed, though he sat on the far side of the fire. He'd strolled around to her side to ask if she was all right. Had demanded to know if she'd been foolish enough to drink from any of the mountain streams. Then he'd gone back to the chow line to fetch her another biscuit and an apple, when he saw she could manage that.

And when he wasn't watching out for her, it seemed he was simply...watching. More than once she'd looked up from joking with one of the other cowboys, with Anse Kirby or with Adam Dubois, her own line man, who'd turned out to be an attractive midthirties cowboy with a wicked sense of humor, to find Tripp scowling and swinging away before she could meet his gaze.

Or maybe it only seemed Tripp was watching her, because she was watching him. Tripp in his own world, dealing with other men, going about the business of being a cattleman, was an endlessly fascinating subject for study.

Set him against his own kind and Tripp didn't just measure up—he shined.

Coming to the far end of the meadow, she guided Pancake in among a mixed wood of aspen and juniper interspersed with high thickets. With this cover the animals might be quite near, or possibly they'd galloped on ahead.

Abruptly Pancake's ears swiveled to the left. Kaley could see nothing in that direction but bushes and the shimmering golden leaves of a young stand of aspen—then a scrap of pale hide beyond the gold. "Oh, no, you don't!" The half-Brahma cow erupted from the thicket where she'd been standing motionless. Angling off to the east, she headed back toward the meadow. The rest of her herd sprang from the bushes to follow her charge.

"No way!" Pancake spun and shot after them, with Kaley bent low over his shoulder. *"Ouch!"* A leafy limb whacked her cheek. Her hat spun off her head to hang by its rawhide chin strap. They burst into daylight—the meadow again—and she slapped Pancake across the rump with the ends of her reins. "Get 'em!"

You weren't supposed to run the cattle, but when they didn't respond to tact, there was nothing for it. She cut off to the left, hoping to circle them, but the Brahma ran like a deer.

Then a bay horse raced in from the far side of her stampede. Tripp barely moved in the saddle, except for his right arm, which whirled a loop above his head.

His rope shot out and settled around the lead cow's neck.

Capture in one loop! Kaley's admiration was mixed with a fair dose of irritation. She would rather have handled this badly herself than efficiently with Tripp's help. But then, who'd asked her? She loped on in her curve to head the rest of the rebels, but with the loss of their leader, the run had gone out of them.

Tripp dallied his catch to a slow halt. His bay backed as needed to hold the line taut. "Send the rest on ahead," he called to Kaley. "Including her calf if you can. I'll bring her on in a bit."

Kaley gave him a curt nod and herded her charges toward the west.

She stayed on their tails for half a mile through brush and meadow, collected another half-dozen cows, and now she had a grudging consensus; they drifted before her, bawling their discontent.

She looked up as the gray cow loped past, calling her

calf. "Thanks," Kaley said briefly as Tripp loomed alongside.

"Think nothing of it." His eyes swept over her and she was abruptly aware of her dishevelment. She'd ridden out with a neat braid this morning, but that last bit of bushwhacking had taken its toll. Leaning across, he touched her cheek with the back of a rawhide-gloved finger and scowled. "You've cut yourself."

"Oh...yeah...a branch back there..." His touch went through her like ripples expanding out from a tossed stone, silver rings widening across a pool of forest water. *I don't need to remember this, the way it was.*

Or if she did, then she should remember it all: he'd left her in the end. Left her brutally, without even the kindness of allowing her to plead her case. *However much you loved me, it was never with your heart.* But she was a girl no longer, mistaking hot sex in the hayloft for lasting love.

Still, those ripples of sensation rolled outward from his touch, sensations setting off emotions, which in their turn triggered deeper sensations.

The only weapons she had to hold these yearnings at bay were her good sense and her anger. "I've been wanting to ask you for days..." For weeks, actually. Instead, she'd waited in fearful limbo for him to speak. Well, she'd be a coward no longer. "What have you decided about my paying you back?" Once they'd brought the cattle down from the mountains, they'd cull and ship them. Then, by the terms of Tripp's contract, he could insist on total repayment.

And she'd found no teaching job in Cortez or Durango these past several weeks, though she'd tried. "Well?" she prodded when he frowned off into the distance. *Do you enjoy this, keeping me in suspense?*

"I...haven't decided yet," he rasped, so low she had to lean close to hear him.

"Oh, that's nice! You'll just keep me hanging and hoping till the last minute? That gives me *lots* of time to make other plans."

"And my plans, Kaley?" His scar blazed pale on his cheek. "You don't think you knocked th'hell out of mine when you came waltzing back to Trueheart?"

"But I—" Her protest fell on thin air. The bay had spun on a dime and surged away. Horse and rider plunged into the bushes without a backward glance.

ROUNDUP ENDED that evening at Big Rock Meadow. It was a natural alpine bowl, some ten acres of lush mountain grass, encircled by low cliffs on the uphill end, rimmed with dense forest below. A shallow brook ran chuckling down its middle.

As always they pitched camp at the top of the creek, upstream of the herd. Willy, Suntop's oldest hand at eighty-one, had pulled off his usual magic, outflanking the slow-moving cattle by paths known only to him, to drive his mule-hauled chuck wagon into camp hours before the cowboys. As the riders straggled in, they found a fire ablaze with a two-gallon coffeepot steaming on an iron hook above it. Half a dozen Dutch ovens were buried in the coals, giving off a rich fragrance of meat and spices, while a folding table had been set up and heaped high with brownies and apples to hold the hungry till supper. The sight was enough to bring a smile to the weariest cowpoke's face.

Riding into camp, Tripp scanned the stiffly moving figures milling about the fire. He looked past the ancient chuck wagon, a relic almost a hundred years out of date that Suntop Ranch counted among its treasures. Nobody with girl-moves walked out from behind it into view, or stooped with the other riders to wash her face and hands in the rippling creek.

Still out there, then. Tripp swung his horse around to stare off to the east. *Come on, Kaley.* His tension eased as half a dozen cows dribbled out of the trees to merge with the lowing herd. Then a pale horse hove into view, ridden by a slim figure with a fine seat in the saddle. She lifted her Stetson—giving Tripp a glimpse of brown hair that looked almost red in the late slanting light—to wipe a forearm across her forehead, then settle her hat again.

"So now you can relax," said Rafe Montana, standing on the ground beside him, his gaze following Tripp's.

What do you mean? Tripp started to say, then he shut his mouth and shrugged. The manager of Suntop was nobody's fool and he didn't miss much. Protesting would only broaden his smile. "She's holding her own for a girl."

"And then some," Rafe agreed. "But then, she's quite a girl." He flattened a hand on Dodger's shoulder and looked up. "How 'bout you take the first two-hour shift and choose five to help you?" he asked, which was his courteous way of saying, "Take it."

Since Suntop was far and away the largest ranch on the roundup, with the most cattle, and since Suntop made this event possible in half a dozen ways, from providing its wonderful chuck wagon to allowing the herd to trail down over its land, Rafe was the unspoken leader.

"Sure thing," Tripp said easily. He'd been looking forward to planting his boots on the ground and unbending his knees, but that would have to wait. The herd had to be circled, would need to be watched through the night, or the cows would wander back to their familiar range.

Two hours meant he'd be late for supper. Tripp rode alongside the snack table and leaned down to scoop up a

couple of brownies. He reined Dodger sharply away from
the bowl of apples, but took the hint and snagged one; he'd
feed it to the horse later, once he'd forgotten his lapse of
manners.

Heading away from the fire, Tripp tapped two JBJ riders
coming in before they had a chance to unsaddle, then Sean
Kershaw. "Looks like we've got the first shift." The boy's
face fell, but he nodded, and Tripp smiled to himself, riding
on. Good kid. Rafe was shaping him up nicely. He'd been
a rank beginner last fall, but this year he was making a
hand. Two rules of which were never complaining and accepting without question that the youngest and greenest
cowboys drew the worst chores.

Tripp's eyes switched ahead to another beginner incom-
ing. Kaley. By all rights he should choose her to ride this
shift. He opened his mouth to speak as she rode into range,
then changed his mind as she gave him a wan smile. She
was looking a trifle pale around the gills. He'd wondered
the night before if she might have a touch of food poison-
ing. Not that she'd ever admit it. "Have a brownie," he
said, instead, for something to say, holding it out to her.
His own stomach rumbled its outrage at this betrayal.

But her head jerked back as if he'd offered her a rattler.
"No, thanks." Her gray surged into a trot and passed him
by.

Tripp frowned after her. *Still mad at me from this afternoon?* She had every right to be; he sure owed her an
answer about the loan.

But she'd smiled. He rubbed his unshaven chin, then
narrowed his eyes as Anse Kirby walked out to greet Kaley, caught her gelding's bridle and held it while she dismounted, grinning wide as a hound who'd caught a glimpse
of an unguarded pie. *Like she needs that kind of help!* Or
needed it, anyway, from Kirby. Tripp gritted his teeth,

turned his back and rode on toward the milling herd. He was starting to feel he'd made a bad mistake inviting Kaley on roundup.

I should close her down pronto! Ask for my money back the day we ship, and that's the end of it. Clearly she didn't have the means to pay him back—or a hope in hell of paying her debt in the future. The sooner that bitter truth was faced, the better for all of them. She'd move on sooner rather than later.

And he? Well, at least he'd go back to sleeping nights without dreaming.

WHEN JON KRISTOPHERSON relieved him at nine, Tripp rode straight for camp. Maybe half the riders still lounged around the fire, basking their full bellies in the glow of its banked red embers. The rest had already rolled themselves in their blankets a ways apart or were now out riding herd.

He followed his shift mates to the tailgate of the chuck wagon, where Willy ladled out tin plates of steaming chili, then topped each serving with a thick slab of buttered corn bread. Refusing the offer of a cold beer, Tripp served himself from a bowl of salad, then trudged toward the fire. A long day.

Automatically his eyes searched for Kaley—and found her at the far side of the circle, seated cross-legged between Anse Kirby and Adam Dubois. *And I have the nerve to dream about her!* Kaley could have her pick of the men, wherever she went. Still, he stood for a moment, trying to recall if, in his dream of last night, his cheek had been scarred. Couldn't bring that detail to mind, only the sensation of soft lips questing tenderly across his face.

Whatever. He stopped at an empty spot before the fire, but couldn't help glancing across at Kaley.

She grinned and beckoned.

Damn her, did she really think all she had to do was crook her finger and he'd come running?

He walked.

"I believe this is yours?" she laughed, resting a hand on Martha's head. The Border collie lay snugged along her thigh, chin propped adoringly on her knee.

"Beggar's eaten more of Kaley's supper than she has," observed Dubois with a lazy grin from where he lounged on her far side.

Tripp would have never guessed the line camp cowboy would appeal to women. He was as weather-beaten as an old elk-hide boot. But then, what did Tripp know about these things?

He did know that Dubois worked half-time for him. He looked down at the man steadily, silently warning him off. After a moment, the cowboy shrugged and rose. "'Night, Kaley."

Anse Kirby also stood, muttered something about checking the herd and strode off into the dark.

Apparently that ended the party for Kaley. She uncrossed her legs. "Reckon I should help with the cleanup."

Out of sheer reflex, Tripp offered his hand, and supposed she took it the same way. She came up lightly, gracefully, like a mariposa lily rising toward the sun, then stood there, handfast, looking up at him. The flames at her back haloed her hair with glints of rough gold, wavering lines of ruby.

Damn, but he never should have invited her!

"She really did eat," Kaley said, breaking the too-long silence to glance down at the collie. "So I guess it was just a touch of morning sickness, huh, girl?"

Tripp had found the dog puking her guts out at breakfast this morning. She'd looked so shaky on her pins that he'd left her in charge of Whitey and Willy, to ride in the wagon. "Or something dead she got into." Though Martha

lacked that telltale perfume of a good carrion roll. So likely
Kaley was right.

He sat, and the collie inched into striking range, then
gazed wistfully up at him. "It's a dumb dog that steals
from a wolf," he told her, baring his teeth till she backed
off. He sighed and set to his meal, his eyes fixed determinedly on the play of the flames. The next time he let
himself look, he could see Kaley standing over by the folding table, where Whitey had set out a couple of tin tubs
for the dishes. She was up to her elbows in soapy water,
laughing up at one of the JBJ boys who stood by her side
and pretended to rinse.

It was bad enough that he'd put himself in the way of
Kaley's charms for a week straight, Tripp told himself
gloomily, downing four-alarm chili without tasting a bite.
He'd gotten over her before; he could do it again.

He'd have to.

But he'd made a far worse mistake than that—a mistake
that could wreck all his plans and dreams.

*How many cowboys here on roundup are riding for other
men's brands?* Anse Kirby of Suntop, for sure. Adam Dubois made two. Throw in a couple of the JBJ hands. And
one of the middle Kristophersons looked at Kaley the way
Martha was eyeing his corn bread—Tripp let out an audible
snarl and the collie hunched her shoulders and looked
away.

Half a dozen unlanded men had now met Kaley. No
doubt had sniffed around discreetly till they'd learned she
was divorced. Learned from Dubois or Montana or her pal
Sean that she was the owner of the Circle C, as pretty a
little ranch as could be found around Trueheart.

A ranch that might be had for the courting.

In one swoop Tripp had introduced her to half a dozen
cowboys who'd be delighted to park their boots under her

bed, to marry Kaley for both her sexy self and for her ranch. *Could you be more of a fool than that in a month of Sundays? What were you thinking?*

He'd thought he was making sure she wasn't hurt, rounding up her cattle.

Instead he'd shot himself in the foot—in both feet. *Yeah, that was smart!*

Wrenching his gaze away from her radiant face, Tripp looked down at his plate as he reached for his corn bread.

No corn bread. Just a collie crouching at hand with an expression of horrified guilt—and a smear of butter on the end of her nose.

CHAPTER ELEVEN

ON THE EIGHTH DAY of roundup, they trailed the cattle down from the summer range. Riding left flank, Tripp reined in and looked back the way they'd come. As fine a sight as a rancher could wish to see, a line of moving cattle more than five miles long. Red and cream and black in the foreground as they neared, then passed his station, they dwindled in the distance to dark, tiny shapes winding down out of the mountains. Miniature cows and calves and bulls trudged along five and six abreast, with tiny cowboys flitting along their flanks, tucking a bunch-quitter back into line here, pushing a suller along there.

His heart expanded with the sight: *this,* here it was; it was this he was fighting to keep.

To keep and pass on. The words rang in his heart like a vow made so long ago, he didn't remember making it.

But pass on to who? jeered a tiny voice at the back of his mind. Mac might never come back to the M Bar G, and knowing his brother, if he ever did, he'd either bring no woman or twelve.

Even if by some miracle Mac did settle down to ranching someday, Tripp had no ambition to be anybody's dried-out old uncle, pushed farther and farther to the family sidelines, year by passing year. He'd seen enough wistful old bachelor cowboys, practically spinsters in blue jeans, teaching other men's sons how to rope and ride.

No, that wasn't what he wanted from life.

But then? He shrugged the thought aside—too damn

pretty a day to get the glooms—and looked for Kaley. But the tail of the herd hadn't yet twisted into view, was still buried up in the pines beyond an open ridge. Since the greenest hands rode drag, she'd be back there eating dust, shoving the slowest and stubbornnest cows down the mountainside. He grinned, imagining her masked by her red bandanna, blue eyes shining in a dirt-streaked face, yelling with the best of them.

Some of the older cowboys had grumbled at first about Tripp's inviting a woman along. But she'd done him proud, carrying her weight without a whimper. He'd heard no complaints from the old guys after the second day.

And the young ones sure weren't complaining. One of the blasted JBJ boys, Jamie, had picked her a bouquet of daisies at breakfast this dawn! She'd knotted the flowers' stems and tucked them into her braid and was probably wearing them still. Tripp touched his spurs to his horse's sides and the animal shot off along the margin of the moving herd—high time he returned to his post, he reminded himself. But his worries outran his mount's drumming hooves.

Such a mistake, bringing her along. By next week, no doubt about it, she'd have half a dozen cowboys knocking on her door, bouquets in hand. Tripp could just picture 'em standing on her back stoop, rigged out in their town-going Stetsons and snakeskin boots, their eyes hungrily roaming her barns and pastures while they waited.

Well, think again, he told them all savagely as he leaned back and reined Joker to a sliding, dust-raising halt. Reflexively, he patted the startled gelding's neck—*good boy*—and eased him into a saner pace, a ground-eating walk. It had come to Tripp this morning, what he'd have to do to put a stop to all this nonsense.

He had to close Kaley down before somebody got to

her. Demand every cent of his money on shipping day, which meant she'd have to fold her hand and sell.

No ranch to tempt her suitors. That would slow them down some, if it didn't stop them entirely.

No home for Kaley. Which meant she'd have to leave Trueheart. He felt his face warm with the shame of it, but what else could he do?

And in the end, wouldn't he be only helping her on her merry way? Making what would happen sooner or later happen soonest?

Pretty women never stay. Not with a man with an ugly mug they don't, sneered a faint and faraway, half-drunken voice.

Hard to argue with firsthand experience.

THEY STOPPED in late afternoon where they always stopped the last day, on Suntop land, halfway down Blindman's Canyon. There was graze and water enough on the wide canyon floor to hold the cattle overnight, and its high, unclimbable walls made this the perfect arena to split the herd. Rafe assigned three riders to the downhill end of the cliffs where they narrowed to a chokepoint, with two of the JBJ hands waiting south of that line.

Before the tail end of the drive had even arrived at the holding ground, Ben Jarrett and his brothers waded into the combined herd and started cutting their brands out, sending them on down the canyon to the waiting riders. Since the JBJ Ranch lay northwest of Suntop, the Jarrett cattle were always first to go. They'd trail them down to the main valley before stopping for the night, turn clockwise around Suntop Mountain in the morning, then swing north again. Would be grazing their home range by sundown tomorrow.

The remuda had arrived under the care of the youngest and oldest Kristopherson and had been turned into a small box canyon to the east of the holding ground. Tripp went for a remount. Now that Loner was gone, his best cutting horse was Loner's twelve-year-old dam, the buckskin Dancer.

He saddled her and rode out to cut some cows.

In the midst of the herd, riding knee-deep in milling cattle, Tripp would scan their broad backs and tossing heads, looking first for a white face, then a JBJ brand on a red flank—the Jarrett stock was all Hereford or Hereford crosses. Once he'd spotted one, he'd ease Dancer through the press toward his chosen victim, while he scanned the surrounding animals for a calf to pair with his cow. When he'd found them both, he'd slide Dancer in close, her ears constantly pricking, then swiveling back at him, asking, *Which one? Which one? This flat-footed sucker here? Oh, piece of cake!*

Once she'd homed in joyously on their target, he'd loose the reins, sit back and let her work. Sitting lightly in his saddle, hips planted deep and still, the rest of him swaying in sinuous harmony with each twist and check and spin and halt of the cutting horse, he felt half-hypnotized. Dust rising around him, he'd soften the focus of his gaze to gain peripheral vision. Cow and calf became a twisting, dodging, never-escaping blur of movement as Dancer cut them off from their fellows and out of the herd. To where outlying riders waited to receive the pair and hustle them on down the canyon.

Cutting cattle, you couldn't help but dream of making love to a woman. So many of the sensations and movements were the same—the living heat of your horse clasped between your knees…the sound of panting and soft grunts…the pelvic slide and thrust of your hips…the tensing and relaxing leg and groin muscles…the tightness in your belly as your head and shoulders were left behind the mare's sudden spin and you flexed your torso to bring them back in line…the sensuous, unceasing rub of polished

leather along butt and thighs. The checks and feints and
setbacks of the game. Your target's ultimate surrender. The
flush of victory as you swept cow and calf out of the herd.

And all the while your body was saying, *Yes, it's like
this, but this isn't enough. Not nearly enough.* The sensations crisping along your nerve ends…your excitement rising to a higher and higher pitch behind a stern, expres-
sionless face…building to a sexual tension that, at last,
begins to plateau when no relief is to be had. Then the
inevitable letdown, a stealthily creeping—

The sun had dropped beyond the west wall of the canyon, and they were working in a blue twilight now, Tripp
realized, coming out of his trance. And he was tired and
full of dust. As must be poor Dancer, with her nose down
there among the cows. He patted her foam-spattered neck
and swung her out of the herd.

He walked her along the creek to the north end of the
canyon, in search of unmuddied water, assessing her condition along the way. She was twelve, after all, and even
in her youth she'd never had the stamina that her famous
son had shown. But then, Loner's sire was an Arab, one
of the Suntop studs. Tripp had chosen that crossing for
precisely that reason; Arabs had bottomless endurance, as
well as brains and sweet temper.

Could try again, he told himself, rubbing her sweaty
neck. He could breed Dancer this coming spring to the
same stud. Not that a full sibling to Loner would necessarily match him. Loner was a horse in a million, a stroke
of genetic luck, as all exceptional horses were.

But even if Tripp cared to try his luck again, it would
be an expensive gamble. Rafe had doubled Salud's stud fee
after Loner swept all four rounds of the NCHA World
Championship Finals, and he hadn't come cheap before.

Tripp didn't have that kind of money to splash around.

He'd need every penny he'd realized on Loner, to make the down payment on Kaley's ranch.

And even if he didn't have a use for that money, using Loner's sales price to try to replace him would have stuck in his craw. *Never, never, never should have sold him.*

The only thing that made sense of Tripp's loss, that would justify his loss, was buying Kaley's ranch.

"I'VE NEVER EATEN so much dirt—dust for breakfast, lunch and supper," Kaley grumbled, scooping up creek water with both hands to splash her face. Not that she was really complaining. What a day it had been! Even riding drag, she wouldn't have traded this day for any other in her life. To look down the mountain at all those cattle winding before her into the distance! To be a part of this purpose and beauty! She sat up and tucked damp strands of hair back behind her ears, glanced at Sean, who stood nearby, holding their horses, then grinned at his blissful smirk. "That bad?"

"Worse," he assured her. "You look like a raccoon wearing warpaint."

So did he. "Fine. Okay." She grabbed her hat, scooped it full—and dumped the contents over her head, scrubbing vigorously at the corners of her eyes and nose. Leaned down blindly to rinse again and sat up. "Better?"

"Better than a drowned rat," answered Tripp, reining in just beyond Sean and their horses. Martha had already discovered him and was standing on her hind legs to sniff his buckskin's nose, then backing off to yip a high-pitched, tail-waving welcome, probably telling him about the day she'd had helping Kaley.

Looking like a drowned rat before Sean was one thing, before Tripp quite another. "Hey, you're a fine one to talk! Looks like somebody dipped you in cinnamon sugar." She had a split-second, delicious vision of herself licking his face, of how sweet he would taste. Except his coating was red dust, not sugar.

"Been cutting some cows." Dismounting, he led his buckskin to the water downstream of Kaley's rock.

"Darn!" Sean dropped on his boot heels between them. "I was really wanting to watch you." He glanced at Kaley. "You've gotta see this guy. He's the wizard of cutting cows, and his stud Loner—yeow! If you crossed greased lightning with a tango dancer or..." He screwed up his face, at a loss for a description. "Put it this way—he lost the NCHA World Championship by a sneeze, last year. Loner's the best there is in this country."

"He did," Kaley murmured, studying Tripp's profile as he stooped to splash his face. Not a muscle moved; he might have been made of iron. No, she was wrong; there was a tiny muscle fluttering above his cheekbone. "That's wonderful." Except that clearly it wasn't.

"Where is Loner?" Sean wondered belatedly, studying Tripp's mare.

"Never pays to ride a stud on roundup." Eyes fixed on the dark canyon wall to the west, Tripp wiped his face.

"Oh, yeah, I remember. Last year you used him down at Suntop in the traps, for the final cuts, and to help Rafe cull his calves. You should have seen him, Kaley."

"I'd like to. Will you do that again this year?" Kaley probed.

He rose abruptly and ducked out of sight behind his mare's neck, then swung up into her saddle, gathered her reins. He was going without a word? "Tripp?"

"Can't," he said, heading back down the canyon. "That's the stud I sold."

THE NEXT MORNING the cutting continued. The Kristopher-son hellions were split out of the main herd—and what a job that was!—then they went their surly, ill-mannered

GET FREE BOOKS and a FREE GIFT WHEN YOU PLAY THE...

Just scratch off the silver box with a coin. Then check below to see the gifts you get!

SLOT MACHINE GAME!

The Harlequin Reader Service® — Here's how it works:

Accepting your 2 free books and gift places you under no obligation to buy anything. You may keep the books and gift and return the shipping statement marked "cancel." If you do not cancel, about a month later we'll send you 6 additional novels and bill you just $4.05 each in the U.S., or $4.46 each in Canada, plus 25¢ shipping & handling per book and applicable taxes if any.* That's the complete price and — compared to cover prices of $4.99 each in the U.S. and $5.99 each in Canada — it's quite a bargain! You may cancel at any time, but if you choose to continue, every month we'll send you 6 more books, which you may either purchase at the discount price or return to us and cancel your subscription.

*Terms and prices subject to change without notice. Sales tax applicable in N.Y. Canadian residents will be charged applicable provincial taxes and GST.

If offer card is missing write to: Harlequin Reader Service, 3010 Walden Ave., P.O. Box 1867, Buffalo NY 14240-1867

BUSINESS REPLY MAIL
FIRST-CLASS MAIL   PERMIT NO. 717-003   BUFFALO, NY

POSTAGE WILL BE PAID BY ADDRESSEE

HARLEQUIN READER SERVICE
3010 WALDEN AVE
PO BOX 1867
BUFFALO NY 14240-9952

NO POSTAGE
NECESSARY
IF MAILED
IN THE
UNITED STATES

way, driven off to their home range in the foothills southeast of Trueheart. Next it was time to separate Tripp's and
Kaley's cattle from the Suntop stock and say goodbye.
Tripp had suggested this morning, curtly—he seemed still
in a black, wordless mood—that Kaley agree to the method
he and her brother had followed these past few years:
they'd drive their combined stock together as far as the
M Bar G, at which point Kaley's modest herd could be
winnowed out and sent on to the Circle C.

With no better plan to suggest, she'd readily agreed. And
at the moment, she had more pressing concerns. She'd been
trying to corner Rafe Montana—alone—since the night before. Because if there was one man on roundup whom
Tripp seemed to count as friend, it was the trail boss and
manager of Suntop.

Most of the morning Rafe was beyond her reach, up to
his knees in cows, out in midherd cutting along with Tripp,
Anse Kirby and three other Suntop hands. But she found
her chance at noon when he rode off for a remount. Con-
signed to the sidelines as an unskilled cow catcher, she
abandoned her post and spurred after him.

"Hey!" she called, riding up beside him.

"Hey, yourself." Rafe's excellent teeth gleamed white
in a dusty smile. His dark blue, miss-nothing eyes flicked
over her face, a black eyebrow twitched, then he gazed
ahead, riding easily toward the box canyon, waiting for her
to speak her piece.

"Sean was telling me about Tripp's stallion Loner," she
said, gathering her courage. "About how wonderful he
was. How he nearly won the National Cutting Horse Championship."

"He did," Rafe agreed, not making this any easier.

"And I've learned that Tripp sold Loner." She'd known
he'd sold a stallion before this—he'd told her so himself—
but like an idiot, she hadn't delved into the implications of

that bare fact. Tripp should never be taken at face value; whatever he was feeling, he would always downplay it or even conceal it if he could. She didn't remember him being quite such a closed box that first summer. But she'd known so little of men back then. And she'd been so dazzled by his surface; maybe she just hadn't realized his depths.

The brim of Rafe's Stetson tipped an inch and rose again in agreement.

No need to explain that Tripp had sold Loner in the hope of buying her ranch. She wasn't sure anyone knew that—or even knew that Jim and Tripp had made such a deal. "What I was wondering was, could you tell me Loner's breeding?"

The corner of Rafe's mouth that she could see kicked upward. "Easy enough. Loner was by Suntop Salud, our top stud, out of Dancer, that buckskin mare he rides."

"Ah." That made things easier—and harder. Suntop was top drawer all the way to the bank. A Suntop stud would cost the sky. "Is Salud still standing at stud?"

"He is. Entertains quite a few of the ladies nowadays, but his dance card isn't quite filled for this coming spring." He glanced at her inquiringly, but there was a ready sympathy in his eyes that warned her.

Still, she had to try. "Mind if I ask what you get for him?" She sucked in her breath as he named the figure. "Oh." She'd been a fool to hope that somehow... It had crossed her mind that possibly she might sell her car; it was only five years old... But that wouldn't put her even halfway there. *You're a fool even to be thinking about this, Kaley Cotter. You'd better look to your own troubles.* If she had an extra dime, it should go to paying her debt to Tripp—and Tripp would be the first to tell her so. "Oh, well, I was just wondering. Thanks." She started to rein in, but Rafe touched her elbow, urging her to stay with him.

"Kaley, you do understand? I'm the *manager* of Suntop. I don't own Salud. He's a resource I manage and make the most of for the Tankersly family. If he was my stud..." His eyes said the rest.

"Of course." Something about his sympathy, or just her own too-wobbly emotions, brought the tears to her eyes. She brushed them angrily away. Oh, it was humiliating not having enough money to make things right. To be too poor to do what was needed.

Better get used to it, Kaley Cotter. She was a rich lawyer's wife no longer. Not that she regretted *that* for a single minute. "Thanks, Rafe." She reined in and let him ride on.

TRIPP WAS DOZING on his couch after supper when the telephone rang. He sat up with a grunt to glare at it. A telemarketer, without a doubt. Except for their pestering, he could go weeks without a single call. None of his friends was the chatty type, and Mac didn't phone home once a month. He reached for it and growled, "Hello?"

"By any chance are you missing something?" asked a warm, familiar voice full of teasing laughter.

As her smiling face formed in his mind, the muscles in his stomach and groin clenched. *You! I'm missing you!* He hadn't seen Kaley since he'd helped her bring her cattle home the day before yesterday. Wouldn't see her again till tomorrow, when he'd told her he'd come help sort her cattle and ship them out.

His mood had been as gray and bleak as the weather these past two days, since he'd come home to an empty house. But it was only natural to feel a letdown, he supposed, after roundup. For a week or more he'd been surrounded by friends, blood brothers who shared the same fears and hopes as he did, all of them united in an urgent and joyful mission.

Then he'd returned to this…silence.

He didn't remember it ever hitting him quite as bad as it had this year. But then, this year he'd had a hard choice to make. A choice that would leave somebody hurting.

"Well, let me give you a hint," Kaley continued when he didn't respond. "She's black and white and she runs on four—"

"You've got *Martha?*" The Border collie had been with him all afternoon. Had helped him sort out the prime heifer calves, those that he'd keep for future breeding stock, and move them to a separate pasture.

"Scratched on my kitchen door not an hour ago, then offered her paw when I opened it. Right now she's sitting here with her head on my lap."

Lucky damn dog. "Reckon she drew herself a map when we brought your herd home. That dog is nobody's fool." Trust Martha to know the difference between a house and a home. Though he'd not set foot inside Kaley's place since the day after her return, he knew instinctively how it must be by now. Vases of wildflowers set here and there, a smell of cooking to make a man's taste buds stand up and salute, bits of feminine color splashed around on the walls and chairs, a patchwork quilt thrown on the couch, good books stacked on the table, a fire crackling in the fireplace—it would be a cozy nest to keep the night at bay. A night promising frost.

"Mind if I keep her till tomorrow?" Kaley coaxed.

He shivered, images flowing through his mind of other times so long ago: Kaley lying with her head pillowed on his arm, her lips warming his ear, murmuring words of drowsy endearment. "Why not?" A pang of disappointment blossomed inside his chest as he spoke. *Dope!* He could have said he'd come get the collie, and Kaley would have asked him in for a few minutes, maybe offered him a cup of hot chocolate for his trouble. Was it too late to change his mind?

"Great! I've been missing…everybody so much since we got back home. Seems so *quiet* every night without twenty-three guys sawing logs all around me."

"Yeah." So he wasn't alone with this feeling.

"Tripp…"

If he closed his eyes, this could be anytime—could be nine years ago. She'd sounded just the same when she'd call him late at night from her dorm room at college. Nothing urgent to talk about, just Kaley filling him in on her day, the things she'd studied, the people she'd talked to, how much she'd missed him. Her voice talking over the miles had always made him feel like this, as if his stomach had gone all hollow, with a cold wind blowing through. To *need* something so much—need someone—when day by day she was growing apart from you, growing away. The distance spinning out between them, like one person looking back from the deck of a departing ship, while the other stands on the dock, growing smaller and smaller and colder and then…alone.

That he'd been warned, that he'd known from the very start it was bound to happen, didn't make his final loss one damn bit less painful.

"Tripp," she said again coaxingly, "you *are* going to give me one of her puppies, aren't you?"

He should have realized she wanted something more than just to chat with him. "By the time they're weaned, you'll be gone."

He heard the hiss of her indrawn breath. "I *won't* be! Unless you—" She let out a long sigh, then said on a harder, cooler note, "Reckon that means you want all your money tomorrow?"

That means I want you to make it easier on both of us. I want you gone before you lose your shirt playing at ranching or you break my heart again! What the hell was wrong with a man protecting himself?

"Look, I've got to go," he said hoarsely. "We'll talk about this when I see you tomorrow."

When somebody was bound to be hurt.

CHAPTER TWELVE

NOT THAT THEY HAD MUCH leisure to talk on shipping day. Even starting at dawn, the day was always a race against time.

A race against the rancher's worst enemy—shrinkage. Once you moved your stock from the little pastures called traps and into the shipping pens, the cows stopped grazing or drinking water, the calves stopped nursing; they all started losing weight. Shrinking. And since a rancher was paid for his beef by the pound, his profit was shrinking along with the cattle.

The solution was to do your final sort of the cows at the last minute before the stock trucks arrived. But of course you couldn't delay too long and leave the drivers cooling their heels and grumbling about the wait.

And all the while you worked, you were constantly wondering: what will they weigh? And what is a pound of prime steer bringing today? Because fall shipping day was payday for the entire year, the day you learned if your twelve months of painstaking labor had earned you a profit—or a bitter loss; if you could continue doing what you loved for one more hard year, or if you'd be wisest to pack it in.

Tripp had helped Kaley sort out her Beefmaster steers—the steers her brother, Jim, never should have bought—the day they brought her herd home. They were scheduled to go first this morning. A buyer from Amarillo, Texas, had already arrived and stood waiting outside the scale pen, smoking a ten-dollar cigar and eyeing the scale readout as if it might leap up and bite his wallet.

Riding Dancer, Tripp cut out fifteen steers one after another from the herd in the corral and hustled them down a chute to the weighing pen, with Kaley and Adam Dubois manning the gates between. Martha soon got the idea and helped them along. Tripp would indicate a victim and she'd skulk in to nip at its heels till it bellowed and fled this bossy black devil for the safety of the chute. Each time she brought in a steer, the collie would stop by Kaley to collect a crooning word of praise and a pat on the head. For *his* efforts, Tripp only earned a white-faced and wary smile.

A smile he was in no mood to return. What the hell was Adam Dubois doing here? Tripp had paid him off yesterday for his summer up at the line camp; he wouldn't be needed tomorrow for the M Bar G's shipping day, since Tripp always traded out work with the Kristopherson crew.

Kaley must have asked Dubois to lend a hand, since he was half-time her employee, too. But where had the cowboy slept last night? Tripp couldn't help wondering. Somewhere down in Trueheart? In Whitelaw's house, out back of the barn? By the way the bastard smiled at Kaley, you'd almost think...

Only if you were a jealous fool, he warned himself sharply, spinning Dancer after another steer.

Oh, but he was all of that, envious even of a damned Border collie. But Martha might have for the asking what he craved and would never have again. Still, she couldn't wreck his dreams the way Dubois could.

For these past two months, Tripp had been so certain Kaley would leave Trueheart. Yes, she'd shown more sand and stick-with-it-ness than he'd ever dreamed she would on roundup, but still, in the end, she'd go. Would be gone by Christmas for sure. Give her a taste of feeding cattle in the snow—an endless drudgery that nearly broke the back of the strongest man. Give her a month alone and snowed-in, no way to get to the amusements of town, and she'd be thrilled to go...

But he'd never considered, till roundup, what might happen if some landless cowboy came along and persuaded Kaley to stay. Some good-looking, smooth-talking cowhand with an unmarred mug and forty thousand saved up, to pay off her debts. Let a spoiler like that come along, and Tripp could wake up to find the Circle C out of his reach forever.

Losing Kaley's ranch, losing his best chance to survive and even prosper as a rancher would be the least of it, he was starting to realize.

Oh, that would be bad enough—but to live for the rest of his life, having to *see* Kaley happy in another man's arms? To have her living smack-dab on his doorstep forever? Haunting him with what might have been if...if only...

He chased another steer into the chute; Kaley slammed the gate, and beckoned. He kneed Dancer alongside and scowled down. "Yeah?"

"Do you have a headache, Tripp?" Her beautiful blue eyes were troubled. "Because if you do, I have—"

"No, thanks." He spun the mare and loped away, taking deep gulps of the dusty air to calm himself. *Stop worrying. It's under control.* Dubois couldn't court and win Kaley all in a day, and by this afternoon he'd have lost his chance forever to marry the Circle C.

But damn him to hell, he's forced my hand! He and all the other cowboys who'd been mooning over her this past week.

Tripp would rather—would much rather—have given Kaley the time to decide for herself that she wasn't cut out to be a rancher. To remember why she didn't want this

hard life. That there was a reason she'd fled to the bright
lights of the city, and that the reason still held.

But with these coyotes sniffing down her trail, he didn't
dare take the risk of being patient. It was time to close her
down.

AT LAST the trucks bearing the Beefmaster steers rumbled
off over the ridge toward the county road. Kaley and
Whitey walked the Texan up to her house to do their final
figuring at the kitchen table. Tripp ached to follow. The
buyer would try to beat her down; buyers always did, and
a young woman would look easy pickings. But he couldn't
help if she didn't ask and she hadn't. *And she has Whitelaw,* he reminded himself. That old cuss had seen every
buyer's trick in the book and outlasted them all.

Tripp shrugged and glanced at Dubois. "We'll bring in
the cows with steer calves first."

"You don't want to ask Kaley which she wants?"

"No." He'd bring her what she needed. Steer calves
fetched higher prices than heifers. So sort them and send
them off first, before they lost another ounce.

"Fine by me." The line camp cowboy shrugged and
went for his horse.

They'd pushed the first cow-calf herd from its trap into
the corral by the time Kaley and her companions reappeared. Tripp reined in Dancer to watch as she shook the
buyer's hand and he drove off in his yellow Cadillac, a pair
of chrome longhorns for its hood ornament and a Lone Star
flag decal stuck to its back bumper. Tripp couldn't see
Kaley's expression at this distance, but her whole body
seemed to wilt as she stood there, the dust of the buyer's
wheels drifting back over her.

Then she squared her slim shoulders and even from the
corral he could see her chin tip up an inch. *Didn't get the
price you hoped for, sweetheart? Welcome to ranching in*

the twenty-first century. It was only for the toughest of the tough, not someone as soft and hopeful as Kaley.

All the same, Tripp entertained a wistful picture of himself running that Caddie down with Dancer, of dragging the Texan out by his collar and punching his lights out on Kaley's behalf. Whatever he'd paid her, it hadn't been nearly enough.

Mind your own business, he warned himself, and went back to cutting cows. Dry cows and old cows to one pen, bulls to another. Unweaned steer calves down the chute to the scale pen, then onto the waiting truck; their bawling, protesting mothers went back to the trap, to live and breed for another year. Oh, it was a day when you needed to harden your heart.

In all kinds of ways, Tripp reminded himself, looking up from cutting to see that Dubois had taken a break and now stood over by the gate talking with Kaley. He was standing way too close for Tripp's comfort, if not for hers. And he'd draped a muscular arm along the top plank of the corral, then turned slightly to half encircle his quarry.

Kaley smiled, nodding her consent to whatever that grinning damn Cajun crocodile was proposing. Tripp jammed his hat an inch farther down over his nose and swerved Dancer after the largest bull he could find.

But if he was looking for a fight, the bull wasn't. He ambled amiably off to his side pen, content that he was an essential part of the operation—plenty of willing ladies in *his* world.

The next time Tripp looked up from his cutting, only Whitey and Kaley were working the gates. He herded a high-tailed, bawling calf down the chute; she shut the gate, then smiled up at him. "Feel like taking a break?"

"Not till this bunch is loaded and gone. Where's Dubois?"

"He went with that last truck. Caught a ride to Durango.

I said I thought you and I and Whitey could handle it from here.''

''Bet your boots we can!''

He finished the steer calves with a lighter heart, then accepted a ham sandwich from Kaley without dismounting. Ate it as he and Dancer and Martha brought in the herd of cows with heifer calves. At first he looked for the prime heifers, the ones he'd advise she keep back for her own breeding stock, then he realized what he was doing. Kaley wouldn't need them two years from now when they were breedable.

And he wouldn't want them. Jim Cotter hadn't upgraded his herd enough these past few seasons. Tripp would use his own stock and expand from there rather than build on Kaley's cattle. *So ship 'em all out.*

Kaley didn't agree, of course. ''Choose me the twenty best?'' she asked the first time he shunted a heifer through her gate.

You won't need them, he told her with a bleak stare.

She stared back. ''Please?'' she added finally. ''You're a better judge of cows than I'll ever be.''

He shrugged and set twenty prime ones aside. He could only drop the ax on her loan extension, then let the chips fall where they may. A month from now, he'd be sending these calves to the livestock auction. But for now, let them go to winter pasture. A waste of good grazing.

Finally the last calf was sorted to the scale pen and weighed. The job was done. Kaley and Whitey and the buyer for all her calves again walked that ritual walk to her kitchen table. Tripp shooed the last load of heifers up the ramp to the last truck and watched as the tailgate slammed shut. He shook the trucker's hand, then stood, thumbs hooked in his belt, arching his stiff back as the truck swung ponderously around and braked to idle by Kaley's back door.

The buyer stomped down the steps, walked around to the passenger side of the cab and climbed in. Kaley stood on her stoop with one hand lifted in wordless farewell as the truck pulled away.

You could hear the calves calling over the sound of the big engine climbing the ridge.

Their mothers answered from where they crowded along the trap fence, close as they could come to their departing offspring.

Kaley stood gazing after the truck, then trudged down the steps and across the yard.

Bad price, Tripp realized, studying her face. Not just bad, apparently, but awful. His stomach lurched. It would be his turn tomorrow. The cows called their lost babies and the calves answered one last time; then there was only the rumble of a big rig rolling off into the distance.

Without realizing he'd moved, he'd gone to meet her, drawn by the look on her face, his need to take it away. They met midway across the yard and he saw the streaks of her tears through the dust on her face. "Aw, Kaley." He wrapped his arms around her and pulled her to his heart. "*Kaley,* babe…"

She burrowed her face against his shirt and he hugged her closer—closed his own eyes as he rocked her, lost in her sweetness, the hay and honey scent of her hair, the feel of her heart pounding in time with his. "Was it that bad?" he whispered.

She nodded blindly against him, then heaved a sigh up from her toes.

The cows were still calling, though no one answered now.

"What'd he give you per pound?" he asked, stroking a hand through her rich and silky hair, massaging her head with his fingertips. Maybe it wasn't as bad as she thought. No way to really comfort her till he knew.

"Give me?" She raised her head and laughed up at him through streaming tears. "Oh, it's not that, Tripp! I reckon his price was fair."

A cow let out with a particularly mournful bawl, one last desperate attempt to call her calf home, and Kaley's smile wavered, then crumbled. She let out a squeak and buried her face in his shirt. "It's th-th-the *cows!* They've lost their— Lost their— They'll never—"

Her shoulders shuddered; his shirt grew noticeably damper. Tripp looked up helplessly to see Whitey standing on the back porch, frozen with surprise. As their eyes met, he jerked in his grizzled chin and did an abrupt about-face, then whisked back inside—the old goat was pretty damn nimble.

"Kaley, sweetheart, the cows..." Tripp murmured, rubbing his face against her hair, trying not to smile—so hard not to smile, holding Kaley. "They're used to this. They go through it every year. By next week they'll have forgotten, won't have a care in the world."

Unlike him. A week from now, a year from this day, he'd still remember this. Holding her, her softness molded to his urgent hardness, the way her hands had locked fiercely behind his waist, her need of his strength and his need to give it. Oh, when the cows were smiling again, he'd still be regretting. But still he didn't have the sense to let her go and step back and save himself.

"I know, I know, I know! I'm being a silly fool. I guess I just never knew before, how a mother'd feel..." She shuddered against him.

Maybe now was the time and the way to make her see. "Kaley, you're not cut out for this life. It takes a tough heart. That's why I want you to sell out to me. You'll be better off without this."

"Better off with—" The same thing he'd said in his kiss-off letter nine years ago! *You'll be better off without me*. She jerked upright in his arms. "Who says so? Who the *hell* are you, to tell me that?"

His tender half smile faded to bewilderment. "Hey, I'm just trying to—"

She brought her hands around to his chest and shoved, arching her back against his hold. "That's right! You're just doing this all for my own good. Taking my ranch from me. You're *such* a considerate guy!" She shoved him again, but still he held on. For just a moment there—oh, she was *such* a fool to feel safe and loved in his arms! Nothing but her old longings betraying her—just as they'd betrayed her the first time all those years ago. *It isn't me he gives a damn about. Tripp takes what he needs for himself, then tells you he's done you a favor.*

Well, not this time. "So tell me. I've got my money now and it's time to settle up. Are you—or are you not—going to extend my loan another year?" Oh, this was no way to ask for a man's mercy, but she couldn't help herself. She would have shoved him all the way across the barnyard if she could have. "*Are* you? I am so damn *tired* of your wait-and-see!" She flattened her hands on the wall of his chest and pushed.

He didn't budge an inch. His scar looked like an oncoming comet in his darkening face. He clapped his hands over her fingers, trapping them against his warmth. "Cut it out, Kaley!"

"No, *you* cut it out. Is it yes—or no? Are you going to help me out here—or try to squash me flat?"

Something scraped her knee; she glanced down. Martha sat close between them, staring anxiously up at their faces, pawing first her knee, then Tripp's. Doing her best to make peace.

"Martha!" Tripp roared. "Go sit *down!*" He jerked his chin to the side and the collie slunk away ten feet and sat. "Don't you take it out on that dog!" Hands trapped against his body, Kaley shoved him again. "You want to yell at someone, you yell at me."

"I'm *not*..." His eyes shifted over her head.

She glanced over her shoulder in time to see Whitey peering through a crack in the screen door—and the door closed with a bang. No help from that quarter, not that she needed it.

She flexed her fingers beneath Tripp's, feeling the tear-soaked warmth and hardness of him—such a hard, hard, *hard*-hearted man! How she could ever have been such a fool as to love him... "Are you going to shut me down or not, Tripp?" she demanded, trying to tame the shake in her voice. "I've got a right to know. No more stalling." Her fingers flexed again, like a cat's paws kneading someone's lap. Couldn't seem to stop herself; her palms itched with the feel of him. *"Well?"*

"I'm...not." Tripp blinked.

"Oh..." she said in a tiny voice, sounding ridiculous even to herself, after all her yelling. And why was *he* looking as surprised as she felt? She'd been so sure he meant to shut her down.

"That doesn't mean I think you should stay," he rasped. His hands slid down to her wrists and curled around them. "You *should* go. Back to the city."

Oh, yes, she should. She could feel her own pulse where his big thumbs encircled it. Feel it in her throat and between her legs, like twin echoes of her runaway heart. What was she thinking—that she could live happily forever next door to this man and pretend she'd never loved him more than life itself? *You are plumb crazy, Kaley Cotter.*

But better crazy on her own ranch than sane anywhere else in the world. "No, I shouldn't." She gathered her strength and stepped back from his warmth, though still he held her wrists. "But thank you for not driving me away." She licked the tears off her lips and felt him sway toward her an inch or two, a sensation more of rising heat between them, than that she saw him move. "I'll...um..." She was finding it hard to marshal her thoughts. His eyes were intent as a cougar's she'd seen once as a child, staring down at her from the limb of a pine tree. "If...you could give me a day to go over my books, I'll tell you what I can pay and—"

He shrugged, let go her hands and stepped back. "Pay me what you can."

"I will. Every last cent I can scrape together." She wiped her eyes with the back of a hand and found a smile. "And *thank* you! I...I don't know how to thank you. You're being more than fair."

He didn't return the smile. A muscle fluttered above his scarred cheekbone. "Don't thank me yet—not till I tell you the new terms of your loan." He snapped his fingers at Martha and she leaped to her feet, coming to heel as he turned and stalked off.

The collie looked back once over her shoulder in mute apology, then trotted soberly on.

All that night, through a night of hard frost and glittering stars, Kaley heard the cows calling. She didn't find sleep till dawn.

"YIPPIE-YIII, COWGIRL!" Michelle greeted Kaley with an exuberant hug the following evening, welcoming her back to another session of Girls' Night Out. "We've missed you. How was roundup?" She ushered her into the kitchen, where Dana stood at the sink washing red peppers.

"What's not to like," Kaley teased as she slipped out of her coat and hung it over a chair at the table. "Me and twenty or so Marlboro Men. Though all *they* were thinking about was cows."

"Uh-huh," Dana said skeptically. "Rafe tells me you were the queen of roundup."

"Not that hard a title to win since I was the only dad-blasted human female in thirty miles. Still, they did treat me like royalty—let me wash the dishes whenever I pleased."

"Apparently, that's not all you did." Michelle whisked something from beneath a phone book that had been lying on the table. "Ta-da!" She held up an eight-by-eleven photo of Kaley masked like a bandit, face streaked with dust, leaning down from her horse to smack a bolting cow with her Stetson.

"Where did you *get* that?" Kaley remembered the cow, one of the Kristopherson hussies who'd been determined to go her own way that last day when Kaley rode drag.

"It's wonderful!" Dana added, crowding alongside her to see.

"Should be," Michelle agreed with a twinkle. "It was taken by that budding photojournalistic genius who clomps around *your* house wearing a milk mustache."

"Sean!" they said together.

"As was this one," Michelle added, holding up a photo of Tripp in the act of roping a steer. His horse and his target were charging straight toward the camera; his twirling loop caught the light in a mystical swirl above his head.

"These are beautiful!" Dana breathed, holding the prints.

He was beautiful. Kaley tried to swallow around the sudden lump in her throat. Tripp's face was as serenely intent as a knight's charging into battle for God and country.

"Uh-huh." Michelle took the portrait of Kaley and smiled down at it. "If you're not taking that man seriously, then I think you'd better start."

If he'd ever taken me seriously... Kaley mourned. But all he'd wanted from her the first time was a roll in the hay. *And this time all he wants from me is my ranch.*

"Sean shows us so little of his work," Dana murmured

ruefully. "He shot a portrait of Rafe's daughter, Zoe, holding Peter when she came home to visit this summer that just about breaks my heart..." She sighed, then smiled. "But this..." She shook her head with the wonder of it.

"Well, he won't be able to hide his talent much longer," Michelle gloated. "We've worked out a trade. He's doing me a blowup of these two plus another ten for my walls downstairs. Portraits of my favorite customers at work doing whatever they do."

"He traded you photographs for what?" Dana asked with a mother's native suspicion.

Michelle's smile broadened to a mischievous grin. "Ah, now, *there's* a mystery!" She took the photos from Dana and propped them against a wall for all to admire. "Now, if we plan to eat shrimp Sambal before midnight, ladies, we'd better get chopping."

As always, they gossiped while they cooked. Kaley's friends wanted details about roundup, and in turn they told her the latest Trueheart doings. A divorced divorce lawyer, Jack Kelton, an acquaintance of Rafe and Dana's, had moved up from Durango to town, and his ten-year-old daughter was a tomboy terror.

"She came in here with some of the other kiddos after school for sodas," related Michelle, "and the little fiend challenged the biggest hunk in the group to arm-wrestle! Naturally, he doesn't want to wrestle a *gir-irl,* but the brat calls him a coward, shames him into it. So he gives up and figures he'll end the grief fast, beats her in five seconds flat—and she goes all pink in the face and dumps her water glass over his head!"

"So Michelle saves her from annihilation—then makes her mop the floor," Dana said, laughing. "And naturally, when Jack comes looking for his meanie munchkin, he ends up bagging *two* wild women. He asked Michelle for a date."

"Not my type," Michelle insisted. "A divorced divorce lawyer? Now, there's the King of Commitment! But he should be good for a laugh or two."

The conversation faded into a comforting buzz around her. Kaley stood at the counter chopping green onions, facing Tripp's photo across the room. She'd stopped by the M Bar G on the way into Trueheart, with a check to give him. After much agonizing, she'd calculated that she could pay back half Tripp's original loan and still survive—assuming she had no real disasters this winter, ranching or personal. And she'd decided to sell her car and give him that money, too, soon as she could.

But eager though she'd been to settle her debt, she'd found his ranch deserted. Apparently he'd completed his own shipping day earlier than she'd thought he would. Must have gone into town to celebrate. *Wonder who Tripp sees when he celebrates?* Her stomach knotted with the question. He'd always been a dream of a slow dancer. Had won her heart all in one dance, after a rodeo. *Wonder who he's dancing with tonight?*

"Move over, Marlboro Man," murmured Michelle.

Kaley looked up to find a silence had fallen and her friends were following her gaze.

"Did you...know Tripp before that night I braked for a varmint that will forever remain nameless?" Dana asked with her gentle good humor.

"We...used to date," Kaley admitted, eyes on his photograph. *Now why am I telling this?* Because she'd bottled it up so long inside? Because maybe the pain would never heal till she'd poured it out before caring friends? "Actually, once upon a time we were engaged to be married."

"You were!"

"Tell! Oh, tell," begged Michelle.

"There's not much to say, really. I was fresh out of high school, not even eighteen, and he was a man of the world.

Twenty-three. He'd been off on the rodeo road, riding broncs and showing cutting horses for the past three or four years, so we'd never even noticed each other, though our families only lived a few miles apart...." She sighed, remembering. "We met after the rodeo down in Cortez... There was a dance."

Oh, that dance. She felt the tears gathering. That dance—the feel of his arms around her, his lips brushing her temple, the blossoming certainty that she'd found her way home at last—felt the tears sting and hurried to finish. "We...dated hot and heavy all that summer. Got engaged, but Dad made me promise I'd finish a year of college before I married. So we set our day for the following June, the Congregationalist church outside of town."

"Where I was married," Dana said with a dreamy smile. "There's no place prettier for a wedding."

"But in the end we postponed the date till September. I got a grant to study theater in London for the summer, and it seemed smart to go..." She paused, wanting to justify, knowing she had no need among friends. "So I went, but the first week I was there, he wrote me a letter and broke our engagement. Said he'd changed his mind."

"The skunk!" Michelle exploded. "A Dear Joan letter? Breaking up long distance is the lowest of the low. I hope you phoned him and scorched his ears off."

"Never could reach him," Kaley admitted, retreating to the refrigerator for a new bottle of sparkling water. She'd been wrong; telling about it didn't help the pain. "He went back to rodeoing. Was long gone by the time I returned to the States."

"Did he ever explain?" Dana asked, her dark eyes troubled.

"Only what he said in his letter. That we weren't suited for each other. That we'd be happier apart." She shrugged and fixed her eyes on her glass as she poured. "And I reckon, in the end Tripp was right. I think it had just begun to hit him, as the date drew closer, what a wedding would really mean. That marriage lasts about fifty years longer than a romp in the hay. I don't think he'd been exactly…celibate all those years in rodeo…."

Not the way he'd loved her, he hadn't. She'd been too young to appreciate his skill that first summer. Had blithely assumed that all men would bring the same passion and finesse and laughter to bed. She grimaced. Richard had soon taught her otherwise.

"And I reckon it finally had begun to hit home that he'd be giving up all those buckle bunnies a winning cowboy meets rodeoing, for just one woman, and one not all that special…." Though she'd thought the sun rose in *his* eyes.

"One very special indeed," countered Dana indignantly.

"Too good for him," growled Michelle. "Oh, what's wrong with them all? Isn't there *one* one-woman man on this planet?" She grinned as Dana bridled and started to speak. "Okay, there's one. But why can't there be two— or better yet, three?"

"They're out there someplace," Dana assured her with the maddening optimism of the happily married.

"Well, if you find 'em, trot 'em right over," grumbled Michelle. "We'll be here waiting. Meanwhile…" She reached for the wine and topped up her glass, then turned to Kaley. "Guess you were right about Tripp McGraw. Looks like another King of Can't Commit. That was— what, almost ten years ago? And look at him—he's never married."

"You're right," Dana murmured, dark eyebrows rising to some private thought.

CHAPTER THIRTEEN

WHEN TRIPP WAS BLUE and needed to distract himself, he didn't resort to bars or television as some men do. He bred imaginary cutting horses—planned out a line of supersteeds that someday he'd never ride. Paper matings. Pipe-dream foals. Bring this mare, which he didn't own, to this stallion, whose twenty-five-thousand-dollar stud fee Tripp could not afford. Cross this stunning speed with that willing temperament—but no—that mare was a tad too long in the back; look for something more short-coupled. "The dapple gray that won Best of Show in 1982," he told Martha, who looked up from her basket in the corner of the living room and thumped her tail. "She'd do the trick. Now, where'd I see her photograph?"

Martha was used to his mumbling and shuffling papers by now. He'd been distracting himself every evening since Circle C shipping day. Had needed to fix his mind on something neutral, because every time he turned it loose, he started thinking about—

Shut up, he warned himself, and got to his feet. The gray mare would be in an '82 magazine, of course, since that was the year she'd won the national title. As a kid he'd had all the breeding magazines going back to the seventies. They'd been good distractions nights when his old man was crashing around downstairs with a bottle of rye and it was too cold for escape outdoors.

"Nineteen eighty-two," he muttered to himself. When he'd hit the rodeo trail the day after he graduated high school, his brother had gleefully cleared out the room they shared and stuck his possessions up in the attic. Years later when Tripp returned to the M Bar G, he hadn't bothered retrieving his outgrown treasures. His magazines from those years were bound to be somewhere up there.

"Might as well bring 'em down," he told the collie. He had the nineties issues arranged by month and year in his office bookcase. But there was room on the shelves for the older stuff. No reason not to have it at hand.

And no reason not to do the job now. He was in no mood to cook supper. Would grab something later—bowl of cereal, maybe.

He lit a kerosene lantern—there was no wiring in the attic—went to the second floor, then pulled down the trapdoor and the folding stairs. Climbed up into dusty darkness going golden with his advancing light. Motes of dust swirling like fireflies. He hadn't been up here in over a year.

"No. Dogs don't climb ladders," he told Martha, who stood below, whining, her forepaws on the third narrow rung. "Sit and wait for me." He grinned over his shoulder as she sat. Talk about matings, maybe Mac *should* marry her. Her brains and his brother's looks...what a litter they'd have.

"All right, Mac, where'd you put my mags?" He held the lantern high and winced as it revealed the rows of boxes stacked on all sides, leading off into the shadowed eaves. He chose a direction at random, then a box with a layer of dust on its top that seemed thick enough.

But that one turned out to be old kitchenware. Salad forks, a French whisk and cut-glass vases—who needed vases around here? And a fancy fluted cake pan that he didn't remember—would *not* remember—though, as he lifted it, a peal of some dark, unspeakable emotion tolled through his bones. *"Have a piece of cake, my handsome?"*

Shut up! he told himself frantically, and closed that

box—shoved it back into darkness, then sat, not thinking. Blanking his mind out.

But not thinking always came around to Kaley in the end. What the hell had he done, he found himself asking for the fiftieth time since her shipping day. *Had the chance to end it all, to shut her down, and I didn't. Threw it away, and why—because she cried?*

Women cried at the drop of a hat, over the darnedest things.

That didn't make their tears any easier for a man to bear.

So you threw your chance away and now Dubois or Anse Kirby will marry her and laugh every time he sees you coming.

But that was the chance he'd have to take for being a coward, Tripp told himself brutally. He just hadn't been able to demand his money. Not while he held her in his arms and the tears hung like crystal on her lashes, he couldn't do it.

Oh, he was a fool, no doubt about it, but fool that he was, all he could do was take the risk. Pray that she'd come to her senses and go before some blasted cowboy persuaded her to stay.

But, oh, it's gonna be a long, cold winter, holding my breath.

Down below, Martha barked, one sharp yap of inquiry.

"Yeah, yeah, I'm still up here. Keep your fuzzy pants on." He shook himself and stood. "Where was I?"

Quarter horse, 1982, right. He opened more boxes—shied away from one that was full of women's clothes—found another that looked promising. He lifted out a broken set of encyclopedias, several novels, was just coming to the conclusion that it was the dregs from the living room bookcases cleared out years before, when he uncovered a layer of narrower books, dog-eared and brightly colored.

Picture books. His mother had read to them each night,

a bedtime story, both boys curled up and leaning against her in Mac's narrow bed. He grimaced, helpless to stop the flood of memories as he sorted through the stories, then laughed softly aloud as he came to "The Little Red Hen."

It had been Mac's favorite fable. At four he'd fixated on it the way kids sometimes do, and he'd insisted each night, despite Tripp's disgust, that their mother read it. All one summer, he couldn't, wouldn't, go to sleep without it, the tale of the gallant little red hen who cared for her chicks all by herself.

Faced with a task like planting the corn, and having no helpers, what had she always said?

"Then I'll do it myself!" Tripp murmured, grinning as it came back to him. And by God, she'd done it. She feathered a fine, cozy nest for herself and her lucky brood. He thumbed to the last page, which showed the red hen and her chicks gathered contentedly around her well-provided table, while the lazy animals who'd refused to help her peered through the kitchen windows with awe and envy, shut out forever from her circle of loving warmth.

He closed the book, smiling, set it gently back in the box—then remembered the rest. His smile slowly faded.

His dad had surprised his mother on her birthday that summer with a teasing gift—a little Rhode Island red hen. She'd been the prettiest thing, with feathers red as a blood bay; they'd gleamed in the sun. And plump and industrious as her fictional namesake, she'd been a fine layer, a fierce defender of her nest.

But Tripp's mother hadn't liked chickens, though that chore usually fell to the wife on a ranch. Sometime that fall, in a hurry to drive into town, she'd rushed their feeding. Had forgotten to close the door of the coop securely on her way out. A fox or coyote hadn't missed the opportunity. The little red hen had vanished from their lives, without the trace of one shining feather. So much for guts and hope and gallantry.

At the foot of the ladder, Martha barked three times, then departed, racing heavy-footed down the stairs. Tripp frowned and cocked his head, then heard her whining below in the kitchen at the back door.

Company at this hour? *Mac,* he told himself as he hurried downstairs.

Wagging her tail, Martha ran to meet him and nipped at his boots, trying to herd him toward the kitchen. "Cut it out. I heard you the first time." He opened the back door and his brotherly grin wavered.

Kaley! Standing there with a cautious half smile and a wicker picnic basket hooked over one arm. He stood stunned with the shock of seeing her, the way he always reined in when he rode over a hill and found an elk standing on the far ridge, silhouetted against the evening sky. Just a simple *yes,* sounding deep inside him, keeping time with his heart.

"Could I come in?" she asked after a moment, then laughed as Martha caught the sleeve of her jacket and tried to tug her inside, growling with impatience. "Well, I reckon somebody's missed me!"

We both have, he wanted to cry, swinging the door wide.

"I just dropped by for a second," she added quickly when still he couldn't find words to welcome her. "Brought you a check." She pulled an envelope out of a pocket and handed it over, still chattering. "Sorry to come so late...you're probably ready for bed...but I tried two or three times this week and you were always out."

The moon had been waxing toward full this week and he'd ridden each night till it rose, reluctant to face the silence of his own house. "You could have mailed it." He was in no special hurry for the money, though he'd sent her a new loan contract for the coming year, with the terms he'd decided upon. The sooner she understood those, the better, he'd figured. Most likely she'd get that in tomorrow's post.

"Uh…yes…I reckon I could have." She sighed and stooped to receive a kiss from the collie.

He looked down at them wistfully, laughing woman and wriggling dog and clenched his hands so they wouldn't reach for her and lift her up to his lonesome heart. Finally, he found the words. "Want a cup of coffee?"

"Oh, I don't think so, thanks. Got things to do still at home. I'm painting the kitchen this week. Got to choose paint chips."

Making herself a cozy nest. Her hair gleamed red in the overhead light as she rose.

She set her basket on the table. "I'm afraid I got carried away cooking last night and made way too much soup, so I thought maybe you could use some. Don't boil it. Just heat it till it simmers. Then shred a bit of this cheddar and throw it in—I brought you some, in case you haven't shopped this week."

He hadn't. "You didn't have to do that."

"No…" She shrugged. "But…" She touched his forearm with two fingertips and sailed toward the door. Flying away from him.

Pretty women never stay, he reminded himself as she looked back over her shoulder.

"'Night, Tripp." She smiled and was gone.

He stood listening to the sound of her car pulling out of the yard, while his heartbeat gradually steadied. Martha whined and sniffed at the back door, then looked over her shoulder accusingly. "You're right. I should have made her stay. Seems like I'm always one jump behind her." He blew out a breath and turned to the basket. "She said soup?"

His stomach rumbled. He hadn't fed it a bite since noon.

Careful to follow instructions, he warmed the soup on the stove, diced and threw in some cheese, then carried it into the living room and sat before the fire. Ventured a wary mouthful, then sighed and dug in. It was like nothing he'd ever tasted, full of corn and cream and onions and what was this—zucchini? Spiced with jalapeños and maybe nutmeg, it delighted the tongue, then went straight to the heart, driving the autumn chill before it, filling emptiness with contentment.

He ate two bowlfuls, and found himself smiling as he went off to bed.

DRIVING BACK FROM DURANGO two days later, Kaley considered stopping off at Michelle's Place on her way north, then changed her mind. She'd had a long, busy day, and she was tired to the bone.

All the same, the expedition had been productive. She'd found a dealer willing to pay fair value for her car, after dickering with two others whose final offers had been barely more than insults. *Poor little car.* She patted its steering wheel. She'd give it up tomorrow, when Whitey could follow her into town in the pickup, then drive her back. *They'll find you a good home, I'm sure.* And she would have more money for Tripp.

Tripp... She frowned, picturing him standing there in his cold, stark kitchen, a room to strike a chill to any woman's heart. Not that it had been messy—quite the contrary—but it sure needed repainting, and not in muddy bachelor shades of maroon and tan. Its tired old brick-pattern linoleum needed replacing and it cried out for some bright, cheery pictures on its walls. *Maybe I could bring him a cyclamen for his windowsill next time.* Or better than a flower, an herb—say, rosemary or chives; men always had to be practical.

But whatever, she was quite sure after seeing his place

last night that there would be a next time. How much she owed Tripp was starting to hit her. Any way at all she could find to pay him back...

"And meanwhile," she said, touching her stomach, "I don't know if you were paying attention back there..." After the dealers, she'd gone on to Dr. Cass Hancock for her monthly checkup. "She says we're still looking good."

A shadow crossed over her face and she bit her lip. Next month came their first real hurdle, a blood test that could reveal many—though not all—possible defects. Other potential forms of damage might—or might not—show up during an ultrasound viewing. That depended on the skill of the technician and the subtlety of the damage.

"But she says we've got a very good chance." No guarantees, Dr. Hancock had warned quietly, her wise gray eyes brimming with compassion. She couldn't promise, but there was plenty of room for hope.

"So we'll settle for that." *Hope and faith and fingers firmly crossed.* Kaley touched her stomach again. "And you are now approximately four inches long, the doctor tells me, and you weigh about two ounces. And she says we don't need to worry if I feel faint from time to time, that that's perfectly normal."

She'd risen too suddenly from a nap on the couch night before last and half blacked out. Luckily, she'd dropped straight back on the cushions and not cracked her head on the coffee table. "Reckon Whitey would think I was crazy if I started wearing a football helmet instead of a Stetson for the next month or two?"

At some point she would have to tell the old man what was going on. She'd hurt his feelings the other morning upchucking his huevos rancheros. And he couldn't understand why she no longer drank coffee. Now that Tripp had renewed her loan, she supposed she didn't have to keep her pregnancy such a secret.

Though Tripp's not going to like it when he finds out, she knew instinctively. He'd extended her loan out of kindness, not because he believed for a minute she could make a go of her ranch. Learning she was pregnant would hardly make him rate her chances higher. *I just hope he doesn't think I tricked him.*

She hadn't. Carrying a baby who needed a home, she'd fight all the harder for the Circle C. "No way are we quitting." She touched her stomach.

Still, in spite of all her brave talk, she greeted the sight of the Circle C name board with a grateful sigh. A bowl of soup, then straight to bed, she promised herself. She braked, turned into the ranch road and steered alongside the mailbox. Made a face as she found the letter from Tripp. New terms, he'd said. She shifted into neutral, opened the letter and read.

Peace, gratitude, a future she could build on all flew out the window in a heartbeat. "You son of a—!" She slammed the car into reverse, then headed back down the road to the M Bar G.

HE'D RATIONED HER SOUP these past two nights, making it last; a bowl of it at the end of the day was like the first sight of the sun after a three-day blizzard. The thought of it had lured him home before dark. Tripp was unsaddling Joker, when Kaley's little car came bucketing down his road. His heart leaped at the sight of it, then he frowned. *Where's the fire?*

Hoisting his saddle over a railing, he turned to greet her as she braked to a dust-raising halt before the corral. She was scowling, he realized, as she popped out of her door— and dropped like a stone. Her head banged the side mirror as she fell.

"Kaley." He stood thunderstruck for half a heartbeat, then lunged into motion—way too late. *"Kaley!"*

Kneeling in the dirt beside her, he touched her face; she was pale, almost greenish, except for—his breath went out in a *whoosh*. Blood on her temple! "Kaley, sweetheart!" He framed her face with his shaking hands. She was out cold. *Tell me, God, she's only fainted, not dead!* He laid his cheek to her lips and felt her breath. It was even and slow. He let out a groan of relief.

Fainted, then, but why?

And more urgently at the moment, what to do? When a friend was knocked cold out riding range, you generally gave him a few minutes to come to and collect himself before you panicked. Sat your horse and waited, hiding your worry with gruff teasing and jokes till he blushed and scrambled to his feet and stomped back to his horse.

But that was a cowboy and this was Kaley, fragile, infinitely precious, nothing to joke about.

Don't move the victim was what they always said in emergencies. But this wasn't the city, with an ambulance only minutes away. And a raw frosty dusk was falling like a shroud. "Kaley..." He brushed his fingertips over her cheeks, her soft lips. "Come on, honey. Talk to me." He bent farther over her, trying to see the cut on her temple. Faints weren't so bad in themselves, but she'd knocked her head as she fell. Concussions, skull fractures... *Not likely,* he told himself. She hadn't fallen far. But still...

She needed warmth; he needed light to see the damage. *So stop your dithering.* Gently he slid his arms beneath her and gathered her up. "Come on, sweetheart." Legs dangling long and limp over his forearm reminded him of foals he'd carried in the past. She was light in his arms; he could have carried her forever. Wished he could. He dropped his face to her hair and kissed her temple, then started toward the house, walking on eggshells.

Martha met them as Tripp eased Kaley's legs through the back door, and turned to kick it shut. Whining, she danced on her hind legs to study his burden. "Yeah, it's Kaley. Now, sit. Nothing dogs can fix."

He carried her on into the living room and sat on the couch, cradling her in his lap, their faces only inches apart. Ought to set her down and find a blanket, but his arms had a will of their own. "Kaley, baby..."

Her eyelids were starting to flutter. Gratitude swept like a hot rushing tide through his heart and he bent to brush his lips through her shivering lashes. "Come back to me, sweetheart... Come on."

Her lids trembled and opened—stayed open—and she looked up at him, drowsy and bewildered and adorable. "Tripp?"

He couldn't help himself. He kissed the tip of her nose. "Hey, there."

She frowned, turning her head from his chest to the room. Then arched her back tentatively, testing his hold. "What happened?"

"Darned if I know. Reckon you fainted." What he did know was that he shouldn't be holding her, and any minute she'd be telling him so. Tripp deposited her gently on the cushions. "Don't budge."

He hurried off to the kitchen and found that Martha had relocated her "sit" from near the back door to the living-room doorway. She sat there craning her neck toward the sofa, quivering with impatience. "Sit," he repeated ruthlessly while he dampened a clean dish towel and drew a glass of water, then hastened back.

Contrary to his expectations, Kaley lay as he'd left her. *Doctor,* he decided. If she hadn't her normal spunk, then something was definitely wrong. He switched on the lamp on the side table, then sat next to her. "How do you feel?"

"Fine." She frowned as he leaned over her. "What are you looking at?"

"Your pupils." They were of equal diameter, pools of

midnight to drown a man. He held a fingertip before them. "Can you follow this?"

"Oh, for Pete's sake, Tripp! I fainted, that's all."

"You banged your head a good one when you fell." But she seemed to be tracking fine. "What day of the week is it?"

"Thursday and I don't have a concussion, Doctor. I just passed out."

"Yeah, but why?" He reached for the dish towel and dabbed at her wound, biting his own lip with sympathy. It wasn't bad; nothing he'd have thought twice about for himself. But this was Kaley. "This could use a stitch or two. Reckon we'll see what the doctor says."

"*Doctor*—what are you talking about?" She tried to sit up.

He rested a broad palm on her forehead, holding her flat. "The E.R. in Durango, unless you've got somebody else you'd rather see? You don't just faint out of the blue. Somebody's got to look into this."

"I've *been* to the doctor already today. Don't need to see another."

She caught his wrist and reluctantly he let her lift it aside. "You've already—? Then what's the matter?"

"*Nothing's* the matter. I'm just—" She stopped and her hand clenched on his wrist. Tears welled in her beautiful eyes.

"Just?" He smoothed a fingertip of his free hand under her long lashes; it came away wet.

"Pregnant," she said flatly, and closed her eyes.

She could have kicked him in the heart and he'd have felt less...winded. He sat for a minute before he remembered to breathe. *Pregnant*...the word echoed through his brain, a searing sense of loss spreading out from its bomb site, ashes overlaying all.

Pregnant and not by me. Oh, if he'd had the sense that

God gave a bull, he'd have bred her himself that first summer—made her his, at least for as long as she carried his
child. Any bull on his range would have told him that.

Instead, he'd done what was expected of a good man—
of a damn fool!—and waited for a wedding that had never
come, hoping against hope for a promise of forever that he
knew she couldn't keep.

Pregnant... His eyes traveled to her flat stomach.
"How...when..." Who, that was the question. *Whoever it
was, I'll kill him.*

"The usual way," she muttered, opening her eyes. "And
you can quit staring, there's nothing to see yet. It's only
three months and a week."

He counted backward: all of October, September, August, a bit before. "Then it's your husband's." No one
she'd met since her divorce. *"Ouch!"*

She jabbed his thigh again with her elbow. "Who did
you think? Whitey? The mailman? Santa Claus–come–
early? Now, let me up!"

"I just meant—"

"I know *just* what you meant, thank you. And by the
way, he isn't a husband. He's an ex. And now—"

He caught her upper arms and helped her to a sit. "Calm
down." Pregnant women weren't supposed to get themselves in a tizzy. Even he knew that much.

"Ha! That reminds me." She patted her shirt pocket,
glanced around at the cushions. "Oh, it's in the car. Your
contract—your *despicable* contract."

His temper was rising to meet hers. "The loan extension
I never should have given you?" *And she was pregnant!*
Could not possibly handle a ranch. If he'd known, he'd
never have—

"It's your terms. Only one month to take outside bids
from other buyers was bad enough—but you've shortened
that to one week? Come *on*, Tripp!"

"I'm supposed to make it easy for some developer to buy your ranch out from under me?"

"No, of course not, but the real worth of the Circle C is what people are willing to pay. If you don't give 'em time to make an offer, how is that fair?"

How was it fair that she could sit on his couch and lambaste him about money, when all *he* could think about was scooping her up and carrying her off to bed? Her cheeks had regained their color; her lips were parted; her hair seemed to crackle with passion. And he desperately needed to imprint himself on her body, try somehow to erase the marks of the man that had come before him. *Oh, you damn fool,* he cursed himself. Once again she'd ducked entirely under his defenses.

"One week isn't enough," Kaley insisted when he just looked at her, "but it's the other clause that I can't abide. You can call your loan *at any time from here on out,* Tripp? Strip me of all my year's operating cash with only two weeks' notice?"

"That's right," he rasped. It was the only way he could think of to protect himself. If some cowboy came seriously courting her, the bastard would have to be pretty damn quick. Because the minute Tripp smelled danger, he could demand his cash, and quite likely Kaley's ranch would fail. She'd be forced to sell.

And assuming she didn't get a bid he couldn't match within one week, he'd be the buyer. "That's precisely right."

"It's not fair!" Her lips trembled; her eyes welled. "How am I supposed to build a...a life—a home—when you could wreck it on a whim? Wreck it anytime you please, on just two weeks' notice?"

"Who said life's fair?" *You think you didn't wreck my life, coming back to Trueheart? Coming back with another man's baby?* His eyes swept down over her body with wincing tenderness. But how could he fight her? She held every weapon against him. What the hell was fair about that? His contract terms didn't begin to level their playing field. "Fair or not, you can take it or leave it."

"But—"

"That's not negotiable. Those are my terms." He stood. "And since you're feeling well enough to argue, reckon I best get you home. Or…" He touched her wounded temple, couldn't help himself. "Sure you don't want a doctor?"

"*Quite* sure." She bounced to her feet—wobbled—then growled when he caught her.

"Yeah, you are." He scooped her off her feet. "I always heard pregnant women go a little bit crazy."

"You say one word about hormones, Tripp McGraw— one peep—and I'll never speak to you again."

"Think I'd complain about that?" Angry as he was, that didn't seem to account for all the warmth around his heart when he carried her. A smile trembling somewhere deep inside him, like sunshine on rippling water. "Sit, Martha," he said as they passed her.

"Come, girl," Kaley cried, eyes flashing rebellion.

Martha whimpered and danced in place.

"So, come," he said, releasing the collie before she exploded. "No wonder you two get along, both of you broody."

"Mmm…" Eyes faraway, arm hooked around his neck, Kaley sighed, then leaned her head against his shoulder as he carried her across the yard. She trailed her other hand over his forearm so Martha could leap and lick it.

He glanced down at her and his arms tightened of their own accord. "What are you thinking?" he half whispered. She looked so damn…accepting…as if she knew as well as he that here in his arms was where she belonged.

"I think…" Her mood and her thoughts seemed to

swerve fast as any cutter's, from anger to teasing. "I think if I have to accept those two terms of your dadblasted contract, then you have to agree to a third."

"Which is?" Without putting her down, he opened the passenger door to her car.

"Clause three—I get a puppy." She smiled as Martha hopped onto the seat, claiming the middle position.

Damn the dog. "You can have the pick of the whole misbegotten litter if you're still here by Christmas." He stooped to set her on the seat, then stayed, one knee braced beside her, their noses nearly touching.

"But you won't be."

CHAPTER FOURTEEN

"I HAVE BEEN OUTED!" Kaley announced ruefully the next Wednesday while she unloaded her contribution to Girls' Night Out—bags of almonds and crystallized ginger, candied orange peel and two kinds of raisins—onto Michelle's kitchen table.

"So I heard." Dana laughed. "I stopped by Hansen's for a gallon of milk on my way here, and Josie Hansen told me you seem to be expecting a 'happy event,' is how she put it, with much up and down of the eyebrows."

"*Aaagh,* it's everywhere! Mo wouldn't let me pump my own gas at the truck stop. I feel like somebody painted a bull's-eye on my tummy!"

"It gets worse," Dana assured her. "Wait till they start patting you."

"It's all Tripp McGraw's fault," Kaley growled, folding her shopping bags.

"*Is* it." Michelle exchanged a glance with Dana. "How did he come to find out?"

"I was stupid enough to faint on his doorstep." While they set out their utensils and ingredients, Kaley gave them a severely edited version of the mishap. "So Tripp insisted on driving me home, and when we got there..." He hadn't allowed her to walk into her own house. "He made such a fuss about it..." And wouldn't you know it, Whitey had still been puttering around her kitchen. "He demanded to know how Whitey was taking care of me. Before I could stop him, he'd spilled the beans." She sighed. "So I suppose Whitey told his sister, Emma Connelly, when he went for Sunday dinner—I have a bun in the oven is the wonderful way he describes it—and I'm sure Emma took it from there. I reckon they know in Hong Kong by now that Kaley Cotter's baking up a storm.''

''Another month and the rumors would have started anyway,'' Michelle consoled her while she arranged cookbooks on stands where they all could read the recipes. She opened an issue of *Bon Appétit* on the counter, then another of *Gourmet*. ''Unless you were planning to wear a sack over your head every time you come into Trueheart—the Masked Mama rides again?''

''And speaking of baking…'' Dana drew a stained, dog-eared index card out of her purse. ''This one has to be in the running. It's my grandmother's. She brought it from Ireland, and who knows how far back it goes over there.''

Tonight's mission—to cook and compare fruitcake recipes—was Dana's idea. She'd decided that the ideal way to remind past guests of the delights of the Ribbon River Dude Ranch was to send each and every one of them a small but marvelous fruitcake each year before Christmas. ''Repeat business is the name of the game in the guest-ranch industry,'' she'd insisted when they'd groaned at the thought of baking hundreds of half-size fruitcakes. ''You guys help me find the perfect recipe, then Sean and Willy and I will take it from there.'' Kaley had learned over the past month that Sean was Dana's partner in the dude ranch, having inherited a quarter share from his late father.

The night passed in the usual flurry of chopping and mixing and laughter and moans, garnished with the latest news. Sean had completed his delivery of photographs to Michelle and they were being framed in Durango. ''They'll knock your eyes out,'' Michelle promised. ''I'm serving nothing but western dishes all next week in their honor—barbecue, chili, enchiladas, buttermilk chocolate cake, et cetera.'' And she'd grinned like the Cheshire cat when Dana demanded to know what Sean had received in exchange. ''Wait and see!''

Kaley's contribution to the night's entertainment was mail. Her brother, Jim, had sent a homesick, hilarious letter describing air force basic training. She read it aloud: '''And please tell Michelle that I miss her breakfasts, especially the pecan muffins. I plan to do a fly-by, over Michelle's Place, one of these days. Tell her that'll be me up there, doing loops and snap rolls in her honor.'''

''What a sweetie,'' Michelle murmured. ''Can't resist those flyboys. And when they wear cowboy boots? *Rrrrowrr…*''

''And,'' Kaley added, plunking another postcard down on the chopping block with a grimace, ''guess who else wrote me this week.''

''Who?''

''Richard.''

''Your skunk-of-an-ex?''

''The very same.'' Kaley held up a postcard, an *Arizona Highways*–style shot of saguaro cactus.

''Thorny subjects to discuss?'' hazarded Dana.

''You might say that. He says hello, says he was just thinking about me. Then he wonders rather delicately if perhaps, now that three months have passed, I might have taken his advice and had a change of heart.'' When her friends frowned in question, Kaley translated grimly, ''He means, did I change my mind and get an abortion within the first trimester?''

Michelle snorted. ''In other words, that choice of a post-card is *no* accident. Even he knows it deep down inside— the man's a prick!''

''And what shall we send him for that?'' purred Dana. ''A gift-wrapped mackerel?''

''A two-hundred-and-fifty-pound sadistic clown with a

crate of cream pies for the next time he goes to court,"
suggested Michelle. "I'll bake them myself!"

Kaley laughed as she pictured it. Trust her friends to
draw Richard's spiteful sting. "Better yet, I ignore him
completely. Being ignored is the one thing Richard could
never take."

"Done," agreed Dana. "We leave him stranded in the
State of Ignorance. And now, ladies, to change the subject
to something good and important—Thanksgiving is only
three weeks away!"

DRIVING HOME late that night, her old pickup trailing a
fragrance of fruitcakes through the streets of Trueheart that
probably had people drooling in their dreams, Kaley still
smiled. Another lovely night, and another problem solved.
She'd been wondering rather mournfully what to do about
Thanksgiving. Now she and Michelle had an invitation to
Dana's.

Wonder how Tripp celebrates the day? she asked herself
as she neared the turnoff to his ranch. She had an awful
suspicion that he treated Thanksgiving like any other day.
*Maybe eats a frozen dinner, Turkey à la king, if he remem-
bers to buy one.* She grimaced. He didn't take care of himself the way he ought to be cared for. *If he were mine...*

But he isn't, she reminded herself. *The man passed on
that chance, remember?*

Somehow it had really hit her the other night when he
made her tell about her pregnancy. *This baby could have
been ours, if only he'd wanted.* If he'd wanted her and all
she brought with her.

"You," she said softly, touching her stomach.

When she told Tripp, the tears had sprung out of nowhere, along with a ridiculous feeling: she'd felt like a
traitor. As if she'd betrayed him—betrayed their love—
conceiving another man's child. "Which is about the

dumbest notion a woman could have," she said aloud. "I mean, who left who? Whom?"

Still...

"Get over it," she advised herself. Guess he just wasn't the marrying kind. Another King of Can't Commit, as Michelle would say.

Hard to get over it when she could still feel Tripp's arms branded across her shoulders, on the underside of her knees...feel the solid warmth of his chest, her breast pressing against him as he carried her. Remember that heavenly sensation of being cherished and protected. And how was she to get over that odd notion that he'd kissed her, before she came to the other night?

Wishful dreaming, she scoffed at herself, and even if it was true, it meant nothing. Sex—good sex—in fact, wonderful sex—had never been the problem between them. *But turning great sex into lasting love, how do you do that?*

The woman who came up with the surefire answer to that tiny problem had better patent the process. She'd make a gazillion dollars.

Kaley sighed, then brightened as Tripp's mailbox came into view. Swerving to the side of the road, she stopped beside it. She found a scrap of paper and a pen in her purse and wrote a short note, then left it inside his box on top of a foil-covered cake: *For the kitchen of Mr. Tripp McGraw. Do* not *eat for one week. It has to ripen.*

She drove on her way with a smile.

ALL WEEK LONG, Tripp had looked for an excuse to see her. The plastic container that had held her soup—maybe he should return it. But in truth it was just a recycled half-gallon ice-cream tub, not even a piece of Tupperware. His motive would be transparent.

Stop by to thank her for her cake? But then he'd have

to admit that he'd eaten every crumb of it, despite her injunction, by the third day.

Still, he needed to see her. See for himself she was thriving, not driving herself too hard. He had trouble putting his mind to his own work while he worried that she was out riding range as he was, checking the herds, clearing brush from the watering holes, fixing the last fences before the ground froze till the spring. And she with only an old man to help her.

For his own peace of mind he needed to see her, and after a week of groping for excuses, two landed in his lap all in a day. Kaley mailed him an additional payment on her loan, a check for five thousand dollars. And Martha disappeared.

Reasons enough. That afternoon found him standing on her back stoop, rapping smartly on her door.

But it was Whitelaw who opened it. "McGraw. You always could smell a fresh pot of coffee." He limped back into the kitchen.

Taking that for invitation, Tripp followed and found the old man pouring out two steaming mugs of his famous brew, black and thick enough to stand a spoon up in it. He nodded his thanks, tried a cautious sip, then after a few comments about the snow holding off, added casually, "I'm looking for m'dog. Seen Martha around?" Which was a roundabout way of asking for Kaley.

"Reckon she's prowling Cottonwood Pasture with Kaley. Hound showed up here for breakfast this morning. Ate more flapjacks than Kaley did."

"You let her ride out alone?" After he'd made sure the other night that Whitelaw knew she was expecting. Fragile.

"Let her!" Whitey snorted, then his eyes dropped past Tripp to the floor. "Hear that, Chang? We're supposed to tell Kaley what to do."

His ancient, moth-eaten Pekingese stood in the living-room doorway, goggle eyed and grumpy, snuffling his contempt at the question.

"She's just like her mother, bless her sweet soul," Whitey grumbled. "Can't tell that girl nothin'. Busy from dawn till dark. Painted the kitchen this week. Like she didn't have enough to do." He waved his cup at the surrounding walls, which gleamed with a fresh coat of creamy white. And the kitchen cabinets and window trim had turned buttercup yellow, Tripp realized. "Then last night I found her up in the attic, dragging down that old crib. Same one her mother used for Jim and for Kaley herself."

"You've got to slow her down," Tripp insisted, though he was breaking one of the oldest rules between men. You didn't volunteer advice unless it was asked for. But this was important. This was Kaley.

"Huh! I've been meaning t'come talk to you 'bout that." Whitelaw shuffled over to the window above the sink, peered out toward the barn, then nodded to himself and turned. He scratched his unshaven jaw, made a wry face. "A fella don't like to give advice, but sometimes…" He peered sternly at Tripp from under his grizzled eyebrows. "Seems I recall that once 'pon a time you thought that girl hung the moon. I seem to recall something about wedding plans that fizzled, though nobody ever told *me* why." He cocked a considering blue eye at Tripp over the rim of his mug.

"Turned out we weren't suited," Tripp said briefly.

Whitey snorted and consulted his dog, who'd stumped halfway across the floor, then sat for a breather. "Weren't suited! And who's trained more teams of horses and mules to wagon than me, huh, boy? Some of the pairs I've hitched together—well, you'd be amazed. Had a mule and a half-buffalo steer once that made a dadblasted fine team. Harness those two together and they'd pull a load sweet as you please."

"Is that a fact." Tripp buried his face in his mug and gulped the last of his coffee. "Well, reckon I best be on—"

Whitey rode right over him. "You best be thinking long and hard. Whatever happened last time, well, son, here she's come round again, prettier than ever. With a baby that'll be needing a father."

This baby had a father and Kaley threw him aside.

For the flimsiest of reasons.

But how about pregnancy for a reason? An extended, hormone-induced tizzy? A feminine brainstorm that had caused her to blow her and her husband's differences out of all proportion?

That seemed to make sense of this nonsense.

But then that conclusion led to a new thought—a thought that had hit him like a two-by-four between the eyes: Had Kaley known she was pregnant when she flew the coop?

Surely not! Because even the flightiest woman knew that a baby sometimes mends the cracks in the shakiest marriage. If Kaley had been aware she and her husband had made a child, surely she'd have stayed in Phoenix and given her marriage another chance.

But now that she's learned she's pregnant? What now?

It didn't take a college degree to figure that one. Tripp knew Kaley's mule-stubborn pride as he knew his own. *She made her bed, leaving her husband, and now she's telling herself she'll have to lie in it.* That was what Kaley would be thinking right now.

But give her a month or two of feeding cattle in the snow, barely able to see around her own burgeoning belly... *And even if she toughs it out past Christmas, it'll only get harder and harder.* Calving season would hit about a month before she herself was due to calf, and it was a brutal schedule for the healthiest, strongest man. A rancher hardly slept during calving season, for all the cows needing help. *She'll never make it. She'll come to her senses. City life will look better and better.*

Meanwhile, back in Phoenix, Kaley's husband had to be missing her. No doubt the man was begging her daily to come home, try again.

Sooner or later he's bound to learn that she's making his baby. And then he'll come get her, if he has to carry her kicking and screaming all the way to Arizona. Tripp couldn't imagine a man—a father—acting otherwise. Not when the runaway wife in question was Kaley.

Slouched back against the counter, Whitey stirred. "So, son, what do you think?"

I think you're dead right, old man. Her baby needs a father—but it's not going to be me. By spring at the latest, Kaley would be back in Phoenix, back in her husband's arms, giving the lucky bastard another chance. Tripp shrugged. "Reckon she's old enough to know her own mind."

Whitey snorted. "You think that, then you've got a truckload to learn about pregnant ladies. She's of three minds at once on a good day. And on a bad? No mind a'tall—just bees in the bonnet."

Tripp set his mug down on the table and glanced down, to see Chang doing his tottering best to lift his leg on Tripp's boot. He backed hastily toward the door. "Keep an eye on her for me, will you?"

CHAPTER FIFTEEN

THANKSGIVING MORNING, Kaley was flying around her kitchen. With four pies baking in the oven, the air seemed almost golden with the scents of caramelizing sugar and toasting pecans, pumpkin-pie spice and browning crusts. She pulled her French apple cakes out of the fridge and packed them for travel.

"Don't see why we have to leave this early," grumbled Whitey, loosening the knot in his tie that had cost them both ten minutes of swearing. Since they had one vehicle between them, she was dropping him off at his sister's on the way through Trueheart, though clearly he'd prefer to miss "the fuss" as he'd put it, timing his and Chang's arrival for when the turkey hit the table.

"I promised Dana I'd help with the cooking," she repeated, hanging on to her patience. "Hey, was that the door?"

It was. Whitey returned from the mudroom with Tripp striding at his heels, inhaling blissfully.

"Heaven will smell just like this," he declared.

And heaven would look like him, Kaley privately thought. About that wide across the shoulders and narrow through the hips, standing tall in his best Sunday boots, with that same crooked grin. She hadn't seen him since the night she fainted, though he'd stopped by the Circle C two or three times to collect Martha, and she'd left a container of chicken stew in his fridge last week. But it seemed they'd been star-crossed throughout November, always missing each other. "*You're* all dressed up," she noted. In town-going slacks and a burgundy western shirt, wearing a turquoise bolo tie. So she needn't have worried, after all; Tripp had someplace to go for the holiday.

And someone to go to. A stinging sensation shot through her breast, as if someone had grabbed and plucked a heart-string.

"No more than you." His hazel eyes gleamed with appreciation as he surveyed her dress—a simple knit of blue-gray jersey that crossed at the bodice, then flowed softly down over her ripening body. "'Bout ready to go?" When she cocked her head in question, he added, "Dana said you'd want me to pick you up early, but maybe I'm too early?"

"No-o-o...no, you're just about right. Let me pack these pies and we're out of here." *Why, Dana, you little con-niver! Matchmaking, are we?* Still, it was the season for forgiveness, and Whitey, at least, was delighted by this turn of events. She dropped the truck keys in his triumphantly outstretched palm. "So, guess I'll see you tomorrow. Be sure to take Emma that pecan pie I made her, okay?"

He snorted. "Like I'm gonna forget!"

THANKSGIVING WAS ENTIRELY unforgettable, one of those treasured days to be tucked into the scrapbook of Kaley's memory. The Ribbon River Dude Ranch rocked with joy-ous life, from the laughing, busy women in its roomy kitchen, to the children squealing and romping upstairs, to the menfolk roaming from the football games on TV in the living room, to whatever it was they had stashed out in the barn.

"They're up to something," Dana insisted, watching them troop out the back door with wide, innocent grins, to saunter too casually up toward the corrals. Sean's grand-father had just arrived from California, and apparently it was now necessary that Dr. Swenson be initiated into the masculine mystery. "It started last night. I came back from shopping and Rafe informed me the barn is strictly off-limits, but the beast won't say why and all Sean does is gloat. I've a good mind to hold this turkey for ransom till they tell me what's up."

Michelle glanced up from the broth she was skimming for gravy. "Maybe they've got a keg up there."

But she doesn't believe that, Kaley realized, noting the mischief in her eyes. *In fact, I do believe she's in on it.* She lifted an inquiring brow at Michelle, but the blonde simply smirked and put a shushing finger to her lips.

The dude ranch wrangler, Willy, who'd been cook on roundup, strolled in from the living room with baby Peter riding his shoulder and toddler Petra pattering at his side, clinging with both tiny hands to his big, gnarled thumb. "Got my hands full of varmints here, so can I get one of you ladies to check my sweet-potato pie? Don't want it brownin' too much."

Sean banged in the back door, shared a grin with Michelle, then ambled over to the computer in the corner and sat. He typed a few keystrokes, then called to Dana, "It's Zoe again. She wants to know if she's supposed to sauté the onions *before* she mixes them into the dressing, or does she stick them in raw?"

Zoe was Rafe's daughter by a previous marriage, Kaley had come to learn. She was presently a freshman at Harvard, and she and several classmates were cooking their first Thanksgiving dinner away from home. With Sean's intercessions, Dana was coaching her through the creation of a traditional corn bread stuffing, via e-mail. This was her third query within the past hour.

"Sauté them in butter till they're soft, along with the bell peppers," called Dana in the midst of basting a twenty-pound turkey. "And remind her that once she mixes in the eggs she shouldn't sample the dressing any more till it's cooked.''

Sean typed, then looked up. ''She says, 'Yeah, yeah, yeah.' There're three premeds in the kitchen with her and they've already licked the bowl she used to make fudge brownies, so salmonella is a done deal, except that wine sometimes prevents it.''

''Then I imagine she's safe,'' Dana said wryly. She walked across the kitchen to read Zoe's message over Sean's shoulder, then tenderly ruffled his sandy hair and went back to her cooking.

They were fourteen at table by the time they sat down, counting two of Dana's dudes—Hans and Anna Goetz from Germany, plus the lawyer Jack Kelton, who'd arrived at the last minute with his ten-year-old terror, Kat, she of arm-wrestling fame. Kaley hadn't had a chance all day to accuse Dana of matchmaking, but she had to smile now that it was Michelle's turn to wince and roll her eyes.

But if the divorce lawyer was earmarked for Michelle, she wasn't cooperating. Throughout the sumptuous meal she devoted herself to Sean's grandfather, flirting outrageously and drawing him out with wide eyes and breathless questions, while Kelton glowered and the rest of the table was roundly entertained by Dr. Swenson's scandalous tales of life as a plastic surgeon to the vain and the beautiful of Hollywood.

From there the conversation veered to Sean's photographs that now graced the walls of Michelle's Place. His work had drawn in viewers—and diners—from as far away as Durango, inspired by an art critic who'd mentioned them in a newspaper article on local artists. There had been several offers to buy Sean's prints, and the librarian in Cortez was asking if she could borrow them for an exhibition.

''You're that masked cowgirl he shot, aren't you?'' Jack Kelton asked Kaley, openly admiring. ''All boots and spurs and attitude—a dominatrix on horseback, just *whacking* that bull. Yippie yiii ki-yay!''

''Except that was a cow,'' added Tripp in a gravelly voice.

''Oh.'' The two men measured each other for a moment that seemed to stretch, then stretch again.

To break that implacable gaze, Kaley picked up a bowl of mashed potatoes and waved it under Tripp's nose. ''Have some more?''

''No, thanks.'' They'd hardly spoken to each other all day, though Kaley had been intensely aware of him every time he passed through the kitchen. Then, sitting next to him, she'd felt that side of her body…prickle…throughout the meal. He took the bowl from her and their fingertips touched. He reddened and turned away to pass them on; she curled her fingers into a fist and hid them in her lap.

Silly, she told herself, that she'd be more aware of him in company than she was when they were alone. Maybe it was simply because Dana had tried to pair them. *I'll have to ask her not to do this again.* She prayed that Tripp hadn't realized their hostess was matchmaking—or worse yet, that he might have thought she'd done so at Kaley's request!

''You're looking sort of rosy,'' Tripp murmured at her ear, his breath stirring the tendrils that had escaped her French braid. ''You're not getting too warm in here, are you?''

A shiver sifted down her nape…down her spine… blossomed to warmth in her stomach. ''No, I'm fine, thanks.'' He'd been quietly, unassumingly, gallant all day, helping her in and out of his truck, insisting on carrying her pies, reminding her by a dozen tiny acts of consideration—just by the searching way he studied her—that he knew she was with child. That he was looking out for her. She'd thought several times of telling him that she wasn't made of glass, that she wouldn't shatter if bumped, but she wasn't really annoyed by his concern. Far from it.

"No more turkey for anyone?" inquired Rafe from the head of the table.

His challenge was met by universal, laughing groans.

"Maybe we should take a walk before desserts," suggested Michelle.

Sean glanced at her, then he grinned at Dana. "Why don't we walk to the barn."

BY THE TIME they'd all donned their coats and scarves and hats, it had started to snow. They trooped up the hill, laughing and talking and tipping their faces to the sky to catch the first fat flakes of the season whirling down. When they reached the barn door, Sean came to stand beside Dana. "This is your Christmas present, Dana, so close your eyes."

"Christmas in November?" she protested as Sean took one elbow and Rafe the other.

"Couldn't wait any longer. And they're not quite finished yet, anyway," her stepson told her, teasingly mysterious.

Kaley and the others followed them into the dimness, down the dirt aisle between two rows of stalls. Kat Kelton muttered her impatience at the slowpoke adults and wriggled past, and someone caught Kaley's arm. She glanced up to find Tripp beside her, smiling down. "What is all this?" she whispered, but he only shook his head.

In front of her, Dana stopped before a stall door, while Rafe opened its upper half. She peered in. "What? Why would you give me—"

"Oh, wow!" breathed Kat, standing on tiptoe at her side.

Dana turned to stare at Sean. "They *aren't* deer—too shaggy. And they can't be elk, with horns like that. What in heavens are they?"

Sean laughed aloud. "They're Ribbon River reindeer! To pull your sleigh, which is over...there. Merry Christmas, Dana!"

THEY LINGERED as long as they dared, but the snow kept on falling, and finally, about eight in the evening, Tripp declared they should go, before they were drifted in for the duration. Still, it took them another half hour to make their farewells, wrap up all the leftovers that Dana insisted they take, then escape. The edges of the private road out to the highway were barely visible beneath several inches of fluffy white, and the truck's windshield wipers labored to sweep the flakes aside. "Reindeer!" Kaley reminisced delightedly. "Who'd have ever imagined?" The pair had turned out to be shaggy little beasts the size of ponies—a doe with odd, forward-slanting horns and a buck without horns. Sean had explained that he'd shed his after mating season and would regrow them by the spring.

Their acquisition had been something of a shaggy reindeer story, which Michelle had related over wedges of pumpkin pie and ice cream. She'd accepted the pair finally, grudgingly, as barter from a customer who'd owned a petting zoo in the hills south of Trueheart. His wife had left him for a guitar-playing truckdriver. Entirely disheartened, the man had decided he was sick of feeding llamas and goats and ostriches and reindeer—the petting zoo had been his wife's idea—that he'd rather raise something sensible like sheep.

"And besides that, he couldn't cook a lick," Michelle reported ruefully. "So he moped around my café claiming he was starving to death and offering me all sorts of exotic beasts in exchange for a year's worth of breakfasts—like I really needed a baby buffalo—till I finally figured out a trade." She grinned at Sean. "I met this fabulous photographer who just happened to want a Christmas gift for his stepmother—''

''Who owns a guest ranch.'' Sean had taken up the tale. ''And I figured what could be better for business than to offer reindeer sleigh rides to the dudes?'' Along with the pair of reindeer, he'd found an old dogsled somewhere in town. He'd shown them photographs of Laplanders in Scandinavia with reindeer harnessed to just such a sledge.

''But you haven't heard the rest of it,'' Tripp assured Kaley as he swung carefully out onto the highway. ''The shaggy reindeer story goes on and on.'' Rafe had pulled him aside that afternoon while they were out in the barn admiring the animals. ''They aren't trained to harness, you understand. They've never even seen a sleigh. This is just Sean's notion he got from that encyclopedia article, and though the kid'll make a cowhand someday with Rafe teaching him, he didn't even learn how to ride till a couple of years ago. No way is he going to be able to train those critters.''

''Then who is?'' Kaley asked, catching the excitement in his voice.

''Well, Rafe could do it. But between managing Suntop and helping Dana at the dude ranch, he's kind of busy this year...so...''

Kaley burst out laughing. ''He talked *you* into taking this on?''

Tripp looked indignant. ''We worked out a trade and I figure I got the best of the deal. You know that Suntop Ranch has a stallion—an Arab, Salud—that stands at stud?''

Kaley's heart gave a tiny skip. She clasped her fingers tightly in her lap. ''Reckon I might have heard that somewhere.''

''Well, one of Rafe's perks as manager of Suntop is that he gets to bring two of his own mares to Salud each year.

And this year he only has one mare that he thinks measures up to the horse. Which means he either has to sell that second service he can't use—"

"Or trade it for reindeer training," Kaley murmured, almost singing it. *Bless you, Rafe Montana, oh, bless you!* "I see. So who do you think you'll send to Salud?"

"My buckskin, Dancer, of course," Tripp said, his voice going husky with emotion. "Which means her foal will be a full brother or sister to that cutting horse I sold, Loner."

Her eyes were filling with foolish tears of gratitude. It was really Rafe Montana she ought to kiss, but Tripp seemed a reasonable substitute—an excellent substitute. She leaned over and brushed her lips along his cheek. "I'm *so* glad, Tripp! You've cut yourself a wonderful deal."

THE PLOWS HADN'T CLEARED the highway yet, so they crept on at a snail's pace, straining to see through the oncoming flakes. "Turkey sandwiches with dressing and cranberries tomorrow," Kaley gloated after a while. "I think I love the leftovers even more than the main event."

"Yeah, but I noticed you managed a plateful back there. Feeling better than you were on roundup?"

She touched her stomach and smiled. "I am. Seems like the morning sickness is easing up a bit, thank God." She stretched contentedly and sighed. "*What* a lovely day, thank you, Rafe and Dana. I wasn't much looking forward to celebrating it alone."

"Reckon..." He cleared his throat. "Reckon you always celebrated it with your husband before this?"

"Mmm." Happy as she was, she didn't need to think about Richard.

Tripp, for some reason, did. "What d'you figure he's doing today?"

She shrugged. "I'm sure his mother is taking good care

of him." Phyllis would be delighted to have him back, all to herself, to cosset and spoil.

Tripp snorted. "Not quite the same as a wife, though, is it?"

For Richard, maybe even better. Endless devotion without a need to reciprocate. She unrolled her window a few inches and turned her fingers to the wind, caught a few flakes and touched them to her tongue.

"Do you...ever hear from him?" Tripp asked, eyes on the road.

What is this? "Once or twice." Well, once—that horrible postcard. She shifted restlessly in her seat.

"When do you mean to tell him about your baby?" Tripp asked all in a rush.

Kaley glanced at him, frowning perplexedly. Even in the darkness she could tell his teeth were clenched. "He knows about my baby, Tripp. Knew from the very start." She lifted her chin, waiting for the old hurt and sorrow to come rushing in, that monstrous sense of rejection. *My husband didn't want me enough to welcome my baby, blood of my blood, soul of my soul.*

But tonight when it came, the pain was soft and faraway, something that had hurt somebody else—another Kaley.

This Kaley wasn't so achingly vulnerable. This Kaley was now safely at home in a world full of friends and family, driving through a gorgeous white night with a man who maybe could not love her...but he noticed what she ate at table. His hands had been strong and careful and caring when he lifted her into his truck. Maybe Tripp couldn't give all that she wished for, but in some way— she was coming to feel it more and more—in some way he cared for her.

This man she could trust enough to tell at least one of her secrets. "Richard wanted me to abort my baby and I wouldn't. That's why I left him."

Tripp's hands must have jerked on the wheel. The truck swerved as she gasped and looked up. Scowling with concentration, he steered into the skid and after a heart-stopping half minute, the truck straightened to the road. "But you said…" He flicked a frowning glance at her, then stared straight ahead. "You told me—that night at Mo's—that he was selfish, was why you left him. That you squabbled about TV channels and such stuff."

"Well, he was—is—just like that. But he wanted his way in the big things as well as the small. And when I finally got pregnant, he didn't want children. And no *way* was I dumping my baby. So I left him."

"Oh…" Tripp didn't say another word all the way home.

CHAPTER SIXTEEN

THREE DAYS AFTER Thanksgiving, Tripp couldn't stand it anymore. How was Kaley faring? With a foot of snow on the ground, cattle-feeding season was upon them and there'd be no letup in the grinding work till spring.

He started feeding his own herds at dawn and was finished by midafternoon, with plenty of light left in the day. A beginner like Kaley would not be so efficient, could possibly use some help, he told himself. And since Martha had vanished the night before when he let her out, he had his excuse. He grabbed a chunk of bread and cheese on his way past his house and ate lunch in the truck, driving to the Circle C.

Her private road had been plowed, he noted approvingly, and when he reached the ranch house, the plowed track led up and away toward her winter pastures. No one answered his knock in the main house, but smoke rose from the tin stovepipe of Whitelaw's cottage, back of the barn.

He thumped on the door and the old man opened it. "Yeah?" His snub nose was rosy as a department-store St. Nick's.

"Kaley around?"

Whitey whipped out a yellow bandanna, blew emphatically, then leaned out to study the sun, which was sinking fast toward Suntop Mountain. "Out feeding. Always finishes with the hay meadows to the south. That's where she'll be by now."

"Thanks. Caught a cold, huh?"

The old man grunted. "From m'dang sister. Nothin' to speak of, but Kaley won't let me come near. Says her baby might catch it. So me and Chang—" He glanced down at his slippers, where the Pekingese peered suspiciously around the doorjamb. "We're in quarantine."

"Then reckon I'll go see if she needs a hand."

Whitey shifted his chaw and nodded judiciously. "You could do that."

If he skied over, then he could ride back with Kaley. Unclipping his cross-country skis from the rack atop his truck, Tripp stepped into them. He strode up the track toward the pastures, setting himself a steady pace, breath coming in slow, steamy huffs in the blue-shadowed silence, skis rasping rhythmically on the snow.

Kaley…what she'd told him the other night, about her son of a bitch of a poor excuse for a husband…Tripp was still trying to wrap his mind around it… Reaching the top of a long rise, he tucked and glided down the far side, exulting in his silken, swooping progress, eyes watering in the cold wind… That a man could not want his own child… It was hard for Tripp to credit, but if Kaley said so, then it must be true.

And if—since—this was the truth, it changed everything. He was still coming to grips with all it changed, coming around corners and glimpsing new vistas and implications…

Reaching the bottom of the slope, he scanned the turnoff to a gate on the left, which led to Cougar Rock Pasture, where she penned her yearling and two-year heifers. Tracks of a truck led in and back out through the new layer of snow that had fallen during the night, so he kicked on over a level stretch, then the road rose to the next ridge.

His breath was coming harder now, but he felt good. Felt better than good. Felt almost excited, the way a man felt when he rode into wild new country with no idea what

lay beyond the next hill. Kaley... So she hadn't flown away
from her marriage on a whim... She'd had the best of all
reasons to leave her man—to protect her child...

*Here I figured her for a quitter, but if you look at it
another way...* She'd run from an easy life in the
city...marriage to a rich lawyer, was the way Jim Cotter
had once described the man... Kaley had taken her baby
and run from that—

To this. He reached the top of the rise and paused, panting, searching the ragged black-on-white landscape ahead
for her truck. His eyes swept over the line of naked cot-
tonwoods that marked the course of the river to the south
of the road. He could see cattle gathered at the first and
second of the long wooden troughs, but her truck was out
of sight, somewhere beyond the trees. He pushed his pole-
tips in and shot down the slope—came to a stop in a
shower of powdery snow by the gate, and stepped sideways
over to open it—grunted with the effort of pulling the posts
together and grimaced; this would be so much harder for
Kaley.

This whole life was hard, an exhausting and scary struggle, but she'd come running back to it. She'd shown a
fierce and selfless loyalty, choosing the hard path over the
easy, choosing to keep her baby, then fighting to make a
home for it. Struggling to save her baby's birthright. *Can't
see how she'll ever do it.* But still, he had to admire her
courage in trying.

He skied a wide, wary circle around the feeding cattle,
then came back to the plowed track, kick-gliding on down
the gently rolling contours of the valley. When he heard
the truck coming, he stopped, spiked his poles in the snow
and stood, breathing hard. Like a dark, humpbacked beetle,
with its snowplow raised before it and its feeding box jut-
ting up behind the cab, the pickup heaved itself over the
brow of a distant white hill. Seeing the dark figure riding

beside the driver, Tripp glowered—then laughed to himself as he realized. Martha, riding shotgun. When they neared and Kaley rolled down her window with a flashing smile, he stuck out a mittened thumb. "Got room for one more?"

ON THE WAY BACK they talked as if they hadn't seen each other in a month, about nothing important, just idle chatter, but it flowed like a creek after snow melt. They mourned the last of their turkey leftovers; discussed skiing—something they'd never done together, Tripp realized, since theirs had been mostly a summer romance. Compared the virtues of home-built feeding boxes, Kaley's hydraulically driven dispenser versus Tripp's gasoline-driven device. Sobered as they wondered how long they could hold off before they had to give the cattle hay, as well as protein feed. Before Tripp knew it, they were pulling into the barn.

He helped her load the box with cottonseed cake for the morrow, then picked up his skis and sighed. Sundown. He had no more reason to stay.

Kaley pulled off her wool watch cap, shook out her red-brown mane and cocked her head in question. "Got time for a cup of chocolate?"

He built a fire in the living-room fireplace while she heated the cocoa, then he came to stand in the doorway, watching. Humming to herself, she stood at the counter, slicing something and arranging it on a plate. She swerved gracefully toward the refrigerator, then startled as she saw him; she smiled, but quit her singing.

"What's all that on the counter?" He nodded toward a collection of clay pots and what looked like a mound of onions and another of garlic.

"Daffodil and crocus and hyacinth bulbs. I'm potting them up. Gonna force 'em—persuade them that spring's come early and it's time to bloom."

He shook his head, marveling. Where did she find the

time or energy for these unessential graces? Taking the loaded tray from her hands, he followed her into the living room.

She chose to sit on the braided rug before the fire and he settled beside her. After handing him a mug of cocoa sprinkled with cinnamon, she offered a plate on which she'd arranged slabs of a thick, coarse-grained bread slathered with butter.

He tried a piece and groaned with pleasure. "Where did you find bread like this?" It was nothing like the white, marshmallowy stuff he bought at the supermarket.

"Baked it. My mother used to bake, and I thought I'd give it a try." Kaley examined a slice, then shrugged. "Needs a bit more honey, I think."

"It's perfect." No flattery in that, just God's simple truth. He took a second piece and, savoring it, glanced around the room. She'd painted the walls and trim in here also, he noted. A big vase of dried golden and orange leaves glowed on the coffee table. She'd draped a yellow woolen blanket over the sofa to change its color and she'd rearranged the furniture. The place seemed warmer, cheerier, homier... "Where's Martha?" he asked suddenly. She'd entered the house with them.

"In her closet, I expect." Kaley nodded to a door standing ajar in the hallway that led to the rear of the house. "She's taken quite a fancy to it this past week."

"Has she." He stood and walked over to see.

Suspended from a wooden rod, coats and summer wear created a dense, soft overhang, with a shadowy space beneath. Tripp dropped to his heels and peered into this dusky cave, and found the Border collie curled on a mound of blankets, staring back at him.

"There was a box of old newspapers and magazines in there, which she's been shredding and pushing around for the past week. I finally threw them out and gave her these old blankets.'' Kaley came to kneel beside him. ''She seems to really like it in there.''

''She's nesting, Kaley. Choosing the place she means to whelp.'' No wonder the dog kept straying back to the Circle C.

''So that's it!'' Kaley laughed. ''We always had male dogs around here. I've never been in on a delivery before. *Clever* mama,'' she crooned, then accepted his hand and let him raise her to her feet.

The dog was no fool, Tripp had to agree as they returned to the fire. He sat and helped himself to a third slice of bread and butter.

''More cocoa?'' Kaley lifted a flowered teapot from the tray and, when he nodded, poured him a second steaming cup.

No, the collie was no fool, choosing to nest in this cozy refuge, he realized, looking around the room. Flowers, fresh bread, warm happy colors, a fire on the hearth, a woman singing in the kitchen… *It's not just the dog that's nesting,* it hit him suddenly. *Kaley's nesting, too.* She leaned to stir the fire and it blazed up suddenly. Her hair swayed like a silken shawl with her movements; the leaping light danced along strands of ruddy copper, threads of glittering garnet and ruby.

Like the wings of the little red hen his father had given his mother—precisely that same banked-ember color, he realized. *And that's who you remind me of… Feathering her cozy nest… Show her a hard, thankless task and no one to help her and what does she say?* ''Then I'll do it myself,'' he murmured.

''Hmm?'' Kaley looked up over the rim of her mug, her big eyes in shadow, long lashes fringed with sparks of copper.

He put down his mug and rose. ''Said I reckon I'd better go.'' Before he begged her to let him stay.

"DARN, I WAS REALLY LOOKING forward to tonight," Kaley mourned. Snuggled under her down comforter, she'd called Dana after Michelle phoned her to cancel Girls' Night Out. A blizzard was forecast. She glanced at her bedroom window. Snow was falling already, thick and soft, though the northeast wind had yet to rise.

"Me, too," agreed Dana. "Shrimp curry with coconut milk. My mouth has been watering all day."

"Chicken with lemongrass," Kaley lamented. Their menu for the night was to have been Southeast Asian; they'd special-ordered their ingredients weeks ago, from an ethnic-cooking catalog. "Guess it'll keep till next week." She sighed. "If we don't get snowed out again." For the next four months, they'd be at the mercy of the weather.

"Or aren't still snowed in," Dana agreed. "We've got six inches already, I'd say, and Rafe isn't home yet. He trailered Donner and Blitzen over to Tripp's this afternoon."

"Did he." Kaley had been wanting an excuse to visit the M Bar G. Tripp must be keeping Martha penned lately; the collie hadn't come calling in days. Kaley missed them both.

"Mmm. Guess I shouldn't worry. That four-wheel-drive monster of his will plow through just about anything." Dana yawned hugely. "And you've got to get down to Durango for an appointment with Dr. Cass this week, don't you?"

"Next Monday," Kaley corrected her grimly. "Time for a blood test." The test for fetal abnormalities, though it wouldn't necessarily reveal them all. She felt her heart rate kick up, just thinking about it.

"Cass does that to all the moms," Dana assured her, catching the tension in her voice.

"Yeah…" But how many of those moms had taken a whopping cycle of tetracycline just before and after con-

ception? She drew a long breath. "I've been meaning to
ask you…" Thank God she had Dana, sane, kind and twice
a mother, to guide her through this. "When did you…"
She swallowed. "Did you first feel your babies move?"
She cupped her hand to herself, but the round, warm curve
held no hint of life within.

"I think that varies quite a bit from baby to baby," Dana
said after a hesitation.

"But when did yours?" Kaley insisted.

Dana sighed. "Petra…she moved first in her fifteenth
week."

Kaley's teeth pressed into her bottom lip. This was her
seventeenth week, give or take a few days. "And Peter?"

There came a longer pause. "I…seem to remember that
Peter moved in his sixteenth week."

Kaley squeezed shut her eyes against the easy tears of
pregnancy. "Oh." She tipped her face to the ceiling in
supplication. *Oh, please…*

"And that proves absolutely nothing," Dana said firmly,
"except that all expecting mothers worry about their babies
when they shouldn't. You ask Cass and she'll tell you.
Now, don't be a goose. Think happy thoughts. Happy
thought number one—shrimp curry next Wednesday.
Now—number two?"

Kaley laughed and wiped her lashes. "All right, all right.
A puppy for Christmas." She cocked her head against the
pillows, then sat up. Had that thought spurred her imagination, or…

"There you go—Christmas," Dana applauded. "A white
Christmas! Big beautiful fir tree, with cranberry and pop-
corn strings, and gingerbread men hanging all over it."

"That's what we should make Wednesday after—" Kaley stopped and frowned, listened, then laughed. "You
know, speaking of pregnant moms, I think I've got one at

my door. Sounds like Martha barking out there. Talk to you soon, okay?''

IT WASN'T TILL Rafe drove off through the gathering dusk that Tripp realized Martha was missing.

Blast the dog! She'd been such a help this afternoon when the buck reindeer escaped while they were unloading the pair. Rafe and he had been unable to move fast through the knee-high snow, and he'd had no horse saddled to give chase. But needing no signal to trail the frantic beast, the Border collie had skulked behind him like a small, fat, black-and-white single-minded wolf. Predator and prey, they'd vanished up the hill and into the trees while Rafe stood swearing and Tripp ran for his skis and poles.

By the time he'd laced into his cross-country boots and Rafe was grimly handing him a lariat, they'd looked up— to see the pair plunging back down the slope. Donner had rolled his eyes and tossed his head as he danced over the snow's crust on his enormous, splayed hooves; nose almost touching the ground, Martha had plodded relentlessly in his wake.

Thank God the reindeer hadn't set out for the North Pole. Tripp could just picture himself explaining to Mac how he'd lost his collie.

She'd chivied her charge through the gate and into the corral. From there they'd hazed the reindeer into the barn, then finally into the same stall as Blitzen, his anxiously waiting mate.

This miraculous reindeer restoration had called for two cold beers in the kitchen and a steak bone for Martha. When she carried it to the back door and scratched, Tripp had assumed she meant to bury it in her usual fashion and he'd let her out. He'd not thought to check on her till Rafe drove away through the fast-falling flakes. Even then, he'd been hopeful that, good stock dog that she was, she'd be lurking in the barn, studying her latest responsibilities.

No such luck. He'd just finished searching the outbuildings, was stamping the snow off his boots on the back stoop, when the phone rang in the kitchen. "Hello?"

"Sorry to call you so late, but I guess you're gonna have to talk me through this," said Kaley's voice, shimmering with its usual laughter.

He found himself smiling. "Through what?"

"I think tonight's the big night for Martha-girl. I know they always boil water in the movies, but then what d'you do with it?"

"When did she show up?" He stretched the phone cord over to his boots and stepped back into them.

"Half an hour ago. She seems exhausted, poor thing, slogging all this way in a blizzard. She went straight to her closet, but she's restless. Keeps circling out, pacing and whimpering, then goes back in again. And she's panting nonstop."

"I'll be right there." He pulled his jacket off the hook.

"Tripp, don't! The roads have got to be awful by now. Why don't you just tell me what to do."

"Put a pot of coffee on and listen for my knock." He hung up on her protest, shrugged back out of his jacket and went for his long johns and down vest. If he put the truck in a ditch on the way, he'd better be dressed for it.

THE ONLY REASON Tripp didn't end up in a ditch was he couldn't find one, for all the scudding, swirling white. It took him almost an hour, creeping along at dead low, to blunder his way through the rising drifts. By the time his headlights picked out Kaley's back door, his shoulders were rock-hard from tension; his eyes ached from peering through the oncoming flakes. He cut the engine and sat listening to the wind's monstrous howl. Another half hour and he'd have been in real trouble.

The door banged back on its hinges and a white figure flew down the steps. Kaley—in a bathrobe? He lunged out of the truck to meet her and she ran straight into his chest, hands clutching at his shoulders. "Kaley, honey—what?"

"Martha!" She buried her face below his chin and clung to him, shuddering.

Bad, whatever it was; Kaley was no hysteric. He scooped her up out of the drift and noted grimly that she wore no shoes, only socks. "Come on, sweetheart. Whatever's the trouble, pneumonia won't help it."

"Nothing's going to—" The rest of her words were drowned out as the wind rose to a roar.

He strode up the steps, then had to drop her to vertical, hooking one arm around her waist while he held the door from flying to kingdom come with the other. He nudged her inside before him, wrenched the door shut despite the gale and let out a gasp of relief. Tears streaming, she swayed back against him and he caught her upper arms. "What is it?"

"Martha, her puppy—it's..." She shook her head blindly, staggered over to the sink and yanked open the door below it—pulled out a garbage pail and threw up.

Worse than bad. He eased her down into a chair, set the pail before her, dampened a dish towel at the sink. "It's okay, sweetheart," he soothed, washing her face. "Goin' to be fine." All the while swearing at himself. Never should have let Martha help with the reindeer. And then the trek here after that. If she was too exhausted to push... *And it's not like a cow, where I could reach in and help her out.* The fourteen miles into Trueheart to the vet might as well be fourteen thousand tonight. "She's going to be fine," he murmured, stroking Kaley's forehead.

"It's not her." Kaley hid her face in hands that trembled. "It's her...p-puppy... Would you *please*—"

He threaded his fingers through her hair, massaging her fragile skull with his fingertips. "I will, I will, soon as you settle down." He kissed the top of her head, turned and rewet the towel. "Here, take this. Wash your face, honey, and I'll go see."

A lamp stood on the floor next to the open door of the closet, along with a pillow, where Kaley must have been keeping vigil. He kicked it aside and crouched down, peered into the dimness—

His stomach heaved. Not one puppy by now, but five stillborn pups, if these poor, bloody little...abominations could even be called— He clapped a hand over his mouth and looked aside, breathing hard through his mouth. He steeled himself and looked again. "Aw, Martha-girl."

Too tired to lift her chin from the bloody blanket, she blinked up at him. Managed a faint, apologetic thump of her tail.

"I'm so sorry, girl." She'd gotten into something behind a barn, Mac had said, that night he brought her to the ranch. Pesticide, he'd thought possibly. All too damn possible. They never should have assumed that once she'd seemed to recover... "I'm sorry, sweetheart." He stroked her ears. "Let me get Kaley to bed, then we'll clean up this mess, okay?"

He found Kaley slumped at the table with her forehead resting on her crossed forearms. "Bed for you," he announced. A shock at this stage in her pregnancy? He'd no idea how dangerous that might be; was taking no chances. He gripped her waist and noticed for the first time that she was expanding. Her bulky winter clothes had hidden the change, but tonight she wore only pajamas and a terry-cloth robe. "Come on, honey." She rose so shakily, with face so greeny-pale, that he changed his mind about her walk-

ing. Last thing she needed was to faint and whack her head.
"Upsy daisy."

"I can walk," she protested—even as she buried her
face against his shoulder and snuggled into his arms and
sighed.

He smiled against her silky temple. "Sure you can, but
why bother, with Tripp's taxi service in town?" And this
way she could close her eyes while he carried her past the
dreadful closet.

Still, he hurried his steps, did his best to distract her. "I
thought you were supposed to be getting fat." Then swore
at himself. Reminders of pregnancy tonight were the last
thing she needed. Her imagination had to be running wild,
inventing horrors to match Martha's misfortune.

"I am. I've gained eight pounds," she growled against
his shirt as he climbed the stairs.

"Good for you." He stopped at the top, breathing hard.
"Which way?" He'd never been up to her bedroom before.
Back in their dating days, her father would have unracked
the shotgun had he tried.

She shivered and lifted her head. "Let me off at the
bathroom."

When she insisted that she could walk from there to her
bed, he left her and returned downstairs to the collie.

Martha lay as he'd left her. Looked as if five was the
total litter. Quite enough. Clamping his jaws against the
nausea, averting his eyes as much as he could, he helped
her to her shaky legs, then guided her out of the closet.

With all the instincts of a good mother, she tried immediately to return. Blocking her with one shoulder, he
folded the blanket into a soft, damp shroud and picked it
up. "Next time, girl, you'll have some keepers," he
crooned as she lifted her nose to his burden. "This wasn't
your fault."

She trailed him piteously into the kitchen, but he man-

aged to slip out the back door without her. He stowed the
bundle in the rear of his truck, to be buried back at the M
Bar G.

Once he'd offered the collie food and water and made
her a new, clean nest in the closet, there was no more
comfort he could give. Time would have to heal the rest.
He rubbed her ears till she heaved a sigh and closed her
eyes, then he half shut the closet door and climbed the
stairs.

HOPING THAT KALEY had fallen asleep, he peeked around
the doorjamb.

She lay in her bed, propped up against the headboard on
a mound of pillows. Her eyes were wide-open, fixed on
some awful distance, her teeth clamped in her lush under-
lip. One teardrop after another rolled down her pale cheeks.

"Hey," he protested softly, venturing into the room. He
sat on the edge of the bed and lifted her hands from her
lap; they were as cold as the white world outside her window. He chafed them between his own palms, but felt no
rush of answering warmth. She stared right through him.
"Honey, hey…hey…don't take it so hard." He lifted her
fingers to his lips and blew on them, then kissed her knuckles, the backs of her hands.

No response. Where, oh, where had she gone?

"Kaley, sweetheart…" He kissed her palms, blew on
them, brought them to his cheeks—colder than icicles. He
nuzzled against them, scraping her deliberately with his
evening beard. *Come back to me, darlin'.*

Her face crumpled suddenly, her shoulders shook.

"Aw, honey!" He shifted to lean on the pillows beside
her, wrapped his arms around her…held her while she
cried.

CHAPTER SEVENTEEN

SHE HELD MORE TEARS than a man would have thought possible—enough tears to last a dozen men a dozen lifetimes. While her tears soaked his shirt, Tripp stroked her hair and her shaking shoulders, searching his mind frantically for what he might say to stem this terrible flood—that he'd find her another puppy by Christmas...that he'd bring her flowers and jewels... Would never try to buy her ranch again—hell, he'd give her *his* ranch if only she'd stop weeping! That he loved her more than man could or should love woman, and that her tears just might drown his heart.

Some last shred of common sense bade him shut his mouth and let her cry herself out while he kissed her hair...her temples...her salty eyelashes...the tip of her nose, when finally she pulled back to look at him.

Eyes deep and velvety blue-black as the sky on the night of a full moon. Framing her solemn face with one hand, he thumbed away a tear from below her spiky lashes. Gave her a shaken smile. "Better?" he whispered hopefully.

"N-n-not—" Tears welled and overflowed. "Not yet. Not for months and months!" She ducked in against his chest, hooked an arm under his, then around his ribs to wedge herself closer.

"Sure...that's okay... Whatever it takes..." He slid a hand under her hair, massaging her nape in a slow, soothing rhythm.

She pulled a deep, shivering breath; let it out in a sigh

that warmed his skin through his drenched shirt. "Were...there any more?"

Puppy, she'd said when he first arrived, Tripp realized. He nuzzled her hair. "Five, in all."

"And they were all..."

"Yeah...fraid so." He traced the intricate bones of her spine through her pajamas, down to her waist and up again, soothing, caressing.

"But *why?* What could have caused—" She shuddered and pressed against him, as if she could fuse her body to his, leaving no room between them for nightmares or loneliness.

He told her as gently as he could about the pesticide, or the poison, or whatever it had been that Martha had eaten. "Mac and I both figured she was fine once she stopped being sick... The next morning she seemed right as rain... We figured maybe it had been no more than a bit of bad food...."

"But it wasn't." She'd gone very still against him.

"No..." Splaying his hand, he rubbed it up from her waist, then down again. She'd gone too still, too taut. What had he said? "I'm sorry... Reckon I should have warned you when you asked for a pup...but I never dreamed..."

"No, you don't dream at the time... It's supposed to be good for you, so you swallow it, never dreaming..." She shivered and writhed in his arms. "Oh, *God!*"

"Reckon that's what we have to tell ourselves," he agreed softly, rubbing his cheek across her forehead. "If it wasn't meant to be, then it was ended for good reason..."

"Don't tell me that!" She shoved at him, suddenly furious. "I don't want to *hear* that!" She tried to twist away, but entangled as they were, she couldn't. She fisted her hand and thumped his chest. "Shut *up!*"

"Easy!" She was going to do real damage if she kept kicking. He rolled half on top of her, hooking his leg over hers, pinning her shoulders with his forearms, framing her face with his hands. "What is it? What did I say? Kaley, calm down!"

She burst into tears. "Don't you *ever* say that! Not ever!"

"What?" He swept her cheeks with his thumbs—the tears overflowed them. And now, to stack one problem on top of the other, he felt himself hardening...rising. Her sorrow had called to his tenderness, kept him damped down to a manageable state of arousal. But somehow this anger and wriggling roused an instinctive need to quell it, an urge to subdue and surmount this seeming rebellion...

He rolled hastily off her. "Reckon maybe I'd better— Don't you need to sleep?"

"No!" She grabbed his shirt with both hands. "Oh, *please,* Tripp, don't...would you..." Her throat convulsed on the words; she bit her lip; her eyes begged him mutely.

Fingers shaking with his arousal, he swept the hair off her forehead. "Whatever it is you want, Kaley, I would. You know I would."

Her voice was tiny and timid and tremulous. "Then... would you just hold me?"

SOMETIME LATE THAT NIGHT, asleep in the magic circle of Tripp's arms, safe from all sorrow, Kaley stretched and stirred and half awoke.

But there was danger in waking; safety here in this dream of belonging and love. She dived deep again, nuzzling into this warm corner that smelled of home. She inhaled, sighed happily, tasted the living walls of her haven and found it good...vital... She lipped it again, her kisses trailing up over contours of scratchy hardness and musky resilience, till she found the source of all delight. Murmuring wordless wonder, she blindly explored— silky...salty...a heated, honeyed pressure responding slowly at first, then quickening...mouth molded hungrily to mouth.

They rolled like dolphins in their sleep, this bed their ocean, a delicious vast weight of water pressing her down... Mouth plundering mouth... Rough fingertips sliding through her hair, cradling her head. She arched like a dolphin to meet this wave, kissed him deeply—then dragged her mouth apart with a waking gasp. Lay, heart pounding, looking up into hard-breathing darkness... *Tripp, here in her arms again.*

She put a hand up to his face and he kissed it. *"You..."* she whispered. No dream, this, only happiness come 'round again, like rain to long-parched earth. Her legs slid luxuriously, inevitably, invitingly out over the sheet. She hooked her ankles over the back of his calves and her body rippled beneath him, boat on this bed of an ocean, ready to carry him wherever he steered.

He shuddered against her, hard, vibrantly alive. Framed her face with trembling hands. "You awake?"

"Mmm..." Her kiss was her answer.

He laughed shakily against her lips. "I'm sorry...Don't know how this...I didn't mean to..."

She pulled his head back down and murmured into him. *"I'm* not sorry." No regret was possible before this floodtide of delight.

"Oh, Kaley..." He kissed her eyes, her nose, came back to her lips to dance, tongue to tongue. "You're sure you're awake?"

"Mmm..." A groan containing rueful laughter. She searched for his shirt buttons and he lifted just far enough to let her. At last she peeled the garment off him and threw it aside...worked another layer up and off him and tossed it, her hands seeking eagerly the hard, never-forgotten contours of his stomach and chest, the enticing curly roughness of hair...

He groaned, rolled to one elbow and fumbled her pajama buttons. She laughed as one gave and spun away into the dark; he growled his exasperation, then triumph, as the last button surrendered. His lips found her breast and she cried aloud, her back arching like a rainbow, body pulsing with the need for him... Her fingers buried in his hair.

He came back to her mouth, caught her lower lip between his teeth, surged against her. "I never thought to bring...I don't have any—"

She found his belt buckle and tugged, frantic to undo it. "What are you going to do—get me pregnant?"

"Wish I could!" He yanked the belt free, whipped it out between them; it fell to the floor.

Me, too, me, too! Oh, if only...but babies were the last thing she wanted to think of tonight; that way lay sorrow. She narrowed her focus, centered every sensation and emotion on now, on here, on Tripp...his scent as familiar as wood smoke on her hearth...his strength lifting her, covering her, at last surging into her...his tenderness and laughter and passion—hers for the asking...every time that she asked...all through that white and roaring night.

SHE ROSE FROM SLEEP like a diver rising from the depths... Silvery bubbles trailing upward...happiness deep and wordless as the ocean...daylight somewhere overhead, coming nearer, brighter... Warm lips lingering on hers, then leaving too soon. Moaning a protest, she found the strength to lift a hand, thread it up through his thick hair, drag his mouth down to hers again. *More*...

He laughed against her lips. "Whoa, cowgirl, don't get me started. I've got cows to feed."

"Cows?" She wrinkled her nose, turned her face to the window, squinted through drowsy lashes at a white, blinding light—sunshine bouncing off a world of snow. *"Ugh!"* She pulled the comforter over her head.

"'Bout sums it up.'' Tripp slid out from under the bed-clothes and sat. Blew out a startled breath at the cold. "The keys to your truck—are they in the ignition?"

"What," she mumbled as she rolled to her stomach. "You're going to feed my herd? Don't be…" The thought trailed away like a dream unraveling. "I mean that," she added haughtily as his weight lifted off the bed and the mattress rebounded.

"I know you do. I'm just heading for the bathroom," he assured her on a note of laughter. "Keep the bed warm."

"I can do that." She smiled into the pillow—and slept.

AND WOKE SOMETIME after noon. She lay for a moment, blinking, then bolted upright. "Tripp!"

Silence reigned within the house and without, in that world of dazzling white. Throwing a robe over her naked-ness, she hurried downstairs; shied as she came abreast of the closet.

Its door was closed entirely and she couldn't bring her-self to check. She padded on into the kitchen and found his note on the table:

Sleeping Beauty,
The cows couldn't wait. I've fed yours, and looks like they came through the night fine. Now I'm off to check mine. Will call you tonight. Now, go back to bed and stay there all day. Tripp.
                    P.S. Martha's with me.

Not "love, Tripp," but simply "Tripp." But still… "Thank you," she whispered, and kissed his name. She folded the paper and tucked it in her pocket, then pulled out a chair and sat, exhaustion cresting like a sudden wave over her head. "Not a whole lot of sleep last night," she admitted aloud, a hand creeping to her stomach.

She glanced down. "I hope we didn't disturb your sweet dreams."

No answering kick, not even a flutter. She bit her lip and pressed harder, eyes turned inward, listening, feeling... *Oh, please...*

The thought came creeping inevitably, dragging its hateful shadow across the lovely day: *How long were those puppies dead before Martha bore them?*

"But I'd know," she whispered. "Wouldn't I know?"

SHE SLEPT most of the day, waking once from a delicious dream of Tripp, then once from a nightmare so terrible that she woke in tears, though she remembered none of it.

Finally she rousted herself out of the sack to make a pot of onion soup and bake some corn bread. No telling if she might have hungry company tonight. Her body pulsed at the thought. She closed her eyes for an instant, tipped back her head and sucked in a breath, simply surrendering to the sensation.

Touching her kiss-swollen lips, she opened her eyes... blew out a breath and squared her shoulders. Even if he didn't come, she still had Whitey and herself to feed.

The sun had blazed its way beyond the mountains, turning its back on a world gone lilac blue, when Kaley slogged out across the yard to Whitey's cottage. The snow had blown into drifts high as her head where building or tree or fence had impeded its frigid flow; unsheltered areas were scoured down to the sugary crust of earlier falls.

Whitey stumped to the door when she knocked. "This is pure foolishness," he grumbled when she handed him his supper at arm's length. "Chang's got cabin fever so dang bad he's going to start biting hisself if I don't give him a run."

She grinned down at the Pekingese, who sat warming his bottom on Whitey's buckskin slippers. "You tell Chang that there're drifts out here that'll swallow him up. Three days more and I'll believe you're both past the contagious stage."

"Bossy women…" Whitey fished for his bandanna and wiped defiantly. His shrewd, faded blue eyes studied her over its folds. "Cold germs or not, I'da come out and helped you with this morning's run, 'cept I noticed you had all the help you needed…that McGraw. And *danged* if he didn't show up early. Truck was out there when I looked at dawn."

"Yes, he's a good neighbor." Before the blush could rise to her cheeks, she retreated down the steps, then sniped back from a safe distance, "I gave you enough corn bread for morning, too, so don't you feed it all to that chowhound!"

SHE WAITED her own supper till nine that night, her ears tuned for the ring of the telephone, or even better, for the sound of an approaching truck.

Finally Kaley had to admit it: he was neither coming nor calling. *You silly fool.* Dadblasted wishful woman. *What did you expect?* Tripp had shown her before that to his mind, sex and love didn't run hand in hand. Why should she have expected him to be any different this time?

Hopeful Kaley, hoping against all common sense.

Idiot! she called herself bitterly. Clattering the dishes into the sink, she started to wash them. Because life had to go on, hope or no hope, love or no love.

Scrubbing grimly at the final pot, she felt the draft as the back door cracked open. She spun around, almost dizzy as her emotions spun with her, swinging from despair to hope to—

"Hello the house!" Tripp leaned in the door, letting in a gust of cold air—and Martha, pushing past his knees.

"Come in!" She caught the lapels of his jacket and drew him into the mudroom, but he wasn't smiling to match the sunrise in her heart. Solemn and watchful, almost wary, his eyes scanned her face. Her impulse to step straight into his arms faltered. "Hey," she said softly. But still, he'd come, he'd come! She cupped a palm to his cheek. "Hey, you!" Noting the shadows beneath his eyes, the drawn muscles at forehead and jaw, she frowned. "You look beat."

Martha surged between them and stood on her hind legs, sniffing lustily at Tripp's jacket.

"Yeah. A long day." A spark of rueful laughter lit his eyes for a moment. *You know how long,* was the silent message. "Sorry I didn't phone, but me and Martha just made it back from Trueheart. Roads are terrible. Down, girl!" he added to the whining collie.

Resting a big hand on her shoulder, he guided Kaley back to the kitchen. "Shouldn't have dropped in on you this way, but I thought you'd want to see this." He shrugged out of his jacket, revealing a cloth bag hung from his neck. Martha whined and pawed at his thigh.

Carefully he lifted the bag's drawstring over his head, then he set the bundle on her table. "I phoned Sam Kerner…"

The veterinarian for Trueheart and the surrounding ranches, Kerner was mostly a big-animal man, but he'd tend any sick patient when need called. "To have him check Martha," Kaley assumed. She caught the dog's collar as Martha reared to brace her forepaws on the table. "What's the matter with her?" The dog's usual good manners seemed entirely forgotten.

"This…" Tripp opened the neck of the bag…unfolded a layer of soft cloth, then another. "Kerner told me that there was a husky bitch in town, whelped two days ago.

She had a litter of ten—too many to give them all a good
start. The owner's been going half-crazy, trying to bottle-
feed the three smallest. This one's the runt.''

As he lifted the last fold of cushioning towel to reveal
a puppy—a squirming, squeaking, cream-colored handful—Martha burst into frantic barking.

Kaley burst into tears.

Tripp looked at her worriedly. "Maybe I shouldn't
have…''

''No, you should, you should! I'm *so* glad you did!'' *I
love you.* All the trouble he'd taken to console a dog. The
trip into town over unplowed roads would have been a
nightmare. *Oh, I do love you!* She didn't dare say it, but
Kaley brushed past the prancing, pleading collie. Stood on
tiptoe and kissed his cheek. *''Thank* you!''

''Don't thank me yet,'' Tripp warned her. ''Let's see if
she accepts him. Will you hold her for me before she has
a conniption?''

While Kaley held the struggling collie, Tripp rubbed the
puppy back and forth over her flanks and belly. ''Get as
much of her scent onto him as we can,'' he explained. ''I
saved a bit of the afterbirth from her litter if we have to…''

Kaley shuddered, then refound her smile. ''Don't think
you'll need it. She's going to have a fit if you don't let her
at him.''

At last Tripp led the way to the closet. He placed the
puppy in the nest of new blankets and they crouched to
watch as the collie surged into her cave.

Blinking through her tears, Kaley watched as Martha
nosed the squeaking baby. It oriented immediately toward
her, weaving its tiny blind head. The collie nosed the pup
again—flipped it over—sniffing passionately.

''Easy,'' Tripp soothed, gripping her collar.

Martha's tongue flicked out to test the baby's fragile,

hairless belly. The puppy squeaked and writhed itself upright.

With a long grunting sigh, the collie settled beside it, nudged it with her nose.

"Home free!" Tripp whispered.

Tentatively, almost shyly, the collie rolled farther onto her side to expose her stomach. She nudged at the puppy again; his blunt nose touched her breast, setting off a flurry of frenzied activity. Blindly rooting, greedily searching, he brailled his way to a nipple, latched on—all squeaking ceased. Martha groaned and half curled around him, steadily licking, her whole world contracting to one furry, thrusting back.

"So..." Tripp let out a long, satisfied sigh.

"So..." Kaley rubbed his spine, then used his broad shoulder to help herself rise. She stood behind him, Tripp resting his heavy head against her thighs while he watched the puppy feed, she caressing his hair with slow, loving fingers. "Have you eaten yet?" she murmured finally.

Silently he shook his head against her.

Her happiness deepened, if that was possible. "Then come to the kitchen."

HALFWAY THROUGH his second bowl of a wonderful onion soup, Tripp fell asleep at the table. He woke with a start when he nodded—to find Kaley sitting across from him, her graceful fingers clasped around a mug of steaming tea, her eyes warmly laughing. He pushed back his chair; he was hammered. Two ranches doubled his load—clearing snow out to twice as many pastures, then feeding both herds. Plus that exhausting trip into Trueheart—he'd had to dig the pickup out of three drifts on the way in, and winch it out of one ditch on the way back. All that on top of a sleepless night in heaven. "Better go," he muttered, shoving himself to his feet.

"Uh-uh." Coming around the table, Kaley shook her head. "You're asleep on your feet. No way I'm letting you drive. Come to bed."

He stood swaying, tempted beyond words, fearing... *This is so dangerous. I shouldn't.* But, oh, he wanted.

Her smile went a little lopsided as she sensed his hesitation. "I promise I won't jump your bones," she said, wryly self-mocking.

"Now *that's* a relief," he agreed, making a joke to match her own. That wasn't what worried him. He worried that he wouldn't be able to keep his hands off her. Because one more time of loving Kaley, and he was a goner—his heart her slave for life.

If she didn't own it already.

But he was too tired, too tempted, to resist, and he found himself following her in a daze of contentment, up the stairs.

First into the bathroom, he was first to climb into Kaley's soft bed. Snuggling under covers that held her entrancing scent, he had to lie on his side, facing away from the middle, else his erection would have peaked the comforter like a tent pole. Seemed a shame to hide such a rock-hard tribute to her charms, but he could not, dared not, presume. Kaley had offered him a bed—and made it clear she wasn't offering more.

Unless, womanlike, she was leaving the asking to him?

He didn't ponder that mystery long. Was no longer awake when the lights went out, the mattress bounced gently; when deep in a delicious dream, he felt Kaley's lips move against his spine—trailing a string of moist, hot kisses from between his shoulder blades to his nape. But there was nothing new in this to wake a man. Kaley had been coming to him in dreams since the summer they met. Tripp let out a slow, blissful sigh—and slept.

HE WOKE at his usual time, half an hour before dawn. What wasn't usual was the warm, shapely bottom pressed to his stomach, the hot velvety breast he held cupped in his hand, the weight of a head, pillowed on his arm, the storm of silk in which his face was buried. Afraid to open his eyes and banish this dream, he breathed in the scent of her hair...*honey and hay*... His fingers were moving before thought had formed, teasing her nipple; it grew like a bud, swelling to the heat of spring sunshine. His hips rocked a question of their own accord as he rose and hardened against her.

Her hips rolled...slender thighs parted ever so slightly to form a satiny, snug divide. Her hand reached back over her shoulder to cup the back of his head, her fingers twining, caressing. Kaley made a small, soft, languid sound, deep in her throat. Tripp needed no further invitation. The door to heaven was open wide....

AFTERWARD THEY LAY for a long time, wrapped in each other's arms, face-to-face, not speaking, simply gazing into each other's eyes...smiling dreamily. Tripp had a thousand questions...he didn't dare say a word. Words were dangerous, slippery, clumsy things—heavy enough to hurt something precious and fragile. He'd have just as soon never spoken again...just as soon stayed where he was, tracing her perfect mouth, feeling the sun rise again, each time she smiled and kissed his fingertip.

But finally Kaley sighed, sat up, brushed her wild mane of hair out of her laughing blue eyes and said, ''Well, cowboy...'' She drifted off to the bathroom.

From there on, she was one step ahead of him. By the time Tripp showered and dressed, she had breakfast waiting. She served him a bowl of steaming oatmeal topped with walnuts and bananas, with slices of homemade bread on the side, while she listened to the weather channel on

the radio and frowned. "Snow again. By ten, they're saying. Maybe another six inches before it quits."

Not good. Unlike horses or elk, cattle would not paw
through heavy snow for grass. They'd be doling out their
precious hay before Christmas, it looked like. "We'd better
get a move-on then," he said. "We'll do your herd first,
then I'll get on down to my—" He paused; she was smiling
and shaking her head.

"You don't need to feed my cows, Tripp. That was a
treat yesterday, but you know I can do it myself."

Like the little red hen. Gutsy, self-sufficient...standing
alone. Tending her own nest. Reaping her own paradise.
He looked down at his bowl as his smile started to waver.
"Sure you can, but I thought—"

She dropped a kiss on the top of his head on her way to
the toaster. "And bless you for it. But don't worry about
me. Feeding one herd is hard enough."

Worry was just what he'd do. "If you say so." Suddenly
desperate to escape, he finished his bowl as quick as he
could. "Well, reckon Martha's yours for the next week or
two, if that's all right." When she nodded, he gave her
brisk instructions about feeding a nursing bitch. He plunked
his mug and bowl into the sink, then struggled into his
jacket, jammed on his watch cap. "Thanks for..."

For what? Taking in a starving soul for one—no, make
that two—delirious nights?

He couldn't find the words to thank her for that bound-
less generosity, not without admitting how much he'd
needed it. And somehow a man was shamed by his needs
and wants—or shamed by the fact that he hadn't been able
to fill them.

Besides which, her rejection of his help still stung. Let
him open his mouth and maybe she'd hear his hurt. "Uh,
thanks for breakfast," he said abruptly. "See you..."

When? There was no guarantee that he'd ever be back this way again. Not as her lover.

That depended entirely on her and what she wanted of him. And being that much at another's mercy, damn sure shamed a man.

Still seated at the table, eyebrows drawn together into a tiny frown, Kaley tipped up her face for his kiss.

He dared not kiss her lips. One real kiss would tell her everything, how much he longed to stay. He pecked her on the cheek and strode out into the cold.

KALEY SAT, smoothing her spoon back and forth across her congealing oatmeal, trying not to cry. "What did I do?" Or not do.

Looked at him with too much love in her face? But how could she have hidden it? Why should a woman have to hide it?

"Or maybe I'm imagining things." She glanced down at her rounding belly. "Maybe I'm just in a weepy mood and he was just in a hurry to hit the pastures, no more than that. What do you think?" She prodded her navel with one fingertip.

No comment. She'd met bowling balls with more to say for themselves.

"Ten minutes ago, I thought I owned the world," she mused, filling in the lagging conversation.

And now?

With a sigh, she pushed herself to her feet. Lovers might come and go, but cows remained. She had four hundred-plus critters looking for their breakfast before snowfall.

CHAPTER EIGHTEEN

ALL THAT LONG, lonely, cloud-covered weekend, Tripp stayed away. He called every night, but their conversations grew increasingly awkward. Once they'd exhausted the obvious topics—Martha and pup were thriving; the weather continued snowy and they were both now feeding hay; Whitey had recovered—after they'd covered all that, their conversation stumbled and sagged. Kaley had no idea what Tripp might be thinking at his end of the line, but at hers, she was clenching her teeth over the question she longed to ask: *Why don't you just come over here and hug me?*

She had too much pride to ask it.

And too much fear—if she insisted on an answer, she might not like the one he gave her.

Better to simply wait and hope and meanwhile get on with her own life, but, *oh,* it was hard.

MONDAY THE SUN returned at last, lightening Kaley's mood, lighting her way to Durango, to her appointment with Dr. Cass Hancock. On her return trip, it burnished the snowy landscape to rumpled gold, shining bright as the hope in her heart. *At last, at last, oh, thank you, God, at last!* With news this good she had to tell *somebody,* but when she pulled into the parking lot at Michelle's Place, the café was locked up tight and Michelle's car was gone.

Still, nothing could daunt this mood. And it only surged higher when she stopped off to collect two more husky pups. Tripp's original arrangement had stipulated that if

Martha would agree to play wet nurse, Kaley would take the three smallest and weakest of the oversize litter to raise. She drove north out of Trueheart with a well-padded box of squeaking, indignant puppies on the seat beside her—and her heart singing counterpoint.

She just might pop with all the good news. And she knew with whom she wanted to share it. When she reached the turnoff to the M Bar G, there was no way she was passing it by; she slowed and made the turn, then bumped down his private road.

Driving into the ranch yard, she spotted Tripp leaning against the corral, arms crossed on the top rail, studying whatever lay within. At the sound of her truck, he swung around—and his face lit up in an unabashed grin. He raised an arm in greeting.

"Thank you, God!" she whispered. Whatever was awkward between them, still he was glad to see her. As he approached, she slid out of her seat. Walking straight into his arms, she caught the back of his head and pulled him down for a kiss.

She'd intended a short, brisk, unassuming, thank-you smack, but once their lips touched, they took on a mind of their own—clinging, sipping honey, molding tighter. She found herself arching against him, shuddering with desire. He ripped off her cap and plunged his fingers into her hair and tipped her face back for another plundering kiss as she pressed up against him on tiptoe.

Finally they dragged their mouths apart, to stand, arms locked tight around each other. "What was *that* all about?" His laughter was shaken as he smoothed a hand through her hair.

"That was by way of saying thank-you, for starters." She cupped his scarred cheek. "I stopped by Petersen's to collect his other spare puppies, and he told me that you bought Hans Solo."

"Who?"

"Martha's number-one son. You didn't just borrow Hans. You bought him." She'd been appalled when she learned for how much; pedigreed huskies didn't come cheap.

"Oh, yeah…" Tripp's face reddened with more than the cold. "Petersen had this notion that Martha might bite the squirt in half. Some mothers won't nurse any baby but their own. The only way I could persuade him to let me try was…" He shrugged.

"And am I right in thinking you bought him for me?"

"Don't know if he'll be as useful around a ranch as a Border collie, but yes, I got him for you. Merry Christmas."

Which seemed excuse enough to them both for another kiss. When they found their breaths again, Kaley added, "And I've got other good news—wonderful news! I had an appointment with my ob/gyn today…"

His eyes dropped as his hands moved to her waist, thumbs fanning against her stomach. "You're all right?"

"Oh, yes, this was just a routine exam. Plus a blood test." Which she'd been dreading for weeks, since it screened the fetus for defects. Cass would be calling her with the results of this test tomorrow, but today Kaley was too giddy with relief to worry. "A-a-and she found my baby's heartbeat! I got to listen to her through a stethoscope! She's *alive*, Tripp!"

"Well, of course she is." He rocked her backward on her heels and leaned down to place his cheek against her stomach. "Has your silly mom been worried about that?" Grinning, he glanced up at Kaley, then nodded judiciously.

"What's she say?" Kaley half whispered.

"*Rub-dub, rub-dub, rub-dub.* Practicing for a rock band, it sounds like in there. Better start saving for a drum set."

He straightened to smile down at her. "That's the very best news. Anything else?"

Only that you are the most gorgeous man in all southwest Colorado, if not the world, and I'm crazy about you! But happy as he seemed to see her, still she didn't dare say it. She wasn't going to make the mistake again of pushing too fast or of pushing at all. Smiling, she shook her head.

"Then come see my news." Arm around her shoulders, Tripp led her back to the corral.

Dana's two reindeer stood harnessed together, heads up, necks arched as they stared haughtily back at her through their big, intelligent brown eyes. "Like a Christmas card!" she murmured, entranced. "And what's that they're dragging?" Donner and Blitzen had turned away, were striding shoulder to shoulder across the corral.

"Just a half sheet of plywood with a sandbag nailed to it, to give it some weight. This is all improvisation, you understand. Reckon I'd have to go to Lapland to find somebody who could tell me how they train reindeer to pull." Standing side by side, shoulders touching, they watched the animals wander the corral while Tripp explained his methods.

Since they seemed to be a mated and amiable couple, happier together than apart, he'd harnessed them together, letting them teach each other that they must travel as a pair, and that it was useless to fight the harness. "And since they're bored in their stall, I've got them forming an association between harness time and playtime. They have to put up with one to get the other." Today he'd attached the plywood to their harness to give them a feel for pulling a weight over the snow. So they'd learn not to panic when chased by an inanimate object.

"Next step, I'll teach them to answer to reins," Tripp finished, smiling at her. "I've made two reindeer-size hackamores—don't think they'd care for a real bridle with a bit. Then once they learn that, it's time for the sleigh.''

''By Christmas?'' she teased him. ''In case Santa needs a spare team?''

Tripp shrugged. ''If I can. I'm sure Rafe and Sean would like to take Dana for a Christmas spin.'' He rubbed a knuckle along her cheekbone. ''Meantime I'm standing here racking my brains, wondering what I could give you for supper if you'd stay. Somehow hash seems a poor return for the meals you've cooked me.''

''Hash would be fine, but I guess I shouldn't,'' she admitted. ''Petersen hadn't bottle-fed the pups since morning, so they've got to be starving.'' As a shadow crossed his face, she added quickly, ''But I've got a pot of leftover stew at my place. Why don't you come on over once you're done with your reindeer.''

''You're sure?'' Whatever he was asking, it wasn't a question of stew.

Fingering the collar of his jacket, she looked him square in the eye. ''Absolutely.''

BUT LATE THAT NIGHT, after her last cry had shivered out into the darkness, after Tripp had thrust deep and shuddered, then stilled, Kaley wondered. Lying beneath him, holding him deep within her, caressing him with the tiny aftershocks of her passion, she stared up into his shadowed face. *What do you want of me, Tripp? Anything beyond this?* Her fingertips trailed down the hot, muscled contours of back, waist, then buttocks—memorizing, cherishing...

Swooping down out of the dark, Tripp laid a lingering kiss on her chin...another on the tip of her nose. He kissed her eyelids, right then left...

Such tenderness, such generosity—always—in his loving...and yet? She sighed and he sipped the sound off her lips. Their tongues spoke a language all their own, a sweet, yearning sign language that Kaley herself couldn't quite understand. *What are you telling me? Why no words of love, Tripp?*

She found herself needing them...waiting for them...and yet he stayed silent.

HE DIDN'T TRUST such happiness, Tripp realized, shaving in Kaley's bathroom mirror at dawn. It had to be a trick— a trap set by the gods for hopeful fools. He studied the scarred, ugly mug in the glass, frowning back at him. *Who are you to expect Kaley to love you?* Just because he'd stumbled along at the crucial moment, the night of the blizzard, when she'd desperately needed comforting?

She didn't need comforting last night, he argued with the doubter in the mirror. *She was happy from the get-go.* Though he'd made her happier. He felt himself stiffen, remembering how happy.

But that proved nothing. She'd loved loving nine years ago; loved it still. And probably needed it more, after eight years of marriage, of never going without. Just because he could serve as her stud didn't mean she *loved* him. Needed *him.* It was just that he was available and that she trusted him. Probably looked on him as a friend. *As a good neighbor,* he told himself bitterly.

And so he was.

But that was a far cry from what he longed to be.

"WHICH IS *YOUR* favorite?" Kaley quizzed Martha late that afternoon as she held one of the new puppies to her cheek. It gave a breathy, tiny grunt and nuzzled her face, seeking something to suck.

Martha watched with apprehension, ears pricked, tail thumping nervously, while Kaley fondled the puppy.

"I know you think I'm a klutz, but I'm not going to drop her," Kaley soothed. "Promise. And this *was* part of

the bargain, you know.'' The breeder had asked her to handle his pups daily, accustoming them to the scent and feel
of humans from the very start. Resting the baby on her
knee, she fingered each foot in turn. ''Doesn't it just kill
you—their teeny-tiny paws? Each perfect toe and toenail?''

Martha couldn't bear it anymore. She let out a yodeling
growl and stretched her nose toward the puppy.

''Okay, okay.'' Kaley set it back at a nipple. ''But see
if I trust you with mine next spring.''

She glanced down at herself with a smile. After hearing
her baby's heartbeat yesterday, she was finally beginning
to believe, to move past fear to faith. Amplified by the
stethoscope, it had been such a decisive, confident sound,
unstoppable as an acorn stirring under the soil.

She jumped as the phone rang.

Let it be Tripp, she prayed, hurrying to answer. He'd
given her no hint at all when he left this morning about
when he might see her again. But then, actions spoke
louder than silence, she'd been telling herself all day. So
let it be Tripp, come up with some excuse—any excuse—
to visit her again this evening. ''Hello?'' she cried, packing
too much hope and welcome into two short syllables.

''Kaley, it's Dr. Hancock...''

''D-DANA!''

''Who is— Kaley? Is that you?'' Coming down the telephone line, Dana's voice was warm as a hug. ''What's the
matter? Where are you?''

''H-home. I'm home. I just got a call from Dr. Hancock...'' Kaley found herself at the end of her phone cord
and swung back into the kitchen. ''Sh-she said...''

''Sounds like you're hyperventilating,'' Dana said sooth-
ingly. ''Slow down...relax...I'm right here. Are you sitting
down?''

''Yes.'' She pulled out a kitchen chair and sat—drew a

shuddering breath and popped up again. "No." Kaley paced as far as the door to the mudroom, till she hit cord's end, and turned back. "She called to tell me—" Her voice cracked into a sob. "To tell me the protein...the what d'you call it? The alphafetoprotein—my baby's protein level—was too high. She wants to test it again in seven days. Monday, that means Monday. A week from now."

"Yes..." Dana was silent for a moment. "But what does that mean when she says it's too high?"

"I guess your babies tested normal both times?" Kaley swallowed around the lump in her throat. Of course they would have, lucky Dana.

"Er...yes. But that doesn't necessarily... Tell me what Cass said. Why does she want to test again? Could the test result simply be wrong? Labs do make mistakes, you know."

"She said that. She did say that." Kaley shivered. "The results could be wrong—or the date could be wrong. If the date of conception was miscalculated, if my baby's a week older than Cass thinks, then the protein level would be higher than expected."

"Seems to me that that would be an easy mistake to make," Dana observed, the voice of reason. "You are sitting down, aren't you, sweetie?"

"Yeah..." Kaley sat again, wiped the tears off her cheeks. But if the conception date was wrong, was actually a week earlier than originally thought, it meant that Kaley's baby had been bombarded with her mother's antibiotic for nearly *two* weeks instead of one, doubtless doubling the chances of— She shot to her feet. "And sometimes she said they just never know why it's high."

"Anomalies," Dana agreed. "Life hiccups and we all think the sky is falling. We can live with anomalies."

But some of the other conditions that high levels of protein might foretell...! Kaley squeezed her eyes shut, trying to squeeze the image of that pitiful, dreadful travesty of a puppy out of her brain.

"Listen," said Dana decisively. "Are you in shape to drive over here? I can't come to you, I'm afraid—got six dudes who'll be wanting their supper—but I don't think you should be alone. Why don't you pack your bag and come over. Stay the night? Or you know, I could send Sean to get you when he—"

"No..." Kaley smiled through her tears. "Thank you, but—" But maybe if she stayed here, Tripp would come and hold her. That was where she longed to be tonight, safe in his arms. Let him stand like a knight, his sword drawn between her and the dragon. "I think maybe I'll just take a bubble bath, go to sleep early. Get a grip."

"Could you call Tripp to come over and cheer you up?" Dana suggested, effortlessly reading her mind. "I'm sure he would if you called."

If she called, yes, he would; Kaley didn't doubt for a second that he'd come running if he thought her in need.

But she needed him because she loved him, and confessing her need was to confess her love—and ask for his in return.

Asking was the one thing she could not, would not, do.

Because the last time she'd offered him her heart, he'd thrown it back in her face.

The next time—if there was ever to be a next time—Tripp must come to *her,* needing and wanting and, most of all, loving. The next time—this time—she was playing it safe.

She wiped a tear from her chin. "Reckon a tub and a book will do me. But Dana? Thanks so much for being there."

"Any and every time, sweetie. Now, *please,* try not to worry."

TRIPP TWITCHED the reins to the left. *"Haw!"* The command came out in a raspy croak, but the reindeer responded anyway. They swung left, dragging their board behind them, with Tripp walking directly behind this improvised sleigh. "I think you've got it," he muttered, and swallowed again—felt as if his throat was coated with sixty-grit sandpaper.

"Gee!" he called after they'd traveled straight for the length of the corral. He tugged the right-hand reins; the reindeers tossed their heads and swung right along the fence line. Yeah, they had it! Tripp grinned and found himself wishing that Kaley were there to see.

Heat coiled deep in his stomach. *Kaley...* She'd hovered at the back of his mind all day—a slow, fuzzy mind stuffed with cotton wool—and she the angel bouncing on these puffy white cotton wool clouds, while he trudged through his daily chores. *"Whoa!"* he called, pulling back on the leathers.

The reindeer halted and stamped. He could picture them up on a rooftop, hitched to a sleigh, dancing and prancing in place while Santa hoisted his sack and stumped over to the chimney. "You're trained," he informed them. "And I'm done for the day."

Up at the house, wrestling himself out of his cold-weather garments, Tripp found himself propped against the mudroom wall, breathing hard through a painful throat. The thought slowly coalesced. *I'm coming down with something.* An unfamiliar sensation; normally he was healthy. And not something he generally cared to admit. Ignore sickness and it would go away was his credo. But this bug wasn't taking no for an answer; it was coming on like a freight train.

"Hansen!" he swore to himself. He'd stopped by the general store in Trueheart two or three days back, and Han-

sen had been honking and blowing at the cash register
Tripp had hated to accept his change from the purchase
but he'd seen no way out that wouldn't insult the touchy
storekeeper.

Kaley, it hit him a moment later. He'd made love with
Kaley last night! Kissed her a thousand times. If he'd given
her and her baby something, she'd have his hide—look at
the way she'd quarantined Whitey. He gritted his teeth and
walked to the phone and dialed. Nothing to do but take his
licks.

The busy tone drilled into his ear. He hung up and put
the kettle on to boil. Maybe tea would help; he sure didn't
feel like eating.

The next time he tried her phone, it was busy again.

Same for the next. *Who the heck is she talking to?* If
she wanted to talk to someone, she could always call him.
He felt surly and jealous and oddly forlorn. After taking
his tea into the living room, he made a fire and slumped
on the couch, trying to sip around the chunk of hot glass
jammed in his throat.

The room wasn't warming as fast as it should. He
dragged a blanket off the arm of the sofa and stretched out
under it. He'd give her another ten minutes or so, then try
her number again.

He woke to a dark room, the faintest glow of dying
embers on the hearth. Staggering into the kitchen to consult
the clock, he swore aloud in a cracked and rasping voice
Midnight! Way too late to call her now.

HE HADN'T CALLED. The night of all nights when she'd
needed to hear his voice and Tripp hadn't bothered to
phone.

Let that be a lesson to you, Kaley told herself ruefully
slamming the back door behind her and stomping out into

the crackling dawn. Tripp McGraw was a lesson she seemed doomed to study forever, but never quite learn. Maybe it was hope that kept clouding her vision.

No more hope, she told herself crossly. *Only cows.*

And praying.

She had five days to live through before her next blood test. Let her focus all her prayers on that.

"YEAH? Who's this?" growled the voice at the end of the line.

"Hello, Whitey?" Shivering, hunched over the phone, Tripp tried not to cough. "It's Tripp. Can I speak to Kaley?" He'd missed her this morning, calling apparently after she'd gone out to feed the herd. After he'd come in from feeding his own, he'd slept the day through. Now it was evening.

"She's upstairs napping," said Whitey to the sound of a pot being smacked onto a burner. "My turn to cook. You want t'call her later."

"Yeah." Except that he desperately needed to crawl back to bed. "Look, would you tell her…" Tripp hesitated. Didn't want to sound as if he was whining; men didn't call each other up to complain they had a cold. "Tell her I've caught a bit of a bug." He couldn't say more to Whitelaw without admitting he and she had spent night before last in the same bed. And that message should be enough for Kaley to put two and two together and start taking extra vitamin C. "I'll call her in a day or so."

"You do that. Dad*blast* it, Chang, you tryin' to break a man's neck?" The phone clattered onto a hard surface.

"So long," Tripp muttered, then winced as the receiver was slammed down, cutting the connection. He wandered over to the sink, drew a glass of water, thought dimly about food—and went back to bed.

"OH, 'FORE I FORGET," said Whitey, dishing out a bowl of beef stew. He plunked a biscuit fresh from the oven on top of it and thumped it onto the table before Kaley. "That McGraw called, while ago."

"Oh?" Reaching for the salt shaker, Kaley barely hesitated. "What did he want?"

"Not much t'speak of. Said he was a tad under the weather."

A tad. Frowning, she split her biscuit in half. A tad meaning a tiny bit. "Did he want me to call him?"

"Didn't say so."

Teeth buried in her bottom lip, she cut a slice of butter, spread it with exquisite care on the bread.

Tripp had gotten in the habit of phoning her this past week. She'd gotten in the habit of feeling he cared, since he bothered to call.

But now this break in the pattern...first last night, then again tonight. *Even if he really is sick, clearly he can use a phone.* So maybe this message was more by way of an excuse... A way of backing off, of putting some distance between them...

If so, he must have been delighted to reach Whitey, let him pass the bad news on. She sighed and took a crusty nibble, dust on her tongue. *Or maybe I'm just worrying too much about everything, this week.*

Time would tell her.

Meanwhile she'd been the forward one, dropping by his ranch uninvited, inviting him back to her place for supper.

No more of that. *If he wants me, he knows where to find me.*

CHAPTER NINETEEN

ON MONDAY, Kaley stopped at Michelle's Place on her way back from giving blood.

"How did it go?" Michelle asked, bringing two cups of hot chocolate over to her table. She sat and passed the one with a triple serving of tiny marshmallows over to Kaley.

Kaley grimaced. "I don't know—won't know till tomorrow. I do know I'm not crazy about Hancock's partner, Dr. Calloway. A cold fish, and I think he was annoyed with Dr. Hancock's insisting he work me into his schedule." She'd discovered on reaching the office that Cass Hancock had been called off to California on a family emergency; brother had been involved in a car wreck last night, her nurse had confided. Meanwhile, Dr. Calloway was handling all appointments that could not be deferred. "So he rushed in to poke my tummy, told me he was sure Cass had explained everything about this test, which she had, sent me off to give blood and rushed out again. Said he'll call me tomorrow."

Michelle nodded. "Dana and I were thinking that maybe you'd want some support. That maybe one or both of us should try to be there when you get the results."

Kaley could feel the tears stinging the back of her lashes as she reached across and touched Michelle's hand. "You guys are such wonderful friends! I can't tell you how much that means. But I haven't a clue when Dr. Cold Fish will call. He wouldn't say. And it's not like you have all the time in the world to hang out at the Circle C." She tipped

her head at the surrounding tables. With less than tw
weeks to go till Christmas, all Trueheart seemed to be i
a holiday mood. The café was bustling with lunchtime din
ers.

"Yes, but—"

"I can handle this, Michelle." She would have to. It wa
her baby, her chosen path; she'd reap the consequence
Friends could warm the way, but in the end she stoo
alone. *Might as well get used to it.* Tripp had not phone
since the night he spoke with Whitey.

Michelle made a face. "Okay, Supermom. But I wa
you to promise that you'll call at least one of us once yo
hear. Okay?"

So she'd promised and set off to spend her last twenty
four hours in purgatory, with nothing to be done for it b
pray.

WITH WHITEY'S HELP, Kaley fed the herd at crack of daw
so that she could spend the rest of the day hovering ove
the telephone. After she'd paced a mile or more throug
the house, she flogged herself into the kitchen. Might a
well kill the time productively. She started a batch of bread
then made two pans of lasagna. The minutes ticked pas
each second a prayer bead sliding down the string of he
life. *Oh, please.*

At five, she looked at the clock and almost wept. Tha
coldhearted bastard hadn't bothered to call! By now Cal
loway must have gone home for the day, blithely consign
ing her to another night in sleepless limbo. Still, she picke
up the phone and punched out his office number in Du
rango.

An answering machine clicked on, inviting her to leav
a message, or if this was an emergency she could...

"Damn you!" She smashed the phone down and bur
into tears. Martha, who'd just padded into the kitchen t

drink from her bowl, looked up—then came straight over, brown eyes worried, tail waving heartfelt sympathy, to sit at Kaley's feet. She lifted one forepaw, offering to shake.

"Oh, Martha-girl!" Kaley sank to the floor and threw her arms around the collie, hugging her while the dog kissed her face. "You've been there, too, haven't you?"

And found happiness on the far side of sorrow, she reminded herself.

She squared her shoulders. She'd better remember: tragedy only threatened; it hadn't come home to roost. "You're crying too soon, Kaley Cotter," she said aloud. "Show at least as much guts as a Border collie."

She pulled herself to her feet with the help of a chair, then the table—movements that once had been easy were now getting awkward. She'd gained three pounds this week alone.

"And that's got to be a good sign," she informed her belly, rubbing it as she moved to the sink. *Keep on growing; don't give up.* She cupped her hands and splashed water over her face; dog kisses were more heartening than hygienic. She started violently as the phone rang.

Oh, please, oh, please! She snatched it up. "Hello!"

"Mrs. Cotter? Dr. Calloway, here. I have your lab results."

"Yes?" she half whispered, one hand rising to her heart. *Please...*

"I'm afraid your result bears out the previous test, adjusted for another week's growth, naturally. The alphafetoprotein level is...higher than I like to see it. Substantially higher."

"Oh." Kaley dragged a chair out from the table and sat. "Oh." *Oh, God.*

The sound of faint clicking came down the phone line—possibly a pen tapping impatiently on a desk. "I don't have your entire record before me, but I seem to recall that Dr.

Hancock sent you for an ultrasound when you first came
to her, to determine a conception date.''

''She did, but—''

''So that would rule out our underestimating the age of
your fetus, which can be one explanation for such a high
level of AFP.''

''Cass—Dr. Hancock—said that there was always a possibility that the date could be incorrect, with such an early
scan. She said—''

''That would be grasping at straws, frankly. And since
that scan showed only one fetus, we can rule out twins,
which is another benign explanation for an elevated level
of alphafetoprotein—two fetuses, therefore twice the normal amount of protein showing in the mother's serum.''
He sighed heavily and somewhere in Durango a chair
squeaked. ''So the next step is a high-resolution ultrasound
and we'll see what we'll see. Um...I can schedule you for
a scan the week after Christmas—Tuesday, the twenty-
eighth, 3:00 p.m.''

''That's more than two weeks away!'' She could not
bear it! Could not. ''Haven't you *anything* sooner?''

He didn't speak for almost a minute. ''Mrs. Cotter,
there's no rush here. You wouldn't want to schedule an
abortion directly before Christmas. I wouldn't advise any
patient of mine to—''

''I wasn't even thinking about that!'' Her voice wobbled
perilously close to a sob.

''Well, maybe you should,'' he said quietly. ''Think
about it, I mean. I'm sure Dr. Hancock will be recom-
mending that you see a genetic counselor to sort out your
options after this scan if it shows—''

''I meant I'm not sure I can wait that long to *know*.
Don't you have any openings for a scan earlier than that?''

He didn't, not with the ultrasound technician that both
he and Dr. Hancock considered the very best tech in the

city—the one most adept at reading questionable scans, the one with the best record of picking up structural deformities. He promised that if any opening arose, he would certainly have his office contact her, but in the meantime...

"Okay," Kaley agreed bleakly. She did want the best technician. She wanted no mistakes.

"And of course, meantime, as I'm sure Dr. Hancock explained to you, one reason for an elevated level of AFP could be that a spontaneous abortion is...a very real possibility. So any way that you can minimize stress and strain for the next two weeks... Try to put your feet up, take it easy. I don't advise that you overdo it, preparing for the holidays."

Kaley had to press her fist to her mouth to contain the bitter laughter. *Right, Doc, I'll go easy on baking all those plum puddings! Cut back on the old Christmas-card list.* What would he say if she told him she had four hundred–some cows to feed every day? "Sure," she said faintly. "Thanks. I'll be careful."

She sat, dial tone buzzing in her ear, hand soothing her stomach, her eyes fixed on some point far, far beyond her kitchen walls.

Finally she sighed and stirred herself to phone Dana, who dragged every last word of Dr. Calloway's call out of her. "He sounds like a miserable man," Dana growled, banging pots and pans in her kitchen beyond Suntop Mountain. "A pinheaded, arrogant nerd—all brains, no empathy. And a doctor without a heart is about as useful as—as a tone-deaf diva!"

Kaley smiled wearily against the receiver. "I guess he meant well."

"The road to hell is paved with meant-wells." More banging of pots and pans, then Dana said, "So how are you going to take it slow for the next two weeks?"

"Whitey helps me. I've got the easy job, driving. He

shoves the hay bales out the back.'' A strenuous job for an old man. Though he refused to admit it, she was sure that other years Jim would have taken that chore, while Whitey drove the truck.

''*Not* good enough. Oh, I wish Cass were in town. She'd tell you to stay in bed and read mysteries and eat bonbons till your ultrasound. No, don't laugh at me, I mean it.'' Dana blew out a breath, thinking. ''I'll have to talk to Rafe, see what he—''

''Don't,'' Kaley said firmly. ''I mean it, Dana. Everybody's overworked this time of year. If I'm going to run my own ranch, then I have to do it. I can't collapse on my neighbors.''

Dana didn't agree, but she had to go; she had a dining room full of cross-country skiers plus her family to feed. Before hanging up, she promised to pass Kaley's news on to Michelle.

Kaley sat listening to the silence. Such heartbreaking silence. *This wasn't what I pictured driving here from Las Vegas.* She'd pictured a kitchen alive with her brother and Whitey and Chang, herself plus a healthy, happy, adorable toddler. A house that was a home; a loving family to fill it.

Wearily she stood and shuffled into the hallway to stop by the open closet door. She kicked into place the two pillows that she always used and sank down, then lowered herself to lie on her side. ''Mind if I join you guys? I could use a laugh or two.''

Curled halfway around her puppies, Martha thumped her tail in welcome. Hans Solo was sucking fiercely on his sister's ear, so Kaley lifted him and settled him against her cheek. ''Hey, beast.''

He squirmed into the warm hollow beneath her chin, suckled on her throat for a few minutes, then heaved a milk-fed sigh and slept. Kaley smiled, closed her eyes and drifted off after him.

SHE WOKE to the sensation of a delicate touch—the barest caress drifting along her temple. "Mmm?" She stretched and sighed and looked up—to find Tripp kneeling overhead. *"Oh!"*

"Did you fall, honey?" His fingertips explored lightly down over her neck, her spine.

You're here! You're back! She shook her head against the pillow. "Nothing like that. I'm just catnapping with the hound dogs."

"Whew!" Tripp blew out a breath. "You scared the blue blazes out of me. I knocked and when nobody answered, I stuck my head in your door and called. Figured I'd come as far as the living room, to see if you were napping on your couch. But when I spotted you lying here…" He brushed his knuckles tenderly along her cheek. "You've got to be careful." His eyes traveled her length and he scowled. "Wandering around in socks. They're slippery, you know."

"I *didn't* slip." She caught his hand and tugged, and he helped her to a sit. "But if it makes you feel better, I'll wear ice crampons around the house from now on. Though the first time I step on one of Martha's darlings, she'll go for my throat." She was babbling, wasn't she? But, *oh,* the feeling at seeing him again—as if her heart were dancing along a rainbow, color flooding back into her dreary world.

Feasting her eyes on his face, she cocked her head, then frowned. "Have you lost weight?" He'd always had high cheekbones, but now the hollows under them…

Tripp shrugged. "Might have. Didn't eat much this week. I've had the flu or some-such." He touched her cheek again. "You didn't get it? I've been waiting for you to come over and shoot me if I passed on a germ to you and your baby." He'd meant to call her for days, but hadn't found the energy to lift a phone. Just to keep feeding his herd had taken all his strength.

He didn't own a thermometer, but for sure he'd had a fever—how else to explain that his father had ridden beside him in the feed truck for three of those days, swigging whiskey, then throwing his empties out into the snow, the way he used to do? Considering the old man had been in his grave for five years, Tripp damn sure hoped that had been a fever! His dad hadn't thought much of any son of his training reindeer, either....

"You look like you need feeding up," Kaley decided. "Want to cook me supper?"

"Uh...sure. Scrambled eggs, maybe?" He'd have been happy to eat cardboard as long as he ate it at Kaley's table.

Her smile curled wickedly. "I was thinking something fancier...say, lasagna?"

Tripp gulped. "Well, I've never— Sure, I could do that. Got the ingredients?"

She nodded smugly. "Go grab the pan in the fridge and stick it in the stove at four hundred degrees, Chef. Then come back here and look at these puppies. Their eyes are starting to open."

THEY WERE THREE at supper that night—or four, counting Chang, who received his own saucer of lasagna at Whitey's boots. Tripp found himself wishing the talkative old man and his surly yap-hound were on the far side of the mountains. He didn't really have anything important to tell Kaley, but even so, Whitey was a distraction. A breach in their previous intimacy, which Tripp longed to reestablish. He'd missed her all week and now he had to share her.

After supper he leaped to volunteer doing the dishes, figuring that, freed from that task, Whitelaw would stump off to his cabin. No such luck. The old man settled in an easy chair before the fire in the living room and switched on the TV. Tripp gritted his teeth and set to soaping pots and pans.

Kaley leaned against the counter beside him for a while, talking of this and that, but he could see the dark shadows under her eyes. Making a baby just had to drag her down. "Go put your feet up," he finally said.

But once he'd finished the washup, Tripp had no further excuse to stay. It wasn't as if he could saunter upstairs to wait for her, with Whitey and his goggle-eyed partner looking on. Kaley was slumped into one corner of the couch, her long lashes drooping. He leaned down, almost close enough to brush his lips along her cheek. "Reckon I'm off now. Thanks for supper."

"You're going?" She struggled to her feet.

"S'long," Whitey grunted blithely. With his broken-down boots up on a hassock, he was undisputed king of this hill.

Tripp could have cheerfully grabbed him by the scrawny scruff and tossed him out in the snow. "'Night, Whitey." He drew Kaley along with him as far as the back door. "Thanks for supper," he repeated huskily—and kissed her.

Everything he couldn't say was surely clear in that kiss—*I want you. I need you. My heart aches every time I walk away from you.* He dragged his mouth aside to kiss her soft cheek...the satiny, sensitive spot below her ear...giving her air and space to say that she wanted him, too. That he should return in an hour or two, once White-law had gone home to bed.

She didn't, though she clung to his jacket with both hands and arched against him, her rounding belly pressed against his plain and plaintive desire. Finally Tripp realized she wasn't going to ask.

He drew apart, breathing hard, heart thundering. *Ask me,*

Kaley. If you want me the way I want you, all you have to do is ask. Heaven's waiting.

But tonight it waited behind a locked and enigmatic door. He hadn't a clue what she was thinking. She cupped his cheek, kissed him sweetly one last time—this time with closed lips!—murmured, "G'night, Tripp." Then eased backward into the mudroom, like a morning glory closing its petals for the night.

Leaving him standing on her stoop, made a fool by his own desire.

BY NOW she and Whitey had their rhythm down, feeding cows. Starting their day's run with the heifers in Cougar Rock Pasture, Kaley drove the truck in close, alongside a long wooden trough. She had to proceed at near idle, since the most aggressive animals were already grouped around the feeding station, determined to shove their noses in first. "Get along," she growled, and beeped the horn. "How am I s'posed to feed you if you stand in the way?"

"Hi*yaaw,* you hussies!" Whitey yelled from where he stood behind the feed box.

The roadblockers snorted, put up their tails and trotted off a length or two through the trampled snow, then swung around, pricked their ears and drifted back.

But now Kaley had the truck in position, with the side chute slanting down from the feed box to hang over the trough. She engaged the clutch that set the hydraulics in motion; a worm-driven screw in the box started turning, shoving cottonseed cake down the chute. She drove along at dead slow, distributing the manna in a line down the trough. On the opposite side of their lunch counter, the cows crowded in, eager for their fair share—and every other share they could snatch, as well.

Meanwhile, at the rear of the truck bed Whitey snipped the wire off bales of hay, broke them apart with his hay hook, then heaved them off the back end into the rutted snow. A procession of heifers followed the truck, then paused to gaze after them, munching stolidly, hay sticking out both sides of their black, wet muzzles.

Kaley worked on automatic; her mind could go its own way while her hands shifted gears and her feet stomped pedals. Tripp... Had she been crazy not to invite him to stay over last night?

As sad and frightened as she'd been—still was—she'd been in no mood for lovemaking. But she'd have foresworn ice cream for a year in return for one night of Tripp's simply holding her. She always felt so cherished in his arms. *So loved...*

Whoa, cowgirl, she warned herself. Mistaking fabulous sex for true and lasting love? That way lay heartbreak. At least nine years ago, it had.

Reaching the end of the trough, she steered the truck along the south side of a steep and wooded ridge, toward the next station a quarter mile on, with its own set of bovine customers mooing for service.

It was easy to be confused, she thought as the truck bumped and heaved itself over the plowed track. The way he looked at her sometimes. And those looks came at the oddest times, not just when they were naked in bed. She'd glanced up from her plate at supper last night and surprised him in *such* a look of yearning tenderness.

Or maybe this was all wishful thinking and that hadn't been a look of love—that had been Tripp pondering if he dared ask for a third helping of lasagna?

"Get on there, you wall-eyed, knock-kneed, ring-tailed ol' hussy! Hi*yaaw!*" yelled Whitey as they approached.

Kaley slowed down and leaned on the horn. The cows parted like a dark, disgruntled sea, then surged back toward the trough.

But suppose...just suppose... Kaley thought, *that some-*

thing's changed in nine years. I've changed, so why can't he? Maybe he's grown up, or decided it's time to settle down, or... Or some other unspecified miracle had occurred. He'd been struck by lightning. Fallen on his head out riding range. Her fairy godmother had sat him down and given him a serious talking-to.

Somehow miracles seemed in very short supply in this season of miracles. Kaley touched her stomach, closed her eyes for a second. *Oh, please...* She grimaced. *And here I'm asking for not one miracle, but two? What are my chances of that?*

Done with this trough and this pasture, she swung the truck around and headed for the distant gate. They drove back to the barn, reloaded with cake and hay, then set out again for the main herd down at Hay Meadows Pasture.

While the protein feed thumped into the troughs and flakes of hay hit the ground in their wake, her mind drifted away again. Tripp...here he'd been gone from her sight for less than a day and already she missed him.

Missed his dry humor, his warm smile, his hard arms... *And other assorted hard parts!* she admitted with a rueful grin and a delicious inward shiver. His kindliness and his sexiness. His quiet, unassuming competence. His *dad*-blasted reticence. If he loved her, why couldn't he say so?

Or maybe he *was* telling her so, in the only way he knew how—sign language. Tripp was a man who placed his faith in action, not words. And when she thought of all the acts of kindness and consideration he'd shown her...his tenderness in bed. Maybe she was overlooking the truth.

Or was this only foolish, wistful hope *blinding* her to the naked truth—that Tripp loved to make love and she was available?

I don't know, I don't know, I don't know!

The truck bumped on slowly down the slope toward another trough, another huddle of hungry cows.

Well, with all the things she didn't know, Kaley told herself bleakly, there was one thing she did know.

If by any miracle of miracles Tripp *was* trying to reach out to her in the only way he knew how—reach out for something lasting this time—it wouldn't be fair to let him come any closer.

Not till she'd had the scan.

Because if her baby turned out to be—she shied away from the word *deformed* like a colt shying from a tumbleweed. But her mind couldn't escape the vivid image that it held—that pathetic little lump of flesh that had striven so hard to be a puppy and failed. *If my child...*

"You plannin' to drive, or we just gonna sit here and admire the view?" Whitey called rudely from the bed of the truck.

Kaley startled and refocused on the outer world; she'd come to the end of this trough and simply stopped. She put the truck in gear and rolled on.

If she gave birth to such a tragedy, then it was her tragedy. Her burden. And she'd carry the load herself.

Because if Richard could not accept even the risk of having an imperfect child—much less the thought of raising it—how could she ask that of a man who was not her baby's father?

If the ultrasound proved what the blood test foretold, she was looking at heartache. No way would she dump that on the man she loved. A man she wished every comfort and joy.

Which means, she promised herself as the truck pulled away from the last trough, *that I can't let Tripp come any closer. Not till I know for sure.*

"Dad*blast* it!" Whitey yelled. "Stop the damn truck!"

Braking, she glanced in her side mirror, but the feed box blocked her view of the truck bed and the ground close behind it. She rolled down her window and leaned out into the frigid air. "What's the matter?"

Whitey's voice came from a distance. "Dropped m'dang hay hook. Hold on." He stumped into view, walking away from her, his breath smoking as he picked his way gingerly through the ruts and cowpats.

He leaned down for his hook, and she noticed one cow lift its head in the group that was tearing at the hay, dropped some forty feet beyond Whitey.

Not a cow—a bull. He snorted, pricked his ears, lowered his massive neck— "Whitey, *run!*" she screamed, and threw the truck into reverse.

The truck bounced on its springs—then banged into something solid as a boulder.

"Son of a blue-bottomed ba*boon!*" Whitey raged, out of sight. "You consarned, dadblasted, piss-poor excuse for a—now *stop* that! Hi*yaaw!*"

Kaley collapsed against her steering wheel, laughing, then let out a yelp as something banged them again, shaking the whole truck.

"Would you for Pete's sake *drive?*" Whitey yelled.

Laughing so hard it hurt, she stepped on the gas. As they drew away, she could see the bull in her side mirror, one of the two-year-olds. Pawing the snow, he was considering a third charge. But the gap widened and he changed his mind. His broad, hornless head came up; he snorted—*so much for you!*—turned haughtily back to his hay, moving with a rolling strut.

Another hundred feet and Kaley stopped, leaned out. "You all right back there?"

Whitey appeared outside the passenger door, glanced warily over his shoulder, then scrambled in, his face scarlet, his week-old beard bristling with outrage. "That was that dang bull with the tipped brand. I *told* McGraw— And what the blue blazes are you grinning for? He nearly had me!''

She leaned over to kiss his bristly cheek. "As fast as you are on your feet? Never!''

"I *told* McGraw we oughta cull that cocky son of a gun!'' Whitey fumed while she circled back toward the gate and home. "Said he was too big for his britches, didn't I say so?'' Tripp and he had argued all the last day of roundup whether the two-year-old should be sent to the packer or kept for breeding stock.

Whitey had thought him too aggressive to be safe.

Tripp had argued that he had brains and balls and a magnificent conformation, just what you'd want in a range bull, and that he'd settle down once he was given his own allotment of cows. He'd offered to buy him on the spot, but Kaley had vetoed that. The Circle C herd needed upgrading, and she wouldn't have the money to bring in new blood for years. She should conserve what good genes she had.

"Reckon you were right,'' she said peaceably while Whitey muttered dire threats and she aimed the truck for home.

Or maybe he wasn't. Cattle were used to cowboys on horseback; a person on foot was a much more tempting target, especially for a bull in the first flush of testosterone. Just as likely Tripp was right and the bull would settle to pleasanter pastimes this coming summer.

Either way, it was too late to do anything before spring roundup, since she had no intention of letting Whitey shoot him and turn him into a thousand pounds of hamburger, as he was currently threatening. And the bull was too much animal for her and Whitey to rope and drag to a trailer; that chore would take two crack ropers on extra-heavy horses, preferably not in the snow. *We'll just be careful till*

spring. She patted his knee when they reached the gate.
"Sure you're all right?"

"No thanks to that black bastard!"

Watching the old man struggle with the gateposts
through her windshield, Kaley was thankful all the same.
Somebody's looking out for us.

If only this luck could be spun out like a thread of gold,
running through the next few weeks... She'd had one miracle today—whoever would have dreamed Whitey could
move like that?

Now she needed two more.

CHAPTER TWENTY

"DANA CALLED ME," Tripp said bluntly that night, the moment Kaley answered the phone. "She tells me the doc said you're supposed to be taking it easy for the next few weeks. That you shouldn't be out feeding cows."

"Dana shouldn't have—"

"She damn sure should have." *Why the hell didn't you ask me yourself?* "So I'll be there at seven tomorrow to help Whitelaw with feeding, and you'd better still be in bed."

She blew out a breath. "Tripp, look, I don't need—"

"Too bad. This time you're going to take." He hung up the phone on further protests and turned a tight circle of anger around his kitchen. What was she trying to prove? That she was the toughest cowhand in Trueheart?

That she doesn't want my help. Pain sifted through his bones as the thought settled in and took hold. A man *was* his help. Was his hands and his brains and his ability, translated into action, realized as accomplishment. This was the gift he offered her—himself.

And this was what she was rejecting.

If Kaley wouldn't come to him when she needed help, then she didn't want him. Didn't need him. He stood, staring at the floor, eyes bleak, shoulders slumped. This was the message he'd feared she was sending him last night, when she didn't invite him to stay.

And now this.

Except she does need me. To feed her cows, if not t
warm her bed.

AT SEVEN the next morning, Kaley was picking her wa
cautiously across the sun-glazed yard when Tripp's picku
rumbled into view. He parked by the barn and stalked bac
to meet her, breath smoking, eyes narrowed. "What ar
you doin' out here?"

Not waiting for her good-morning kiss, that was sure
"I was just going to help Whitey load the truck."

"No. You're not." He left her standing there, mouth aja
to argue.

Mitten-clad hands clenching to fists, she glared afte
him—then stamped a foot in frustration. It made a satis
factory *crack* as she broke the crust of the snow. *What*
got into you, Tripp McGraw? The Christmas grinch him
self.

She stood debating for a full minute. She could ignor
his high-handed ways and press on to the barn.

He'd looked angry enough to carry her back to th
house, and wouldn't that just entertain Whitey?

A pregnant woman had a scarce—and diminishing–
supply of dignity. She wasn't in a mood to risk hers; nc
when she'd lose in the end. *I'll reason with him at luncl*
time, she told herself, and stomped back to her house.

THERE WAS NO REASONING with Tripp. Once he'd made u
his mind, he was as stubborn as any bull. Worst yet, White
backed him up.

Of course he would, Kaley fumed as she smacked a plat
filled with a hot sloppy joe sandwich on the table befor
each of them. *Now Whitey gets to sit in a heated cab an*
Tripp heaves the bales!

After which he'd go home to the M Bar G and heav
hay *and* manage the protein feed, with no one to help *hir*

And Tripp had more than five hundred in his herd. "You won't be done feeding before dark," she protested. That was a brutal load, working all day out in the bone-chilling cold, and he'd lost a good ten pounds the week he was sick, she'd noticed last night. "I can't let you do this!"

"You can't stop me," Tripp said calmly, finishing his sandwich in four businesslike bites. "See you tomorrow," he added to Whitey, and he was out the door.

"And thank you for your support," she growled, banging dishes into the sink.

Whitey cut a plug of tobacco and stuffed it in his cheek. "Way it's s'posed to be. Glad *some*body knows it 'round here."

"If we're going to trade work, then the custom is both parties work," Kaley phoned Tripp that night to announce. "If you're really coming tomorrow, don't you dare show your face without an armload of mending for me to do. Go through your closet right now and find all the shirts that need buttons and the pants that want patching."

"You're s'posed to be resting, is what Dana said," he protested. She was canceling out his gift with one of her own. The red hen, determined to do it all herself, closing him out of her charmed circle.

"Sewing is very restful. Bring me some or I'll go over and paint your kitchen while you're out feeding cows."

He wheeled around, scanning the walls. "It was painted last year." Well, sometime in the past three or four, maybe five years.

"Painted bachelor brown," she sniffed. "I was thinking cream cabinets and trim, then the walls a medium ocher?"

What the hell color was ocher? "No, thanks." It wasn't paint that brightened up a kitchen, he'd come to realize; it was a woman singing in it while she went about her work. That was what this room cried out for. No wonder his old

man had taken to the bottle. Sometimes, lately, Tripp felt
as if his own heart would—

"What are you doing right now?" she asked, her voice
going softer, losing its bossy edge.

"Figuring out some cutting-horse bloodlines." The table
was strewn with yellowing magazines, scribbled sheets of
paper showing family trees of an imaginary dynasty, starting with a Salud/Dancer colt.

"Oh, sorry I interrupted. Me, I'm playing with the puppies. They can walk—well, wobble—all the way across the
room now. And Hans knows his name—I'm almost sure
he does."

"I'll have to see that to believe it." *Invite me over, Kaley. I'll come in a heartbeat.*

"I'll prove it tomorrow," she assured him, rising to the
challenge.

"You do that," he said heavily. "Look, I've got to—"
What? Step outside and howl at the moon? He felt mournful as a whole pack of coyotes. He'd made *such* a mistake,
letting himself love her again. But it was too late to know
that now.

"Oh, sure," she said as quickly. "Don't let me keep
you. Reckon I'll see you tomorrow?"

"You will." And he'd see her tonight.

In his lonely dreams.

WHATEVER TRIPP had thought Kaley might feel for him
during those two blissful nights in her bed, well, he must
have been wrong.

And he'd been here before, he was coming to realize.
Nine years ago he'd come to this same bitter fork in the
road. Oh, Kaley was grateful for his help and she showed
him that she was, feeding him lunch whenever he'd let her.
Sending him home with pies and home-baked bread and
other treats. Mending his clothes.

But she didn't want him in her bed anymore. Didn't want his loving.

Did not love him. He'd been every kind of fool to hope something had changed between them. Something to make happiness possible.

And this time was worse—far worse!—than the last. This time Tripp couldn't run away from heartbreak, losing himself on the rodeo trail, leaving his father and brother to take up the slack at the M Bar G.

He could not even go to ground—hole up on his own land for the winter like a bear in his cave. Forget about smiling till spring.

Because Kaley might not need him, but she was in need.

Each day he had to feed her cows, then eat lunch at her table, all the while pretending he didn't care. Pretending that loving Kaley was the last thing on his mind.

Seeing her like that every day, wanting what was beyond his grasp, he had to harden his heart like a man tempering a red-hot horseshoe on an anvil, blow by blow by ringing blow, till it was hard enough...and cold enough...to withstand stone.

"JUST THINK," Kaley said aloud to her baby as she carried two bags of groceries into Tripp's kitchen. She'd gone shopping in Durango, leaving just as soon as Whitey and Tripp had set out for the pastures this morning. Since Tripp was too busy these days to shop for himself, she was making it her business to stock his fridge as well as her own, and who cared if the man fussed when he found out? "Just think," she repeated, unpacking the bags on the kitchen table. "Three days ago I was actually dithering about how unfair it would be to let Tripp become involved with us, before we know where we stand. Do you remember?"

No comment from the kiddie gallery.

She carried the perishables over to the fridge, clucked

when she saw the wasteland within—no wonder he was losing weight—and started stacking cartons of coleslaw and macaroni salads, a roast chicken, a pound of ham and as much roast beef. Milk, a block of cheddar, butter, a dozen eggs. Two gallons of milk and one of OJ.

"I mean, I was even thinking I should warn him not to get too close. To guard his heart. Ha! As if Tripp McGraw needs lessons in guarding his own heart! Can you imagine how humiliated I'd be by now if I'd told him that—when he never had the least intention of coming close enough to love us?"

Like an amorous porcupine, Tripp had come just close enough to mate, then had as hastily withdrawn. He hadn't touched her in days. Hadn't tried to kiss her. He'd hardly even meet her eyes across the table.

To think for a day or so there, I thought maybe, just maybe... Fighting back tears, Kaley shook her head angrily, thumped shut the fridge door and cupped a hand to her stomach. *But I thought wrong.* "Looks like it's just you and me, kid." For better or worse.

DRIVING TO TRUEHEART the next morning, Tripp felt like a dog who'd snapped his chain. Rafe had called the night before to announce that Dana would be visiting Kaley this morning, bearing Christmas gifts. And that she was dragging her menfolk along. "Last thing Sean and I want to do is hang around a house listening to gossip and recipes," Rafe had confided. "So save us. Let us do the feeding tomorrow—Kaley's herd and yours, too. And you take the day off. Sleep in."

Even though he'd recognized Rafe's too-long explanation for what it was, charity in disguise, Tripp had leaped at the offer. He needed to buy a new drive belt for his feed box engine; the old one was fraying, he'd told himself. But in truth, he welcomed the chance to avoid Kaley. It hurt too much to see her these days. She'd hardly look him square in the eye when he came in her kitchen.

But day by day the bitter truth was taking shape. Coming clearer. He understood now where he'd put his foot wrong. Those two nights in her bed had been a gift—two brief, unforgettable moments of bliss born of her need for comfort, his proximity, their old sexual sizzle. But that didn't add up to love, and Kaley, womanlike, knew it, even if he did not.

So here he was precisely where he'd been nine years before, when he'd wanted to press ahead even while Kaley had been backing away, putting off their marriage from one summer to the next, then to the following fall.

This time she couldn't fly away to Europe, but still she was doing it again—smiling and treating him kindly even while she withdrew. *She just can't look me in the eye and tell me no, she doesn't love me. But I've got the message all right.*

For the very last time.

Pretty women didn't stay—not the one pretty woman who mattered. Whatever it was such a woman wanted, it wasn't a man with an ugly mug and an aching heart.

Fair enough. What else could a man do, but play the hand he was dealt and not complain?

But no more would he lay his heart on the line.

WITH HIS SHOPPING accomplished, Tripp had nothing else to do in town. But if he returned to the M Bar G, he'd just get sucked into helping feed the cattle, spoiling Rafe's gesture. Might as well take the day he'd been given. He stopped into Michelle's Place; it was only ten, but he had room for a second breakfast.

He'd cleaned his plate; Michelle had whisked it away with a warm smile and a wise glance that said she knew when a man wanted to be left alone. He sat, head down, hands clasped around a mug of coffee as if its warmth might seep into his frozen soul.

A woman came in the door and walked by his table, passing him by before he'd thought to look up; she headed for the back of the room. He sat breathing the faint perfume of her passage—and shivered, old memories whirling like a drift of dry leaves. Love and hatred and loss...the taste of the butterscotch brownies his mother used to bake suddenly bursting on his tongue.

Who *was* that? He turned to look toward the counter, to where she stood talking with Michelle.

From the back she was slender, dark haired, too expensively dressed to be someone from these parts... Hauntingly familiar.

"Oh, yes, the M Bar G still exists," Michelle was saying. Her eyes flicked to Tripp's face, then back to the stranger. "But there's the man to ask." She nodded at Tripp and the woman turned.

No! a voice—voice of a child—cried deep down inside him. Oh, no, it could not be! That pain was over and done with, buried too deep in his heart for resurrection. He leaped to his feet, all his instincts crying *Run!*

He stood, trembling, as she stopped before him, older yet still the same.

Her slender hands lifted toward him...fell away... clasped themselves in a twisting knot. Her hazel eyes— same color as his own—brightened, then brimmed with tears. "Oh, my handsome..." Words spoken in a whisper of a Southern drawl.

"Not anymore," he grated out through his closing throat. *Not yours. Not handsome.*

"No..." She shook her head. "You've grown *way* past handsome." Her eyes traveled slowly over him from head to toe and back again, as if she was storing up memories for the next twenty-five years. "You're as drop-dead gorgeous as your father was. His very image." Her hand lifted toward his face.

He shied back an inch, then held his ground, trembling.

Her hand paused...then came on with that strange soft courage of women—rose till her knuckles brushed his scarred cheek in the lightest, most tender of touches. "And even this...I cried myself to sleep every night for a year, thinking what I'd done to you, your poor little face. But you came shining through, didn't you? Makes you look tough and dangerous and manly, like a pirate."

Tough? He was cracking apart, an icefall shattering over stones.

"We're stopping in Durango for a day or so. David is visiting old friends," she continued, tears rolling down her face. "I couldn't stay away. Had to come ask."

"Well, now you know," he said harshly.

"Not nearly enough, but..." Her mouth, beautiful as he remembered it, drooped. "But as much as I deserve, I guess." She nodded once, confirming some inner thought, sighed—and reached almost absently for his shirt.

With the blood pounding in his ears, he stood while she tugged a collar point, which had been twisted under, free, straightening it for him.

"Goodbye, sweet darlin'." Lips quivering, eyes aglimmer, she started for the door.

He could let her go. Ought to let her go... *"Wait!"* He caught her arm, then groped blindly for words as she halted, head down. "Would you...would you sit with me a while?"

DRIVING NORTH to the ranch a short while—a lifetime!—later, Tripp was no longer shaking. But he felt as if a big motor was idling deep down at his center—his whole life warming up; fixing to change gears. The things his mother had told him...nothing monumental...just the little things… But somehow something had changed…was changing. Might take him a year to figure out all that had changed…to rearrange his thoughts. Fit the new pieces of the puzzle she'd given him to the old, to make a new picture.

Right now he needed to talk to someone to make it real. If only Mac would call him right now to share in this miracle, or if not Mac, then even better: *Kaley*…

The passing thought lodged and grew in his heart. He wanted to see Kaley. Tomorrow might be too late.

Reaching his turnoff, he braked the truck by his mailbox and collected his mail: a bill, invitation to a Cattlemen's Association doo-dah in Cortez, a camping-gear catalog—and a red envelope. A Christmas card. He didn't get many of those. He ripped it open on the spot.

The front of the card showed a delicate illustration: a team of tiny reindeer flying over a snowy, starlit world that looked much like Colorado. He opened the card to find feminine handwriting:

Wishing you all the happiness in the whole wide world! Kaley.

Down at the bottom of the page she'd added:

P.S. if you get back in time today, would you consider coming over here and helping me cut a tree? It's only six days till Christmas!

Today? He glanced at the envelope again, then realized. No stamp. She must have driven down to put this in his mailbox. He glanced automatically to the west. The sun was barely an hour above the peaks, then figure another two hours of twilight after that.

So what? Kaley had asked for his help.

Or asked for his company? A Christmas tree wasn't so much a need as a desire, when you thought about it. He felt the motor inside him idle down—and shift.

SOMETHING ABOUT SEEING Dana and Rafe together, their laughter and surefooted happiness, had struck a chord of loneliness in Kaley's soul.

They made it look so easy.

For her it was so hard.

There was nothing harder than wishing and hoping for love when it wouldn't come. When Tripp wouldn't come.

Let him just come and say that he's been thinking, and last time he was wrong—we did have something special. That he'd like to try for love again. Let him say that, and he wouldn't have to say more. I'd fly into his arms!

Or was this foolish pride talking, insisting that he come to her? What had her mother said once years ago? Something about love walking out the back door when pride walked in the front?

But pride wouldn't fill this icebound silence with caring talk. Pride wouldn't hold her in its arms when she was frightened, or tease her to laughter when she was sad. Pride wouldn't feed her soul. Kaley found her box of Christmas cards she'd been too blue to send out and wrote.

SHE WAS SEATED on the kitchen floor with three puppies growling and tussling in her lap, when the knock sounded on her door. "Come in!" Her heart flew into her throat. Nobody would be knocking at this hour, except—

"Kaley." Tripp looked brighter and brisker than she'd seen him in days, his cheeks flushed with the cold. He stood looking down at her, not smiling, but his eyes were both hungry and tender. First time he'd looked at her that way in too long. "You want to cut a Christmas tree?"

"I do, but—" She glanced out the window at the pin-kening sky.

He read her mind. "Full moon tonight, if we stay out that late. But you'll need to bundle up."

"Let's do it!" She gave him her hand and let him lift her to her feet. She touched his cheek. "Thanks for coming."

"Thanks...for asking." He turned his head to kiss her fingers.

Their eyes connected and drank deep; her pulse rocketed. *Yes.* Whatever had stopped between them was starting again, her heart singing with it. "I'll be quick as I can."

WHEN SHE WALKED out on the stoop ten minutes later, Tripp had already unloaded the reindeer from his trailer and hitched them to the sleigh. Her face lit like a torch with pleasure. "Oh, Tripp!" She darted back inside.

Minutes later she reappeared with two dark leather straps draped over one shoulder; he heard a chiming jingle as she hurried down the steps. Sleigh bells!

He moved quickly to the reindeers' heads and caught the reins close to their hackamores. "Easy," he warned as she approached. "Where did you get those?"

"They're for Dana, her Christmas present. I found them in Durango last trip, in an antique store. I meant to ask you to attach them to Donner's and Blitzen's harnesses, before you take them back to Ribbon River."

"The sound may spook them," he cautioned. But there was no way he could deny Kaley when she looked like this, sparkly as sleigh bells in the sun. So he took ten minutes to drive the sleigh by himself around the yard, with the bell straps tied with twine to the front of the sleigh. Donner and Blitzen skittered along, snorting and tossing their heads and rolling their eyes as the silvery sounds pursued them, then gradually they settled down. From a reindeer's point of view, whatever this nonsense was, it didn't sound like wolves.

Finally he reined in the sleigh beside Kaley. "Reckon they'll put up with it, but if you don't mind, let's leave the bells tied to the sled today. I'll stitch the straps to their harnesses, then let them wear 'em around their stall for a day or two, before I drive them out in the open."

"They sound lovely where they are." When he patted the sled beside him invitingly, she scrambled into place.

He tucked her in beneath the black bear hide, a trophy of his father some forty years old, a bit moth-eaten but snuggly warm. She looked as delighted as if he were handing her into a golden fairy-tale coach and four, instead of a battered old dogsled.

"This is perfect!" Laughter ran rippling under her words.

Could perfection be this easy? Nothing had ever come easy to him before, but now… "Hi*yaw!*" he called, shaking the reins, and the reindeer clattered away.

"Oh!" She caught his upper arm with mittened hands. "Oh, lovely!"

Bells chiming sweetly, they glided out of the yard, waving merrily to Whitey and Chang when the two came to their door to stare.

"They really can pull us both?" she marveled as they flew along the plowed track toward the pastures.

"Sean came up with an encyclopedia article that claims they can handle three hundred pounds apiece, do fifty miles in the snow each day. And they don't seem to be straining, do they?"

"They look marvelous. You've done such a wonderful job with them."

"They're still pretty skitzy. I mean to tell Rafe that he or Willy better be the driver for the rest of this winter, till we're sure they've settled down."

He'd thought to tell her about his mother's visit while they drove. But with the bells chiming, the hooves stomping and Kaley bubbling, and him needing to concentrate on the road and the reins, he decided it would keep. He'd tell her tonight. If there was a tonight.

He glanced down at her; she rode with her head pillowed against his shoulder, still holding his arm; her fingers flexed against his muscles like a cat kneading its owner's lap in a slow, absent caress. If he hadn't needed to watch the road, he'd have leaned over and kissed her. *If she doesn't ask me to stay tonight, damned if I don't ask her!*

All the things he had to tell her. He had two half sisters he'd never known existed. His mother had written him about them, she'd said, many times, though he'd never seen the letters. *Dad,* he thought more in pity than anger.

No time for anger today. He felt more as if old scars were healing. His mother hadn't walked out on him without looking back. She'd looked back plenty. Had left him and Mac, not because she didn't want them, but because, though she could not love his father, she couldn't bear to strip him of his family. And because she'd known that her sons would be happier growing up on a ranch they'd someday inherit than cooped up in an apartment in New Orleans. His eyes scanned the rugged mountains to the north, the closer velvety snow-draped pines. *And she was right.*

"I forgot," Kaley murmured, rubbing her cheek along his shoulder. "Rafe told me to tell you. He and Sean found a stretch of fence down, two fence posts' worth, just east of the Hay Meadows gate. They propped it back up, figured it would hold fine till morning, but he said you'd want to bring more posts, set up some sort of tripod brace for each, till new holes can be dug."

"Any sign that cattle strayed?" That stretch of fence gave into Cougar Rock Pasture, he concluded, visualizing the enclosures. Which meant if there had been any strays, they were still penned in a pasture where they'd find feed troughs. Not so bad.

"He couldn't tell. There was that four inches of powder that fell last night over all."

"I'll sort it out tomorrow." Today was a cow holiday. A holiday from worries and sadness. "Now, where do we find your tree?"

She had in mind a stand of fir a quarter mile inside Cougar Rock Pasture. Not sure that Kaley could hold the team if they bolted, Tripp tied the reindeer to a fence post while he opened the gate. He led them through, then reversed the procedure while he closed it again.

As they neared the grove of planted firs that sheltered this stretch of the pasture from drifting snow, he kept a sharp lookout for any heifers. The reindeer were still skittish around cattle. But this late in the day, the herd had cleaned their troughs and drifted off to seek cover in the brush down along the river to the west.

"There!" Kaley put a hand on his arm. "That one! I've been ogling it for weeks, every time I drove past."

He halted the reindeer some twenty yards back, by a birch big enough to hold them. While he hitched them to the tree, then fetched his ax from the sled, Kaley slogged on ahead. Here, where the evergreen shadows blocked most of the day's sun, the snow was soft. She kept breaking through the crust, sinking almost to the tops of her knee-high boots.

Arms spread and flapping for balance as she cruised past tree after tree, she looked like a chubby angel trying to take wing. "Hang on," he called laughingly. She shouldn't be exerting herself.

"This one!" she cried. "No...no, maybe not. Its backside is skinny. Then maybe—um—no..."

"Not too big," he warned, catching up with her. "It's got to fit on the sled with us. Limit six feet, okay?"

"Okay," she agreed, laughing up at him. "Then-n-n—"
She carried the word out all the way around a fir, studying
it from every angle, then looked back at him mischie-
vously. "*This* one."

You're the one. Forever and always. He'd chop down
the whole forest if she asked him. "You've got it."

He used the side of his ax head to clear the snow down
eighteen inches or so along the trunk, then set to cutting.
The sun had sunk far beyond Suntop; the world was all
lilac snow and black-green forest. There would be a stretch
of near dark before the full moon cleared the eastern peaks,
but he'd brought a thermos of tea. They could drink it on
the sled and wait for moonrise. The tree shivered, shuddered; his ax bit out a four-inch wedge.

"Timber," Kaley called as it toppled into the snow.
"Perfect," she said quietly, eyes shining. "It will be perfect."

Say you love me, then—and only then will it be perfect.
He hadn't put anything to the test yet. For all he knew,
nothing had changed between them. Maybe it was the oncoming dark causing his courage to falter. Nothing had
ever come easy before. How could he be certain that now
his life had turned around?

"It will be perfect," Kaley repeated, wading close and
reaching up to touch his face.

He leaned down and kissed her—cool lips softly opening. Heat and honey within. She shuddered and pressed
against him, humming a small welcoming sound deep in
her throat. He didn't know if that was her love song or just
a mating cry she'd give to any man who pleased her. But
damned if he didn't take her right here in the snow and
figure that out later.

But she was fragile, Dana had warned him. He dragged
his mouth away with an effort. "I should get you back to
the house."

"Yes," she agreed, breathing hard, smiling soft. "You should."

She slogged silently along at his side as he dragged the tree. He was debating how to drag the fir up to the sled without panicking the reindeer, when their heads shot up from the snow and turned as one to face him. To face something beyond him.

And he felt the first faint vibrations.

"Oh, God," Kaley said quietly, looking over her shoulder.

CHAPTER TWENTY-ONE

THE BULL WAS a hundred yards back and closing. Advanc
ing at a deliberate trot, he breasted the drifts in the ope
meadow like a blunt black plow, waves of snow crestin
and curling back along his shaggy sides.

"It's the two-year-old. The one that went for Whitey,"
Kaley murmured.

"Yes." This was what had come through the downe
fence—had probably downed the fence in search of heifers
What the hell was I thinking of?

Kaley. He'd thought only of Kaley. As he must now
"Go to the sled, sweetheart. Take it and get the hell ou
of here. I'll meet you the far side of the gate."

"No!" she cried on a thread of sound, catching at hi
arm. The bull was fifty yards off, forging with brutal in
tention through the powdery white.

"Yes," he whispered, eyes locked on the beast
"You've got a baby to think of. Meet you at the gate."
God willing. *"Move!"* He felt her lips pressed to his arm
then heard the rasp of the snow as she retreated.

The bull's massive head swung to track her.

Tripp rotated the ax so that the blunt end of its head
faced outward, positioned his hands along the haft—and
stepped forward to meet him. "To me, you black devil."

Forty yards…thirty…

Tripp sucked in a deep breath, held it, let it out slowly.
Behind him the sleigh bells chimed. She'd made the sled,
must be untying the team. If they bolted before she'd set-

led into her seat... *She'll hold them,* he assured himself. And he'd hold this bull.

The bull stopped, lowered his hornless, battering ram of a head, pawed the snow. It feathered over his bunching shoulders, white on black.

"Come on, then."

And on he came—like a half-ton train through the snow, drifts exploding before him, not easy to see, just a black, murderous force bearing down. Tripp swung back the ax...stepped to the side. *"Uhhh!"* The flat of the ax smashed the bull's shoulder as he stormed past not a foot away.

The force of the blow rebounding spun Tripp around in the snow and he fell—then scrambled frantically to his knees, gripping the ax.

The brute had halted some ten yards on, had spun half-way round. He stood rubbing his muzzle along his bruised shoulder.

Like it? There's more where that came from. Shaking with adrenaline, Tripp gained his feet. He spared one glance for Kaley and clenched his teeth. The sleigh still stood by the birch—a flurry of motion there in the dusk—what the hell was she doing? Couldn't she untie the pair? He groaned as the bull caught some movement and swung his evil head toward the tree.

"*You!* This way." He swung the ax in a swishing arc and that did the trick. The bull turned, lowered his head, pawed—and charged.

Barely had he time to swing the ax back before the bull was upon him. Tripp stepped to the side—one second too late. The brute's shoulder smashed into him and he flew through the dusk. *"Ooff!"*

He landed badly, and the ax, the ax, the ax, where was the ax? His hands groped frantically—gripped it—and the last light in the sky turned to black; the bull was upon him.

The beast crunched his middle and he flew through clouds
of snow, darkness exploding inside him and out.

Then a starburst of white…he lay facedown, half buried
in a drift. If he lay still and played dead?

But there was Kaley, forever and ever. *Get up, get up,*
he cried silently, wheezing for air that wouldn't come. *Get
up before he turns to Kaley!* Somehow he found himself
on his knees—

And the bull was there, waiting. He nudged him almost
gently, a bull's game.

Tripp fell back into the snow—and smiled. He could
hear sleigh bells jingling and jangling. She'd untied them
at last and was getting away. "I won," he assured the
darkness blocking the sky.

The bull stared down at him—then lowered his head.

THE TWINE was too strong—too cruelly, horribly strong! It
bit into her fingers as she broke one loop after another,
keening her anguish. The straps chimed and jingled as she
wrenched at them. The reindeer danced around the birch
on the end of their tether, jerking the sled this way and
that, making things harder. "Oh, God, oh, please, come *on,*
oh, *please!*" The last bit of twine broke; she dragged the
strap free and turned—in time to see Tripp fly through the
air like a broken doll, the ax spinning away.

No-o-o! she screamed inwardly, stumbling back through
the snow. Twenty yards that seemed like two thousand.
Snow sucking at her knees. Wind tearing out of her lungs.
Heart breaking. *Not Tripp, not Tripp, you cannot have him!*

The bull had him. He'd stopped, head lowered to the
crumpled shape in the snow—then he dropped to his bony
knees for the kill. He'd use his armored forehead to grind
his prey into the ground.

But she was upon him. "*No-o-o!*" she shrieked, swinging the strap of sleigh bells over her head, then bringing it

jingling down with a hellish *whack* across his rump. She raised it again. The jangling lash whomped bull-hide again; she was making a jingle-jangle, chiming, screeching racket that no bull in Colorado had ever heard before.

Or ever cared to again. The bull scrambled to his feet, shying away. She caught him before he got moving—"Get out of here!" *Whack!*

He bellowed his astonishment and fled.

"Tripp, Tripp, oh, Tripp!" She fell to her knees beside him, weeping.

He was making a dreadful sound. Much like…like…he was laughing. Groaning, wheezing for breath—laughing too hard to find it.

"D-d-damn you, you idiot! If you'd come with me…" Then the bull would have caught them at the sled and had them both, most likely. He'd bought her the time and room she needed…

At what cost? "You dadblasted, crazy, pigheaded… cowboy! Think you're a damn matador?" She kissed his chin, his mouth, his eyes, his ear; her hands flew over his chest. No bones out of place that she could find. "Are you all right?"

"M-more or less. Would you stop kissing me and look for that damn bull? If he comes back…"

"Then I'll do it again," she growled, rising to her knees. "He's not having you. You're mine!" And no bull in sight to dispute this, the big coward.

WHICH WAS a good thing in the end, since Tripp could not walk. His left leg was sprained or broken. Also, she suspected some ribs were cracked. No more damage than he might have suffered in a fall out on the range, he pointed out, panting and white with pain, while she brought the sled to him and somehow they got him aboard. "It's nothing to speak of,'' he insisted each time she asked how he felt.

Since she could barely speak herself, for rage and her chattering teeth, this was just as well. Some sort of delayed reaction had her nerves sizzling and her hair almost standing on end, especially until she'd closed the pasture gate behind them.

Then it was dashaway, dashaway, dashaway home, the reindeer sweeping them on through the moon-silvered night, Tripp's heavy head resting against her shoulder. God, oh, God, he could have been killed! How close she'd come to losing him!

The sled bounced over a rut and he groaned. ''I'm sorry!'' She bit her lip and slowed the team to a prancing walk.

''I'm fine.''

''Yeah, right.'' She ducked sideways to kiss his eyebrow, then his warm mouth with fierce possession. Oh, God, so close!

''What you said back there,'' he muttered after a moment, ''about me being yours. Did you...mean it?''

''I whomped on that bull because I *didn't* mean it?'' She glanced at him sideways, then stopped the sleigh and turned to face him fully. No more pride, no more holding back. She'd almost lost him, before she had a chance to tell him. ''Tripp, maybe I'm a fool for caring, but you are the love of my life. No way was I going to let that bull have you.''

''But...'' His eyes searched her face. ''How can you say that when you went off to Europe and left me like that?''

''Europe? We're talking *Europe?*'' she cried on a rising note. ''I didn't ever—*ever*—leave you! I mean, my body flew over there for a summer, and I told you why I had to do that, but the whole time, Tripp, my heart was right here in your pocket, true as true can be. You're the guy who tossed it over your shoulder and walked—remember?''

"After you'd put off our marrying for the third time. You think I couldn't read the writing on the wall?''

"The writing on the wall said—*still* says, 'Kaley Cotter loves Tripp McGraw forever and ever, amen,' you big—'' She shook her head wrathfully, at a loss for words. "Goof!'' She burst into tears. "If you had half the brains that you have courage, you'd be so dangerous, I...I...'' She shook her head, slinging drops like diamonds, unable to wipe her eyes for the reins in her hands. "*That's* why you left me all those years ago, because you thought *I* didn't love *you?* For *that?* I could just...I could... If you weren't bull bait already, Tripp, I'd...''

He rubbed his knuckles along her quivering mouth. "You'd what, sweetheart?''

She blew out a frustrated breath. Couldn't shake him, couldn't shoot him, which left nothing but... "T-take you back to my bed and love you till you yelled for mercy, and...''

"And?'' he challenged huskily, looking less than terrified.

"*No* mercy, McGraw. Not ever!''

"Well, that's a start,'' he allowed, a slow smile rising to his eyes.

"Maybe for you, cowboy, but there's something I've got to say—that you've got to hear—before you come back to my bed. If you ever do.''

"If you love me, Kaley, there's no fence that'll keep me out!''

Donner stamped and looked back at them. "Easy to say,'' she muttered, and shook the reins. The reindeer set out again at a clopping walk. "But it's about my baby... It's not just me anymore who needs your love. This time I'm a package deal.''

His hand slid over to curve warmly against her stomach. "Reckon I might have noticed that. But, Kaley, I love you and yours, and if I could ever make you mine..."

And I am! "But you might not want us when you—" She squared her shoulders. "Let me tell you about this particular package...."

"THIS MAY BE a little cool," the technician cautioned as she spread a film of gel over Kaley's bare stomach. "Not too bad? Good. This helps the conduction of sound...is why we use it."

"Yes." Kaley smiled wanly. *Oh, please, please...* She'd barely been able to speak, the whole trip in from the Circle C, she'd been praying so hard. Tripp had tried to distract her with talk for the first few miles, then given up and simply rubbed her nape with a slow soothing hand for the rest of the way.

Please, I know I've had more than my share of miracles already, but if You could just see your way to one more?

"There. Now, you said you want your husband to be a part of this?" the technician asked, cocking her head.

"Yes!" Though they'd not slept apart since the night of their sleigh ride, Tripp wasn't her husband yet. But they'd set their date and this time there would be no postponements. No hesitation. Not a doubt in the world.

They would be married in the white church on the hill above Trueheart at four o'clock on New Year's Eve. Afterward Dana and Michelle planned to throw them a wedding party out at the Ribbon River Dude Ranch that sounded as if it might well stretch into the new year—at least for the wedding guests, if not the bride and groom.

"Fine, then I'll call him in," said the technician.

Dr. Cass Hancock entered the exam room first, with Tripp swinging behind her on his crutches. His broken ribs were taped and his left leg was encased in a cast from the knee down, but his injuries didn't seem to slow him much. Already he was grumbling that their neighbors and friends had done enough. That he was perfectly capable of driving a feed truck, that he and Whitey could handle the herds without further help.

So far Rafe and Sean and Jon Kristopherson and Anse Kirby just nodded agreeably and kept right on showing up each day at dawn to feed the cows. Kaley didn't doubt they'd continue until Tripp had recovered to their own satisfaction and not before. Such good friends.

"We take care of our own," Rafe had said with a shrug when she'd tried to thank him. "Someday we'll need a hand, too, and when we do, Tripp and you will be there."

The technician moved a chair close to the exam table for Tripp to sit on. "For you, Dad."

"Thanks." His eyes met Kaley's, sharing the magic of that word. He sat and clasped her cold, clenched fingers between his two big, rough palms. "All right?"

She nodded jerkily and his hands squeezed comfort.

"So...Kaley." With her wise elfin smile, Dr. Hancock took her other hand for a moment. "Ready to do this?"

"P-please." As wildly, wondrously happy as Kaley had been these past few days with Tripp in her life, this one shadow remained. It was time to face it.

"We'll be bringing the image up in a moment," Cass said, nodding at the screen positioned near the foot of the bed. "And I know this will be hard, but I'm going to ask you to be patient. It will take us several minutes to examine your baby. We'll be looking very carefully, very closely, taking our time. And I don't want to speak too soon, you understand?"

Kaley swallowed around the lump in her throat and nodded. "You don't want to say she's all right, then notice something that means she..." *Isn't.*

"That's right. No off-the-top-of-my-head opinion. Give me and Joan a minute or two, okay?

"But what I really mean is that my silence doesn't necessarily mean bad news—and I don't want you to jump to the conclusion that it does. All my silence means is I'm still checking. So, if you're ready..." Her glance signaled the technician, who stepped forward with the transducer.

Kaley shivered as the instrument touched her bare skin. Her eyes locked on the screen, the window on her fate, on happiness or sorrow. *Oh, please...*

Tripp's palm cupped her cheek, turning her face gently toward his. "Look at me, sweetheart," he insisted tenderly, his eyes as serene as hers must be terrified. He brought her hand to his lips and kissed it. "I want you to remember. Remember and never forget, Kaley. Whatever's coming— *whatever*—we're in this together. No more little red hen by herself. Okay?"

"Hen? Wh-what are you talking about?" She rubbed her knuckles along his hard jaw. Smiled shakily as again he kissed her fingers.

"I mean you're not doing it yourself. You're not facing this alone. You're with me—I'm with you. For better or worse. For always. And don't you forget it."

The tears sprang to her eyes. How could a woman ask for more miracle than that, and yet... And yet—

The transducer glided over her stomach, then, "Ah," said Joan.

Kaley's eyes flew toward the screen.

"Oh," murmured Dr. Hancock on an odd note. She moved closer to the technician, blocking Kaley's view of the screen entirely.

Doctor and technician exchanged a long, earnest look— then swung as one again toward the screen.

What is it? Oh, what is it? Kaley couldn't help herself, she had to know! She bit down on her lip to keep from crying out that someone should move and let her see! Then Cass did move, drifting intently toward the screen, and beyond her arm Kaley could see half the monitor.

The swirling darks and lights made no discernible pattern, no baby that she could see. Like Martha, she held chaos, heartbreak, not a child at all. Her hand was clamped tight on something warm.

More warmth stroked her clenched fingers—Tripp, soothing, caressing her. "Easy...easy, sweetheart. I'm with you. We're gonna be fine..."

Dr. Hancock and the technician again turned to share a look—and Joan chuckled. Nodded vigorous agreement to some silent question.

"Kaley." Dr. Hancock swung around with a laugh dancing in her voice. "The very best of news! You've got twice the normal alphafetoprotein level—and twice the usual payload. It's twins."

"B-but— But you said—" Her voice was squeaking off the register; a smile was flowering somewhere around her heart. Or perhaps beneath her navel?

She turned, seeking Tripp's face beyond her flowing tears—found his shock just turning to a grin as wide as all outdoors. Bright as the sun.

"Healthy twins, as far as we can see," the doctor continued. "They look perfectly fine and their protein level is precisely normal for *two* kiddos." Dr. Hancock was beaming. "And you're right. We missed them back in October with your first ultrasound. Somebody in there was playing peekaboo, hiding behind his or her sibling."

"Overlaps happen," agreed Joan, also beaming. "It even happens sometimes at this stage, if one fetus happens to be lying right in line with the other."

"So let me show you how they're situated here," Cass said briskly, moving back to the screen. "And, oh, do you want to know their sex?"

Kaley's heart was just about bursting; she was so giddy it was good she was lying down. To go from terror to bliss in less than two minutes... She squeezed Tripp's hand. "Shall we?"

"As much as you talk to your tummy, might be good to know who you're chatting with," he agreed, smiling. "But it's your call, sweetheart."

"Then, yes, please, Cass." *Make it real for me. I keep wanting to pinch myself!*

"Then here's your son, Kaley." Cass's fine-boned finger traced a pale, rounded, gently moving shape. "And here, cuddled up with him, Tripp, this is your daughter. They're fraternal twins, not identical."

"Full house," Tripp said on a note of quiet triumph. "Full *nest.* Well done, sweetheart!"

Not done quite yet, but oh, now there'd be delight in the doing! No more fear. Only anticipation and joy and a chance to make their own little piece of paradise, right here on earth.

"And a ranch big enough now to hold 'em and keep 'em all busy," exulted Tripp, running to his own thoughts. "Room enough for them, and even more, maybe, someday. Sure sounds like a family to me."

As he leaned down for a kiss, Kaley hooked an arm up around his neck and hugged him close. "And to me," she whispered against his lips. "But reckon I'll call it a miracle."

HARLEQUIN *Super* ROMANCE

Old friends, best friends...

Girlfriends

Your friends are an important part of your life. You confide in them, laugh with them, cry with them....

Girlfriends

Three new novels by Judith Bowen

Zoey Phillips. Charlotte Moore. Lydia Lane.
They've been best friends for ten years, ever since the summer they all worked together at a lodge. At their last reunion, they all accepted a challenge: *look up your first love*. Find out what happened to him, how he turned out....

Join Zoey, Charlotte and Lydia as they rediscover old loves and find new ones.

Read all the *Girlfriends* books! Watch for *Zoey Phillips* in November, *Charlotte Moore* in December and *Lydia Lane* in January.

HARLEQUIN®
Makes any time special ®

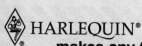

HARLEQUIN®

makes any time special—online...

eHARLEQUIN.com

shop eHarlequin

♥ Find all the new Harlequin releases at everyday great discounts.

♥ Try before you buy! Read an excerpt from the latest Harlequin novels.

♥ Write an online review and share your thoughts with others.

reading room

♥ Read our Internet exclusive daily and weekly online serials, or vote in our interactive novel.

♥ Talk to other readers about your favorite novels in our Reading Groups.

♥ Take our Choose-a-Book quiz to find the series that matches you!

authors' alcove

♥ Find out interesting tidbits and details about your favorite authors' lives, interests and writing habits.

♥ Ever dreamed of being an author? Enter our Writing Round Robin. The Winning Chapter will be published online! Or review our writing guidelines for submitting your novel.

**All this and more available at
www.eHarlequin.com
on Women.com Networks**

HINTB1R

Harlequin *Romance*®
Love affairs that
last a lifetime.

HARLEQUIN *Presents*®
Seduction and passion
guaranteed.

Harlequin®
® **Historical**
Historical
Romantic
Adventure.

HARLEQUIN®
Temptation.
Sassy, sexy, seductive!

HARLEQUIN *Super*ROMANCE®
Emotional,
exciting,
unexpected.

HARLEQUIN®
AMERICAN *Romance*
Heart, home
& happiness.

HARLEQUIN®
Duets™
Romantic comedy.

HARLEQUIN®
INTRIGUE®
Breathtaking
romantic suspense.

HARLEQUIN® *Blaze*™
Red-Hot Reads.

HARLEQUIN®
Makes any time special®

CALL THE ONES YOU LOVE OVER THE HOLIDAYS!

Save $25 off future book purchases when you buy any four Harlequin® or Silhouette® books in October, November and December 2001,

PLUS

receive a phone card good for 15 minutes of long-distance calls to anyone you want in North America!

WHAT AN INCREDIBLE DEAL!

Just fill out this form and attach 4 proofs of purchase (cash register receipts) from October, November and December 2001 books, and Harlequin Books will send you a coupon booklet worth a total savings of $25 off future purchases of Harlequin® and Silhouette® books, AND a 15-minute phone card to call the ones you love, anywhere in North America.

Please send this form, along with your cash register receipts
as proofs of purchase, to:
In the USA: Harlequin Books, P.O. Box 9057, Buffalo, NY 14269-9057
In Canada: Harlequin Books, P.O. Box 622, Fort Erie, Ontario L2A 5X3
Cash register receipts must be dated no later than December 31, 2001.
Limit of 1 coupon booklet and phone card per household.
Please allow 4-6 weeks for delivery.

I accept your offer! Enclosed are 4 proofs of purchase. Please send me my coupon booklet and a 15-minute phone card:

Name: _____

Address: _____ City: _____

State/Prov.: _____ Zip/Postal Code: _____

Account Number (if available): _____

097 KJB DAGL

PHQ401